THE
STRICKEN FIELD

PART·THREE·OF·A·HANDFUL·OF·MEN

BY DAVE DUNCAN
PUBLISHED BY BALLANTINE BOOKS

A Rose-Red City

West of January

Shadow

Strings

Hero!

The Reaver Road

THE SEVENTH SWORD
The Reluctant Swordsman
The Coming of Wisdom
The Destiny of the Sword

A MAN OF HIS WORD
Magic Casement
Faery Lands Forelorn
Perilous Seas
Emperor and Clown

A HANDFUL OF MEN
The Cutting Edge
Upland Outlaws
The Stricken Field
The Living God★

★*Forthcoming*

T H E
STRICKEN FIELD

PART·THREE·OF·A·HANDFUL·OF·MEN

DAVE DUNCAN

A DEL REY BOOK

BALLANTINE BOOKS • NEW YORK

A Del Rey Book
Published by Ballantine Books

Copyright © 1993 by D. J. Duncan
Map copyright © 1993 by Steve Palmer
All rights reserved under International and Pan-American Copyright
Conventions. Published in the United States by Ballantine Books, a
division of Random House, Inc., New York, and simultaneously
in Canada by Random House of Canada Limited, Toronto.

LIBRARY OF CONGRESS CATALOGING-IN-PUBLICATION DATA
Duncan, Dave, 1933–
The stricken field / Dave Duncan. — 1st ed.
p. cm.—(A handful of men ; pt. 3)
"A Del Rey book."
ISBN 0-345-37898-9
I. Title. II Series: Duncan, Dave, 1933–   Handful of men ; pt. 3.
PR9199.3.D847S77   1993
813'.54—dc20   93-3174 CIP

Manufactured in the United States of America
First Edition: October 1993
10 9 8 7 6 5 4 3 2 1

CONTENTS

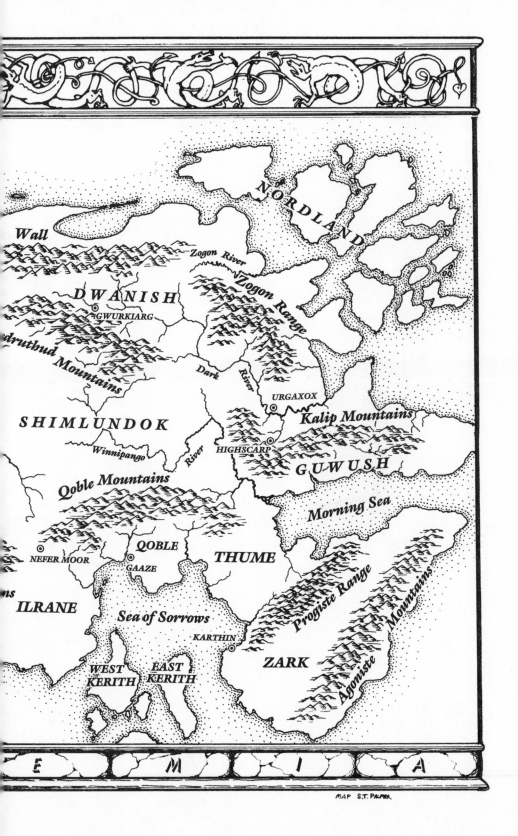

N'ORDLAND

Wall

Zogon River

Zogon Range

DWANISH

GWURKIARG

druthud Mountains

Dark River

URGAXOX

SHIMLUNDOK

Kalip Mountains

Winnipango River

HIGHSCARP

GUWUSH

Qoble Mountains

Morning Sea

QOBLE

THUME

NEFER MOOR

GAAZE

Progiste Range

Mountains

ILRANE

Sea of Sorrows

KARTHIN

ns

WEST
KERITH

EAST
KERITH

ZARK

Agoniste

E   M   I   A

MAP S.T. PALMER

THE
STRICKEN FIELD

PART·THREE·OF·A·HANDFUL·OF·MEN

PROLOGUE

A BLUSTERY WIND RIPPED AND BUFFETED AT THE OLD house, making roof creak and casements rattle. Clouds streamed through the night sky and played tag with the moon. The air smelled of rain now, not snow; spring lurked outside in the damp woods.

The old woman wandered the empty galleries, clutching a dancing candle in knotted fingers. She listened to the whisper of the Voices and cackled at their amusement and their joy.

"Coming, is he?" she said. "Well, you said he would."

She paused, thinking she had heard a living sound, but there was nothing more. It might have been the child, restless with a new tooth, perhaps. It might have been the soldier. She had forgotten his name, they all just called him Centurion. He prowled at night, sometimes, but the Voices warned her where he was and she avoided him. Dangerous, that one.

The Voices were joyful tonight. The duke was coming, they said, coming to claim his lady, coming to fulfill his destiny as they had known he would, these many years.

She wasn't aware of it yet, the lady—didn't know he was coming. Pretty, she was. Lovely as a dream, even if she was mother to the brat. And cold. The old couple had a name for her, but they called her Ma'am when they thought they weren't overheard. They were a count and countess, so what did that make the lady, that they would be so respectful toward her? She had a husband somewhere. Not the duke. Husbands had never stopped lovers much, now, had they?

The old folk wouldn't either. Nor the centurion. The Voices knew that.

Cold, she was, but a lover would soon melt the ice.

He was on his way at last, the duke. Coming to claim his lady, his destiny. And hers. The Voices knew.

Wind rattled the casements.

CHAPTER ONE

AULD ACQUAINTANCES

1

LORD UMPILY HAD NEVER EXPERIENCED ANYTHING IN HIS life as bad as the dungeon. He did not know how long he had been lying there, alone in the cold, stinking darkness, but when he heard the clatter of chains and locks and saw the flicker of light through the peephole in the door and could guess that they had come to take him away ... well, then he did not want to leave.

Probably he had been there for no more than a week, although it felt like at least a month. In the darkness and silence he would have welcomed even a rat or two for company, but the only other residents were the tiny, many-legged kind. He itched all over; there was a lot of him to itch. He had developed sores from lying on the hard stone, for the straw provided was rotten and scanty. He had lost count of meals, but they seemed to come only every second day, or perhaps twice a week. He had passed the time mostly in thinking of some of the great banquets he had attended in his time, mulling them over in his mind, dish by dish. When he had exhausted even that fund of entertainment, he began reviewing all his favorite recipes, planning the perfect meal, the one he would arrange in celebration were he ever to be restored to court and a normal existence again.

The mental torment was much worse than the physical. He was no stranger to hardship. As advisor to the prince imperial, he had journeyed with Shandie to almost every corner of the Impire, living in the saddle for weeks on end, bedding in army camp or hedgerow hostel. He had survived forests and deserts, blizzards and breakers—he had never tasted anything worse than this prison gruel, though. At least on those expeditions he had understood why he was there and what he was doing. Life had made sense then, and even if warfare itself sometimes seemed nonsensical, there had always been the consolation that he was helping a future imperor learn his trade.

He wondered how Shandie was managing now, deposed and dispossessed within minutes of his accession, a hunted outlaw battling omnipotent sorcery. Ironically, when Legate Ugoatho arrested Umpily, he had not ordered him searched, and the magic scroll still nestled safely in the inside pocket of his doublet. Writing in the dark was trickier than he had expected, but he had scrawled a warning that his spying days were ended. *Disregard future communications!* He could not tell if Shandie had received the message or had replied.

Always Umpily's thoughts would return to the dread vision he had seen in the preflecting pool. That prophecy had been fulfilled. A dwarf now sat on the Opal Throne. After more than three thousand years the Impire had fallen, and almost no one knew it. With its immense occult power, the Covin had overthrown the Protocol, deposed the wardens, replaced the imperor, and yet had managed to hide the truth from the world. The sorcerous would know the secret, of course, or most of it—practically all of them had been conscripted into the Covin anyway—but no mundanes did, except for a tiny handful. Zinixo undoubtedly intended to keep his triumph secret indefinitely. What would he do to those who knew it?

Umpily was about to find out. Light flickered outside the spy hole, chains rattled, the lock squeaked.

Blinded by the lanterns, he was dragged along a corridor and up a flight of stairs. When the cruel hands were removed, he toppled limply to a bare plank floor.

"Oh, you needn't be so formal," said an odious, familiar voice.

Umpily forced himself to his hands and knees. Squinting, he made out a pair of smart military sandals in front of him, and shiny greaves above them. "How long?" he croaked. "How long have I been in there?"

"A little more than a day."

Aghast, Umpily registered the reflection on the polished bronze before him. Thinned down by the curvature until it seemed narrow and bony, his own face stared back at him. It wore no beard. He felt his chin and found only stubble. One day?

"The imperor wants to see you," Ugoatho said. "Can you stand?"

Grimly, grunting with the effort, Umpily heaved his bulk upright. His eyes were adjusting, even if his mind would not. Swaying, he stared at the hard, hateful face of Legate . . . no, not Legate. His cuirass was set with gems and gold inlay. The horsehair crest on the helmet was scarlet. Legate Ugoatho had been promoted.

"Congratulations. Was I responsible for that?"

The new marshal of the armies had a grim chuckle. "Partly. I was told to bring you at once, but nobody said anything about passengers."

"Passengers?"

Ugoatho wrinkled his nose. "Wash him!" he snapped. He spun around and headed for the door.

•   •   •

The court was still in mourning for Emshandar IV. Statues and pictures were draped in black crepe. The corridors and halls were almost deserted, and spooky in scanty candlelight. Apart from that, the palace seemed eerily normal. There were no dwarves in sight. Guards, secretaries, footmen . . . mercifully few spectators saw Lord Umpily being conducted to the imperial presence.

The clothes that had been found for him were absurdly tight. He could not fasten the doublet, and he was certain things would rip if he tried to sit down. His escort of Praetorian Guards could have no inkling that they served an imposter. Umpily would be dismissed as a raving lunatic if he ever tried to explain that the imperor he was being taken to see was not Shandie, but his cousin Prince Emthoro, sorcerously disguised.

In silence the prisoner was conducted across the great expanse of the Throne Room, deserted and huge. There was no sign of Marshal Ugoatho. The usual challenges and responses were proclaimed, all very normal, and then the big door swung open, and Umpily was ushered through into the Cabinet.

This part of the palace dated from the XVth Dynasty. The Throne Room was for show, the Cabinet was the inner sanctum. A score of imperors had ruled the world from this room. Emshandar had sat at that great desk for half a century, and his grandson had ruled there for half a year as unofficial regent in the old man's last decline. He had never had a chance to sit there in his own right as Emshandar V.

Defiance! Umpily thought. *I know he is a fraud, and he knows I know it. I will be true to my loyalties. I will not concede.*

The door closed. The big room was scented by the beeswax candles burning over the desk. Heavy, soft shadows outside their oasis of golden light could not conceal the opulence of the chamber—fine carved woods, fabrics of silk. Peat smoldered in the hearth, adding its friendly odor to the candles'. The fake imperor was alone, sitting at the desk, head resting on a hand, studying one of the endless papers that flowed into this center of power. In a moment he marked his place with a finger and looked up.

It *was* Shandie!

For a moment he seemed tired, and worried. Then a slow,

familiar smile of welcome spread over the nondescript features. He sprang to his feet.

"Umpy!"

Umpily's heart twisted in his chest. His eyelids prickled. Shandie—the real Shandie, Umpily reminded himself—the real Shandie had not used that foolish diminutive in ten years. Back when he had been an awkward, friendless adolescent, yes. Never since then.

Umpily hinted a bow. "Your Maj—*Highness.*"

The fake Shandie winced. "Lord Umpily, then. What in the Name of Evil have they told you?" He strode over, with Shandie's urgent walk. He spread his arms, as if to embrace his visitor, then peered anxiously at him. "You're all right? Believe me, it was a mistake! I had no idea the idiots would put you in a cell! 'Find him,' I said. I meant that you needed help! I never intended that you should be thrown in jail, old friend!"

"I am as well as could be expected, your *Highness!*"

The imposter shook his head sadly, disbelievingly. "Come and sit down."

He led the way over to a green kidskin sofa. Umpily eased himself onto it circumspectly. Fabric strained, but held. His waistband tightened like a tourniquet. The disguised Emthoro settled at his side, studying his visitor with obvious concern.

"Perhaps you'd better tell me exactly what you believe."

Gods! It was Shandie to the life—an ordinary-looking, serious young man, with nothing remarkable about him except a burning intensity in his dark imp eyes.

"Believe?" Umpily said. "What I know of the truth, you mean?"

The imposter nodded. Shandie never wasted words, either.

"You were . . . his Majesty was sitting on the Opal Throne when word came of your, er, his grandfather's death. We were rehearsing the enthronement. The warden of the north appeared and warned you, him . . ." Umpily went through the story, struggling to believe that even sorcery could produce so perfect a likeness. Eyes, mouth, voice . . . The telling was unnecessary, but he kept talking, describing how North and West had acknowledged the new imperor, but South and East had not appeared at all. The destruction of the four thrones, the meeting with King Rap of Krasnegar and with Warlock Raspnex again, the escape to the Red Palace and then to the boat . . . It was old history, months old. The enemy must already know far more than he did.

As he talked, Umpily was surprised to realize that he had another listener, back in the shadows. Someone was sitting in the blue silk armchair to his left, although he had been certain that there was no one else present when he came in. He glanced quickly that way, but the chair was empty. He was quite alone with the incredibly convincing imposter. An odd trick of the light . . .

When the tale was done, the fake Shandie shook his head sadly.

"I knew it must be something like that. Shall I tell you what really happened?"

"Er . . . Please do." The vague, half-seen shape was back in the corner of Umpily's vision again. If he looked directly at the blue armchair, it was empty.

The imperor sprang up and began to pace. "Ever since Emine set up the Protocol, three thousand years ago, the wardens have ruled the world. Witches and warlocks, the Four have been the power behind the Imperial throne, correct?"

Umpily nodded. The real Shandie would not move around like that when he talked. He sat still always, inhumanly still.

"It is a terrible evil!"

"Evil, your Maj . . . your Highness?"

The imposter paused to look at him with a raised eyebrow, then shrugged and continued his restless pacing. "Yes, evil. If it is not evil, why does the Impire rule only part of Pandemia and not all of it? We have a stable, prosperous civilization. The outlying races are for the most part primitive, or even barbarous. They fight among themselves and between themselves, constantly. Time and again we have tried to take the benefits of enlightened rule to the lesser breeds. At some times and in some places we have succeeded—but only for a while. Always we have been driven out again, although we have the greatest mundane military power, and the greatest occult resources, also, in the Four. This does not make sense, does it? Do you not see? Ostensibly the Four's job is to control the political use of sorcery. But who controls them, mm? No one, of course! They play with us, Umpy!"

Again that long-discarded incivility! "Play with us?"

"We are tokens in the longest-running game in the universe. The Four amuse themselves by playing war games with mundane mankind."

The only warden Umpily could claim to know even slightly was Warlock Olybino. As ruler of the Imperial Army, East had certainly enjoyed playing at war. Umpily had not thought the others did, though. He said nothing.

"At last one man arose who saw the terrible truth," Shandie continued. He paused and for a moment seemed to be studying that mysterious blue chair in the shadows. "Twenty years ago, a clear-thinking, peace-loving, well-meaning young man succeeded to the Red Throne. You know to whom I refer?"

"Warlock Zinixo?" Umpily did not recall the dwarf as *clear-thinking, peace-loving,* or *well-meaning.* More like crazy, deluded, and murderous.

"Zinixo, correct. He became warden of the west, and resolved to stop this evil senseless slaughter." Shandie—Emthoro—resumed his restless movement to and fro. "He was very young. Perhaps the others tolerated him at first because they thought he would grow out of what they regarded as juvenile idealism. When they realized that he was serious in his intent, they closed ranks against him. They ganged up on him. He was overthrown."

"I understood—"

Shandie nodded sadly. "They had help, yes. Even all together, the other three were not strong enough to prevail against him, for he had the Good on his side, and the Gods. They enlisted to their misbegotten cause a sinister, perverted accomplice—a sorcerer of frightful capacity, a faun mongrel who went by the name of *Rap.*" He spat the word, scowling.

"But he cured your grandfa—"

"A sadist!" Shandie shouted. "An evil, power-crazy barbarian, who mocked at law and flouted the Protocol! With his help, the other three wardens overturned and dispossessed the rightful warden of the west!" He paused and then smiled almost bashfully, as if ashamed of his strange show of anger.

"Fortunately," he continued more softly, "the Blessed One survived. He was driven from Hub, out into the darkness, but he did survive. For many years he gathered strength in secret, never flagging in his dream of bringing justice and peace to all of Pandemia. Eventually, of course, the Four learned of their danger. The events you witnessed in the Rotunda were a frantic effort to impose their ancient evil system on yet another imperor—me!"

Umpily licked his lips and said nothing. This man might look exactly like Shandie, and his voice might sound like Shandie's, but Shandie would never talk with such vehemence.

Neither, for that matter, would the foppish, languorous Emthoro, who had never been known to work up a passion over anything or anyone: masculine, feminine, or neuter. Whoever this Shandie-figure was, real or fake, he was not his own master.

"Hoping to forestall the reformer," the imperor continued, pausing for a moment by the fireplace to adjust the Kerithian figurines on the mantel, "the Four chose to preempt the enthronement ceremony. Two of them would be enough to confirm my accession, of course, and even one of them could bind me to their will."

"But—"

"But you thought the imperor was sacrosanct? You thought the Protocol defended him against all use of sorcery? Oh, you poor dupe! And yet millions of others have believed that lie, for thousands of years. No, the imperor has always been a puppet of the Four. That was why Raspnex and Grunth appeared in the Rotunda, as you saw. South and East were elsewhere, attempting to hold off the Godly One long enough for the dwarf and troll to complete the rite. When they failed, when they saw that they were not strong enough to prevail, then they destroyed the four thrones. It was an act of desperation, and of desecration."

The dwarf Raspnex had admitted doing that, or at least the faun had said he admitted . . .

"My wife and I escaped in time," Shandie said, walking faster now. "You and a few others were not so fortunate. One of those who fell into their clutches was my poor cousin, Prince

Emthoro. Do you understand? The dwarf sorcerer who stole you away cast an occult glamour on him so that he appeared to be the rightful imperor! He believed it himself, of course, and so did you, but neither of you is at fault. Whatever Warlock Raspnex may have told you, he sought only to uphold an ancient evil, whose time has now—thank the Gods!—has now passed. The man you thought to be me was actually Emthoro." The burning eyes turned back to Umpily. "I do not blame you, old friend. You were deluded by a hideous evil."

Shandie? Umpily's heart had started to pound. He could feel sweat trickling down his ribs. Which of the two was the real one? Had he been misled all this time? Had he betrayed his best friend, his liege lord?

"Fortunately," Shandie said, smiling grimly, "there is little harm done. Their mischief was of no avail, except to deceive you and a few who were with you. I reign, as you see. The Four are all still at large, but we shall run them down in time, and they will suffer for their own sins and the sins of all their uncounted predecessors, back for three thousand years. The Almighty is with us."

Umpily shot a quick glance at that blue chair. It was empty. When he looked back at Shandie again, it wasn't.

"But you did have an enthronement . . ."

"You were there?" Shandie looked surprised, annoyed, and then amused, in fast succession. "My, you are a dedicated old snoop, aren't you? Well, yes, we did. And yes, it was a total fake. It seemed wisest to follow the ancient practices until the people can be educated in the new ways. That's all. Why not?"

"S-s-sire?"

Shandie's smile broadened at the word. "After all, what they don't know won't worry them. Not everyone will understand the truth at first. People can be misled so easily . . . even yourself. What you thought you knew was not very probable, now was it?"

"No, Sire!" Gods, what a fool he had been! What a witless, misguided, idiot!

Shandie waved his fists overhead in triumph. "And we shall prevail! The Almighty is with us, and we are his chosen vessels! Can you see the glorious future that awaits us, Umpy?

No more will the evil Four crouch in their webs and roll dice with human lives. We are blessed among all generations! We shall see the Impire spread out to the four oceans and all men shall know the benefits of universal peace and tranquility. Did you meet the faun?"

"Yes, Sire."

"Did he . . ." Shandie was suddenly very intent. "Did he display his powers at all?"

"Very little. He made some garments. He claims that he is only a very weak sorcerer now, Sire."

The imperor nodded, as if that were a satisfying piece of confirmation. "Mm? But do we believe him, eh? Well, no matter. Time will tell."

With difficulty, Umpily heaved himself to his feet. He had been cut almost in half by his belt and it was wonderful to breathe again.

Shandie threw an arm around his shoulders. "I shall be the first imperor to rule all the world! And you are my first and truest friend!"

Umpily was blinded by tears. He had never known Shandie to display such emotion—but justifiably, of course! No more wars? Universal justice and prosperity! It was a staggering, awe-inspiring concept.

"Sire, Sire! I have been a fool!"

"But no real harm done. You have missed a few good meals, I expect."

"Worse! I have been tattling all this time to the imposter!" Hurriedly he pulled the little roll from his pocket. "This is a magic scroll, Sire. The imposter has its companion—"

Shandie snatched the parchment and opened it. His face darkened. "He limns a fair version of my hand, doesn't he?"

Umpily had often found his ability to read upside down to be a useful knack. In the brief moment before Shandie rolled up the scroll again, he had made out the message: *I am grateful. The Good be with you.*

Insolence! That the evil charlatan should have the gall to invoke the Good! The scroll always managed a superb forgery of Shandie's handwriting, of course.

"I shall hang on to this," Shandie said thoughtfully. "Have you any idea where we might find him?"

"None, Sire. I left them all on the boat. I suspected that they were heading for the north shore."

"And long since departed elsewhere! Well, no matter. They can cause little trouble . . . Can they? I wonder what they think they can accomplish. Did you hear any of their vile plotting?"

"Oh, yes! They talk of setting up a new protocol."

"A what?" Shandie almost never showed his feelings, but now he turned quite pale with shock.

"A new protocol, Sire! They hope to bribe all the, er, unattached sorcerers in the world to rally to their cause by promising a new order."

The imperor spun around and stared for a long moment at that ominous blue chair. He licked his lips. "New order? Was this the faun's idea?"

"Yes, sir."

"Of course! And what exactly is he promising?"

Umpily tried to remember all the crazy ideas that had been tossed around on the ferryboat. "They will outlaw votarism, Sire. No sorcerer, even a warden, will be allowed to bind another to his will. They hope to establish sorcery as a force for good in the world . . ."

Shandie laughed, rather shrilly. "Well, I wish them luck! The attempt should keep them out of any real mischief, and we shall catch them soon enough. I feel sorry for my poor cousin. When we catch him, he will be restored to his wits and given full pardon. The Four will meet their just deserts. And that faun . . ." He stared again at the blue chair. He did not complete the thought, but Umpily shivered.

"It is good to have you back in our councils, old friend," the imperor said. "I have convinced you? No qualms now?"

"None, Sire! None at all." Oh, what a fool he had been to trust a dwarf and a faun!

"That's good. And should you, in your dallying around the court, hear of any others voicing doubts, or criticism . . . of course you will inform us at once." Again Shandie put an arm around Umpily, a most unusual gesture for him. The audience was over, they were heading for the door. "You will not speak of the Almighty One." That sounded like a statement of fact. "And your old quarters at Oak House are still as they were. We must find somewhere for you in the palace itself—and I don't mean a dungeon! Now I shall let you go. If I know you, a small repast will be uppermost in your thoughts after that unfortunate misunderstanding."

With Shandie's familiar quiet chuckle, the imperor bade his old friend farewell.

2

FAR TO THE NORTH, NEAR THE EASTERN END OF THE PON-dague Range, a galaxy of twinkling campfires nestled within the Kribur Valley. The winter dark was raucous with guttural male voices; the crackle of firewood blended with horses' whinnies and the scream of dying captives.

The goblin horde under Death Bird had met up with the dwarvish army led by General Karax. Now the leaders were planning a combined advance southward, into the heart of the Impire. Four legions had been slaughtered in the last two weeks and there were no more in the vicinity. The road to Hub was unguarded; the capital lay naked and vulnerable as it had not been in centuries.

The dwarvish end of the combined camp was an untidy city of tents, but goblins would sleep under the sky, spurning this puny southern cold. The junction between the territories was an uneasy border, for the two races had never worked together before and their ways were different. Goblins sneered at the mailed dwarves and wondered aloud how fast those little legs could run. Dwarvish nerves were strained by the noise of the goblins' barbarous amusement. The alliance was fragile.

Near the frontier dividing the two forces, but within one of the dwarves' tents, Queen Inosolan of Krasnegar was attending to her toilet with the aid of a bucket of icy water. As she had lived in the same clothes for a week and had no clean garments to replace them, she had little hope of doing much about her disgusting condition. She could do nothing about her crushing exhaustion, either. She ached as she had never ached in her life. At fourteen, Gath and Kadie were withstanding the rigors of fatigue better than their mother, but all three were close to the breaking point.

The tent was shabby and well patched, typically dwarvish. It smelled bad, but it was roomy enough. The floor was muddy grass, and there was no bedding. At least it was shelter—there would be snow tonight, likely—and there was even a dreary little lantern, which qualified as a luxury by dwarvish standards.

"Mom!" Kadie squealed, peering at something she held pinched between her finger and thumb. "What's *this*?"

"If it's what I think it is, darling, it's a louse."

Kadie screamed and hurled the offending parasite from her. Then she burst into tears.

Stripped to the waist, her twin brother Gath shivered over another bucket. He looked around briefly, before remembering that he was supposed to keep his back turned.

"I've got fleas, as well," he remarked wryly. "Want to trade?"

Inos pulled her blouse closed, then enveloped her daughter in a tight hug. It made no difference. Kadie was working herself into hysterics. Not unexpected. Overdue, really.

"Hush!" Inos said. "This isn't going to help, dear."

"Lice! Oh, Mother! Lice! Ugggh!"

"Hush! There are guards outside, remember. Lots of people have lice. There are lice in Krasnegar. And fleas."

"Bet mine are bigger than yours," Gath said.

"You keep out of this! Kadie, stop it! You've been very brave, dear, and I'm proud of you. And of Gath. But you've got to keep on being brave."

Kadie gulped stridently for breath, then resumed howling.

Inos released the hug, took hold of her daughter's shoulders, and shook her, hard. *"Stop it!"* she shouted.

Shocked, Kadie fell into wide-eyed, shivering silence.

"That's better." Hug again, tightly. "Now listen! We're in great danger. You know that, and I won't lie to you. All we can do is try to be as brave as we can. Think of your father and try to do what he would be proud of. Think of Eva and

Holi, back home in Krasnegar. One day we'll go home and tell them of all our adventures. But that isn't likely to happen if you start behaving like a crybaby." It wasn't very likely if she didn't, either, but one must not say such things. Innocent bystanders caught up in one of the worst wars in Pandemia's bloody history had very poor prospects for survival.

Kadie sniffled, dribbling tears on Inos' shoulder. She was still shaking violently, and the cheek she pressed to her mother's felt colder than the wash water.

"That's better," Inos said. What else could she say? "I'm afraid real adventures are not as nice as adventures in storybooks. You're not the Elven Queen of Giapen, dear! In real life people die or get hurt. They go hungry and they get lice. Now, look on the bright side."

"Is there a bright side?" Gath inquired from the background. It could have been Rap speaking. He sounded absurdly like his father when he managed to display his manly new tenor.

Inos must remember to tell him so.

"Yes, there is. First, Death Bird is our friend. He owes your father a lot, and he knows it."

"I killed his nephew," Kadie whimpered.

"Served him right! Don't worry about that. I don't think the goblins will hold that against you, dear." They were more likely to take it as a challenge. Who would demand the next try at taming the killer virgin from Krasnegar? Don't even think about that . . . "And second, we have magic. All three of us have magic. That's very lucky."

"Three of us?" Kadie wiped her eyes and her nose with the back of her hand. "My sword? Gath's prescience? You?"

"I told you," Inos said gently. She thought the fit was over. "Long ago, when your father helped me drive out the jotnar, he put an occult glamour on me. When I give royal orders, people have to obey me."

"Then why don't you just order them to send us home?" Kadie sniveled.

For one thing, goblins became so infuriated at being ordered around by a woman that they might easily react by killing her. Don't say so.

"I could, but how can they? I crossed the taiga in winter

once with a band of impish soldiers. That was bad enough—I don't want to try it with goblins. We'll have to wait until summer and then go home by sea. Meanwhile, we have other problems, don't we? Gath, what can you foresee now?"

"They come for us soon," Gath said. He was dressed again, his bony face pale in the gloom, and he was hovering nearby—longing to be included in the hugging and unwilling to admit such unmanly sentiments even to himself. He was a kid trying to be a man under conditions few men could have handled.

In a sense, both Gath and Kadie were protected by their innocence. If they had any concept of how the world should be, they would not be withstanding this nightmare transformation of it nearly so well. All that two fourteen-year-olds really could understand was that this was not Krasnegar.

Inos detached one arm from her daughter and pulled her son into the joint embrace. "But you're sure about the imperor?"

"Yes. Usually he recognizes me, too."

"What do you mean *usually*?"

"Mean it's fuzzy. Not certain. May not happen that way."

"Thank you, dear. And I tell Death Bird that his prisoner is Shandie?"

"That's solid enough."

Who needed a seer to know that much? How could Inos ever just stand by and watch the imperor being tortured to death without even trying to save him?

"Then what happens?"

"Then they argue." Gath sounded grumpy. Either he disliked being questioned about his prescience or he was unsure of the fall of events.

But again, who needed a seer? Death Bird and his green horrors might choose to torment a royal victim, but dwarves would never squander a valuable hostage. Argument was almost certain. How durable was the coalition? Suppose the argument became a quarrel?

Gath could not foresee the outcome yet, apparently, or at least Inos found she could coax nothing more out of him. She wished his range was days or weeks, instead of only an hour or two.

"How could the goblins have captured the imperor?" Kadie sniffed. "And how can they not know it?"

"I don't know, dear. Perhaps he was leading one of the legions they ambushed." Inos did not want to speculate, even to herself. She did not think the imperor would ever lead a single legion, or even two. It was only three months since the old Emshandar had died, and Shandie ought to be in Hub, tending his inheritance. Why should he be here, in northwest Julgistro, hundreds of leagues from his capital? Could he have been on his way to Krasnegar? Gath had seen him in a vision; Rap had speculated that Shandie might similarly have seen Gath. She hoped the imperor had not been coming to consult his old sorcerer-friend Rap. That would mean that Rap, when he headed off to Hub, had failed to meet up with Shandie. Sorcerers did not make mistakes like that. The implications would not bear thinking about.

Then she heard the guttural jabber of goblins outside, mingled with the subterranean rumble of dwarves. She was summoned to the feast.

The leaders of the coalition were still holding court within a burned-out shell of a barn, but there had been changes in the last couple of hours. The central bonfire roared even larger, and there were more chiefs in attendance. They were sitting in a ragged circle on boxes and barrels instead of the littered floor, which meant that dwarvish customs had prevailed over the goblins'. They alternated—mailed gray men and half-naked greenish men.

Inos sensed a new antagonism. Weapons had disappeared, no one was smiling. The negotiations had not gone well, then.

She was led to an unoccupied nail keg between Death Bird and Karax. Possibly that was intended to be the place of honor. More likely, both wanted to know why she was there and neither trusted the other alone with her. Gath was given a patch of dirty floor on the opposite side of the fire, the smoky side. Kadie had not been included in the invitation. After some grumbling, she was allowed to remain, sitting in a corner by herself. Fair enough!

Inos thought Death Bird looked tired, although the heavy tattooing on his face made it hard to read. His bulky torso and limbs shone greasily, and every now and again she would catch a stomach-turning whiff of rancid goblin unguent. He gnawed on a meat bone in ominous silence.

The dwarvish general was older than she had realized. There was silver in the natural gray of his beard, and his rough-hewn face bore many tiny wrinkles, like cracks in weathered sandstone. Even for a dwarf, he was surly. His table manners were no better than Death Bird's.

Nor were hers, of course. She bit listlessly at her own hunk of meat, wiping her mouth with her hand and her hands on her robe. The fire crackled and sprayed sparks up into the night sky. There was very little talk anywhere in the company, and where there was, goblins were conversing across dwarves and vice versa, not to one another. Language was part of the problem, but distrust was playing a part, also. Again she wondered how long this unlikely coalition could survive.

Gods, but she was tired! Every bone ached. Six days in the saddle!

Eventually the diners began tossing their discards into the embers. She copied them with relief. Then she licked and wiped her fingers as best she could and waited for the greater ordeal to begin.

She wished she could see Gath more clearly. Being an hour or two ahead of her, he could give her hints, were the fire not between them. Sometime soon she was going to be asked what her mission was. To confess that she had blundered into this disaster by sheer accident would leave her very little status to bargain with.

At last Death Bird belched and threw away his bone. He shot an unfriendly glance past her at Karax. "Start entertainment?"

The dwarf scowled as only dwarves could. "Just two."

"Was agreed, two." Death Bird spoke in goblin. He could manage fair impish when he chose, although he still had the jotunn accent he had picked up years ago from Thane Kalkor's crew.

"But first I want to hear from Queen Inosolan," Karax said.

The goblin shrugged his enormous shoulders. "Speak, woman. Why here?"

Inos drew a deep breath. She decided to stick to the truth as far as she could. If she tried lying and was disbelieved, then her later efforts to save Shandie would be made more difficult. "Your Majesty . . . your Excellency . . . I thought I was here by accident, but now I suspect otherwise." She could address only one at a time, and watch only one face at a time.

"Tell where Rap!" Death Bird demanded, in no mood to listen to speeches.

"He went to Hub."

"When?"

"Three months ago, or more."

"Why?"

Inos turned to the dwarf. "My husband is a sorcerer."

"I know."

"He spoke with a God. He was given a warning to pass on to the Impire. And he himself foresaw a great disaster."

Death Bird chuckled coarsely and switched to impish. "His warning was not believed then."

"Not you. Not this. The danger is occult, and it threatens goblins and dwarves just as much as the Impire."

The goblin grunted skeptically. "He told me. This is old news, Inosolan."

"But perhaps still timely. The millennium has not come yet."

"Never mind the sorcerer," Karax rumbled. "Stop evading the question. Why are you here?"

"There is a magic portal between my kingdom and the house at Kinvale. I came through and was captured by Death Bird's troops."

The Dwarf cleared his throat harshly and spat toward the fire. "That's all? Then you are a blundering fool. Your loyalty is to the Impire. You are spies, or will be if you get the chance. We should kill the boy now, then give you and your daughter to the troops."

Inos hoped that was merely an initial bargaining position, although dwarves were notoriously suspicious and untrusting. She turned her head to study Death Bird's reaction. "My husband was a good friend to you once."

"Long ago. For him I spared your town many times, when my young men wanted it for sport. What happened to Quiet Stalker?" His angular eyes glinted with cold anger.

"He tried to rape my daughter. A sorcerer's daughter. That was unwise."

The goblin showed his white tusks, but he did not seem to be smiling. "No, he didn't. Your son gave him the girl for the night to seal a treaty. So it was not rape! Your son knew she bore an occult sword, one that cannot be seen unless she wishes it to be seen. He is a cheat and a murderer."

Inos's heart was beating much too fast now. She could feel sweat streaming down her face, and that was not all due to the heat of the fire. "He did not promise she would submit. The condition was that your nephew could subdue the girl. He failed."

"Against an unmentioned sorcery. Perhaps we should try another man or two, without the sword?"

She faced the threat as defiantly as she could manage, clenching her fists. "Rap is a sorcerer, as you well know. If any of us comes to harm he will hold you responsible, Death Bird. Dare you risk the vengeance of a sorcerer?"

"Yes." The goblin scratched the bristly hairs around his mouth, peering across her at the dwarf. "General, I give you the choice. Tonight one of us will take the daughter and one the mother. Which do you want? All three of them can amuse the troops afterward."

Karax's permanent scowl deepened. "There is more to this than we have heard yet, I think."

"Yes, there is," Inos said quickly. "Bring in your entertainment, your Majesty." For a moment the gruesome assembly seemed to swim before her eyes and she feared she would faint. "I . . . I have a surprise for you."

If Gath was wrong, it would be she who got the nasty surprise.

Death Bird studied her for a moment, then turned to bark an order. He had known about the sword. He was not frightened of Rap. There could be only one conclusion—he had sorcerers of his own in attendance. Suddenly things began to seem a great deal clearer, and a great deal worse, were that possible.

If this ravaging horde was occultly aided, then it might itself be the great evil that Rap had foreseen. Could the Gods Themselves imagine anything worse?

"And summon my son," Inos added.

For a moment she thought the goblin would refuse, but he gave the order.

She heard laughter, then Gath came around the fire, stumbling barefoot on the rough debris, clad only in one of the goblins' skimpy breechclouts. He looked absurdly skinny and pale pink in this company, far taller than anyone else present. His appearance had united dwarf and goblin for the first time that night. They were all laughing.

"Sit here," Inos said, but he stepped around to stand behind her and huddled close against her furs. He might freeze there, but he probably felt safer. His hand grasped her shoulder and squeezed. She hoped that was meant as a sign of encouragement.

There was a brief disturbance beyond the fire, then two burly goblins appeared, dragging an unwilling captive between them. He seemed tall in this company, but he was not big for an imp. His hands were bound behind him, his clothes hung in tatters. Several days' growth of beard obscured his face, matted with old blood and dirt. He was pitched forward at Death Bird's feet. He twisted slightly to take the impact with a shoulder, but then he lay still.

Inos thought her heart would explode, it was beating so hard. This human refuse could not be the man she had expected. Two, the goblin king had said—so this might not be the one she wanted.

"Well?" Death Bird demanded. "What surprise? Will you offer to begin the sport?"

With a mouth almost too dry for speech, she said, "Lift him up."

The goblin gestured, the prisoner was hauled to his knees.

He saw Gath first. His eyes widened in disbelief and he uttered a cry. Then he looked to Inos. She saw mortal despair flicker into unbearable hope.

They had not met since he was ten years old. She would never have recognized him. But he knew her.

She did not trust herself to rise and stand erect. She could hardly curtsey to a man on his knees, anyway. So she just smiled to assure him that she knew who he was.

"Royal cousin . . . your Excellency . . . This is his Imperial Majesty, Emshandar V, Imperor of Pandemia."

Death Bird looked to his right and bellowed. "Long Runner!"

An elderly goblin four or five places along had been picking his teeth with a twig. He spat. "So it is." He stayed where he was and continued poking his teeth.

Karax muttered something under his breath, but he had been exchanging glances with one of the dwarves to his left. There were at least two sorcerers present, then.

Shandie lurched to his feet, awkward in his bonds. His eyes were as wild as his hair, but he seemed to have himself under control. "We meet again, Death Bird. You had another name when last we met—and sometimes another face, also."

The great goblin tusks were showing again. Under his tattoos, Death Bird's cheeks were turquoise with fury. He had been caught off guard in the presence of his allies and senior deputies.

His voice came out as a dangerous low growl. "Explain, imp!"

Inos marveled at the prisoner's courage. A moment ago he must have been steeling himself to die in long agony. Now a glimmer of a chance for life had put his shoulders back and lifted his chin. He smiled grotesquely down at his seated captors and shook his head.

"A private conference—you . . . and the general. And Queen Inos, of course. I bring news you should hear."

"You make conditions?" The goblin was shivering, his fingers hooked like claws. He could tear the prisoner in pieces with his bare hands.

"I know you are not a fool, goblin." Shandie glanced around at the puzzled company. Very few of them seemed to have realized what was happening. Then those dark imperious eyes came back to Death Bird and Karax. "You can't trust everyone here."

"By the Gods, I will skin you myself!"

"Maybe. But not just yet you won't." Filthy and tattered, bound and maltreated, the impish scarecrow was dominating the contest. He repeated his gruesome smile. "I am the imperor. You know that the Council of Four actually has a fifth member, who must be mundane. You know who that one is. I repeat that I bring you news you both must hear and consider carefully. Whatever you decide to do with me afterward, you must first listen to me. And you must make sure that I am telling the truth."

For a moment Gath's teeth stopped chattering and he sighed softly at Inos's back. Things were going to be all right—for the next hour, or even two.

3

A THOUSAND LEAGUES TO THE SOUTH, THE MOON HAD SET over the foothills of the great Mosweeps Range. Dawn was already turning the sky to pearl, but the light was poor for riding. The trail up the Frelket Valley wound through pine woods, staying close to the chattering river. It was reasonably flat but rarely used and badly overgrown. The horses stumbled on rocks, flinching at the touch of saplings and thorn bushes.

Somewhere behind was the Covin, the greatest concentration of sorcerers Pandemia had ever known. Somewhere ahead were the mountains. Most of the time their impossible barrier was mercifully concealed by the trees, but now and again Rap would glimpse the spectral glitter of starlight on rock and ice, a wall that seemed to obscure half the sky.

He could sense the shivering fear of his mount, and hated the need to force it. If he was thrown and broke his neck it would serve him right, he thought. He dared not use power to soothe the horses or spy out the way, for it would reveal his location to the Covin. Fortunately Thrugg had a troll's ability to see in the dark, and every now and again he would calm the animals. It was a necessary risk if the fugitives were to make any speed, and his occult strength was so great that even at such close quarters Rap would catch barely a glimpse of him in the ambience.

The troll was running along ahead at Norp's side, giving the impression that he could keep up the pace indefinitely. Young

Norp was doing amazingly well. Almost certainly she had
never been on a horse in her life. Horses disliked trolls—their
musky scent, most likely, or just their grotesquely ugly faces.
Perhaps they feared such hulking people might try to ride them.
No horse ever foaled could have carried Thrugg's weight for
very long, or even Urg's, who was running at her husband's
back.

Andor brought up the rear, cursing continuously under his
breath. Andor was a fine horseman but no hero. His mount
was scenting his terror and giving more trouble than either
Rap's or Norp's.

Slowly the eastern sky blushed pink. The trail became more
visible.

Then it dipped to a shadowy ford where a frothing tributary
clattered over pebbles on its way to join the Frelket. Thrugg
halted in the middle, calf-deep in the icy water. The others
pulled up also, and the horses dipped their heads to drink.
They were too hot for much of that, of course, but to use
sorcery to dissuade them would be utter folly and the only
alternative was to overrule the troll, who must have some reason for stopping there.

He was a massive bulk in his all-enveloping sackcloth, panting hard like a dog, long tongue hanging out over huge teeth,
but for a moment his image showed in the ambience, a solid
mass of muscle, grinning ferociously.

"Turn off here, sir."

"I thought the trail went a lot farther," Rap said aloud.

"It does. We don't. There's a shortcut."

A troll shortcut through the Mosweeps was a concept to
chill the blood, but it would be better than falling into the
hands of the Covin. Furthermore, sorcery was not the only
danger. There would certainly be mundane pursuit by morning. Dogs would lose the scent in the water, and hopefully the
legionaries would follow the horses' tracks, at least for a while.
Abandoning the road made good sense, therefore.

"I'll send the ponies on," Thrugg added. All three horses stood
at least sixteen hands high, but they did look like ponies beside
him. He lifted Norp easily to the ground. Rap did not think
he could have done that, child though she was.

But if the three barefoot trolls could stand in the stream, then he could. He slid out of the saddle. Icy water surged over his knees and filled his boots with a rush of agony. He shuddered.

"Now will you take this Evil-begotten sorcery off me?" Andor shouted, making no effort to dismount. He had been demanding that release even before the fugitives left Casfrel. He wanted to disappear out of this hardship and danger. For the first time in more than a century he could not call one of his sequential companions to take his place, for he could not invoke the ancient spell while cloaked in Ainopple's shielding.

"I can't risk it," Rap said.

"If you're leaving the horses, you don't need me! Darad'll do better on foot than I will."

Andor did not add that Darad also had a lot more courage. To be exact, Rap thought, Darad was just too stupid and too much a jotunn to be afraid of anything.

"I know that, but if I free you I'll rattle the ambience. I'm not even sure I can."

"Thrugg then?"

"He's better, but it's still a risk."

"He freed you!"

"But that was hours ago. The Covin must have arrived by now. They must be looking for us."

It was very strange that Zinixo's minions had not arrived already. Perhaps they were secretly watching and laughing and biding their time, but there had been no sign of sorcery back at Casfrel since the fugitives departed. Ainopple must be still asleep, unaware that her prisoners had escaped and unaware of the other danger, which threatened her just as much as it did them.

Thrugg waded over to Andor's horse and grinned up at him. As a threat that grin would make a notable nightmare, yet it was completely misleading. Despite his monstrous jaws and bovine muscle, the big man was as gentle as a rabbit.

"You . . . want us . . . to leave you, sir?" If a horse could speak, it might produce something like that slurred trollish mumble.

Andor flinched. "No." He slid from the saddle and stumbled on the pebbles. Thrugg's huge paw shot out and steadied him.

Rap had eased his horse's girths and tied the reins back out of harm's way. Shivering as his legs froze, he splashed over to Norp's mount and did the same for it.

The ambience flickered. He swung around instinctively to stare back down the valley, but of course mundane senses could detect nothing.

Thrugg chortled like a feeding lion.

"What's happening?" Andor demanded shrilly.

"There's a fight going on," Rap said. He could not make out the details. "Thrugg?"

"The mistress was awake. She's giving them something to think about! Oo! See that?"

"Some." Rap turned to Andor. "The Covin's trying to subdue Ainopple. She's playing for keeps."

Andor wailed. "But she'll lose?"

"Certain to, in the end. But it's a standoff at the moment. Like men with ropes trying to capture a man with a sword . . ." He shifted as the din increased. "She's a real fireball, though, no matter what she looks like."

"Then they'll turn her, of course? She'll lead them to us?"

"It's possible," Rap said. Indeed, it was highly probable that the Covin would transfer the sorceress' loyalty from Olybino to Zinixo, for then she would cooperate. "Maybe not right away, though. They may just subdue her and take her back to their master." She was very old, so the usurper might choose to force her words of power out of her for someone else's benefit, and then kill her. Rap was more worried that the Covin already knew about the other sorcerers in the area, Thrugg and himself. There was a very slim chance Zinixo's press gang would be satisfied with Ainopple, if their watchers had not been close to Casfrel.

"Shall I release your friend, sir?" Thrugg asked. *"Should be safe right now, with all that going on."*

"Good idea," Rap said.

With a faint occult pop, Andor's shielding vanished. He said, "Ah!" and disappeared in another faint flicker of sorcery. His clothes rent noisily as Darad's mighty form materialized within them. The jotunn roared in disgust at the icy bath around his legs. The horses shied and the two female trolls cried out in alarm.

"Rap!" Even for a jotunn, Darad was big—a scarred, tattooed, flaxen-haired giant. Although Rap had replaced his front teeth once, at some point in the last twenty years he had lost them again. Now he grinned like a hungry wolf and lurched forward through the water, hairy hide exposed under his rags, huge arms outstretched to embrace his old friend. Nobody could ever make Thrugg seem good-looking, but Darad came about as close as possible.

"You old villain!" Rap gasped as he was lifted bodily in that crushing bear hug. Heavy with water, his left boot fell off, and the other tried to.

"Old times!" Darad chortled. "You got trouble so you send for me, right? Bash some heads, right?"

"Put me *down!* Thank you! Now, meet Master Thrugg, and Mistress Urg, and . . ."

God of Fools! Darad was glowering at the troll. Rap had never considered that the warrior might have the same sort of racial prejudice as the slave-owning imps of Casfrel, but brains were not his strong point. If he was going to treat the sorcerer as subhuman, then there might be very considerable trouble in store.

"Not as big as Mord was," Darad growled. "Can he fight or is he one of those sissy ones?"

Thrugg's muzzle opened hugely. "Try me." He spread his arms and drooped into a wrestler's crouch.

"Hold it!" Rap shouted. He had retrieved his boot, but both his legs were going to fall off at the knees soon. The battle in the ambience was flaring brighter and noisier, obviously headed for a climax as the Covin brought its stupendous power to bear. "Roughhousing can wait until later. Let's get going before I freeze. Urg, Norp, this is Darad. Now come on, all of you. Shoo those ponies, Thrugg. Then lead the way."

Darad was a sadistic killer with the brains of a crocodile and the loyalty of a pit bull—just the sort of companion a man needed in a tight spot. He would be useless against sorcery, of course, but very functional if the legionaries came in pursuit.

And the old rascal would be really handy if there were bears around.

4

AT KRIBUR, GATH WAS WALKING ACROSS THE DWARVISH camp in the dark, helping Kadie around the obstacles—tent ropes and ditches and things. Mom was following close behind. They were doing much better than their guards, except for the ones with lanterns. He couldn't see in the dark like a real sorcerer, but he knew which steps meant *fall down* and which steps did not, so his prescience was almost as good as farsight for this sort of thing. It was hard work, though, and giving him a headache.

He was glad to have his clothes on again. Most of them weren't his, just things he'd picked up in the last week, some of them bloody or burned at the edges and smelly, but it was nice not to feel like a shelled oyster.

Morning was near. The moon was just setting, a blur in the clouds. Snowflakes swirled in the air. There was a lot more daylight here than there was back north in Krasnegar at this time of year. He had stayed up all night! He had never done that before. He and Kadie had tried once or twice, and they'd always fallen asleep without meaning to. Tonight Kadie had slept for a while during the long arguments and the waiting, but he hadn't. It was a funny feeling, sort of dizzy-making.

"Where are we going, Gath?" They'd been told not to talk, but there was no one close enough to hear Kadie's whisper.

"To a little house."

"Why? What happens?"

She was scared. So was he, but he must try to sound brave and cheer her up. His new man-voice was good for that.

"That's where they're going to have their meeting. Don't know what happens inside, though." It was a creepy feeling. He could foresee arriving at the cottage, but when he went inside everything stopped, as if someone was waiting there to bang him on the head with a club. He'd had prescience for almost a year now and he felt blind when it was taken away like this. Fortunately, he'd met that same blankness before, home in Krasnegar. When he was going to leave the castle, he could not see what would happen outside. Outside, he could not tell what would happen when he went in again. Whenever Brak had come hunting for him, he'd had no warning until Brak actually stepped through the gate.

"Why not?" Kadie sounded annoyed, as if he were being difficult. A year ago she'd been taller than he. Now he was a lot taller than she was. He was turning out jotunnish like his coloring, going to be a big man. Bigger than Dad, even, per-haps.

He tried to explain about the castle back home, and how Dad had said it was because the castle was *shielded*, magic-proofed the way a boat was waterproofed with tar. Obviously this runty little building was shielded, too. That seemed to have been what the arguments had been about, or some of them. The old goblin Long Runner had insisted that they all go to this cottage to hear what the imperor wanted to tell them. Some of the dwarves had argued a lot, but Death Bird had agreed with the old man and won in the end. So now everyone was walking to the cottage.

Gath steered Kadie around a pile of firewood. "Must be a sorcerer's house," he concluded. "Or it was a long time ago. Shielding lasts a long time, Dad says." Nice to sound knowl-edgeable.

"You knew about the goblins!" Kadie said crossly. She was grouchy because she had been asleep, and perhaps because she was tired and frightened. He wasn't going to lose his temper with her, though, at least not before they reached the cottage.

Tricky ditch here . . . "What goblins?"

"When Brak knocked you out, you told Mom about the goblins at Kinvale. We didn't believe you."

"Don't remember."

"Well, you did!"

"Must have foreseen it outside then." He'd had his fight with Brak at Oshi's house, outside the castle. Maybe he'd foreseen the goblins then and been too busy to notice. Now he had stopped hurting, he could chuckle when he thought of the fight with Brak. It had been worth being knocked out— although not worth what had happened as a result. Maybe it had been silly. He thought Dad would say so, if he knew.

"Wasn't it wonderful how Mom saved the imperor?" Kadie sighed. "Just like Princess Taol'dor rescuing Prince Ozmoro from the cannibals!"

Gath hoped the imperor stayed saved. The meeting in the cottage must be going to last a long time, because he couldn't foresee coming out again.

The little house must have more magic than just a shielding spell on it; it was the first unburned building Gath had seen since leaving Krasnegar. Just two rooms with stone walls and a thatched roof, it stood a short distance outside the dwarves' camp, all by itself. If there had been sheds or fence or trees, they had gone for firewood. Now there were guards all around it, to protect the goblin king and the dwarvish general when they arrived. Light shone welcomes in the little windows, and the wind swirled sparks from the chimney pot.

Stepping inside, into brightness and heat, was a real shock for Garth. Prescience crashed in upon him—all the things that were going to be said. He couldn't sort it all out. It was like waking up and trying to remember everything that had happened the day before all at once. One of the dwarves was ordering him to go to a corner . . .

He spun around. "Mom! Dad's all right! The imperor met him in Hub—"

The dwarf *threw* him into the corner. He struck a wall and tumbled to the ground.

That hurt! He rolled upright with his jotunn blood bubbling. The dwarf had stopped being an armored soldier and was just an ugly, squat old man a lot smaller than Brak. Gath's legs twisted under him, his hands found purchase on the floor, and he was almost into a leap when Kadie flopped down on top of him.

"No! Gath!"

Then Mom huddled in on his other side and took a firm grip on his shoulders. Maybe he was a coward. Maybe he was smart. Maybe he was just too tired. He didn't struggle much. He pounded the floor a few times with a fist and then forced himself to unwind. He gave Mom a smile and saw her relax, also. He didn't lose his temper very often, but it had been a long day and a man could only take so much from those bow-legged hairy runts . . . He always tried not to behave like a jotunn. He knew that fighting an army of dwarves single-handed was the sort of thing that would make sense to a jo-tunn, but not to anyone else.

He stayed sitting on the ground between Mom and Kadie because there was no furniture. They weren't allowed to talk. Didn't matter to him—he had all the conversations for the next hour or two to foresee . . . fore-hear?

Dad had gone to Hub and met the imperor. They'd parted before Winterfest, but Dad had been all right then. That was good! He squeezed Mom's hand to comfort her.

Now Death Bird was arriving, with the old man, Long Run-ner, and another goblin, Moon Baiter. Stupid names! And General Karax had come in, and more guards brought the im-peror. They'd untied him earlier and given him something to eat. He was still as filthy as a gnome, but he wasn't behaving like a prisoner in great danger. He looked pleased. He should! Without Gath's prescience he'd be a heap of charred pieces by now.

Later there was going to be a big argument about what to do with him and Mom and Kadie and Gath. Sounded—would sound—as if they might be sent to Dwanish as prisoners of war. That would be better than staying with the goblin army.

Everyone else was leaving. No, two dwarves would be stay-ing. One of them had been referred to as Wirax earlier, and the other would be called Frazkr in a few minutes. So three goblins and three dwarves and the four prisoners. That was what all the arguments had been about earlier—where this meeting should be held and who should be there, apart from the two leaders. Little of it had made sense to Gath, because he hadn't heard everything said and people had been meaning more than they put into words. Now prescience told him why those four underlings had been included, and he shivered. They were going to be asked if the imperor was telling the truth.

They were sorcerers! Of course the invaders would want to have sorcerers on their side. Mom had said it was quite likely Death Bird would have sorcerers around, even though they mustn't use sorcery against Imperial legions. The legions belonged to the warlock of the east, meaning only he could use magic on them, and of course he did it only to help them. But even if sorcerers mustn't fight directly, they could still do a lot of things to help an army: cure disease or wounds, spy out the enemy, interrogate prisoners—which was why those four were here tonight. Mom had explained a lot of this in the last few days; things you never bothered with in school came to mean a lot more when you were stuck in the middle of a war.

His own name was going to be mentioned. The imperor had seen him in a magic pool and been coming to Krasnegar to meet him! Wow! That must be why he'd seen a vision of the imperor, of course, although Shandie had been only prince imperial then, and that was how Gath'd been able to recognize him and save him, so the pool must have known that . . . how could a pool of water *know* anything?

The imperor was going to talk a lot about Zinixo. Gath knew the name. When they were kids, Kadie's games had often involved a villain called Zinixo. Gath had usually been the Zinixo, because none of the others had ever wanted to be bad guys. He'd never understood why that had bothered them, it had just been a game. Kadie had usually been the good witch of the south, of course, or Allena the Fair.

Zinixo had been a very evil warden, warlock of the west years and years ago. They'd heard of him even in Krasnegar, although no one had been quite sure exactly how he had been evil. He'd been killed by a faun sorcerer and everyone in Krasnegar believed that had been Dad, but Dad had refused to talk about it even after he'd admitted to Gath that he was a sorcerer, which he'd never admitted to anyone else.

But this wasn't a game, and Zinixo wasn't dead, after all. Now—so Shandie was going to say—he'd gathered an army of sorcerers and made them all loyal to him. The Covin, the imperor would call it. Zinixo'd overthrown the wardens! Holy Balance! Even Kadie had never invented *that*!

That was going to be one of the times the goblin king asked Long Runner if all this was true and the sorcerer was going to say yes, the imperor was telling the truth.

Gath glanced around as the last guard left, wondering why everyone did not look more excited. But of course Shandie was just starting to speak. They hadn't got there yet. The seven men were still arranging themselves in a horseshoe—dwarves one side, goblins the other, and the imperor in the middle, facing the fireplace with his back to the prisoners.

And there was going to be some really ferocious stuff about how the imperor and Dad and the impress and some others had escaped from the Covin with the help of the warlock of the north, who was a dwarf called Raspnex. Kadie would love that bit!

But the bit the goblins and dwarves were going to be interested in was about Zinixo—and Dad was going to be mentioned again.

"So the Protocol doesn't work anymore," the imperor would say. "The wardens all ran away, except Raspnex, and I don't know where he went after he left us. Lith'rian probably headed home to Ilrane, and Witch Grunth to the Mosweeps, but we can't guess where Olybino went."

Gath tried to recall more of the stuff Mom had told him and Kadie in the last few days. Lith'rian was South and an elf. The witch of the west must be a troll if she went to the Mosweeps, because that was troll country. East was an imp, Warlock Olybino.

The bit about Dad ... "King Rap and the warlock have invented a new protocol. It's going to outlaw votarism."

What was *votarism*? Sure was hard to think straight when your eyes felt full of sand. The warmth was making him sleepy. His jaw ached from the effort of not yawning. Sounded— would sound—like votarism was one sorcerer putting a loyalty spell on another, making a slave out of him, like Zinixo had done to all the people in the Covin. Dad would not approve of that, so it made sense.

Trouble was, there was so much of it, and Gath wasn't listening to a bit at a time as the others were, he was trying to take it all in at once. Then he realized that the best way was to concentrate on Death Bird's questions. The general's, too, but Death Bird's would be really sharp.

"How can you hope to defeat this Covin if it's so powerful?"

"We can't, unless we can collect more power than it has."

"But if the Covin's still hunting down all the sorcerers it can find, then how can you hope to find them faster?"

"We can't. What we can hope to do is to spread the word about the new protocol to all the sorcerers still at large. The new protocol is their only hope, because otherwise the Covin will get them all in the end. If they will help us, we can build a bigger army."

"And how do you spread the word?"

"We're telling all the mundane leaders. Like you, your Majesty. And you, your Excellency. You can help us by spreading the news so the free sorcerers will hear of it. This is our only advantage—you couldn't help Zinixo that way, even if he made you want to."

The goblin was going to look very mad then. And he was going to ask Long Runner and, er . . . Moon Baiter . . . what they thought. And he was going to be really mad when they said that it sounded like a good idea to them.

And the two dwarves would agree, too, which wouldn't please the general, either.

And then Shandie was going to tell them they had better call off their war, because there were no rules anymore, no wardens to take their part. The Covin might just wipe them out, and even Long Runner and the others couldn't save them and would just get enlisted in the Covin, also.

Now that was *really* going to make them cross!

Gath felt his hand squeezed. Mom was beaming at him with tears in her eyes. Huh? Oh, now the imperor had got to the bit about the escape with Dad.

He smiled back at her uncertainly.

Trouble? Yes, there was something bad coming after all this argument . . . He couldn't quite see it yet, but he wasn't going to like it. He felt a shiver of fear.

The imperor was smiling at him, everyone was looking . . . Oh, yes. The bit about the imperor coming to Krasnegar to see him.

He puffed out his chest and tried to look useful.

What was so bad at the end, that he couldn't quite see yet?

Dad had gone off hunting for sorcerers. Kadie would say that was romantic. He thought it was very brave, but it worried him. Dad could be just about anywhere now.

Something else was going to worry him much more. It would come after the goblin king and the general announced that they had heard enough and were going away to talk it over. The prisoners were to be left in this cottage—well, it would be a better place to sleep than anything they'd had in a week. Besides, the windows were starting to brighten with dawn, so there wouldn't be much sleep for anyone.

And the last thing discussed would be what was going to happen to the prisoners. Death Bird would insist that they be kept with the army. Karax was going to demand that they be sent off to Dwanish as hostages.

Suddenly it came. Gath foresaw the decision, and Mom screaming and being shouted down. He saw the leaders and the sorcerers all leaving. He turned to stare at his sister, clenching his fists. Intent on the story, she didn't notice him. She didn't know yet. *Oh, Kadie, Kadie! I can't save you this time, Kadie! Don't cry, Kadie!*

5

DEATH BIRD STORMED OUT OF THE HOVEL, WITH THE dwarvish general scowling along at his heels. The four sorcerers followed, the dwarves taking the lanterns. That didn't matter—the fire gave light, and the windows were bright.

For a moment Shandie just sat where he was on the floor, a crumpled heap of weariness older than the Impire, and yet somehow exultant. Or feeling as if he would feel exultant if he could feel anything ever again. Dawn was coming and it was a dawn he had not expected to see. He had survived, and he might even have turned the awful horde aside from the Impire, his Impire. He might have saved thousands of lives. Even if he hadn't, he'd made an evilish good try at it! If he ever got back to Hub, he ought to award himself a medal of some sort. And he had also made a start on promoting the new protocol—he had told four sorcerers about it.

Then he pulled himself out of his pit of exhaustion and peered blearily at Inosolan. She was staring down at him reproachfully, her eyes red-rimmed, her hair a tangle. Not reproachfully—furiously. The two kids were still sitting in the corner. They hadn't moved since they arrived, except the boy was now hugging the girl, and they were both white as ice under their dirt.

He heaved himself to his feet and faced the woman's blazing green stare. "I tried, ma'am! We all tried."

"She is only a child!"

"Do you think Death Bird doesn't know that? We did all we could. You offered yourself in her place, ma'am, and so did I." He wondered if he would have had the courage to make that offer if he had not been so certain it would be refused.

She crumpled suddenly. "Yes, you did." She stared at the floor.

He stepped closer, and for a moment was tempted to lay a hand on her shoulder as he would have done with a man. "It makes sense. It makes sense to move us to Dwanish. In similar circumstances I have always sent important prisoners back to my base. It is better for us that we not stay with this rabble. And it makes sense that Death Bird would not trust his allies with all four of us. Be grateful he only demanded one."

She wrung her hands and turned away. She was admitting the logic, even if she could not bring herself to say so.

"She is a valuable hostage, ma'am . . . May I call you Inos? She is the daughter of a sorcerer, a friend of Death Bird's. She will be well treated, I am sure. Better than any of the rest of us could expect." He was lying, of course, and they must all know that.

Inosolan did not reply. How in the Name of Evil had she ever landed in this Evilish perdition, and with her children? Time enough tomorrow to get the story.

Lucky for him that she had, though.

He walked over to the kids, and they scrambled to their feet. Frightened, exhausted, shocked, they stared wordlessly at him. He spoke to the boy first.

"You've grown since I saw you last summer, Prince Gathmor. I owe you my life. I am very grateful." He held out a hand.

The boy had an unexpectedly powerful grip—jotunn, of course. His hair was a golden bush, but his eyes were the same dark gray as Rap's.

"Your father would be very proud of you."

The kid just licked his lips and nodded, as if past the point of speech.

"I admire the way you're bearing up, lad. I'm a soldier. I know what it takes when you're new to it. If you can handle this at your age, you're going to be quite a man in a couple of years."

The kid squeaked, "Thank you, sir," in a wavery treble.

"Sire!" the girl snapped.

"Sire, I mean."

"Don't worry about that!" Shandie said, and felt his face ache as he smiled. "Now, your father told me you had—"

"Just an hour or two. No, I can't."

"Can you—"

"The building's shielded. Can't know what happens when we go out."

Shandie nodded. "I see. Thank you." He looked to the girl and was tongue-tied. He never knew the right thing to say to women, and what could he possibly say to this doomed waif? Tell her she was going to be a stunning looker like her mother? Not very comforting under the circumstances. Tell her that being raped was better than being tortured? Was it true?

"Princess Kadolan? I . . . er, am honored to meet you."

Like her mother, she had brilliant green eyes, and they were wide with wonder. "Oh!" she said. "Oh, your Imperial Majesty!" She curtseyed low in her filthy fur robe. That was a crazily inappropriate reaction and should have been funny, but his Imperial Majesty had no sense of humor left. Well, maybe he did—he bowed in response. Every bone in his back groaned.

"I am sure that the goblin king is an honorable man and will see that you are well treated, as he promised." *Liar! Liar!*

"And I am sure that someone will rescue me, your Majesty!" *Gods!* What childish fancy was that?

He was saved from having to say more. The door creaked open. The old goblin sorcerer stepped in nimbly and closed it behind him. He folded his big arms across his greenish chest and stared hard at Shandie.

Now what? The great danger was that one or more of those four sorcerers was a Covin spy, of course. Perhaps this man . . . Long Runner was his name. Perhaps Long Runner had come to announce disaster. *You are coming to Hub with me, your Majesty . . .*

"That went very well," he growled.

Shandie felt a surge of excitement. "You mean I persuaded you? You will join our cause?"

The short man chuckled. "I'm part of it already. Sit down before you fall down. All of you."

Exchanging perplexed glances, the hostages obeyed. The goblin leered, his big teeth and black tattoos making a fearsome sight. "Just in case you're wondering, Death Bird trusts me because he's known me a very long time. I've never used sorcery on him, though, or for him. His destiny comes from the Gods and sorcery had no part in it—apart from a little help that Rap gave him once, of course, and Rap was more than just a sorcerer. But we're old friends, Death Bird and me."

"Get to the point," Shandie snapped. "We're too tired to play games."

"Don't get uppity. Imperors aren't protected by the Protocol anymore. But you did very well, all of you."

"If you're trying to be friendly," Queen Inos shouted, "then stop them taking my daughter!"

"I can't. I just told you. I don't dare use sorcery. And you shouldn't, either! Yes, you! That tantrum you threw a little while ago just about deafened me. Good job this cottage is shielded! Some of Rap's old magic, I suppose? It took all four of us to cancel you out, woman! You shout orders like that outside this building, Queen Inosolan, and you'll call down the Covin!"

"Do you think I care? My daughter—"

"You had better care! If you think Death Bird is bad, how much do you suppose Zinixo would like to get his hands on Rap's family?"

Shandie would not have believed she could have turned any paler, but she did.

"Furthermore," the goblin snarled, turning to the children, "you two both have magic, also, don't you? That foresight of yours is not too bad, son. Frankly, if your dad hadn't mentioned it, I probably wouldn't have detected it, and I expect you can't help using it. Not much you can do, but just remember that an unfriendly sorcerer can smell you out if he gets close enough. And you, little missie? Keep that sword of yours well covered."

Sword? Shandie stared at the girl—who was hastily pulling her robe tight around herself but who certainly was not wearing a sword—and then at the goblin, wondering if he'd gone mad. Sorcerers could go mad. They often did—Zinixo, Bright Water.

"It's a very fine piece of sorcery," Long Runner added. "Very old, I should guess, but I couldn't improve on it. As long as it's mundanely hidden, it doesn't register occultly either, understand? So keep it out of sight. I think Death Bird's forgotten about it already. Course, he has a lot on his mind just now."

"Why didn't you use sorcery on him when he was in here?" Inos raged. She was addressing a sorcerer as if he were a wayward tradesman. "You can stop him stealing Kadie!"

"Yes, I could, stupid. But I keep telling you I don't dare use sorcery on him at any time. If you aren't afraid of the Gods, I assure you that I am! And the Covin! The Covin is watching for the use of sorcery. If I had spelled him, it would have shown up when he walked out of here. Or else he would have changed his mind, depending on how I did it. Now be quiet. Your daughter goes with the army, the rest of you go to Dwanish. That's settled."

"Why her? Why not one of us?"

"He thinks he's going to marry her to his son. That isn't likely to happen for a while. Right now she's officially a hostage, and hostages are always well guarded. So are princes' betrotheds. Shut up, because there's nothing you can do about it."

"If you're not here to help," Shandie demanded, "then what do you want of us?" He had had more than he could stand. He needed rest. They all did, and he thought they were going to be thrown on horses very shortly. The sun was up, and the army would move out at dawn. He could hear voices in the distance, the sounds of camp being struck.

The goblin leered again. "I wanted to give you some good news. I thought you deserved it."

"Then tell us, and go."

Long Runner shimmered, like a reflection in a pool. His tattoos faded, his greenish skin turned gray. An iron-colored beard sprouted on his face, and silver hair on his thick chest.

He was a dwarf in a goblin loincloth.

"Raspnex!"

The warlock bowed. "In the flesh. Good morning, your Majesties."

Shandie jumped to his feet with a zest he would not have credited a moment ago. "You old scoundrel! What are you doing here?" He almost leaped over to the little man to thump him on the back, but then he thought much better of it.

The dwarf scowled ferociously. "Hiding out, mostly. I told you—I've been Long Runner often enough over the years. It was my nephew himself who started that, and I found the goblin business interesting. True destinies are rare. Besides, I wanted to keep an eye on this invasion."

"I'll be damned!"

"Probably. I also suspected some sorcerers would show up, and they did. But I didn't expect you. Or you," he added, glowering at the queen. "I wonder if someone's meddling?"

"Meddling?" Shandie said. "Who?"

"I don't know. The Gods, maybe. That preflecting pool has produced some very odd effects, hasn't it?"

"Then you could have saved the imperor without us?" the boy muttered. He looked disappointed, of course. He thought he'd just changed the course of history.

The warlock chortled. "No! I could have done, but I

wouldn't! I didn't recognize this scarecrow. I ignore their nasty little games." He grinned gruesomely at Shandie. "That would have been funny, wouldn't it—you dying joint by joint while a friendly sorcerer twiddled his thumbs nearby, thinking about other things? Of course, if you'd announced who you were, then I'd have done something—but you wouldn't have, now would you?"

Of course not. Shandie had been prepared to die in as much silence as he could, because he'd been certain he would not be believed if he had announced his identity. If he had, it would just have made matters worse, a matter of days instead of hours.

"Good night's work," Raspnex said, nodding his massive head. "I'd spotted one of the dwarves, but we got two, and that goblin. Thanks to you, I got them all inside a shielded building! Didn't know how I was going to manage that."

"That what the argument was about?"

"Of course. Sorcerers don't like potential traps any more than mundanes do. It worked, though. I explained, they approved. Now they'll cooperate, all of them! So we just picked up three recruits. It's a start! There's a goblin mage, too. We'll take him along."

Shandie's legs were shaking. He sank down on the floor again. "And none of them belongs to the Covin?"

"Not that I can see. No, I'm sure. But we're all going to get out of here. We'll come with you to Dwanish, because this invasion is doomed."

"Doomed?" the queen shouted.

"Oh, not right away. Zinixo may enjoy the chaos for a while, but he can't afford to let a horde of barbarians take the capital. Eventually the Covin will move."

"And my daughter?"

The dwarf turned a dark glare on the girl. "She'll have to take her chances, ma'am. Nothing I can do. Besides, my nephew will certainly have left a few votaries behind in Dwanish. We may soon be in worse danger than she is."

6

FAR AWAY TO THE SOUTHEAST, THE SUN STOOD HIGH OVER the rural peace of Thume. It wasn't shining, though. This was still the rainy season and dense clouds obscured the land between the seas. Rain drummed unceasingly on the roof of Thaïle's cottage, cascading from the eaves and the trees, puddling on the grass. Not a drop of it came inside, and that was still a great wonder to her. When rain fell on her parents' home, the roof and walls did little more than slow it down, for Gaib had always been better at growing things than building. He hated to cut down decent timber—he even hated gathering fresh ferns for bedding.

Although she felt shaky and a little light-headed, Thaïle was keeping busy with a wonderful game she had invented. It involved rearranging the furniture to see how it changed the look of the room—the table here and the other chair over there, and so on. She thought Frial would have enjoyed the game. But then her mother would enjoy just having furniture.

Thaïle had not eaten since the previous morning. Twice Mist had come to talk through the door at her and twice she had resolutely sent him away. No one else had disturbed her, and she clung to a thin hope that no one would. The inhabitants of the College were mighty sorcerers, but they were pixies like her. To a pixie any other pixie's Place was sacred. She knew she was defying the Keeper herself and there could be no greater heresy in Thume, but this was her Place and here she felt safe. Perhaps she was crazy.

Had she planned this brash rebellion in advance, she could have stocked up on some of the wonderful foodstuffs available for the taking at the Market, but she had acted on impulse like a child. Now she was apparently being left to suffer her babyish sulks alone.

She must endure at least two more nights, until the full of the moon had passed. Then she might emerge and go in search of food.

The sorcery of the cottage still worked. Hot water came from the spigot, the lanterns lit when she told them to, the stove would grow hot at her command. The cookpots were mundane, unfortunately—she could not get soup out unless she first put vegetables in. Her closet was full of the finest clothes she had ever seen, finer than anything she had dreamed before she arrived at the College a week ago; but her larder was empty.

She did not want riches and comfort. She wanted Leéb.

Whoever he was.

If he walked up to the door, she would not know him.

No one was walking up to her door. No one had come to scold or threaten or chide, which was somehow unnerving. If she wasn't important, why had they brought her here? For a whole day and a night she had spoken with no one except the lackadaisical Mist, and he was only another novice like herself. He knew no more than she did, and cared a great deal less.

She had Felt no one either. That was really very strange. Her Faculty was strong—Jain had said so. Back at the Gaib Place, ever since she had kept Death Watch for old Phain and learned her word of power, Thaïle had been vaguely conscious all the time of the neighbors beyond the hills. The Gaib Place was more remote than most, too. On her journey to visit Sheel she had sensed dozens of strangers in the distance along the way. Here at the College she could Feel only the other novices and some trainees. The others were all sorcerers, who masked their emotions, of course, but the outside world was somehow masked from her, also.

Pixies prized privacy and solitude, didn't they? So why was she complaining?

About noon, she suddenly Felt worry. In a moment she knew that it was Mist again, approaching along the Way. She peeked around the drape to make sure he was alone and did not have some un-Feelable sorcerers with him. Soon he came into sight among the trees, hurrying with long strides along the white path, shrouded in a hooded cloak of cypress green. That was unusually subdued wear for him, the first time she had seen him not clad in bright reds or blues. But he was alone.

She left the window and walked away into the bedroom,

catching a glimpse of herself in the great crystal mirror. She looked fragile and timid, like a fledgling fallen from its nest, yellow eyes stretched wide with fear.

She heard Mist stamp up on the porch. She Felt a twinge of annoyance, as if rain had run down his neck when he removed the cloak. Then he braced up his courage and tapped on the door. She sat on the edge of the bed and folded her hands. *Go away!*

The moments dripped by. His worry begin to mount. He tapped again, louder.

"Thaïle! It's me, Mist. I need to talk to you."

He wouldn't go away, she decided. Mist was brash enough and so convinced of his own lovability that he would open the door and peer in if she did not answer. She could not bear the thought of that violation.

Very shakily, she rose and went out to the front room again. "Go away!"

"It's Mist!"

"I know it is. I don't want to talk with you."

"But I have to talk with you. I have a message from Mistress Mearn. Please, Thaïle?"

Reluctantly she opened the door a crack and peered out at him. He had removed the cloak. His doublet was scarlet, his hose saffron, and he seemed to fill the porch. His butter-colored eyes stared back at her in ludicrous anxiety. Affable to absurdity, Mist was a human puffball—big and soft and of no known use to anyone. There was hardly anything in him to dislike, even. He forced a smile, but she could Feel his worry and nervousness.

"What's the message?" she asked.

He swallowed.

"She says you are being, er, foolish. She says you can come to the Commons and eat and you won't be stopped from coming back to your Place again." He smiled hopefully. "Come and have lunch with me?" All around him silver water streamed from the eaves of the tiny porch.

"No."

"Fried perch and yams and—"

"*No!*"

"Then I'll bring some food here and we can—or you can . . ."

"No. Go away."

He seemed to shrink. She Felt fear, then. He would have to take her refusal back to Mearn, and he was frightened of the mistress of novices.

"Thaïle? I'm your friend, right? Tell me what's wrong?"

Leéb was what was wrong, but how could she explain? Mist would think she was mad. Even if he believed her, he would never understand.

"No."

"Is it the Defile? We didn't go last night, because of the rain. But Mearn says the Keeper will make the sky clear tonight and the moon is full, so this is the best night." He studied her hopefully. "It's only a valley in the mountains, Thaïle! We just walk through to the other side. We'll all be together, you and me and the other three. I'll hold your hand if you'll let me."

Some comfort that would be! She had seen the Defile, or at least the start of it. It was the most evil-looking thing she could imagine. Mearn had admitted it was an ordeal, and that implied a lot more than a walk in the hills by moonlight.

"No, it isn't the Defile," she said, meaning that the Defile was only part of it, and a small part.

"Then what?" he demanded with a show of exasperation. "You worry me, Thaïle. I love you, you know that!"

She knew he didn't. He might think he did, but *loving* and *making love* meant the same thing to Mist. He thought wanting was the same as wanting to be wanted, and it wasn't.

She hesitated, and he rushed on.

"Darling, you can't defy the whole College like this! And the Keeper herself! You know your catechism—*Whom do we serve? The Keeper and the College!* What do I tell Mistress Mearn?"

It slipped out in a flash of anger. "Tell her I want Leéb!"

The buttery eyes blinked with bovine slowness. "Who?"

"Leéb."

"Leéb? That was the name you said when I was . . . when we were . . ."

"My goodman."

Mist's jaw dropped. Then his big boyish face turned pink

and pinker and pinkest. "You never said!" he whispered. "You wear your hair short. You didn't tell me." His emotions clamored like thunder—shame that he had bedded another man's goodwife, fear that her goodman might come seeking revenge . . . and real disappointment. He had been looking forward to the next time ever since the only time. And that had been her fault.

Somehow she was sorry for him, then. It was very hard to stay mad at Mist.

"I didn't know," she admitted, not able to look him in the eye, studying his long yellow legs and fancy boots. "Not at first. They made me forget."

"Who did? Forget what?"

"Forget my goodman. Mist, this isn't your trouble."

"It is if you're unhappy."

How had he stumbled into that touching, un-Mist-like thought?

"Thank you, Mist. I can't tell you very much." But suddenly the story came pouring out of her like the insides of a broken egg and she couldn't stop. "A recorder came and told me I have Faculty and I must come to the College . . . I ran away. I think I ran away. I fell in love with a man called Leéb. We had a Place, I think, a Place very like your cottage, because that was one of the things that started me remembering. I don't know how I came here. I just was here. That day we met—I realized that there was a whole year missing from my life, or almost a year. The recorders must have found me and brought me here, and they made me forget."

"Leéb?" he said. "You didn't know about him, then, when you . . . I mean, when we . . ."

"Yes. But I wasn't a beginner, Mist, was I?"

His blush had been fading. Now it flooded back.

"No. I don't think so. You knew more than I did, I think."

That was an astonishing admission from him. Where had all his smugness gone? Why did he suddenly have to start being so infuriatingly likable? She clenched her fists and hardened her anger.

"That was when I was sure. They stole part of my life and they stole my love! How can the Keeper do that? Where do you find that in your catechism? *I want Leéb!*"

For a moment Mist shuffled his feet. His fright had returned at the thought of carrying this defiance to Mearn.

"What's he like, Thaïle? Anything like me?"

She hoped not. "I don't know. I told you—I don't remember him at all. Only his name."

Again those pale yellow eyes widened. "You mean you're doing this because you're in love with someone you can't remember?"

"Yes!" She slammed the door on him, terrified she might start to weep. She leaned on it, shivering. "Tell that to Mistress Mearn!" she shouted. "Tell her I don't want lunch. Tell her I won't go to the Defile, tonight or any other night. Tell her I want my goodman back and I shan't eat or leave here until I get him!"

She heard a muffled wail through the door and Felt his horror. "Thaïle!"

"I don't care if I starve to death! Tell her that, Mist! Tell the Keeper herself!"

Auld acquaintances:
> *Should auld acquaintance be forgot,*
> *And never brought to min'?*
> *Should auld acquaintance be forgot,*
> *And days o' auld lang syne?*
>> ROBERT BURNS, *AULD LANG SYNE*

CHAPTER TWO

LONESOME ROAD

1

THAT THAÏLE CHILD WAS TURNING OUT TO BE A SERIOUS problem, the sort of flaw that could blight a man's whole career. Her antics were not Jain's fault, though, and he would have to make that very clear . . . Scowling at the brilliant dawn sunshine, he strode out of his cottage and gazed over the dunes. Coarse grass rippled in the sea wind, waves rushed up on the beach, disappearing into froth and silvery sheets of water. He took a deep breath and felt better. At last a fine morning!

As he had foreseen, the children were romping on the sand with an enormous black furry animal. He strode over to them. The monster saw him first.

"Wait!" it said from under the giggling, struggling heap.

"Wait a pesky minute! Daddy's here." Then it shimmered and became a naked woman.

"Trouble?" Jool demanded warily. For a pixie, she was unusually heavy-breasted, wide at the hips, and voluptuous enough to speed his heart even at this time of day—even with his Thaïle worries.

"Just a dull old meeting. Daddy has to leave now, darlings."

The three came running to him for a hug. He knelt, casting a mild charm to keep the sand from sticking to his clothes.

"Stay home today, then," Jool said, stretching out catlike, soaking up the sunlight. Her gaze was seductive. Lately she'd begun to suspect that he was bored with her; she missed no chance to make herself available. How did women know such things? He was a sorcerer. He ought to be able to keep secrets from a mere mundane. She was only guessing about the others.

"I'd love to," he said wearily, and not without truth. "But I can't. One of the novices is being a stubborn little vixen. I recruited her, so they want me at a meeting. That's all." He nibbled and growled fiercely, but a dressed-up daddy was much less fun than a giant sea otter. The youngsters went racing back to their mother.

Jool pulled a sulky face. "Hurry back, lover." She became a furry monster again as she was buried under the shrieking pack. The illusion was a minor magic he'd given her to amuse the kids. It was well within permissible limits. Major sorcery was forbidden; it would distract the archons and the Keeper.

"Best invitation I've had all day," he promised, and went striding off across the sands.

He'd been a farm boy. The College had provided a suitably homey Place for him, as it did for all recruits. When he'd chosen a fisherman's daughter, though, he'd asked for a Place more in keeping with her upbringing. The ancient pixie tradition of honoring the site of the first coupling would have required them to live at his Place. He had not wanted his friends to think that he—an urbane, sophisticated resident of the College—was bothered by such rustic superstition. After all, a goodwife spent all her time at home, while in those days he'd been a recorder, traveling all over Thume. Now he was an archivist, and had work to do in the Scriptorium most days.

He had never regretted the move to the coast, especially on fine salty mornings like this one.

As he left the beach behind, the dunes gave way to moorland and sedge marsh, the sand dwindling to patches and then disappearing altogether. Soon his feet trod a broad white gravel path, winding over the heath ahead until it became the Way itself and then he was encased in sorcery, unable to perceive the ambience. He felt confined and blinded, but that always happened. He called up a mental image of the Meeting Place and strode along at an easy pace. He was in no hurry, although he would be crossing the entire width of Thume, from the shores of the Sea of Sorrows to extreme east; no journey on the Way took very long.

He felt he ought to be rehearsing his defense, yet he could think of no reason why he should need a defense. He'd done exactly what had been required of him. He had been diligent and meticulous, working his assigned area in the Progiste Foothills, month after boring month, talking with all those peasant bumpkins, noting who among the Gifted families had died, which youngsters had kept Death Watch, checking for Faculty, reporting back to the archivists. He had done exactly what a recorder was supposed to do, no more and no less. He had a commendation in his file.

His assignment to the Progistes had been a compliment in itself. His superiors had passed on a warning from the Keeper that there had been a major battle on the other side of the mountains, Outside, and that recorders in the area must keep an eye open for refugees sneaking into Thume. Horses climbed trees with more success than intruders ever evaded the archons' watch, but the posting to that place at that time had been more than pure routine, a sign of trust.

When he had picked up rumors of the Thaïle child and her occult vision of the battle, he had remembered the warning and gone at once to investigate. At once! He made a mental note of that important phrase. He had seen *at once* that her Feeling was extraordinary. He had given her all the necessary instruction, to her and her father. Perhaps he had been a little harsh with the old man, but he had not strayed beyond permissible limits of discipline. He had taken time to explain *very carefully* to the child herself. She had shown no unusual symptoms of rebellion.

He had absolutely nothing to apologize for, nothing to fear.

Any reprimands were going to settle on someone else's performance record, not his.

As it approached the Meeting Place, the Way wound through thick cypress forest, gummy-scented with the trees' response to spring. It emerged into mixed woodland under a veiled sky. The sun shone diffusely, but cheerfully enough. The air sparkled with life and dampness.

Jain's mind drifted back to Jool. She definitely suspected. Why should it matter to her if he indulged in an occasional idle affair? Lots of his friends did. What was the use of being a sorcerer if you couldn't enjoy a few fringe benefits? Why should she care? He wasn't going to walk out on her and the kids, after all. Seven years since their first loving, half a year since he had become a full sorcerer and been promoted to archivist. That fourth word of power must have been a weak one. As an adept he had been exceptional; as a mage still above average, but the final word had not made him the truly powerful sorcerer he had expected. That rankled. He still found it hard to believe that fate should have been so unkind. He might very well remain a lowly archivist all his days. Like Mearn.

Like Mistress Mearn, who had summoned him to this stupid meeting. Would he become bitter, like her? He hoped not. Mearn had never married, which suggested that she had been a sourpuss even in her youth. Her crabby disposition might also explain why she had not been promoted to higher rank, for her power was certainly adequate, much greater than his. Another possibility was that no one else had ever wanted her job as Mistress of Novices. He knew from personal experience how the old cat enjoyed bullying the kids; he still found himself deferring to her. Mearn undoubtedly had enough power for higher rank, even if she lacked the temperament. Power depended on Faculty. Faculty was something one was born with, or without.

The Thaïle child, for example, had considerable Faculty. Even a single word of power—one feeble, attenuated "background" word—had given her an astonishing talent, an occult talent, not just some useful mundane ability. With three more words, she would undoubtedly be a very puissant sorceress. Forty years from now she would likely be an archon. If she was truly extraordinary, she might ultimately become Keeper. Why did she have to be such a stubborn little minx about it? How could Jain possibly have known that she would run away instead of coming to the College as he had directed her? She had not been plotting rebellion that first day he had met her. He was certain of that.

It was not his fault that the archivists had not noted her absence for so long. He had still been a recorder then.

It was not his fault that she had gotten herself with child in the meantime, sired by some nonentity of a peon not even from a Gifted family.

And it was certainly not Jain's fault that she had refused to go to the Defile with the other novices last night.

Everyone went through the Defile! He shivered. The Defile was not a happy memory for anyone, and it would undoubtedly be worse for her with her strong Faculty than it had been for him, but she could not know that.

Stubborn little harpy!

Then the Way had brought him to the Meeting Place, and there it became only a mundane path again. Again he became conscious of the ambience, the other-world, the shadowy plane of the occult.

All around the clearing, spring flowers flamed in brilliant fresh hues. White swans floated on the lake, and the grass was green enough to hurt the eyes. Here and there people strolled or lounged on benches—gossiping, flirting, relishing this fine morning. Perhaps a score of them in all, spread around the glade, none looking more than twenty-five or thirty, young and finely dressed and happy. In the ambience he could see them as they really were, and all the repair work done on gray hair and sagging breasts and wrinkles.

Mearn was standing on the far side of the lake with a blocky-shaped man Jain did not recognize. He set off along the white gravel path toward them. He supposed Mearn would be her usual well-dressed self, but she was too far off for him to make out details of her dress without using farsight. In the ambience her occult image was nasty and scrawny, admittedly very solid-seeming, which was an indicator of her Faculty. She had well-pointed pixie ears, but that was about all she could boast of. Her hair was piled neatly on the top of her head to make her dumpy form seem taller, but her eyes were an ugly brown, sort of mud-color, not good pixie gold. Today they conveyed undoubted worry. Novice trouble was Mearn trouble.

Probably do her a lot of good, humility-wise.

Her husky companion had remarkable eyes, large and very slanted and pure gold. No, Jain had never met him before. That was surprising, but a sorcerer did not forget faces. The man's image was unnervingly solid, like rock. There could be no deception in the ambience—he truly must be as young and husky as he seemed, yet Jain had thought he knew everyone of his own generation in the College at least by sight. Clearly he had been mistaken. This stranger might be a little older than he. He might have been recruited while still very young and progressed very fast through the educational process. But he must have whistled through the junior ranks of recorder and archivist, or Jain would have met him somewhere, sometime. In short, he must be very highly gifted. Could he possibly be an *archon*?

Jain speeded up his approach. If the Thaïle affair had attracted the attention of an archon, then it was serious indeed. He hoped his sudden agitation was not visible, but of course it would be. There were never more than eight archons at a time, and for some reason he had always assumed that they would be very old. He had never met any of them. He knew no one who had. He did not want to meet any of them, either, especially today.

He had never seen the imperturbable Mearn look so uneasy before. Uneasy? She was plain scared!

Long before he was within speaking distance, the man addressed him. *"I am Archon Raim."* His thoughts struck like notes from a great bell. He was violating the College tradition that conversations should be held in mundane style whenever possible, as a concession to those with weaker Faculty.

"Honored, noble sir." Jain had no need to introduce himself, and a strong desire to vanish from Thume altogether.

"Archivist, you interviewed the Thaïle novice on the morning of her arrival."

Jain was starting to sweat, and not only from the length of his strides as he hurried closer. *"I did, sir."*

"You were instructed to establish what she recalled of the period deleted from her memory. You reported that she remembered nothing since before she met the man Leéb."

"That is correct."

"Then explain why she now asks for him by name and demands to be reunited with him?"

Still several paces away, Jain came to a dead halt, panting and gaping. *"Impossible!"*

The archon smiled thinly and dangerously. *"Perhaps, but it is so. You offer no explanation?"*

"None, sir!" Jain realized that he had spoken aloud. He began to walk again. This was what was behind the rebellion? This why the minx refused to go to the Defile? "The memories had been totally wiped. They had been excised as completely as the aftereffects of her pregnancy. I said all that in my report. It was one of the finest pieces of sorcery I have ever seen." Mearn had credited it to Analyst Shole, who was an acknowledged expert in such matters.

"Obviously your judgment was faulty."

"Yes, sir." Jain shivered, and could think of nothing to say.

He was relieved when Mearn intervened—grateful, even, although he would never have imagined himself ever feeling grateful to the old hussy.

"Sir, is it possible that her unusually strong Faculty could have interfered with the results of the operation?"

"No." The ambience flickered with annoyance. Evidently archons could think up such inanities for themselves.

The gold eyes raked Jain as he finally reached the group. "You have not spoken with her since?"

"No, sir! Certainly not!"

"Someone has been meddling!" This time Raim's anger was a rumble like distant surf. "The archons will assemble today at noon. In the Chapel. You will attend."

Cold rivulets coursed down Jain's skin. "I am not familiar with the Chapel—"

"Of course not. You will be summoned." The archon vanished, his departure lighting the ambience with a blinding flash.

Jain and Mearn both jumped. Startled faces looked around everywhere in the Meeting Place. To use such naked sorcery within Thume was a crime of great magnitude. Only the Keeper unleashed power like that. That an archon would do so was more proof of severe trouble, and of more trouble in store.

Jain and Mearn exchanged worried looks. Don't blame *me,* those looks said, and I have *nothing* to fear, and what do *you* think's going on?

Jain cleared his throat harshly. "I don't recall when the archons last assembled."

She pouted. "Are you implying that I do? It was about three hundred years ago."

2

THAÏLE LAY ON HER BED, FULLY DRESSED BUT UNABLE TO find the energy to do anything at all. She would not have believed that a mere two days without food would make her so weak. Visions of melons and cutlets floated in her head. Mangoes and perch and rice cakes and breadfruit and . . .

Where had she ever tasted breadfruit?

If Mistress Mearn marched in now and waved an egg at her, she would crawl on hands and knees all the way to the Defile to get it.

No she wouldn't!

Leéb! My goodman, Leéb! Whoever or whatever you are, Leéb, I want you. I want to come back to you.

I will never give up.

She drifted in and out of a drowsiness that was not sleep.

Never give up.

An explosion of terror jarred her awake. Someone was coming. The Feeling was unbearable, the worst agony she had ever sensed. It grew stronger and nearer. Footsteps thudded like drumbeats before they reached the porch—a heavy man, running hard, his tread uneven and staggering as if he had run a very long way. She soon realized that it was Mist, his normal aura warped off-key and distorted almost beyond recognition by the strength of his fear.

As she struggled upright on the bed, he tripped on the steps and crashed down on the porch. The whole cottage rocked. She scrambled to her feet and reeled unsteadily to the wall, through the doorway, and across the outer room.

She found him curled up as he must have landed, breathing hoarsely. Appalled, she knelt and laid a hand on his sweat-soaked hair.

"Mist? What's wrong?" She could hardly think through the torrent of dread he was projecting. Her skin broke out in gooseflesh.

He shuddered violently, breath croaking and rattling.

"Tell me!" she cried. "Speak, Mist!"

He raised a face the color of old snow. His eyes were round and his lips blue. He drooled like a dog.

"The Defile! You can't imagine! Oh, *Gods!*"

She recoiled as he grabbed at her arm, crushing it with his big fingers.

"The Defile . . . whatever you do . . . don't let them . . . Stay away from there!"

"Mist, you're hurting me!"

A board creaked; a shadow fell across them both.

"That is all the extra trouble we needed!" another voice snapped. A heavyset young man stood there, glaring down angrily at the unheeding novice. Either his emotions were masked or Mist's distress was drowning them out.

"Who are you?" Thaïle shouted. She tried to rise, but Mist still held her arm. She staggered, swaying with sudden dizziness, and had to steady herself with a hand on the floor.

Piercing gold eyes flashed fury at her. "Never mind! We're leaving. I am sorry this young idiot disturbed you. Someone has been very careless."

Her arm was held no longer; both men vanished simultaneously. The door behind her slammed in the wind. She tried to reach it and her limbs would not obey her. She sprawled on the planks. By the time her head stopped spinning and her heart calmed down to something like its normal pace, she had almost convinced herself that she was hallucinating. Just faintness caused by hunger, that was all!

Ignoring the bruises on her arm, the footprints on the grass, and the muddy marks on the stoop, she went back indoors.

3

THE LIBRARY COMPLEX STOOD ON A HIGH CLIFF OVERlooking the Morning Sea. The Scriptorium was one of the largest buildings, and the whole north wall was glass. Sorcerers could read and write perfectly well in complete darkness, of course, but that effort would have added to the occult noise they made in their labors, which was distracting enough already. The work hall was shielded. It would have been more pleasant had each of the many desks had its own shielding. Jain did not know why nobody had ever thought of that. Perhaps everybody did at some time or another and was scared to suggest the idea in case people thought they could not concentrate properly, which was why he didn't.

He was having great difficulty concentrating that morning. He was supposed to be restoring some genealogical records dating from very early in the College's history, not long after the War of the Five Warlocks. Every page had to be freed of the remains of preservation sorcery, upgraded to legibility, and then preserved again. It was a monotonous and yet exacting task, and he was miserably aware that he was making an unconscionable racket doing it. He felt sure that everyone else in the great room was laughing at him.

It was not fair! That fourth word must have been defective, and now he was stuck with the words he knew until the day he died. He might gain a fraction more power from time to time when whoever else shared his various words died, but then he would just have to share that word with some pimplyfaced novice, so any improvement would be very brief.

Eventually he took a rest from his labors. He wandered out to the stacks and consulted some of the historical archives. Mearn had not been far wrong. The last reported assembly of the archons had been two hundred seventy-six years ago and was believed to have debated a shortage of words of power. Whenever there was need of a new Keeper, the archons chose one of their own number as replacement, but apparently they could do so without formally assembling.

Grumpily he went back to his desk.

And now this wisp of a girl had provoked an assembly? Slouched on his stool, he worked it out and his hair stood erect. Archon Raim had asserted—and puissant sorcerers were seldom mistaken—that *someone had been meddling.* No one within the College would or could tamper with its official business, the Keeper's business. Never! So the meddling must originate Outside. So security had been breached. So the work of a millennium was overthrown, and the demons might invade Thume again, bringing all the evils of ancient times. Jain's reclusive pixie heart cringed into a prune.

He decided to go and talk with Mearn, as the two of them seemed to be in this together. He hurried out of the Scriptorium into sunshine and the cool spring wind, and strode off along the Way.

A sorcerer's hunch told him to look near the Commons and he found her outside, in the courtyard. Even a mundane could have guessed she would be outdoors somewhere. Four novices had passed through the Defile the previous night and would still be recovering. They would especially want sunlight. She was sitting at an outdoor table with three of them, in the dappled shade of an arbutus tree, which had not been there yesterday. Apart from them, the courtyard was empty, but it would soon fill up. Lunch was a popular social event.

"How did it go?" he inquired, pulling up a chair.

Mearn pursed her lips at him, but with less than her usual distaste. "Novice Doob had a nice walk in the hills." She glanced at the youngest of the three.

He smiled back shyly. "I'm going home!"

"What's his talent?" Jain inquired. The boy wasn't close to pubescent yet, and looked about as intelligent as an average mango.

"He hasn't any but his Uncle Kulth wouldn't believe it."

"No harm done?"

"No, he saw nothing but moonlight and shadows. Can't say the same for Novice Maig."

The second boy was slouched slackly in his chair, arms dangling, head propped against the wall; he might have been put in position by somebody other than himself. He seemed quite unaware of the world around him. His face was locked into a sick stare of horror, and his unblinking eyes gave Jain familiar shivers.

"Don't look—it's very nasty." Mearn meant not to look *inside*, of course. *"He was half-witted to begin with,"* she said sourly.

"It happens. Will he recover?"

"Probably not. Of course!" she added aloud. "Just takes a little time."

Not necessarily. Jain would certainly never forget his own visit to the Defile, nor the many sleepless nights that had followed. He had gone in with six companions and come out with five. The biggest, toughest-looking novice in his class had died of fright. Admittedly that was unusual. The sneer on Mearn's face showed that she knew what he was thinking.

She turned to regard the third youth. "However, I think Novice Woom may have gained some benefit from the night's activities."

Woom was old enough to show that he had missed shaving. He had been sitting with his arms on the table, staring fixedly into a mug of coffee. Now he raised his head to send Mearn a stare of calculated dislike. He was holding himself under very tight control, so that his whole body seemed clenched. His eyes still bore the wildness of eyes that had looked on unimagined horrors. His lower lip was swollen where he had chewed it. He had also torn the palms of his hands with his nails and was keeping them hidden.

"Do you enjoy subjecting people to that?" he inquired hoarsely.

"Normally, no," she said quickly. "Sometimes, yes. You were an obnoxious streak of slime yesterday. Today you know that there's more to life than poking your betters in the eye."

He flushed, but he held her gaze a long moment before speaking again. "I can go back to a clean slate?"

"Absolutely."

"Good." He returned to his brooding.

Mearn radiated a burst of satisfaction. *"See that? He's ten years older than he was last night!"*

"Would you go through what he did if you could be ten years younger tomorrow?"

"Of course not. Stupid question."

Woom looked up again, frowning. "Where's Novice Mist, ma'am? Is he all right?"

Mearn primped up her mouth as she so often did. *"And concern for others now, see?* He had what I call the panic reaction," she said aloud. "He'll run himself to exhaustion and probably pass out. He'll feel better when he wakens. I'll go and track him down shortly."

Woom's lips writhed into a mawkish smile, while his wild eyes did not shift their expression at all. "And did you make a man out of him, also, ma'am?"

Jain suppressed a grin. Nicely done, lad!

Mearn did not flinch—she had been processing adolescents for longer than a mundane lifetime. "If I give you my opinion, will you keep it to yourself?"

Woom blinked, then nodded.

"I think Novice Mist broke in the kiln. I don't think there were the makings of a man there to start with."

"So what do you do with the pieces?"

"We send them home. He'll find some sucker of a woman to care for him. Perhaps his descendants will be Gifted. The worthwhile ones we keep, and let them help us."

Woom blinked again, and then looked down at his coffee again. "Thanks," he said quietly.

"One out of four—that's well above average," Mearn sent. *"And this one has real promise."*

Her paean of self-satisfaction was interrupted. A clap of thunder in the ambience announced the arrival of Novice Mist alongside the table. He was standing on his feet, but at an impossible angle. Mearn made an occult grab to stop him falling. Jain jumped up to help, and they lowered him onto a chair.

A quick glance of hindsight told Jain that Mist had been dispatched from the Thaïle Place by Archon Raim himself. He shuddered at the implications. Things just kept getting worse, and it was almost noon.

4

THE ARCHON HAD TOLD JAIN HE WOULD BE SUMMONED and there was no denying the summons when it came. While he was helping Mearn restore Novice Mist to jittery consciousness, the world seemed to open under him. He plunged into cold darkness. He staggered, seeking sure footing on uneven, spongy ground.

His first thought was that he had gone blind and deaf, but that was only because the ambience was now closed to him. All his power had been taken away. He felt bereft and vulnerable, because he had come to rely on sorcerous talents far more than on his mundane senses. After a confused moment he established that he was standing in forest denser than any he had ever seen. Enormous trunks soared up to a canopy thick enough to cut off the noonday sun. The damp, fetid air was heavy on his skin—cloying and stagnant, as if no healthy breezes ever penetrated.

His feet had sunk to the ankle in soggy moss; his hose were already soaked by clammy, knee-high ferns. The faint chattering noise beside him was coming from Mistress Mearn's teeth.

As his eyes adjusted to the gloom, a vast building came into view before him, a pile so ancient that it seemed to have sunk into the forest and become part of it, or else to be itself a product of the jungle, something that had grown there over the ages. The old walls were cracked and canted, the very stones crumbling under leprous coats of greenish lichens. Narrow windows once inset with glass were now gaping holes toothed by fragments of columns and tracery. Doors, likewise, had long since rotted away; the entrance archway gawked at him like the mouth of an idiot. The roof must have survived, though, for the interior was even darker than the enveloping forest.

"The Chapel!" Mearn said unnecessarily. "I . . . I did not expect it to be so large." She moved forward, and he hastened to follow. Stumbling on roots and rotten timber, they waded through the drippy undergrowth to the forbidding façade. The building had sunk or the forest had risen; uncertain light revealed a ramp of humus and detritus leading down to the dark interior floor.

Resisting an absurd urge to take Mearn's hand, Jain forced himself to go first. The footing was firmer than he had feared it might be. He paused when his feet reached wet flagstones, and in a moment she joined him, doubtless cursing loss of farsight just as he was. The air was cold and dead. They stood within a vestry of some sort, so black that the forest seemed bright behind them. In the inner corners, two fainter glows showed where archways led through the nave. They advanced cautiously, finding the paving clear of traps or obstacles.

From the sumptuous jeweled church of the College itself to humble rustic shrines, every holy place Jain had ever seen had been designed to illustrate the eternal conflict between the Good and the Evil. Always there would be a bright window and a dark window, and a balance standing upon an altar. Even ancient ruins that he had noted in his travels as a recorder had shown evidence of the same basic plan. This abandoned, forgotten place had none of that; it predated the fashion or had been built by maniacs. There was no altar, no furniture at all that he could see, and the framework itself seemed perplexingly lacking in symmetry. The proportions and angles were wrong, the empty arched windows placed at random, no two quite the same height or shape or size. The roof was a dark mystery.

He had just concluded that the crypt was empty when he made out a small group of people standing in the far corner. He pointed at them. Mearn nodded uneasily, then headed that way without a word. Should they go slowly to show respect, or hasten so as not to keep the archons waiting? He let her set the pace and she went slowly—perhaps she was as scared as he was; perhaps hurry would be impossible in that ominous sanctity. The flagstones here were dry and bare, but uneven. Each footstep was swallowed by a silence that seemed too solid for mortals to disturb, as if the very air had congealed into sadness.

Eight cloaked figures stood in a rough circle, their cowled

heads bent in meditation. All eight wore the same plain garb; Jain could see no significance to their grouping. Obviously they were the archons assembled. He had been worrying that the Keeper might preside over such gatherings. Archons would be bad enough. At least they were human.

As the newcomers arrived, the nearer figures moved slightly, opening a gap. They did so without looking around, which suggested that their sorcery was still operative. Jain and Mearn stepped into line, closing the circle but staying closer to each other than to the flanking archons.

He glanced surreptitiously around the silent figures, wondering why they did not tell him to stop making such a racket, for his heart was hammering like a woodpecker. They continued to ignore him, studying the ground. He saw then that the group was not located at random, or because the archons had wanted to be in a corner. They were gathered around a particular dark patch of floor, about the size of a bed. Its surface was slightly raised, perhaps uneven and lumpy, although he could make out no real detail in the gloom. After a while, as his eyes continued to adjust, he began to suspect that the patch was wet. A leak in the ancient ceiling would not be exactly surprising. Then the chill creeping remorselessly into his flesh made him wonder if water would freeze here.

And finally he realized that of course the black layer was ice. This was why the Chapel was so sacred. He was looking at Keef's grave, last resting place of the first Keeper. That somber ice was composed of the tears the pixies had shed for Keef over a thousand years. This was the very heart of the College and Thume itself.

For some reason Jain thought then of the name the Outsiders were reputed to use for Thume: *the Accursed Place.* He had never understood that term and no one had ever managed to explain it to him, but now it seemed oddly appropriate for a realm that would take a tomb as its most revered relic and then hide it away where almost no one ever saw it.

The vigil continued. Eventually the archon on his left moved slightly aside. Jain heard a faint sound at his back and a woman stepped into the gap, wheezing nervously. Her face was only a pallid blur, but he recognized her as Analyst Shole. He edged closer to Mearn, to make the spacing more even. Stillness returned.

He hoped this assembly would do something soon and dismiss him before he froze to death here in the dark, or died of fear.

"May we serve the Good always," intoned one of the cowled archons—Jain could not tell which.

"Amen!" chorused the others. He jumped, wondering if he should join in.

"May the Gods and the Keeper bless our deliberations."

"Amen!"

Mearn and Shole stayed silent. Jain decided to take his cue from them—he was only a lowly archivist. And an innocent one, he reminded himself. He had done nothing wrong. He had nothing to fear. It was not his fault.

"Analyst Shole," whispered the same voice as before, deadly and impersonal like a winter wind. "You and Archivist Mearn delivered the woman Thaïle of a male child. You removed all physical results of that birth. You transported her to the College."

Shole muttered an incoherent agreement.

"Tell us exactly what power you used on her memories."

Jain waited for the reply and then knew that there was not going to be one. The archons were reading the answer directly from the woman's thoughts. They were, after all, the eight most powerful sorcerers in Thume—except for the Keeper, who was more than just a sorceress. His flesh crawled.

"You have not spoken to the novice, or used power upon her, since that day?" Whoever was speaking, it was not Raim.

"No, noble sir."

"We are satisfied. You may leave."

"I would have used greater power except you . . . except I had been instructed—"

"We know. You may go."

Shole spun on her heel and in seconds her footsteps were lost in the massive, immovable silence.

Jain braced himself. Now it would be his turn! He wished he could make out faces, but they were hidden from him. He could not tell how many of the eight were men, how many women. He was unable even to determine the color of their dark robes.

"Archivist Jain? You received the woman Thaïle at the Meeting Place and spoke with her."

Jain thought back to that meeting on the bench—what he had said, and she had said, and what she had been thinking until Mist arrived and how he had then left the two of them . . .

"You have not spoken with her since." That was a statement, but he nodded. He was chilled through and yet sweating. He hoped he would be dismissed then, but now the inquisitor asked Mearn about her meetings with the girl in the past week.

Silence. Surely he would be allowed to leave soon? He was drowning in this icy darkness. He needed warmth and sunshine, and life. This laborious inquisition was not his business!

"Her Faculty is extraordinary," murmured another voice, as if musing aloud in the middle of an inaudible conversation.

"It might explain her suspicions," another said. "Just possibly. But not her recovery of the man's name."

"Someone has been meddling!" That sounded like Raim, but perhaps only because he had used those words earlier.

"She cannot possibly understand," another said sharply. "She must be compelled to enter the Defile tonight."

"No," said a spidery voice. "No one has been meddling."

The archons turned at once to face the speaker and sank to their knees. Mearn copied them an instant later, then Jain moved so fast he almost overbalanced. He kept his gaze fixed on the floor, knowing that the Keeper herself had joined the meeting. Fear tightened icy fingers around his heart. He could not remember ever knowing worse terror, not even the horrors of the Defile itself. He recalled awful stories of Keepers who had wiped out whole armies of intruding Outsiders, and of the deadly, unpredictable discipline with which they ruled the College. Keepers were laws unto themselves, utterly unpredictable, heedless of precedent, devoid of mercy.

The voice came again, a dry inhuman rustle beyond fear and passion and hope. "I warned you that the drums of the millennium were beating, that Evil walked the world. I warned you that we are threatened as never before. You know that this girl must be the Promised One, and yet we almost lost her. The first night she was here, I found her at the mouth of the Defile."

Several of the archons gasped, but none spoke. The cold of the floor bit into Jain's knees like sharp teeth, but deadlier yet was the thought of the Defile in less than full-moon light.

Trembling, but unable to resist the need, he risked a hasty glance. The Keeper was a tall, spare shape, muffled in a dark cloak and hood. She seemed to be leaning on a staff, but he could make out nothing more. He looked down again quickly, at the dusty, uneven pavement, so comfortingly solid and prosaic. Tonight he would tell Jool that he had met the Keeper!

She spoke again. "Raim, you are junior. Can you advise your older brothers and sisters how they blundered?"

"No, Holy Lady." Raim's voice was much less arrogant than it had been earlier. "Enlighten us."

"You trespassed beyond the limits the Gods set for Keef, my children," said the Keeper's sad whisper. "You broke her word. You offended grievously against the Good."

"There are many precedents!" Raim protested, his voice quavering.

The Keeper sighed. "Not thus. Analyst Jain, when you instructed the candidate to come to the College, did you specifically warn her that she must not fall in love?"

Jain did try to answer. The answer roared in his head: Not *specifically*. His tongue was paralyzed, no sound emerged—but that would not matter.

"Archivist Mearn," the Keeper persisted, "you slew the man."

Mearn screamed. "There are precedents!"

"But the babe? There are no precedents for that! Why did you not find a haven for the babe?"

"I was obeying orders!"

"The fault was mine, Holy One," said a new voice, a woman's. One of the cowls sank forward to touch the floor. "I feared the Chosen One's future power, thinking she would be able to seek out the child wherever it might be hid. I was overzealous. Destroy me."

"It will not suffice, Sheef. If you seek to accept the guilt of ten, you must offer more."

Somebody whimpered, but it did not seem to be the Sheef woman.

After a moment, Sheef spoke again. "Pronounce anathema upon me, as Deel did upon Theur. Expel me to the Outside, to wander there a hundred years among the demons, without power and without speech, in the guise of a gnome."

"That may still not be enough."

The woman moaned. "It is too much!"

"Does my suffering mean nothing to you?" the Keeper asked. "Will you bring destruction upon us all?"

Sheef screamed. "Then two hundred years, and let me also be cursed with all manner of ill fortune and fated to a foul and painful death!"

After a moment the Keeper said softly, "It may serve. So be it."

Out of the corner of his eye, Jain registered that there were now but seven archons. The gap where the eighth had knelt was marked by an empty cloak. He clenched his teeth and tensed his limbs, yet still he shivered. He, too, had only obeyed orders! He had not known of the killings!

The Keeper paused as if to give the others time to reflect on the fate of their missing sister. At last the insectile voice began again, dripping words into the silence as water might drip into an ocean of dust.

"You sinned against an innocent girl, against her lover and newborn child. You will be fortunate indeed if Sheef's penalty assuages the anger of the Gods. In Their pity They gave the girl a hint of what she has lost. Do you understand what she did with that hint?"

After a moment Raim's voice spoke uncertainly. "She did nothing except go to the young man Mist and copulate with him."

"*She made sacrifice!*" the Keeper snapped, shattering the stillness. Suddenly the Chapel seemed to come alive, as if starting awake from its sleep of centuries. The dread voice rolled around the great building. "She sacrificed herself to the God of Love!

She gave her body to a man for the love of another! Fools! Now do you understand?" Her words echoed and echoed in the shadows, finally whispering back faintly from the roof as they died away.

All the cowls tipped forward to touch the floor. Mearn doubled herself over, also, but Jain remained as he was, sitting back on his heels, paralyzed. He stared in rank despair at the edge of the age-old ice over the tomb of Keef. The magnitude of the danger appalled him. Thume's whole existence depended on the Gods' sufferance, the concessions that Keef had won when she sacrificed her lover. He had seen the Thaïle girl as foolish and ignorant and of no importance, and she had won a God to her side. She had given her body to a man for the love of another, *and the gods had accepted that offering!*

He was ruined! They all were!

The Keeper's voice returned to its resigned whisper, sounding as ancient as the Chapel itself, crushed with an unbearable burden of care. "It was the God of Love who restored her memory. Be grateful They have yet done no more! Hope They will not! It is the millennium prophesied. The Promised One has come and you have blundered."

In the long silence that followed, Jain heard some of the archons weeping. He knew nothing of millennia or Promised Ones, which must be lore restricted to the archons, but he could see that he had perhaps been guilty of some errors of judgment, due to his inexperience. He would certainly try harder in future. He would promise faithfully.

At last one of the archons said, "Holy One, what must we do?"

Again the heartbreaking sigh, the hopeless whisper. "Do nothing. If the child suffers more she may yet be taken from us, and she is your only hope. She must give up the man voluntarily, or you are all as doomed as I. Let her be, return to your posts. I shall go and plead with her myself."

The audience seemed to be over. Jain relaxed with a gasp of relief.

The archons had gone. He and Mearn were alone with the Keeper.

"As for you two!" The Keeper's voice burned with contempt and was terrifyingly closer. "You are a disgrace to your training. Look what you have wrought!"

Again Mearn screamed. "Did not Archon Sheef accept our guilt?"

"In the killings, yes. But you have abused your powers and betrayed my trust. You seek to compel what can only be earned, you apply contempt in lieu of affection. Mankin, did you truly expect to win the child's loyalty by torturing her father, or bribing her with things she did not want or even understand? Woman, do you expect your sneers to inspire endeavor? I strip you both of all occult power and banish you from the College forever. Live henceforth as the animals you are. Begone!"

5

LATE IN THE AFTERNOON, THAÏLE AWOKE FROM A DOZE FEELing restored and strengthened. Her hunger pangs had gone.

She was familiar enough with sorcery now to recognize its effects and could guess at the meaning. She did not believe she had won. More likely her rebellion was just not going to be tolerated any longer.

She peered out a window. The forest glade was bright with thin sunshine and apparently deserted, but common sense suggested she would have visitors shortly. She treated herself to a hasty dip in the magical hot water of the bathtub, then dressed in a soft green gown and brushed her hair. She took a chair out to the porch and sat down to wait.

Shadows lay long upon the grass and the western clouds were flushing. In a few minutes she observed a tall figure coming through the trees, walking slowly along the Way. It was the apparition she had met on the mountain path. It bore a long staff, although its gait seemed steady enough. Measuring its approach by her own rising fear, she watched until it came to a halt before the steps. Even then, nothing of the person within the dark cloak was visible—the cowl cast an unnaturally dark shadow over the face, and the hand holding the staff was concealed by the edge of the sleeve—yet somehow she knew it to be a very old woman.

Thaïle could remember strangers calling at the Gaib Place. The visitor would speak first, giving his name and home, then her father would bid him welcome and offer hospitality. But this was no ordinary visitor, and the cottage was the Thaïle Place only because it had been given to her by the College—and thus by this very visitor, if it was who she thought it was. And she had no food to offer.

She slid off the chair to her knees and bowed her head.

The stranger made a little sighing noise, as if approving. A board creaked as she stepped up on the porch. She dragged the chair back a couple of paces and sat down.

For about a dozen heartbeats there was silence, and then the visitor spoke in that same ancient whisper Thaïle had heard in the night. *"What lies Outside?"*

It was the start of the catechism, and it flooded Thaïle's mind with innumerable memories of childhood, of herself standing before her father with Feen and Sheel, learning and repeating the sacred words. She responded automatically. "Death and torture and slavery."

"Who waits Outside?"

"The red-haired demons, the white-haired demons, the gold-haired demons, the blue-haired demons, and the dark-haired demons."

"How do the demons come?"

"Over the mountains and over the sea."

"Who defends us from them?"

Thaïle clasped her hands to stop them trembling. They were very cold. "The Keeper and the College." Now she was whispering also.

"Whom do we serve?"

"The Keeper and the College."

"Who never sleeps?"

"The Keeper."

A longer silence, then the visitor said, "I am the Keeper." Thaïle shivered.

"Well, child? Have you nothing to say to me?"

"Where is Leéb?"

The Keeper banged her staff on the floor in anger. Then she said sharply, "Why did you refuse to go to the Defile as you were told?"

They had destroyed her memory, Thaïle thought. They had stolen her away from her lover and brought her here by sorcery, and the Keeper had transported her back here from the mountains by sorcery . . . They were all-powerful! Why then did they not just force her to go to the dreadful Defile place if it was so important? And what did she have to lose now?

"Because I want Leéb."

"I never sleep," the Keeper said with a sort of dry contempt. "Do you believe that? Truly believe that?"

"Er, yes, ma'am."

"Look at me, child."

Thaïle looked up as a fragile hand lifted back the cowl. She gasped. The woman's face was wizened and shrunken, like dead leaves plastered roughly over the bones of her skull, but the scalp was smooth under silver wisps of hair. Her eyes were shrouded in wrinkles and so full of suffering that they were impossible to meet. They stared accusingly, questioning like the eyes of a tortured animal. Hastily Thaïle looked away, shivering. The Keeper must be hundreds of years old, far older even than Great-grandmother Phain had been.

"Now do you believe that?"

"Yes. Yes, I do, ma'am."

The Keeper sighed, and Thaïle thought she replaced her hood, but she dared not glance up to make sure.

"You are the first to look on me for a long time. My name, when I had one, was Lain. I have been Keeper for seven years. How old do you suppose I am?"

"I don't know, ma'am."

"I am younger than your mother, Thaïle!"

Astonished, she did look up then, but the Keeper's face was concealed again by the cowl.

"Child, I am the Keeper. I watch over Thume and I watch the world. I tell you now that there is a danger out there worse than all those demons you listed in your parrot-talk. He is prophesied in our most holy lore—a dwarf. A gray-haired demon, if you like. He is the greatest threat that Thume has known since the time of Keef herself, a thousand years ago. His army has overthrown the wardens and usurped the Protocol, and even Ulien'quith could not achieve that. If he discovers us we are doomed, for he will assuredly seek to destroy us and even I have not the power to turn him away."

What had this to do with her? Thaïle wondered. And why would the Keeper not speak of Leéb?

"You owe me your help, Thaïle. All Thume requires your help. I ask you to go to the Defile tonight. Will you do that for me?"

That awful, leering gateway . . . "It is an evil place!"

"It is a necessary evil."

"I want Leéb!"

There was a nerve-wracking pause, and then the Keeper uttered a sudden wry chuckle. "You are misguided, but you are most certainly not lacking in courage. Very well, I will make a deal with you, although I am the first of Keef's successors in a thousand years to stoop to bargaining. Yes, you loved a man named Leéb, and yes, he loved you, also."

Thaïle felt a pang of doubt. "Loved?"

"He believes that you are dead, and he weeps sorely for you. But I will make you this promise. Walk the Defile tonight, as I ask, and tomorrow I shall restore you to him. I shall return your memories and remove his memory of seeing you dead. He will be lacking only a few days and will not notice."

Incredulous, Thaïle stared at that mysterious hood, seeing only a hint of the crazily tormented eyes glinting in its shadow. "You will?"

"I will—if you wish me to."

So there was a catch? Of course there would be!

"What happens in the Defile?" She remembered Mist's warning.

"You are given understanding."

"Mist—"

"Mist is a weakling. You are not. All of us in the College have walked the Defile at the full of the moon. Tomorrow you will comprehend why we do what we do, but if you still wish to leave the College and return to Leéb, then I will grant your request. I swear this by all the Gods. I swear it on Keef's tomb."

For a moment Thaïle's mouth was too dry for speech. She nodded and finally whispered, "Thank you." She had won!

Won!

"Go inside now," the Keeper said softly. "There is a meal there, waiting. When the sky darkens, dress warmly and go to the Defile. The Way will take you. Do you want anyone to guide you?"

Thaïle shook her head.

"I trust your courage, then. One warning you are given: Do not look behind you! I will meet you at the far end."

Thaïle watched the Keeper trudge off along the Way and disappear into the darkening woods. Then she rose unsteadily to her feet and went indoors.

She had won! Tomorrow she would meet Leéb, the man she loved, the man who loved her. She had won.

6

THE WAY CLIMBED STEEPLY THROUGH THE FOREST, UNPLEAS- antly familiar. Soon Thaïle was again traversing the upland valley she had discovered on her first night in the College, the stony ground falling off steeply on her right and rising on her left, obscured by shrubbery and trees. The moon was bright through a hazy veil of cloud, and just knowing that she was supposed to be there made her far more confident than she had been the first time. The white path unwound before her feet, the sounds of a torrent below her grew louder. This time she did not try to turn back, so there were no bridges and no delays. Soon the gorge narrowed, the slopes becoming bare and precipitous; she rounded a bend and saw the gateway ahead already.

She paused, then, panting and yet chilled as the mountain air nipped through her heavy cloak. The light was different this time, the ruin less sinister, less distinct, more like part of the cliffs from which it sprung. She could not distinguish the illusion of a face in it. The arch spanning the ravine no longer seemed like a mouth. The empty windows above were not eyes, nor the stunted trees on top hair. She saw only a ruin of white stone—old and sad, but not threatening.

Reassured, she hastened forward. Even when she reached the arch itself, she did not falter or break stride. The exit showed ahead beyond a brief darkness that echoed with the roar of a waterfall in the depths. In a moment she emerged on the far side.

The gorge had widened dramatically. The moon shone clearly from a sky of black crystal, casting harder shadows. Off to the right, a small river cascaded down into unseen darkness but ahead the valley floor was level, and bare, flanked by cliffs. The Way continued, winding between pinnacles and slabs of rock; high on either hand great mountains shone as icy ghosts under the silver orb of the moon. There was no color, only paleness and dark and rare patches of snow.

She hurried on, soon losing the noise of the cataract, walking into silence. Even the wind had stilled, as if the night held its breath. She could hear nothing but the faint crunch of her feet on the gravel and the steady beat of her heart.

It would not all be this easy, of course. Mistress Mearn had admitted that the Defile was an ordeal. Mist had been frightened out of his wits. Yet the Way continued empty and level. The river had vanished completely. Nothing seemed to grow in this desolation except straggly tufts of pale grass, hardly darker than the snowbanks.

The corners were where danger might lurk. Flat though the path was, it zigzagged between the jagged monoliths, and she could rarely see very far ahead.

Crunch, crunch, crunch, said her feet on the grit.

The light was strange, an ethereal blend of silver and jet. Even the stones had taken on a transparent look, the shadows were indistinct and ghostly. Although the air was calm, it was bitterly cold on her heated face. Her breath came in puffs of rainbow-tinted fog.

Crunch. Crunch. Crunch.

An ordeal could not possibly be so easy. She began to use a little commonsense caution, slowing down at each blind corner, edging around cautiously in case some horror barred her path. Always the Way was empty in the moonlight.

Leéb! Think of Leéb! Whoever you are, my darling, I am coming back to you.

How far would she have to go? The great peaks glimmered against the sky, unchanging. Surely the Defile could not take her right through the range, whatever range it was, because then she would be Outside, and pixies never went Outside, where the demons lurked.

She had argued with the Keeper! Talking back like an impudent child . . . She paused at another blind corner, where the Way angled around a wall of rock. Hugging that wall, she peered cautiously, first one eye, then both. She saw rocks and dirt and a few patches of snow and the gravel path. Nothing more.

As she moved away from the wall, her shadow moved upon it. Out of the corner of her eye—

Two shadows!

She screamed and was running before she knew it.

She had not looked back! She had heeded the Keeper's warning! But out of the corner of her eye she had seen the second shadow right behind her own. It had been a trick of the light, hadn't it? Just dark streaks in the stone? Sticks . . . the shadow of a tree maybe! But there were no trees.

She hurtled along the path with her hair flying and the air cold in her throat.

Cru-unch. Cru-unch. Something had changed in her footsteps. They did not sound the same. They seemed to echo off something right behind her.

At her heels.

Keeping pace. *Cru-unch, cru-unch, cru-unch* . . . It was staying with her, at her back. Twigs. Weathered branches. Just a freak of moonlight—not truly bones! Do not look behind you!

She ran until a stitch stabbed her side and she could run no more. Staggering with exhaustion, she slowed to a walk. Nothing ran into her, nothing grabbed her. Over the thunder of her heart she heard those steps still there, keeping time, stepping where she had stepped, following right at her back.

There was nothing there, she told herself firmly, and knew

that she lied. It was right behind her, close enough to breathe on her neck, if it breathed. Close enough to touch her, if it could touch.

Everyone in the College had done this, had walked the Defile. They had not been eaten by monsters! It was a trick to frighten her, an illusion.

"Who are you?" she shrilled, not daring to look around again.

There was no reply, no wind. Only her leaping heart, and those wrongly repeating footsteps.

"Tell me who you are!" she cried, louder. "In the name of the Keeper, tell me!"

This time there was an answer, but whether it was a sigh on the night air or only a thought in her head, she could not tell.

I am your guide.

"I don't need a guide! Go away!"

There was no reply, but she sensed that the wraith or whatever it was had not gone away. It still paced right behind her, matching stride for stride. She walked faster. She slowed down. Unseen, it clung like a shadow. She stopped completely, cringing lest something dry and hard should blunder into her. Nothing did. It was standing still as she was, waiting for her to move again.

It was nothing! She should spin around and she would see only the empty path behind her.

"You cannot hurt me!"

But others can.

She still could not tell if that was a voice or only a thought in her own head.

"And I don't believe that, either!" Raising her chin, Thaïle began to march, swinging her arms vigorously. "Mistress Mearn said she had come this way. Mist came this way. I expect Jain ca—" She stopped.

A shadowy shape stood in the distance, athwart her path.

It was so vague that she could hardly make it out, a hint of moonlight and shadow against the rocks, the image of a man. It was illusion, a trick of vision like shapes seen in nighttime embers or in clouds by day. Yet the more she squinted and strained her eyes, the more definite it seemed to be. Sudden anger replaced her fear—tricks and illusions! The Keeper herself had commented on her courage. She would not let such foolery frighten her. Big, soft Mist, yes. Mist might have panicked at hints of shadow, but she was not going to. She was doing this for love, for Leéb.

She took two or three steps more and the shape was clearer. She stopped again.

"Who is that?" she demanded.

It is a jotunn, one of the white-haired demons.

Her teeth chattered on their own for a moment, refusing to obey her. "Is it alive?" Maybe she did need a guide.

It died in the War of the Five Warlocks. The voice—if it was a voice—was utterly devoid of emotion. No amusement, or anger, or sadness. Just answers.

A thousand years dead? "Then it cannot hurt me!" Thaïle insisted, as much to herself as to the unseen presence at her back. She lurched forward shakily and continued along the path toward the thing . . . the illusion.

If it was a trick of the light, it should fade as she drew nearer. It did not. It grew more solid, although it was still only a silver patch of brightness against shadows, a man in moonlight among the rocks. Against her will, she began to make out detail, a man so huge that her head would barely reach his chest. He wore a shiny helmet, and breeches, and boots. His flowing beard and mustache were the brightest part of him, except for his eyes. His eyes were watching her come. He knew she was there. He was waiting for her, starting to smile.

Moonlight glinted on his helmet, his eyes, his sword.

She stopped again, reluctant to draw near.

Now she knew why there was a wraith at her back. There could be no retreat; she must go on.

"What does he want?" she demanded.

He wants to kill you.

"Then he will be disappointed." She eased forward on absurdly shaky legs.

The white-haired demon grew ever more solid. Moonlight shone on the long blade, and the silver beard, and the heavy, hairy limbs. Teeth gleamed.

Thaïle stopped.

The demon began to walk, and now he was openly grinning at her and hefting his sword in anticipation. She could see his chest move as he breathed.

She almost backed up a step, and then remembered that what was behind her might be a great deal worse than what was in front.

"Go away!" she shouted. "In the name of the Keeper!"

The demon laughed, as if he had heard that. He was striding toward her and now she heard gravel crunch under his great boots.

"What's he going to do?" she wailed.

He is going to kill you.

"No!"

"Yes. You are Stheam. You die now.

She smelled a strange salty tang in the air.

Stheam was only sixteen, a herder of sheep, and no one had ever shown him how to use a sword, but jotnar had come ashore at Wild Cape, and Grandsire had called in all the young men from the hills and issued swords and shields. Stheam had been told to stand watch here by the moorings in case more longships came.

He couldn't fight a *giant*!

Dropping the awkward, cumbersome shield, Stheam bolted off into the rocks. There was no path there. He scrambled up as fast as he could, but in a moment he knew he was cornered. Boots rasped on stone behind him.

He spun around. "Please! I don't want to die!"

The monster loomed over him, grinning, flaxen-haired, with a sheen of sweat on his shoulders and wind-reddened face, a joyous gleam of hatred in inhuman blue eyes. He probably did not understand the words. He would not heed them if he did.

He poked playfully with his sword. Stheam threw up his own blade instinctively and it was smashed aside like a twig, sending spasms of pain up his arm. With a snort of disgust the giant thrust his sword into Stheam's belly, pushing it deep and twisting until the point grated on the rock behind.

The pain was beyond imagining. He fell to the ground, clutching the bloody mess falling out of him. He tried to scream, and that hurt even more.

Oh, Gods! The pain! He whimpered animal noises, feeling blood rush hot through his fingers.

The warrior kicked him a few times to roll him over, then leered down in triumph and contempt. He spat, and even through the awful torment in his gut, Stheam felt the spittle splash cold on his cheek. The jotunn walked away, leaving his victim writhing in death agony.

It was not quick, and nobody came.

Thaïle lay facedown on the path, the gravel hard and cold on her face. She was shaking violently and felt sick. She must not be dead, then. She was a woman again, Thaïle.

"Am I alive?" she whispered to the ground.

You are alive.

"I thought he killed me."

He killed Stheam.

She raised her head. The Way stretched ahead of her, empty. The warrior had vanished and the eerie shadows were deserted. She felt her abdomen with nervous fingers, but found no wound. The awful pain had gone, too.

Her convulsive shivers warned her that she would freeze if she stayed. She struggled to her knees on the sharp rocks and then to her feet. She did not look behind her. She began to walk unsteadily through the frosty stillness of the night. Her shadow walked at her feet, sometimes two shadows.

Was that all? Could that be all? Had she survived the ordeal? Then why did she still see two shadows? Whatever was casting that second shadow was not human. Had some experience like Stheam been enough to drive Mist into madness?

Something moved in the darkness ahead and her heart leaped wildly. She stopped. Not again!

Again. She saw another movement. Hint became form as she watched; form became substance. Tricks of the light became watchers. Three shapes waited for her on one side, two more on the other. She tried to take a step backward and there was a wall there. The rocks were more like corners of buildings, high board fences. The moonlight was yellowish, not so bright now, it was lamplight from a window, but they had seen her. She had no weapons this time. She was a woman, trapped in a courtyard.

Trapped by shadows—but she could see them solidify as they approached, and their voices were becoming audible. They were between her and the gateway. They were chuckling and making jokes in words she did not understand and did not need to. The wall was cold, rough stone at her back. It was not to be death this time, at least not at first.

"Stop them!" she screamed.

You are Hoon, sighed that faint inhuman voice in her mind. *They are imps, the dark-haired demons.*

"They are men!" They were real men, not mere shadows, living bodies, brown-skinned, dark and bearded and armored. They were not as large as jotnar, but every one was larger than Hoon. Hoon could hear her sister-in-law yelling at the children upstairs. She could hear horses and wagons going by in the street. She opened her mouth to scream for help and legionaries rushed at her. She dived for the gap between them. Hands caught her and reeled her in, in to the heavy male laughter.

More hands seized her face and forced it up to meet bearded lips. His mouth was foul. Hands held wrists and ankles. More hands were fumbling with her clothes, stripping them off, fumbling with her body . . . Pain and humiliation. Then just pain. And finally death of course, when they were all satisfied.

Again Thaïle lay on the cold, cold gravel of the Way, and the moon had not moved in the sky.

"How many more?" she whimpered.

All you can endure, and then more.

She was uninjured, except where she had scraped her hands on the ground. Her *body* was uninjured. Her mind was another matter. It would crumble to nothing if it had to take much more of this. She heaved herself up again and stumbled forward. There was no going back.

She had not gone a dozen paces before she was Keem, drowning while a boot forced his face down into the mud.

She was Drume. She was Shile.

"What lies Outside?"
Death and torture and slavery.
All of those, and more.

She died in darkness and in sunlight. She was stabbed, and clubbed, and raped to death by jotnar twice her size.

She was a soldier in a squad trapped by a dragon, rampaging in quest of bronze as the men desperately stripped off their armor and hurled it at the searing, incandescent monster. It roared and flamed, and charred skin from flesh and then flesh and bones, too.

Reen was tending his father's herd when a squad of refugee djinns came by. He did not realize his danger, or he would not have waited to speak with them. They spread him over a stump and sodomized him repeatedly. He lost a lot of blood and died two days later of a fever.

Quole had screamed for help until she could scream no more, and none had come. Clutching her child tightly, she backed into a corner of the cellar. The gnomes knew she was trapped now. They came creeping forward through the gloom, piping in shrill excitement. There was barely enough light even to show the gleam of their eyes and their innumerable little sharp teeth and nails. Gnomes could see in the dark, though. They were tiny and had no weapons, but they were starving.

The red-haired demons were djinns, cruel and ruthless. The gold-haired demons were elves, whose arrows nailed living bodies together.

"We need to make an example," the impish centurion said. "Take that one. String him up and flog him to death."

It was all real, every time. Always it was real death, personal death. It was never Thaïle, never just pretend. It was *Why me?* and *I am not ready!* It was always pain and humiliation and the discovery that a human body was only a sack of fluids that could be made to leak and suffer unbearably. Dying was the ultimate degradation, and sometimes it took days.

And always it was becoming Thaïle again, and realizing that this was not Thaïle's death, not yet, and climbing to her feet again afterward and going onward until the next one came.

Kaim was chained in the cell. He smelled smoke . . .

They were the wraiths of the pixies who had died in the

War of the Five Warlocks. They had been waiting in the Defile for a thousand years for someone to die their deaths again and release them—someone with Faculty.

Looq was a slave, being worked to death as a matter of policy.

"You will talk," the djinn told Reil. "You will tell us everything."

Reil did not even know what they wanted to know.

And it could all happen again! The demons were still there, Outside, waiting. Only the College and the Keeper kept them away.

Thaïle knew that, in the moments when she was Thaïle, staggering along the Way in the moonlight, waiting for the next wraith. She knew that her own death, whenever it came, could never be so bad. She knew why she had been sent to walk the Defile, why everyone in the College was sent to walk the Defile.

She knew who followed her.

She knew also what she would tell the Keeper in the morning—that Leéb did not matter any more.

Lonesome road:
> Like one that on a lonesome road
> Doth walk in fear and dread,
> And, having once turned round, walks on,
> And turns no more his head;
> Because he knows a fearful fiend
> Doth close behind him tread.

COLERIDGE, *RIME OF THE ANCIENT MARINER*

CHAPTER THREE

DOUBT AND SORROW

1

A CRUEL NORTH WIND WAS MARCHING FLURRIES OF SNOW over the moors. The sun had already lost whatever slight warmth it had offered at noontide. The foothills of the Isdruthuds lay ahead, white and inhospitable, while the towering ranges beyond promised much worse.

No defined road crossed the scaly gray landscape. The convoy of wagons was well scattered, as each driver sought the smoothest way. Being neither footsloggers nor good horsemen, dwarves traveled on wheels by preference. Their wagons were always stoutly built, and a single vehicle hauled by six dogged mountain ponies could carry a dozen or more armed warriors all day. In this instance most of the carts were high-piled with loot, but one of them included a couple of prisoners.

Wrapped in several layers of fur, Inos huddled next to the emperor, using him as a windbreak. She wished that those famous Dwanishian craftsmen had thought to provide at least an awning to keep off the weather, plus springs of the superb steel that only they could manufacture—but doubtless dwarves would view both as decadent luxuries. Dwarvish transportation rapidly converted nondwarves into bruised jellies, baked or frozen as the case might be.

Up front, the driver slouched on the bench as if half asleep, yet he bounced at every rock. The next wagon ahead was being driven by Raspnex. Imperors as windbreaks, warlocks driving carts? The world had gone mad.

She twisted her head to make sure Gath was still in sight. He preferred to walk as much as he could, just as she would if she had a decent pair of boots. He was visible in the distance, striding along between two diminutive trotting goblins. The guards did not object because the goblins were allies and could run down any jotunn pup with one leg tied behind their backs.

The caravan's nominal commander, Sergeant Girthar, was a mundane, but he took orders from the warlock. That seemed to be more politics than sorcery. There was another sign of insanity in the world—that sorcery should now be banned as dangerous. Raspnex had discarded his Long Runner goblin disguise; he had refused to use power to save Kadie. And where was poor Kadie now? What was she doing, seeing, suffering, feeling? Inos sighed.

Snowflakes swirled in the air.

"You mustn't brood, Inos," Shandie said.

Brood? She choked back an angry retort, for of course he was right. She had been brooding, about Kadie. She would never forgive herself for what had happened to Kadie—or was going to happen to Kadie, abducted by a horde of savages. Kadie filled her nightmares and was waiting for her when she awoke and haunted her days. She had very little hope of ever seeing her husband again, but the thought of doing so and then having to tell him of her folly and the loss of Kadie was unbearable.

"No," she said. "Who am I to argue with the Gods?"

Shandie raised an eyebrow. The abrasions on his face had mostly healed now, or been covered over by his beard. He was a ragged, dirty, disreputable excuse for an imperor. Not that she was a notable example of queenhood.

"What about the Gods?"

"When Rap spoke with the God, They told him he would have to lose one of the children."

Shandie eased himself to a more comfortable position on the load and adjusted his fur cover. He frowned. "You didn't tell me that!"

She almost asked why she should have, when he kept secrets from her. Discretion prevailed, and she restrained her temper. "Then I forgot. That's all, really, typical divine vagueness. They wouldn't say which child, or how. They implied that all this mess was Rap's fault."

"It's not his fault, but he caused it without meaning to."

"He doesn't know how."

"He does now."

"Well, you didn't tell *me* that!" She had discovered that Shandie was a very taciturn man. He asked a lot of questions and volunteered very few answers. He had not yet told her about the magic scrolls. Raspnex had, and she was grateful to the warlock for that—it was wonderful to know that Rap had been in good health as recently as a few days ago—but the imperor had not seen fit to trust her with that information. In a week, she had not penetrated his shell, and he still refused to say exactly where Rap had gone. She could understand the reasoning, but it rankled.

He grunted. "Sorry. The warlock explained to us, that night in Hub. There used to be an unlimited supply of magic. Rap cut it off somehow. Apparently he thought he was doing a good deed, but he had made it impossible for the wardens to counter Zinixo's Covin. It had something to do with Faerie. I don't know the details—do you?"

She shook her head. "It hurts him to talk about sorcery."

For a few minutes neither spoke. The wagon lurched and jangled over rocks and hummocks. This was the least uncomfortable of the wagons, laden mostly with the party's tents and a mountain of leather. Dwarves had curious ideas about loot. Several wagons carried gold and silver and were unbearably knobby and noisy to ride in. Others were full of rope, canvas, alum, and fuller's earth. Given the same chances, jotnar would have taken spices and dyes, works of art and fine fabrics. Dwarves spurned those as impractical conceits.

"But the God's message is interesting," the imperor said. "Did They say that *Rap* must lose a child, or you yourself must, or both of you?"

"I don't know."

"They can be very cruel, Inos, but They rarely add to Their punishments by foretelling them. Perhaps They meant *only* one child? They may have intended Their words as a comfort for you."

"Perhaps They meant he would lose one and I another? As I recall, They implied that one child was a minimum. Frankly, I think we are all doomed!"

"Don't ever give up hope!" Shandie said sternly. "If They specified one child, then They had reason to do so, and They gave the message to Rap, not to you. If They foresaw these events happening and being important, then the circumstances must be ordained and therefore not your fault. I think you have cause for hope there, Inos. Trust in the Good!"

There was just enough difference in their ages for him to seem young to her. Pomposity and youth were an unpleasant blend. He was imperor by right of birth and he could claim to be on a diplomatic mission at the moment, but in truth he was a penniless refugee and more or less a prisoner of war. He had blundered into an ambush and almost died because of it; he had even lost a letter Rap had written to her, which she resented unreasonably. Again she suppressed a snippy reply.

"I expect you're right. And I am not the only one with loved ones in danger. I think you were doing some brooding yourself."

He smiled weakly. "Perhaps a little. I have had several hundred predecessors on the Opal Throne, and not one of them was ever overthrown by a dwarf!" He had evaded the question.

"Who knows? Your subjects believe you still reign. Who can say what hoaxes may have been carried out in the past?"

"Perhaps. But I am the first imperor ever captured by goblins!"

There was no denying that humiliation. "I meant to ask you," Inos said, making a digression more tactical than tactful. "You had a companion who escaped?"

"A man by the name of Ylo, a superb horseman. I think he escaped."

"So where will he have gone?"

Shandie grimaced.

"Well?" she demanded, shutting the trap.

"I think he will have gone back to tell my wife."

Shandie would lecture for hours about his dreams for the Impire, about justice and equitable taxation and the rule of law, but in the last week he had not once mentioned his wife.

"Tell me about her."

He sighed. "Eshiala? She is the most beautiful woman in the world."

"You love her deeply?"

"Beyond words."

"What's she like?"

He shrugged. "Tall . . . Not as tall as you, but she's pure imp, of course—no offense meant. Dark coloring, naturally. Face, figure . . . How can I describe perfection?"

"Well, apart from that?" Inos persisted. "What does she enjoy?"

"Enjoy?"

"Yes. Does she like music? Dancing? Riding?"

"I . . . I'm not . . . She's a marvelous dancer now. I mean, she was always naturally graceful but . . ." His voice trailed off uncertainly.

"How long have you been married?"

"Three years—but we've been apart a lot of that time, you understand. We were only together a few weeks after the wedding and . . . And I was terribly busy after I got back to Hub last summer."

"Too busy, you mean?" she inquired, wielding her best harpoon smile, spoiling the effect with a sudden grunt as the wagon lurched into an especially bad pothole.

"Much too busy—my grandfather was in his dotage and had almost let the Impire fall apart. Ylo helped me stick it back together again."

Friend Shandie was very good at manipulating conversation. Perhaps it was a military thing—feints, diversions, attacks deflected. Inos thought of several pertinent comments and discarded all of them. Instead she asked, "How old is she, the impress?"

"Er, twenty."

"It must be very hard for her." Married at seventeen to a man who disappeared after a few weeks and left her with child? Married to a man so busy that he didn't have time to entertain her when he got back? Inos had a vague memory that the prince imperial had married a commoner. To be promoted to the highest rank of the aristocracy at seventeen would be a shattering experience for a girl who had any sensitivity at all. Inos also suspected that the imperor did not know his wife nearly as well as he thought he did, or should.

"Tell me about this Ylo man."

"My signifer. A soldier, an aristocrat. He was quite a hero in the army."

"Young? Old?"

"Young."

After a long pause, the imperor added, "A bit of a rogue. Good-looking."

"So that's why you were brooding!"

The imperial eyes flashed angrily. "What do you mean by that?"

"He thinks the goblins killed you?"

"It would be a reasonable assumption."

Inos sighed and then smiled sympathetically at the troubled young man beside her. "We were both brooding and we both have much to brood about."

He nodded. "Yes, I'm afraid we do. I trust my wife absolutely, you understand, but if she believes she is a widow, then she will have to consider our child's welfare." For a while the imperor stared blankly out at the rolling moorland, doubtless imagining his wife married to the handsome signifer.

"She is physically safe, though," Inos said. "Or I assume she is. That's one comfort."

"True. Whereas your lambs are not."

"And few women are as fickle as most men fear. She will be very unusual if she forgets her love for you and throws herself into another man's arms right away. Two years is a normal mourning period—I don't mean legally, I mean it takes that long to recover from a bereavement. You will just have to hurry back to her as soon as you can."

Shandie did not reply to that. He scratched his stubble thoughtfully, as if planning a speech, and then changed the subject.

"Inos, even here we are in some danger, you and I and Gath. When we get to Gwurkiarg the risks will become much worse. I've been talking with the warlock, and we agree that there is no need for you to come all the way to Dwanish with us."

"I understood that we were prisoners of war?"

"In theory. But Raspnex is still warlock of the north. Dwarves don't argue with him. Tomorrow we should arrive at Throgg. I visited it once. It's a mean little hamlet, one of those sorry border places that gets destroyed whenever it grows big enough to be worth fighting over. The buildings are a bedraggled collection and the people are a hard lot. However, this war isn't going to come its way. It's relatively secure this time. We'll leave you there, and you can hide out in safety, if not comfort. By summer the way should be clear for you to make a dash back to the coast and catch a ship. Maybe the summer after, even."

"The prospect does not exactly fill me with rapture."

Shandie chuckled cheerfully. "But any port in a storm, right? Take up weaving or bird watching! You must think of your kingdom, and war is no place for a woman." If he noted her reaction, he gave no sign of it. "You have children to consider," he added. "I think the snow's passing, don't you?"

Nothing ever roused Inos's temper faster than a suspicion that she was being patronized. "Mmm. Spell out the Dwanishian danger for me," she said sweetly.

He shrugged. "Just that the warlock and I plan to appear before the Directorate to spread the news about the new protocol. The meeting will be private, but word of our presence in Gwurkiarg may get around."

She donned an expression of candied innocence. "Dwanish was Zinixo's home ground, right? He went back there after Rap destroyed his sorcery, and he spent almost twenty years there. He built his power base there. Surely all the sorcerers in Dwanish were coerced into the Covin long ago?" *Am I understanding correctly? Can a mere woman grasp such convoluted concepts?*

Shandie shrugged. "Raspnex does not think so. Dwarves are such a suspicious breed that they're not easily trapped, although he doesn't put it in quite those terms, of course."

"Let me guess," she said, still being all virginal and dulcet. "You and the warlock go before the Directorate and make your little speeches, appealing for help. But Zinixo would not have left his home base unguarded, so he has a spy or two on the Directorate itself. The spy sends an occult message to the Covin, and in a flash the hall is stiff with sorcerers. Am I getting close?"

The imperor gave her a calculating look. His beard was salted with snowflakes, which were flying thicker than ever. "You've been talking with the warlock, too?"

"Not about this."

"Well, I'm impressed! Queens learn to think strategically, I suppose. Yes, you're exactly right! Zinixo must know by now what we're up to, and he has hundreds of smart people utterly devoted to his cause. The Directorate will certainly be under surveillance, at the least."

His attitude made Inos' fingernails itch, but admittedly he was making sense. Although it was many years since she had seen Zinixo, the thought of him could still pucker her skin. If half of what she had been told was true, then the vindictive dwarf would dearly love to get his hands on Rap's wife and son. She would prefer to deny him the satisfaction, if possible. A year of concealment in the odious-sounding Throgg might be preferable, and she did have a responsibility to her realm. She shuddered to think what might be happening back there now, with no one to keep peace between the factions.

"If I had only myself to consider," she said reluctantly, "I'd probably come along just for the fun of it. I'm sure Raspnex has something up his sleeve, probably a sharp knife. But I must think of Gath. Perhaps he and I should stay behind and study decorum and social graces at the knees of the nobility of Throgg."

Shandie cleared his throat and avoided her eye. "Actually, we were thinking just of you, Inos. I realize that he is very young, and I promised Rap that I would be bound by your wishes where Gath was concerned—but that was when we thought he was safe in Krasnegar. Now he's caught in the mill like the rest of us, so I don't think my promise is valid anymore."

Inos took a very deep breath and the feathery snowflakes tickled her nose. "Oh? You were planning to leave me and take my son?"

"Well, yes. The warlock seems to think he might be useful, although I'm not sure exactly how."

God of Murder!

"Emshandar?" Inos said in an excessively gentle tone.

Shandie looked around at her in surprise. His eyes widened at what he saw.

"Don't you remember," she continued softly, "when you were a skinny little boy, one night you went to the Rotunda? You saw Warlock Zinixo try to kill the man who is now my husband."

"Rap bursting into flames? I had nightmares for months."

"And then what happened? Do you remember, Emshandar?"

"I . . . You ran to him and . . . and hugged him."

"Yes, I did," Inos said, smiling. "Fire and all. My aunt always told me I was impulsive. *And you think I will desert my son?*" she roared.

The dwarf driver turned around to see what the noise was all about. The imperor flinched. "Be sensible, Inos!"

"No, you be sensible! That is the most insulting suggestion I have ever heard! Gath is only a child. If Warlock Raspnex thinks he can use him, then he comes and asks me, is that clear? And I decide! And you can take your thriving metropolis of

Throgg and shove it up your Imperial toga! Is that absolutely clear, your Majesty?"

"There is no need to be offensive."

"You started it! There is no need for you to patronize me!"

A small smile twisted Shandie's stubble. "Why not? You were trying to mother me!"

"I . . . Well, that's different!" She returned his grin. "No woman ever believes any man understands marriage. I suppose no man ever believes any woman understands warfare. Truce?"

"Truce!"

"How about a treaty of cooperation?"

"What does that mean?" he asked warily.

"Why didn't you tell me you could communicate with my husband?"

Shandie looked out over the moor for a moment, hiding his expression. When he turned back to her, his face was unreadable again. "Lord Umpily has been captured. Right at the beginning, Raspnex warned us that the scrolls might not be secure once the Covin learned about them. Our messages may be intercepted, or even traced back to their source."

"And you thought I was a flighty, feather-headed woman? You thought that once I knew about them, I would jeopardize security by pestering Rap with innumerable love letters?"

"Not that bad. Something on those lines, I suppose."

"Well, I didn't," she said miserably. "I can't torture him by telling him what I've done. I sent him three words on the warlock's scroll: 'I love you!' That's all. He'll know my handwriting. He'll know I've been warned." *He'll think everything is all right. He'll be deceived. Lying by omission is still lying.*

"I'm sorry, Inos." Shandie sounded as if he meant it.

"Apology accepted." She sighed. "Now, how can my son possibly help the warlock when we get to Dwanish?"

"I don't know. I don't think Raspnex does, either, but he's got some sort of vague idea, or hunch, maybe."

"Gath has prescience, but it's very weak. The warlock himself must be much more powerful."

"Yes." Still, Shandie was giving nothing away.

Inos studied him for a moment. "The only way I can think of that Gath might be useful is as bait."

The imperor sighed. "That had occurred to me, too."

2

"LIFTED TO SADDLE!" KADIE SAID. "JUMPED UP IN BACK! Put arms around. Dug spurs in horse. Galloped toward sunset. Kissed warmly."

"Kissed horse?" Blood Beak demanded with open disbelief.

"Oh, of course not! He kissed Princess Taol'dor!"

"Why?"

"Because it's romantic for princes—"

"Must not speak impish!"

Kadie snorted. "Wanted to kiss her," she said sulkily.

"Kiss in bed, when lodge fire banked. Is obscene other times."

Really! Feeling her cheeks burning, she nudged her pony to a canter. Goblins had absolutely no idea of romance! Blood Beak did not seem to know the difference between a kiss and, er, more intimate behavior.

Kadie was astride a pert little gray, now named Allena the Mare. Her companion was running alongside. He had been doing so all day, burdened with a bow and a quiver and a sword, and yet he matched her new pace with no apparent strain. Behind them, their twenty-four-man guard would keep up just as easily.

"Tell more!" Blood Beak demanded.

It was understandable that he would want her to do most of the talking; she could not imagine how he had breath to speak at all. She must have told him fifty stories in the last few days, all the great classics. Yet somehow romances lost something when translated into goblin, and she thought it would be far more appropriate for her to be teaching him impish than for her to be talking goblin all the time. His insistence upon that was ominous and best not thought about.

The sun was shining warmly and a blustery wind smelled of spring. It also made the farmhouses and haystacks burn well.

The eastern sky was muddy with smoke, the landscape in all directions heavily populated with columns of goblins. To spare her mount she was allowed to use the lanes and roads, but the horde itself traveled in a straight line, across the country. The vanguard ran down all the fugitives, even those on horses. The rearguard set fire to anything that would burn. Every few hours the army would reach another town and sack it, raping and killing all who remained there—like trained acrobats, goblins built human pyramids against the walls and were usually over the top before the defenders had notched their first arrow.

Fortunately Kadie rarely had to watch any of these horrors at close quarters. She had not seen King Death Bird in several days, and no dwarves, either. The dwarvish army had gone its own way. She was a solitary captive princess in a mass of thousands of brutal savages, the only prisoner who survived the nightly atrocities. She was a tourist, an enforced companion for the king's son.

"All right," she agreed. "One more story. But I'm going to tell this one in impish. It will sound better. Or will that be too hard for you to understand?"

Blood Beak shot an angry glare up at her. He was bare-chested as usual, his khaki skin shining with sweat, his greasy queue bouncing on his back between bow and quiver. He was not as tall as she was, but very broad-shouldered, and from above she could also see how astonishingly thick he was, too. She sometimes wondered how he would look in decent clothes. His legs would certainly be impressive in hose, but his face! . . . even if he could be persuaded to shave . . . Long nose, square eyes . . .

"I understand very good. What's this one about?"

"It's about Princess Pearlflower of Kerith and how she was captured by jotunn raiders."

"And rescued, of course?" He showed his big teeth.

"Of course."

"Before she was raped?"

"Yes!"

"Sound not like jotnar." He could speak passable impish when he chose, although his accent was thick as mud. "You think someone coming you rescue, Kadolan?"

Of course she did—princesses were always rescued—but he would jeer if she said so. She had a magic sword, which everyone else seemed to have forgotten about, and both Mom and the imperor had promised they would get the warlock to help as soon as he could. Where were they all now? Still, distance didn't matter to sorcerers. And her own father was a sorcerer—just wait until Dad heard that she'd been kidnapped! Of course someone would rescue her!

If they didn't, she would escape on her own, somehow.

Not getting an answer, the goblin said, "No rescue!"

"So? What happens when we get to Hub?"

Blood Beak laughed. Goblins didn't laugh very often, but when they did they sounded quite, er, normal?—*impish.* "Burn it!"

Not very likely! Hub had never, ever, fallen to an enemy. Hub had never been sacked like all other cities had. "And then?"

He seemed surprised by the question. "Then go home, maybe."

They were heading up quite a steep hill now, through trees that she suspected might be an orchard and was certain would soon be firewood. Blood Beak was managing the incline better than weary Allena was.

"Is that all? You have no plan, do you? No purpose in all this killing and destroying!"

"Yes, do! Are doing because is fun! Imps now better know than attack the goblins more times. Maybe do this every year!"

She pulled a face. "Now you're talking stupid! Big-mouth goblin! When the Impire gets you bottled up again, it'll brick up every pass in the Pondague Mountains."

"Then climb over walls! Or not go home. Goblins stay in the Impire and let imps have the forest."

"You admit this is a better place to live?"

He looked up angrily and she thought his cheeks had flushed greener at being trapped. "Is for sissies! Real men grow in forest."

"So you are going back! And you'll see me safely home to Krasnegar?"

"No." He flashed her a sweat-soaked grin. "Will be first wife mine. Promise from Father."

That was what she'd been afraid of, but no one had ever said so and she hadn't asked. That was why he insisted she speak goblin. It was also why she was not being molested, of course. She suspected that otherwise these barbarians would treat even a princess badly.

"And suppose I don't want to be your wife—first or last?"

"Get beaten," he said happily. "Be beaten anyway."

"Suppose you're killed in the fighting?" She had noticed that he was kept well away from danger, but she wasn't about to say so.

"Marry brother, Big Claws or Black Feather."

Marry the next goblin king and be goblin queen, one day? Raise lots of ugly little goblin princes and princesses? Kadie tried to imagine herself turning up at Krasnegar to visit the family, with her green husband and her green babies. Gath would laugh his stupid head off! Again she wondered how Blood Beak would look in proper clothes. Short and thick, all right from the neck down, but imagine him at a ball or a banquet? In candlelight goblins weren't just greenish but really green!

One of the books she had treasured in her childhood had contained a lithograph showing a frog prince—green face, and very wide mouth, and bulgy eyes. She had never seen a real frog in her life, but—

Kadie decided she was *most definitely* going to be rescued! A handsome prince would be best, but Papa would suffice.

3

AS RAP REACHED OUT WITH HIS RIGHT HAND, SOMETHING jerked him off balance. His left foot began to slide. He grabbed blindly, found a flimsy bunch of fronds, and clung tight; heaved his foot back into position on the slippery root and paused, gasping with effort and fright. He was spread-eagled on a slope steep enough to be called a cliff, half buried in a prickly shrub, every part of him soaked. Rain poured at his head and back. Water cascaded down on his face, on his shoulders, and eventually ran out the toes of his boots. Very far below him a lot more of it roared white over rocks.

This was a troll shortcut.

He had been working his way along this almost-sheer face for the last hour. It was upholstered with a dense mat of shrubs and mosses, which was not always perfectly anchored to the rock. Every once in a while patches would peel away in his grasp. Meanwhile, the strap of his satchel had caught on a twig. That was what had jerked him when he moved. In order to free it, he would have to persuade his left hand to release the death grip it held on a vine. The satchel was an accursed, awkward, heavy thing, but it contained his gold, his knife, and the magic scrolls. Just about everything else had gone, even his sword, but he must not lose the satchel.

First step, then—test right hand grip. He tugged gently at the fronds. A whole thicket of fern came away in a shower of mud and pebbles . . .

For three days after escaping from Casfrel, Rap had been very glad that he was half jotunn. The fugitives had scrambled up a water-filled gorge, then an ice-filled ravine, several chimneys, and a scree slope, finally crossing the divide by way of a glacier. He had understood then why the Imperial Army had been so unsuccessful at catching escaping trolls, even if he had almost frozen to death during the lesson. At night he had slept within a mass of three trolls and one jotunn, heaped together for warmth. They had descended the pass into thick snow, slithering down in avalanches. He had been completely buried twice, being dug out by Thrugg.

Now they were down into the forest, so he supposed he should be grateful for the other half of his mixed inheritance. Jotunn Darad was going insane in the steamy, rain-filled, bug-infested gloom, but a part faun should be able to cope. The trolls were in their element. Visibility had been virtually zero for the last two days, and clothes were rotting away in the never-ending downpour. His left boot had almost fallen apart, and his right was little better.

He was not at all sure how much longer he could cling to

this cliff. Of course he was only imagining it, but the roar of the torrent seemed to be developing a hungry tone. It was a long way down. If he fell, he would have several leisurely seconds to review his life before it came to a sudden end.

Trouble was, he would use sorcery. He wasn't brave enough to die without a struggle, but to save himself that way would surely condemn both him and his friends to a slower and much less pleasant death. The Covin was alert now, and he could not count on it blundering a second time as badly as it had blundered at Casfrel.

Powerful though the Covin was, it had failed to subdue the sorceress in its first surprise attack; Ainopple had put up a ferocious resistance and died unvanquished. Even Thrugg had been unable to make out the details, but most likely she had succumbed to simple old age. She had needed power just to keep herself alive, and in the distraction of the battle her resources had run out. The Covin might have suffered some wounds of its own; at first it had made no search for other sorcerers in the district, or had done so perfunctorily. The hunt had begun in earnest only after a lapse of several days, perhaps when someone used hindsight, or just recognized the significance of trolls escaping. Had Rap and his companions still been in the narrow passes, they could have been located easily, but by then they were already on the western slopes, needles in the world's greatest haystack.

Which did not mean they might not be found yet. Day and night, occult vision searched the trees. In the crazy metaphorical plane of the ambience, Rap could see those eyes, hear those ears. He sensed pillars of light or low crooning of voices, and sometimes he thought they were within yards of him. As far as sorcery went, other people were a much more effective cover than trees. A city would be much safer than a jungle.

Which meant he had to do this the hard way. The most insignificant use of magic now might be detected. He had not dared even unroll the magic scrolls in a week.

He thought briefly of Acopulo sitting at ease on a ship. He wondered if his own favorite armchair before the fire in Krasnegar now held the imperor, sprawling back in comfort, chatting to Inos, while Signifer Ylo smothered himself in rustic jotunn maidens belowstairs. He wondered what Warlock Raspnex was up to.

And what he himself was up to. Day and night, something haunted the back of Rap's mind, some brilliant idea that had come to him, some time, some place, and now evaded all efforts of memory to snare it. Something important. Men had gone mad over less . . .

Shrubbery crackled and swished overhead. He looked up and caught a cataract full in the face. He blinked and shouted warnings as a huge bare foot appeared beside his left hand. The undergrowth roiled briefly; the owner of the foot came slithering down to his level in a shower of water and leaves. He caught glimpses of a naked, parchment-colored body, and then Norp's face was level with his. She grinned, displaying enormous teeth and a mouth full of half-chewed leaves.

Male trolls were bad enough. The females were even uglier, possibly because they lacked beards. Thrugg's face was acceptable as an animal muzzle, but a hairless troll was a grotesque parody of what a human being should look like. Norp was only a child, younger than Kadie, and yet she outweighed Rap himself. She was hideous, and a nice kid.

She grunted a question through a mouthful of vegetation. A troll's idea of a snack was to rip off a branch and eat it whole—twigs, bark, and all. He deciphered: "Resting?"

"Admiring the scenery." It was difficult to think under the rain's constant hammering.

Another series of leafy mumbles translated to: "This is a bad part, and it gets worse."

How did she know that? Neither Norp nor Urg had any occult powers; neither had ever come this way before, and yet they seemed to understand the landscape by instinct. Thrugg had gone on ahead. Urg was helping Darad bring up the rear. All three trolls had long since discarded their slave clothes. The sun never shone in this rain-soaked land, and their doughy hides were impervious to thorns and insects. Rap thought he had lost about a quarter of his own skin and was still losing it faster than he could grow it back.

"Just unhook that strap for me, then, would you?" He braced himself to try again. Burying his face in the soggy moss, he stretched out as far as he could to his right. He found a tangle of roots and grasped it with frozen fingers. He tugged, and this time it seemed firm enough. He persuaded his left hand to let go. The cliff was not *quite* vertical, after all. Had it not been so thickly overgrown, he would have called it a waterfall. Then he brought his left foot closer. He had very little skin left on his left foot. He found a purchase, moved his right leg, and everything seemed to let go at the same instant. He yelled in terror as he began to slide.

Norp grabbed for him, and caught the satchel strap. For a moment she took his whole weight as he dangled over the void. Then the strap broke.

Her reflexes were astonishing. A great paw snatched his shoulder in midair and held him bodily until he found better handholds. His heart thundered.

"Thanks!" he gasped. "Good work!"

"You want . . . me carry you?"

"Oh, I think I'll manage. But that was a nice rescue. I thought I'd gone that time!"

She beamed with childish pleasure.

Rap felt rather proud himself, for he had refrained from using sorcery in that little episode. Nevertheless, it had lost him about half his pants, and the satchel. It was long gone downstream now, scrolls and gold and all. A couple of weeks of this, Thrugg said, would bring them to his mother's place. Fortunately, Rap had always believed in traveling light, but he wished now he had headed for Zark and sent old Acopulo to handle the troll end of the business.

4

STAR OF THE MORNING HAD MADE AN EASY TRIP FROM MALFIN to Coopli—easy for late winter, that was. She was a small cargo ship with little room for passengers, but jotunn-built and more seaworthy than most; so her master had assured Acopulo. A lucky vessel, also, he had insisted. Two days out of Coopli, she had run out of good fortune.

At first Acopulo was too ill to mind. He considered it unfair that he always needed three or four days to gain his sea legs, only to lose them again after a few hours in port, but that was how the Gods had arranged the matter. He suspected that They disapproved of imps afloat on principle. He also suspected that he was about to die, but then he always thought that on a ship. The more violent motion added by the storm could do nothing to make him more miserable.

As his faculties began to return, however, he realized that he had never seen a cabin tilt to and fro at quite such remarkable angles. Nor had he ever heard a ship making quite such loud groaning noises. The occasional shuddering motion was new to him, too.

Eventually he dragged himself out of his stupor and vowed to go up on deck and see. Being a cautious man, he sat on the floor to dress, as standing erect was obviously out of the question. Had he tried to dress in his bunk he would certainly have fallen out. Then he set off on hands and knees.

At the top of the steps he stood up and tried the door. It was totally immovable. He had a sudden panicky thought that he might be locked in. The ship heeled abruptly, the door flew open, and he went flying out into madness. Wind and water together bowled him over, sent him hurtling across the deck in a heap, and slammed him into the side. For a moment he was convinced he had been washed overboard, for he was completely submerged. Then the water drained away, the ship tipped at another angle, and he began to slide. Another wave engulfed him, rolled him. Something grabbed his collar, transferred its grip to his arm, hauled him upright, and wrapped rope around him with a deft motion.

Shivering, choking, and blinking, he registered that he was bound to a mast, together with a large wet jotunn.

"Getting a little fresh air, Father?"

Acopulo made incoherent noises, remembered that he was supposedly a priest these days, and shouted, "Thank you, my son."

"Need a line if you want to stay up here, Father," the man boomed cheerfully.

A huge green wave came frothing over the side and buried the men to their waists—more like chest-deep in Acopulo's case. It swept his feet away, and the big sailor steadied him. Then it departed.

God of Mercy!

There was nothing to see but grayness. After a moment he decided that fog and twilight were merely solid rain. It was hard to tell where the sea ended and the air began, apart from a few frothy wave-tops like roofs all around. *Star of Morning* tilted again and seemed to surge straight up.

"Where are we?" he screamed.

"See those rocks yonder?" The jotunn pointed a long arm.

"No. I can't see a thing."

"Landlubber eyes!"

The ship plunged downward. Another wave came roaring across the deck, interrupting the conversation.

"Did you see the lights, then?" the jotunn yelled in Acopulo's ear. He was young and apparently enjoying himself.

"No."

"Pity. Real pretty sight, dragons."

Acopoulo screamed, *"Dragons?"*

"We're about two cablelengths off Dragon Reach. Here, we're going up again. Now look."

Rain and spume battered Acopulo's eyes, and he saw nothing. "We're in danger?"

"Well, they don't fly over water, usually. Course we're getting awful close. They can sense the iron in the ship. Thazz what brought 'em. 'Spect that's why they're blowing so much fire."

How far was a cablelength? Not very far, Acopulo thought. And dragons, while they ravened after any metal, were especially drawn to gold. What had brought them, he suspected, was the heavy moneybelt around his own waist.

"What's going to happen?" he shouted in the next momentary lull.

"I dunno," the youngster said. He shrugged, and the resulting tightening of the binding almost cut Acopulo in half. "She's dragging her anchors, so we'll likely hit the rocks soon. She'll break up quick in this sea. If not, then we'll go aground when the tide ebbs, and the dragons'll get us."

Acopulo looked up in horror at the cheerful grin. "Aren't you frightened?"

"No." The sailor pondered for a moment and then added, "If I warn't just a dumb jotunn I might be, I s'pose." This sudden insight seemed to worry him more than the dragons themselves.

"I think I want to go back to my cabin."

"Good idea. I'll help you. And, Father? . . ."

"Yes?"

The lad looked around as if to make sure that no one was listening and said apologetically, "Pray a bit when you get there, will you?"

Doubt and sorrow:
> Through the night of doubt and sorrow
> Onward goes the pilgrim band,
> Singing songs of expectation,
> Marching to the Promised Land.

B. S. INGEMANN, IGJENNEM NAT OG TRÆNGSEL, translated by S. Baring-Gould

CHAPTER FOUR

REMEDIES REFUSING

1

WOGGLE LAY ON THE GREAT WEST WAY, FOUR DAYS' RIDE from Hub. It was a nondescript place, famous only for the Warlock's Rest, reputed to be the best post inn in the Impire. It offered well-stocked stables, a famous cuisine, luxurious bedchambers, and a wide variety of services to go with them. No one knew why Woggle should be so favored, although there was a theory that outbound wealthy travelers often needed a break after four days' travel. If they did, then the Warlock's Rest could pander to all their wants. It was even rumored to possess a fair library.

Books were not uppermost on Ylo's mind as he wandered into the premier dining room. Wenches were. The sun had not yet set, but he had decided to treat himself to an early night for once. The king of Krasnegar had reported taking seven weeks to ride from Kinvale to Hub, but he had done it in less than four.

Almost. He would still need a couple of days to reach the capital, were he going there, and he had not quite reached Kinvale before running into the goblin problem. So add another week—he had still set a pace that the Imperial post would be hard put to equal. He was pleased with himself, and utterly determined never to try it again.

He accepted a table by the window and demanded attendance by the wine waiter. The Gods knew he had earned a little civilized decadence! In the sleepy red tinge of a spring evening, the gardens were afire with golden daffodils. Of course! The preflecting pool had prophesied that Eshiala would be his among the daffodils.

A buxom damsel shimmered by, smiling hopefully. He considered her thoughtfully and then shook his head. She departed with a pout. A decrepit old wine waiter came tottering over in her place. He beamed at Ylo's extravagant request for a flagon of Valdolaine, and must have passed word quickly backstage, for the next charmer to float into Ylo's field of view could not have been a day over fifteen. This time he was seriously tempted to nod, but again he declined. These were the professionals. He would find an amateur just as good and get what he wanted for free.

He picked up the menu and then laid it down again, letting his eyes wander over the big room. It was early yet, with few diners in attendance. On the way in he had observed quite a few soldiers and a sizable number of couriers. He thought he had detected an air of concern, a gravity unsuited to such surroundings. His breakneck progress had long since outrun the news of the goblin invasion, of course, at least as far as the civilian population was concerned. The government and the army must be aware of it, and the secret could not be kept very long. Wheels would be spinning madly. He had noted a substantial increase in the postal traffic going by him on the road in the last week; the choice of mounts had deteriorated. It could be only a matter of days now before the imperor broke the news to the Senate, and then the dam would burst with a vengeance. Travel would become almost impossible as the panic took hold. He had cut it very fine.

The wine arrived, deliciously cool at this time of year. Ice houses were rarely effective past early summer in Hub.

One more day in the saddle would bring him to Yewdark. And then what? Possibly the wicked had located the impress, of course, and stolen her away. He had no way of knowing except to go and see. The imperor who would make the dread announcement in the Rotunda would not be Shandie, although everyone would assume he was. Zinixo and his Covin knew better, and they knew about the goblins, but only Ylo himself knew the knot the Gods had tied with those two threads.

He was still surprised how much he mourned Shandie—a fine soldier who would have made a great imperor. He had been an inspiring mentor for Ylo, and in those later weeks on the road their relationship had mellowed into something very close to friendship. That had been another ironic twist of fate, because neither of them had been the sort of man who opened his heart to another. Indeed, that had been an alarming development, and it might have led to serious complications. Ylo suspected that by Rivermead he had been having genuine scruples about seducing Eshiala—why else had he procrastinated so long?

No matter now. The Gods had rolled Their dice, the goblins' arrows had chosen one of the two fugitives, and the other had escaped. Pray that Shandie had died at once!

Again Ylo reached for the menu. Again he looked away, this time to stare out at the twilight and the daffodils. For some strange reason he kept thinking of the king of Krasnegar, that cryptic, practical, self-sufficient faun. With his narrow, rustic morality, he had disapproved of Ylo's intentions. What would he say now? Would he not agree that a girl so young who had already seen so much tragedy in her life was deserving of a little joy? She was a sleeping princess awaiting the true lover's kiss to awaken her; a butterfly still locked in the cocoon and in need of liberation.

He could awaken, he could liberate. Her release would be his glad duty.

Married women were usually easier, being less afraid of accidents. The unmarried were more sporting, more of a challenge. He had no experience with freshly bereaved widows. In this case, he must begin by breaking the news of her widowhood. That would make things tricky. Eshiala did not seriously love her husband, of course, but she would expect to mourn him. She might feel so guilty at not being heartbroken that she would convince herself she was. No matter how genuine—and they would be genuine—his offers of consolation might be declined at first. He had never met quite this situation before.

It would take time to wear down her defenses, at least a week. Not much longer, though, because the daffodils were already past their best, and he had an occult promise on that.

But it would take time.

Which was the main reason he had decided to have an early night—he was horny as a herd of giraffes, and urgency always blunted finesse.

"There you are, darling!" said a seductive voice. A slender hand came to rest on his shoulder.

He looked up inquiringly. Oh, yes! Delicious. "Darling?"

"I beg your pardon, my lord! I mistook you for someone else."

Ylo clasped her hand and rose smoothly to his feet. "You found the right man for your needs!" He turned on his handsomest smile.

2

THE NEXT DAY A SPRING STORM CAME ROARING IN OFF Cenmere to rattle the casements of Yewdark.

The following morning the weather was even worse, stripping all the petals off the daffodils.

By midafternoon the God of Spring had repented of Their juvenile tantrum. The rain stopped, the wind dropped, and the clouds rolled away to uncover the sun. That evening Eshiala saw swallows swooping over the gables, the first outriders of summer. Tulips were coming into bloom, but the daffodils had definitely gone.

•   •   •

Dinner was a quiet affair, as always, although the Great Hall would have seated hundreds. Proconsul Ionfeu presided—bent and silver-haired, an Imperial aristocrat in the finest tradition, a truly gentle gentleman. Tonight he talked of noteworthy elvish poets he had met in his time, quoting their more memorable lines.

His wife was fat and apparently as scatter-brained as the hares that danced their mad spring rituals in the meadow outside. Not so!—her wits were much sharper than she normally allowed them to seem, and a large heart beat within her copious bosom. Three months ago Countess Eigaze had taken a very fragile impress into her care and cherished her with affection, concern, and good common sense. Eshiala had developed an enormous respect for Countess Eigaze, and real gratitude.

Centurion Hardgraa was his normal gruff self, perpetually uncomfortable in such exalted company. In that respect he had Eshiala's most sincere sympathy. He contributed little to the conversation, but he listened and she knew that he understood. He was as fanatical as the count, after his fashion, but his loyalty was to Shandie and Shandie's heir, not to the Impire itself.

Maya was asleep upstairs, tended by a nursemaid.

And the impress? The grocer's daughter? Here she was merely the wife of the fictitious Lord Eshern, but she suspected that even the servants knew she was both more and less than that. She was an exile, an outlaw, a fraud, but yet also a much healthier, happier woman than she had been at court. Of them all, only she was totally happy at Yewdark.

Three months at Yewdark? Nearer four! Where had the time gone? And the daffodils gone, also! Ever since the first green buds had opened their golden hearts, Eshiala had been haunted by thoughts of Ylo and the prophecy he claimed to have seen in the preflecting pool. Now the moment had passed. Did that mean she had another year to wait, or had the prophecy been disproved? Or else that dark-eyed libertine had been lying his head off to her, which was far more likely.

"May I suggest that we move over to the fireplace for coffee?" the count inquired. Receiving no argument, he ordered candles and the coffee. The sun was just setting. The fire smoldered, an unnecessary token. In a few more weeks the evenings would be warm enough for sitting outdoors.

As she settled in her favorite chair by the fieldstone hearth, Eshiala saw that more than coffee was brewing. The count was distracted, and even Eigaze showed less than her usual good humor. If the centurion was aware of the problem, his leathery features would never reveal the fact. He brought a stool forward and sat stiff-backed as always. He distrusted comfort.

The coffee tray was brought by little Mistress Ukka herself. Warmer weather had done nothing to improve her choice of apparel. She still seemed more clothes than person, a shapeless sack of threadbare, well-patched garments. Even indoors, she wore three overcoats and cloaks, with several gowns under them, showing at hems, cuffs, and collars. Her eyes peered out blearily between innumerable sagging wrinkles, just as her face itself peered out under a shabby wool cap and numerous woolen shawls. She muttered and mumbled to herself as she bustled around like a runaway laundry hamper.

But she departed at last, still speaking to anyone except the people actually present.

Eigaze sighed as she poured from the silver coffeepot. "Two more chambermaids tendered their notice this morning." Eigaze almost never complained about anything. Seeing bright sides was her specialty. If the world came to an end, she would applaud the welcome reduction in petty crime, or something. Was Ukka this evening's problem?

The count's permanent stoop made him lean forward even when sitting, conveying the impression that he was desperate for his coffee. "It's not just her meddling, is it?"

His wife passed his cup over. "Not at all. She nags and pesters them all the time, but she's very good at her job, and they appreciate that. They can make allowances for her age, or at least the older ones can. No, it's her constant nattering about voices."

Eshiala decided that there was more to worry about than Ukka. This was just preliminary chatter.

Ionfeu shook his head sadly. "She's convinced them the place is haunted?"

"Or that she's mad. Half of each, I think. Cake?"

"I have heard no supernatural voices. Thank you. I have seen no wraiths. Has anyone?"

Everyone murmured denials. The great house was a spooky place, but there had been no reports of hauntings, except from Ukka herself.

"I don't know what we can do about her, my dear. Excellent coffee! She's been here half a lifetime. We can hardly throw her out in the hedgerows."

"I have tried to retire her," Eigaze agreed. "Three times now. She pays no attention at all, just goes on running everything."

A brief silence was broken by one of Hardgraa's rare flashes of humor, delivered poker-faced as always. "The army would transfer her to Guwush."

Ionfeu smiled thinly. "I don't know that even the gnomes deserve that! You must just continue to pray, my dear, that one day she will collapse completely under the weight of her wardrobe. Where does she find all those garments?"

"I pray for the patience not to brain her with a warming pan," Eigaze remarked mildly. "In the attic. More cream, any-one? Honey?"

No one wanted more cream, or honey. The count twisted his head around stiffly, inspecting the hall to confirm that the domestics had withdrawn. Now he was going to get down to business.

"Ma'am," he said to Eshiala. "Centurion." Evidently his wife already knew what was coming. "We have been here al-most four months. So far Yewdark has served us well as a sanctuary. The Covin has not discovered us, the neighbors have been discouraged."

He meant that Maya was safe, of course. This lonely exile they had all accepted so willingly had no purpose except to protect the child upstairs.

"However, I foresee a problem."

Hardgraa nodded. "The grounds?"

Ionfeu raised his silvery eyebrows to acknowledge the hit. "Indeed! They are a jungle, as you know. Years of neglect. And spring is coming. Were we what we pretend to be, we should have done something about them already."

With a steely glance, the centurion deferred to the impress. She did not see any difficulty. "Can we not just hire gardeners?"

"That would be the logical procedure, ma'am. But it will require a small army of them, at least at first."

"Oh. Money?"

"Money," the old man agreed uncomfortably. "We did as we were instructed. We hired servants and set out to live the normal life of country gentry. We live modestly and try not to attract attention. It was what his Majesty wanted. Unfortunately, this establishment is draining our resources at a very alarming rate."

Eshiala had never had to worry about money in her life. Her parents had lived simply, within their means. Her mother had been a frugal homemaker, her father a practical merchant. They had never hankered after luxuries they could not afford. They would not have regarded Yewdark as modest, although now they might. Ever since the prince imperial had wooed and won their daughter, gold had poured into their lives like a spring flood.

The count's embarrassment was mirrored in his wife's face. These two would never have had to fret over money, either. An odd glint showed in the centurion's eye, but he did not comment.

"More coffee, ma'am?" Eigaze said. "The real problem is not money as such, you understand. Everything we possess is at your service. The problem is *getting* money. Honey? We could write to Tiffy and he would bring us gold in a wagon."

Now Eshiala understood. "And bring the Covin also?"

"We fear so," the count said, squirming to ease his crooked back. "We must assume that our household is watched—all our houses, for we have several—and our relatives, also. We can think of no safe way to tap our resources, my lady, much as we are eager to do so."

Sometimes Eshiala wondered if she really believed in that mysterious army of sorcerers. If it did exist, it had proved strangely inept at finding her. Perhaps Zinixo did not much care about the imperor and his family. The Impire seemed to be surviving very well without them.

The centurion laid his cup on a nearby table, the fragile china incongruous in his powerful fingers. "The fault is mine, my lord. I inspected the supplies the warlock had provided. I did not think to estimate our requirements."

The proconsul shook his head impatiently. "You could not be expected to know them. Nor, I regret to say, would the warlock."

He meant that Raspnex was a dwarf, and a dwarf would live a lifetime on what an impish aristocrat spent in a week. Raspnex probably thought he had made ample provision. Shandie knew nothing about domestic expenditures—logistics of armies and whole impires were his expertise. Even the king of Krasnegar, who had not been directly involved, would not be familiar with finances of this kind. Eshiala felt a surge of anger at herself for not foreseeing the problem, but she was no more to blame than any of them.

"It seems very ironic." The count sighed. "We elude a legion of sorcerers and now we face being defeated by something as mundane as cold cash."

"There is no use worrying about what we have done or should have done," Eigaze said firmly. "The problem exists. What we must do is find a solution." Common sense was another of her strong points.

Hardgraa waited for someone else to speak, then said, "Art? Those pictures? Silverware?"

"Possible," the count agreed. "But the servants will chatter, the neighbors will hear of it, and who is to sell them for us? If you ride into Faintown with a wagonload of art, Centurion, you will be accused of theft. You might dispose of a piece or two at a pawnshop, but not very often. The normal procedure would be to summon a dealer from Hub . . . That risks attracting attention and starting gossip. We have no legal right to be here, remember. I agree with your suggestion, but it is a limited one, if you see."

The soldier nodded impassively. "I'd like some time to consider the matter, if I may." He was speaking as Shandie's chief of security, but he must be feeling sadly out of his depth battling a matter of household finance.

And now it was Eshiala's turn. How could she solve a problem that had baffled the wily Ionfeu and his practical wife?

"Move to a smaller place? No, of course not." Shandie and the others might return here, to Yewdark. It had been designated a headquarters, as well as a sanctuary. "Well, why not just let the servants depart? Let them spread the rumor that the place is haunted. We know it's not. The five of us could live here very cheaply, guarded by rumors of wraiths."

"It would be an uncomfortable life," the count said.

"Stranger to you than to me, my lord. My mother never employed more than three servants, usually only two."

He nodded uncomfortably and did not reply. He had thought of that obvious solution already, obviously.

Eigaze nodded, her various chins pulsing. "It may be the only way out, dear. But it will cause gossip in the district, and we hoped to avoid that. Well, the problem isn't urgent, is it?"

Her husband shook his head. "Not very. We have gold enough for a few months; enough for a couple of years if all we need buy is food. But I am disinclined to hire a legion of gardeners."

"If only we could send word to Tiffy!" Eigaze said.

"Let us all think about it." Hardgraa frowned angrily. He probably felt guilty at having failed Shandie.

3

"*AWAKEN! AWAKEN!*"

The shrill voice slashed into Eshiala's sleeping mind like a runaway coach and four. She gasped, struggling to make sense of the candle flames whirling in the darkness over her bed. Who? What? Her door had been locked. She always locked her door. It had been one of the first things she had been taught at court.

"He is here!" The bundled apparition was Mistress Ukka, of course, waving a candelabra perilously near the bed curtains.

"Who? Who is?"

"The duke! He has come!"

Eshiala hauled the covers up to her chin and fought her way back to consciousness. "What duke? How do you know? How did you get into my room?"

"Come, lady! He has returned to you as They promised!"

Maya cried out from her cot in the corner.

Duke? The old hag meant Ylo? But if Ylo had arrived, then Shandie must have come, also?

"Get out of my room!" Eshiala snapped. "Now! Go wait in the corridor! All right, darling, Mommy's here."

By the time the door closed, Maya had drifted back to sleep.

Heart thumping madly, the impress swung her feet to the cold rug. Moonlight drifted through the window. Ylo returned? The tiny old woman was crazier than the hares, but she had never pulled any stunt like this before. It would have to be investigated.

Having dressed warmly and confirmed that her daughter was sleeping soundly, Eshiala went out to the passage. Ukka was waiting there, fidgeting, a rotund mass of clothing under five flickering flames. She might have duplicate keys to fit every lock in the house, and no one had ever thought to ask her.

"Now, tell me."

"The duke—"

"So you said. Where is he?"

"Outside. Not here yet."

"What? Then how do you know?"

"They told me. The Voices."

Eshiala relaxed. Ravings, only ravings! Still, she had better investigate. The old hag probably meant Ylo, who was theoretically Duke Yllipo.

"This way, lady!" Ukka shrilled.

"Oh, no!" The impress went the other way. "First we waken the centurion."

The crone squawked shrilly behind her. "He's not there! He's downstairs." Her candles were following, though.

"How do you know that?"

"Don't want him. Dangerous, that one."

"We do want him."

Hardgraa's door was open and he was obviously not in the bed. Head spinning, Eshiala demanded to be taken to him. Grumbling, Ukka led the way along the gallery and down the great staircase.

•   •   •

The night blurred into a series of disconnected images.

At the foot of the stairs, Hardgraa emerged from the shadows, a lantern in one hand and a naked sword in the other.

"She says *the duke* has returned," Eshiala explained, eyeing the sword nervously.

"There's no one around," the soldier said flatly.

"Where is he?" she demanded.

The old woman raised her shrouded head to peer up at the high rafters. She seemed to listen for a moment. "Out by the gate. He's hurt, hurt!"

"She's crazy!"

Eshiala's heart thundered in her chest. "She's never done this before, Centurion. We must go and see."

"I'll get some men."

"No!" When had she ever tried to overrule Hardgraa before? "He may not be alone!" That ended talk of servants: *Shandie may be with him.* She did not speak her next thought—*I may not be alone when I go back to bed.*

She wanted to accompany Hardgraa herself, but he would not hear of it. He went and roused the count. She knelt by the hearth, trying to blow life back into the embers, shivering with cold and trepidation. The men left. Ukka had vanished. Eigaze arrived and huddled in a chair, swathed in a voluminous housecoat, her hair in curlers. If she said anything at all, Eshiala did not hear her.

Shandie? She was not ready to be his wife again. She needed warning, time to prepare. Or Ylo? The daffodil season was over.

Either way, Yewdark's precious sanctuary had been violated.

She barely recognized Ylo. He was covered in mud, and not completely conscious. Hardgraa carried him in over a shoulder and lowered him into a chair. She marveled at the older man's strength.

"What's wrong with him?" she demanded, staring at the lolling head, the blurry, unfocused eyes.

"Exhaustion, mostly." The count deposited two lanterns on the floor without having to stoop. He handed Hardgraa's sword back to him. "But he's wounded. Hot water, dear, and cloths?"

"Of course!" Eigaze snatched up a lantern and then squeaked in alarm.

A shrouded figure scurried into the light. It was Ukka, bringing a tray with a steaming mug on it. She sank down by the invalid.

Ylo blinked at her and spoke for the first time. "Food? Oh, Gods, food!"

Eshiala forced out the question, dreading all possible answers. "Where is my husband?"

He peered around to locate the voice.

"Wait!" Hardgraa barked. He grabbed Ukka's shoulders and lifted her to her feet. "You go to your room now and stay there! Is that clear?"

"The duke—"

"Go away! Stay away!"

Then Ukka had gone. Ylo was spluttering and cursing as he tried to gulp the hot brew, spilling it on himself in his haste.

"Where is my husband?"

He spoke without looking up, between gulps. "He's dead. The goblins got him."

Later . . . Eigaze kneeling at Ylo's feet, washing mud and dried blood from his leg. He had screamed when they removed his boots. Something had ripped his hose away from the knee down, and ripped his calf, also.

And even as that was happening, Hardgraa had the point of his dagger at the man's throat, demanding the whole story.

Dead? Shandie?

• • •

Later still . . . Eshiala lying in bed staring at the darkness.

Dead?

She was a widow. She was dowager impress.

The two-year-old in the corner was Impress Uomaya I of Pandemia.

4

THE DAY DAWNED HOT AND SUNNY, BUT ESHIALA FELT SHE was moving in a thick fog. The same conversations seemed to take place over and over, always accompanied by cautious glancings around to make sure there were no servants within earshot.

Ylo slept on upstairs and could almost be dismissed as a nightmare that had not happened.

Mistress Ukka jabbered and giggled without ceasing, prattling to all the bewildered domestics that the duke had returned, just as the Voices had said he would. Eigaze trailed after her, explaining that the old woman was hallucinating, repeating the agreed story about Sir Yyan, a friend who had dropped in unexpectedly. There was no Duke Yllipo, just a chance resemblance to someone Mistress Ukka had known in her youth.

The pastry cook gave notice.

Even Eigaze could not find a bright side to look on.

The proconsul seemed to have aged twenty years. He was haggard and his hands trembled. He made the same speech several times, as if the words were going around and around in his head and he had forgotten he had already spoken them aloud. "Prince Emthoro, ma'am. The Law of Succession states that the next in line is regent during a minority. We shall have to get word to the prince somehow."

By the third repetition, Eshiala had her response prepared. "But we don't know whether he's at court or not. And the Impire seems to be running itself without Shandie. You've been to Faintown. You haven't heard any rumors of vanished imperors, have you? The Covin must have bewitched the court somehow, mustn't it? And the army. And the government.

They must all believe that Shandie's still there and in charge, mustn't they? Emthoro will be as convinced as anyone. How can he ever believe us?"

The bent old man just shook his head like a turtle in despair.

Eshiala herself was haunted by lost futures. She could not stay much longer at Yewdark. Shandie would not be coming to take her back to court. She most certainly could not risk returning to her parents at Thumble. There was no way out.

Hardgraa was another sort of ghost, dark and implacable. He hardly spoke at all, and when he did he had no need to repeat himself. "He went with Shandie as bodyguard. Either he betrayed him or he just ran away and left him. I don't believe his story yet and when he does tell me the truth, I will kill him."

"If he betrayed Shandie, why would he come back here?" she demanded.

Hardgraa raked her with a glare of naked suspicion. "You tell me, ma'am!"

Evening came at last and they gathered for dinner, all five together. The world seemed to steady and clear.

Ylo came in, hobbling and leaning on a cane, with Mistress Ukka fawning all around him, babbling and gibbering. He was still haggard, but his marathon sleep had restored his spirits and his old air of mischief. His face was thinner than Eshiala remembered it, and he needed a haircut. He was weatherbeaten and lean and more startlingly good-looking than ever. The Gods should never make a man so beautiful. He regarded his audience with an amused disdain, especially Hardgraa.

They could not wait until dinner was over; their need to talk was urgent and yet they must fit the conversation into the gaps when the servants were out of earshot—or speak in code.

"I told you everything," Ylo insisted. "We did what we said. I won't say where the others went, but ... Yshan ... and I set off for ... the faun's house. He'd agreed, and told us of a shortcut, at a place called Kinvale. So we headed across Julgistro, staying off the main highways, of course."

"Tell me some details," Hardgraa growled. He was sending whole courses back untouched. He still wore his sword, as he had all day.

Ylo shrugged. "Nothing much to tell. We had a little trouble at the beginning, but nothing important."

"What sort of trouble?"

"Nothing important. Apart from that, we had a good ride. In an odd way, I think we were both enjoying ourselves. It was a vacation."

"That doesn't ring true!"

"It is true, though," Ylo said without losing his easy smile. "He had no army to worry about, only one companion. It was a tough ride with no posts to help, and a physical challenge. You know, he relaxed in a way I've never seen him do ..." He chuckled, but his unfathomable dark gaze moved to Eshiala and they were not smiling. "We became friends."

She started. Obviously that remark was meant to mean more than it seemed to, but she could not decide between the possibilities.

Hardgraa had flushed. "I don't believe you!"

"It's true, though—fetch a sorcerer. Unexpected in Yshan, I agree. Near Rivermead we came on the trail of a legion on the move. Dust cloud one day, then it rained and we saw the tracks. The locals confirmed it. He couldn't rest until he'd found out what was going on, so we followed." Ylo sighed and resumed his meal.

As a hovering footman was removing his plate, Hardgraa barked, "And then goblins?" Cutlery jangled on china.

"Goblins. Suddenly the bushes were stiff with them. Arrows going by like mosquitoes." Ylo's smile faded away. "I looked back and saw him go down. The horse fell."

"So you don't really know he's dead!" Hardgraa had been repeating that refrain at every opportunity.

"I hope he was dead." Ylo seemed intent on cutting his meat. "With djinns or dwarves or even gnomes, I would hope he survived."

The proconsul's voice was a ghostly tremor. "Would even goblins kill such a prisoner?"

No, Eshiala thought, they would not kill the imperor himself. Tell me so!

Ylo paused, fork halfway to mouth. "He had no identification on him, sir. As far as I know, in twenty years they have never returned a captive alive."

Eshiala clenched her fists till they hurt. *Please, Gods, let him have died at once!*

"And you have absolutely no evidence!" Hardgraa barked.

Ylo chewed for a moment with a hurt expression. "I will have. The news will be here any day now. Go into Faintown and—"

"I'm not letting you out of my sight!"

Ylo shrugged and accepted a refill of his wineglass.

"Even if some raiding band got over the pass, what then?" the centurion demanded.

The contemptuous smile returned. "Oh, this was no raiding band! We were days away from Pondague. At least one legion was marching. The next day the wind changed, and I smelled smoke for two days after that. The night sky was aglow. This is the millennium! This is the Gods in Wrath!"

"And no Shandie!" Ionfeu moaned, forgetting the eavesdroppers.

"And no wardens," Ylo responded. The other men both flinched.

"But it was not the goblins who injured you?" Eigaze asked hurriedly, hauling the conversation onto safer ground.

Ylo glanced thoughtfully at Eshiala before he answered. She sensed devilry coming.

"No, Aunt. I rode like a dervish down the Great West Way. My troubles began at Woggle. You know it?"

"Of course."

"The Warlock's Rest? Dangerous place!"

"Dangerous? Why, we've stayed there lots of times!"

"Don't. I advise against it."

"But what happened?"

"I got rolled by a whore," Ylo said blandly.

The countess's fat cheeks turned scarlet with shock, and crockery rattled at the serving trolley.

Eshiala suspected that the vulgarity was intended for her, although she did not know why. She never could predict Ylo.

"Now I know you're lying," Hardgraa snarled. "Those girls are employed by the management."

Ylo beamed blissfully, as if springing a trap. "This one was freelancing. Charming young miss. She put something in my wine, I think. And she cleaned me out totally. I came to with a head like a butter churn and nary a kerchief to tie around me."

"You should have complained to the innkeepers. They guard their reputation very closely." But Hardgraa had merely tightened the noose.

"I was about to, dramatically toga'ed in a bed sheet. At the bottom of the stairs, I almost ran into an old friend of mine, Centurion Hithi. Legate Hithi of the Vth, he is now." Ylo raised his raven eyebrows in mockery. "Family influence, of course. Fortunately he didn't see me. I departed by the window."

"You walked all the way from Woggle?" Eigaze wailed.

"I did. I stole clothes from the next room and was gone. I was rained on, eaten by dogs, and chased by a mad bull. I slept in a hedge." He sighed elaborately. "But the pleasure of your company makes up for such trivial hardships."

Hardgraa looked baffled. It was impossible to believe that Ylo would have deliberately put himself into the state of collapse in which he had arrived. His leg had certainly been bitten by something, and the soles of his feet had been raw. He could still barely walk. So part of his story had to be believed, and he knew that. What reason could he have for inventing the rest of it?

Hardgraa thought he knew the answer.

They moved then to the fireplace to drink coffee. The servants were dismissed, even the odiously attentive Ukka. The scene was an eerie echo of the previous evening, long ago when life had been much simpler. Dust motes glinted in beams of sunlight from high windows; ancestral portraits frowned down through the smoke-stain of decades. There was no fire this time, for the Great Hall was still warm from the day, but the same four persons gathered on the same seats.

The fifth, the newcomer, sprawled back in a soft armchair with his feet up on a stool, and regarded their shocked, worried faces with cynical unconcern. His amusement seemed designed to antagonize them all. He was openly baiting Hardgraa at every opportunity, being little more respectful to the count and countess. He had known about Shandie's death for a month and thus had had time to adjust, but his attitude was cruelly callous.

He almost ignored Eshiala; his occasional sultry glances seemed to convey no messages, just curiosity. She was disappointed, somehow. She certainly had not wanted Ylo bursting into Yewdark playing passionate lover, but at the moment she could have used a strong, supportive friend. He had always been good at cheering her up. Now she felt that he was laughing at her.

"I was thinking about the preflecting pool," he said before the count could start the conversation. "I forget how much you were told about it, Aunt." His dark eyes flickered over Eshiala. He knew very well how much she had been told, but only he knew whether there had been any truth in it.

"Not much, dear."

"Four of us got prophecies. Hardgraa, here, didn't want to get his feet wet. We had the choice of the good or the bad, and only old Umpily had the sense to choose the bad."

Eigaze remembered that she was supposed to pour the coffee, and spasmed into action. "Yes?"

"I think its forecasts were probably sound," Ylo said, smirking at the centurion's continuing scowls, "but the poor thing was limited to a single picture. If it could have talked, it would have done better. And dangers are easier to illustrate than opportunities, aren't they?"

The count nodded, although he seemed to be barely listening. No one said anything. Again Eshiala sensed devilment lurking under those long lashes. Surely even Ylo would not drag her into this, naked among the daffodils? She did not trust him, though. She did not trust him at all.

"I think we tend to take such things too literally. No cream, thank you, Aunt. Sir Acopulo described the visions as sign-posts, and for once I think the old crab had a point. Umpily saw a dwarf on the Opal Throne, but as far as we know, he hasn't seen that actual scene, not in reality. It was a symbol, a warning—a signpost. Acopulo himself was directed to Doctor Sagorn, of course, who could have identified Krasnegar for us right away."

"I wonder what good such a device can do," Eigaze sighed.

Ylo beamed, and again glanced momentarily at Eshiala, to see how she was taking this. "It helped me! I saw a woman. But again, you see, she was only a signpost."

"To whose bed?"

"Centurion!" Eigaze protested.

"Away from the grave!" Ylo said dramatically. "Without the prophecy, I would have accepted the honor of Rivermead when Shandie offered it to me."

"So?"

"So I would now be very dead! The goblins overran it. It was still burning the following dawn."

He was saying that he no longer believed the vision of Eshiala among the daffodils? That the assignation was not preor-dained after all? She had never really believed in it, but she had thought he did. He might have invented the whole thing. What woman would ever be fool enough to believe Ylo?

"And what good did Shandie's prophecy do him?" Hard-graa asked.

"None. It led him to his death. But you see, he waited too long. That's what I realized on my stroll in from Woggle. Re-member we got back to Hub a day or two later—after the pool business, I mean—and found the Impire falling apart?" Sud-denly Ylo was starkly serious. "Acopulo failed to track down Sagorn. Shandie failed to track down Krasnegar. He didn't act on the warning soon enough! If he'd gone off to talk with King Rap last summer, then things might have been different, a lot different. You can't blame the poor old pool; it did its best."

He sipped coffee, eyeing them all over the top of the cup.

The count had been sitting hunched forward in his chair even more than usual; now he roused himself with an effort. He seemed frail. "So what do we do now?"

Ylo raised eyebrows in astonishment. "I have no idea what you do, my lord. I know what I'm doing. I'm just passing through."

"Going where?"

"Oh, somewhere with a warm climate." He glanced around to judge reactions. "I've played my part in this. I find history-making a very stressful occupation. I'm going to give it up. Now I shall find me a beautiful rich heiress and settle down. I have a couple of candidates in mind."

Eshiala was not a rich heiress. She was a penniless refugee, bound to a child who belonged to the Imperial government. She must either surrender to the Covin or flee, abducting the lawful impress, which was at least a capital offence. She could see no escape, no road that did not end in disaster.

But of course her decision would be made for her by the count and the centurion. Shandie had left them in charge.

Hardgraa's dislike and distrust of Ylo were palpable. "He's still an Imperial soldier, my lord. You can give him orders. We don't know that he's telling the truth."

Ionfeu nodded. "If he is, then the news will certainly reach Faintown very soon. Ylo, you will remain here at Yewdark until I give you leave to depart."

"As you command, sir. I have no desire to walk anywhere for a while yet. Is there any coffee left, Aunt?"

"We must review our options," Ionfeu said.

"Please!" Ylo raised a hand. "I don't want to hear them! I don't want to know! I don't want to be involved. In fact, if you will excuse me, I think I'll retire and catch up on some more rest."

The others watched in rockbound silence as he climbed painfully to his feet. He looked them over disdainfully. "Don't forget the other prophecy."

"What other prophecy?" Ionfeu snarled.

"The Sisters, when I was a baby. I told you on the boat, remember? It happened as they said. My family was destroyed. Now the Impire, also. The millennium has come, and the world you know is being stood on its head! Remember that when you make your plans, my lord!"

He bowed, then turned away and hobbled toward the stair.

Eshiala wondered how she could ever have thought him charming, or amusing, or attractive. Only—*damn him!*—handsome.

5

HE HAD LEFT HIS DOOR AJAR AND A LIGHT SHOWING. SHE pushed it open without a knock, closed it and leaned against it, her heart thumping as if lions pursued her. Her palms were wet with fear.

He had been reading, or pretending to read; lying on the bed, still wearing his doublet. He laid down his book and regarded her with affected surprise. His lower half was under a coverlet, and she supposed he might have stripped down to his bandages for comfort. But he was respectable, even if this meeting was not. Whatever would her mother say if she knew?

She was too frantic to care about propriety . . .

"I must talk with you!" she said.

"I was afraid of that."

"The count has gone crazy!" She realized she was shouting and lowered her voice. "And Hardgraa seems to agree with him. They're talking of handing Maya over to the Covin!"

That awful news did not appall Ylo as she had expected. He shrugged.

"I thought they might come to that conclusion. There's this mystic thing about the blood that some people have, the line of descent from Emine. Gods, but they have a lot of faith in fidelity, don't they?"

"He says Prince Emthoro will be regent."

And that remark did surprise Ylo. "But . . . But of course you don't know about him, do you?" He yawned. "Well, it won't change anything. In fact it will probably make them more determined. Never mind. I'm too tired to explain now. I'll tell you in the morning."

His indifference stunned her. Did he not understand? *Maya was in danger!* Whom else could she appeal to? Somehow she had always had a sense of Ylo as a friend in the background. She had been misled by his bantering and flirting. Perhaps she had not truly expected friendship, but assumed that because he lusted after her, she could use that desire as a lever. Now he was revealed as the selfish lout she had been warned of, and her disappointment was no one's fault but her own.

Or was he playing some sort of rake's double-game? Was she supposed to plead now—to grovel? *Help me save my child and I will submit to your advances?* How much humiliation would he demand?

"Why did you come here?" she asked. "To Yewdark?"

He ran a hand through his curls, pretending to be at a loss. "I was in the neighborhood. And I did promise you I would return in daffodil time. I hate to disappoint pretty ladies."

"The daffodils have gone. You should have come sooner."

Devilry danced in his eyes. "Should have come sooner for what?"

"That prophecy you described to me so graphically."

"Ah! Then I return your question—why did *you* come here—to my bedroom?"

She felt the sweat on her palms again. Her heart thundered and her mouth was dry. She had come because she must have help and she thought she would pay whatever price he demanded for that help. Was he going to make her put it into words?

"I . . . I thought you cared."

"Cared for your daughter?"

"Cared for me!"

Ylo shrugged. "But I told you. Shandie and I became friends. I tarried too long. I might not have come at all if the goblins hadn't intervened. I've changed my mind about seducing you."

"Your imperor's wife is all right, but your friend's widow is not? You have strange values."

"No." He cocked his head on one side like a bird, and it was mockery. "I always look out for me, you know that. I've decided that ravishing you now might get me involved in more affairs of state, and I've had enough of those. Sorry, you'll have to do without."

Her fear turned to burning anger without warning. She restrained it with a real effort. "You are a boor!"

"Oh, you're better!" he said admiringly. "You are a lot better! The old Eshiala was a timorous little thing, who never argued, never went skulking into men's rooms in the middle of the night. What happens next, I wonder?"

"I'm only concerned with my daughter's welfare!" She could *not* say it more directly than that.

"But that interests me not at all." Ylo untied his cravat. "I told you the first time we talked that I was an unscrupulous liar."

"Yes, you did."

"That's still true." He tossed the cravat to the floor and began unbuttoning his doublet. "Hardgraa thinks I deserted Shandie and came back here just for a romp with you. I did consider it, I admit." With the doublet open, he began unbuttoning the shirt underneath. "At the moment you really don't know if your husband is dead or not, because you have only my word for it, and that's worthless. Now, if you came here to be bedded, get your clothes off, and I'll see what I can do. But don't expect any favors for it. Otherwise, good night, your Majesty."

Monster! Eshiala stamped out, wishing she could slam the door.

6

THE IMPRESS AND HER MOTHER HAD BEEN DOWN AT THE lake all morning, feeding ducks, throwing rocks, and hunting for wildflowers. By the time they made their way home for lunch, her Imperial Majesty was hot, tired, and grumpy; and wanting to be carried.

Eshiala was not much less grumpy herself. News of Shandie's death had shattered the fragile shell she had developed at Yewdark. Her safe little world had collapsed under her feet like ice on a pond. Friends and accomplices had suddenly become jailers, and she felt surrounded by enemies. There was no one she could trust to help her. Down at the water, she had been tormented by a sensation of being watched—that was one of the first signs of madness, wasn't it?

On the way back to the house, though, she noticed tracks in a muddy stretch of the path, with larger prints overlaying

Maya's and her own. So she had been followed, she had been watched, she was not suffering delusions of persecution! In one sense that was good news. In another it was very bad. Centurion Hardgraa could be assumed guilty until the Gods testified otherwise in Person.

Continually persuading Maya to walk just a few more steps on her own feet, she emerged from the woods. Peering over and under the wilderness of runaway shrubbery, she spied Ylo sitting on the terrace in the sunshine like an unpredictable watchdog dozing before the door. Had she been alone, she could have gone around the long way to avoid him, but Maya was too tired and too heavy for such evasions.

At breakfast that morning, he had hurled another thunderbolt as casually as Maya dropped rocks in lakes. The reason the Impire had not reacted to Shandie's disappearance, he explained, was that a fake imperor ruled in his place, with a fake impress at his side. If Eshiala walked into the Opal Palace now, she might meet herself face to face.

Since both her sister and Shandie's cousin had disappeared from sight, the impostors' true identities were not hard to estimate. As soon as Eshiala's first stunned surprise had worn off, she had shocked everyone by laughing aloud. Ashia would be enjoying herself enormously. She would make a far better impress than Eshiala ever would, and have the fun of a lifetime doing so. She had a low opinion of Prince Emthoro, but likely she would put up with him in a good cause—not that either of them could have had any choice in the matter. They would be doing whatever the almighty Zinixo wanted.

Later though, down at the lake, she had realized that Ashia had been a potential ally and now was not.

" 'Lo, Beautiful!" Ylo smirked cheekily. He seemed very relaxed and comfortable in a soft chair that he must have ordered brought out specially. His sore feet rested on another.

Eshiala ignored him, leading her daughter across the terrace, but she had to pass very close to him.

He ignored her ignoring. "What'cha been doing?"

"Feeding the ducks."

"Ah! Nothing tastier than a fat duckling."

She was almost past him when he said, "Eshiala?"

She thought his tone had lost its banter, and stopped. "Yes?"

He was squinting up at her, against the sun, but the contempt and arrogance still gleamed under the long lashes. "Auntie's back."

The countess had ordered up the gig that morning and had herself driven into Faintown. If she was back already, she had not stayed long.

"So?"

Ylo smiled his most perfect smile, oozing self-satisfaction. "She reports the place is a madhouse. The news is out. It's even worse than I thought—goblins grinding up legions like coffee beans."

"You seem strangely pleased."

"I don't like to be disbelieved when I'm telling the truth. I do it so rarely that I want to have it appreciated! Now you can believe my story. Now you can surrender to lust without worrying about Shandie ever turning up to complain."

Contemptible clod! Dragging her daughter by the hand, she swept past him into the house. Somehow she could not be angry with Ylo, merely sad that he was not the debonair rapscallion she had believed him to be. She had never approved of him, could never have trusted him as an ally, but he had been amusing once. Now he was merely disgusting.

The image of ice on a pond came to her again. She had barely seen Maya happily arranged at the tasty end of a spoon when her footing cracked and tilted some more.

In the gloomy, ill-proportioned room the proconsul used as a study, she faced him like an errant pupil called out by the teacher. Ionfeu was old; his crippled back tormented him. He was badly shaken by the dread responsibility now thrown upon him, and looked as if he had not slept since Ylo's arrival. He was nonetheless still a count, still an Imperial politician and officer, and still very certainly the ruler of Yewdark. He was gracious and implacable.

He was behind a desk. She was expected to sit before it. She could not believe that her sister, as duchess or impress, would ever tolerate that from a mere proconsul.

Eigaze was there, too, still wearing the finery she had assumed for her trip to Faintown, also wearing a very strange expression. Her fat lips were pursed white; her thick fingers moved restlessly on her lap. Eshiala needed hear no words to guess that Lady Eigaze disapproved of whatever message was coming.

The centurion stood in a corner with his arms folded. Two nights ago old Ukka had called him dangerous, and Eshiala had disbelieved, seeing in him only a trustworthy guardian, as she had for months. Now he was her jailer. He spied on her movements. He was the proconsul's instrument and weapon, and as open to argument as a razor. He was more than dangerous.

She perched on a chair, clasped her hands to still them, and regarded Ionfeu with her best Imperial stare, poor thing though it was.

He began delivering sentence, deliberate and lucid and cold. "The signifer seems to be telling the truth, ma'am. News of the goblins has reached Faintown. The imperor addressed the Senate yesterday. As we know that . . . know that he could not have been the real imperor, I must accept that Ylo is also telling the truth about the substitution that has been made. In other words, I have decided to accept all aspects of his story. Do you disagree with my conclusions?"

She could say that Ylo was a notorious liar, but the count would not see *that* sort of lying as being the same as *this* sort of lying. Lying to men was a crime; lying to women only a sin. And she did believe Ylo's tale. She nodded her head to agree.

Before the count spoke again, Hardgraa's iron growl intervened. "I'd still like to know why he's here at all."

For the first time in two days, a faint smile appeared on the old aristocrat's face. "Perhaps he's telling the truth there, too, Centurion. I think he met with a little divine justice at Woggle. He certainly wouldn't be the first young man to wake up naked and penniless in a strange bed. Normally he would have appealed to the army for rescue and retribution, and would have suffered no more than ridicule. But this time he daren't. Yewdark was the only refuge within reach, that's all."

"I expect you're right, my lord."

"And we might give him credit for wanting to break the news to us. He has a sense of duty, too, you know. His record shows that."

"I suppose so." But Hardgraa seemed unconvinced. "His record reveals other abilities also." He sneered at Eshiala, and her temper exploded, taking her completely by surprise.

"How dare you!" she shouted. "How *dare* you suggest that there is anything between that lout and me? You actually dare suggest that Ylo came here for my sake? That . . . that . . . *lout?*"

Ionfeu's smile had faded like the winter snows. "I certainly hope that he was not implying any such thing, ma'am! Centurion?"

Hardgraa muttered, "No offense intended, your Majesty!" He seemed suddenly puzzled. Perhaps he had just realized that no sane suitor would behave as Ylo had been behaving.

The count coughed diplomatically. "We are all a little over-wrought. Now, ma'am, with your husband dead, your daughter is titular ruler of the realm."

"The rest of the world would not agree with you, my lord."

"But I must be guided by my conscience." The old man cleared his throat, glanced hesitantly at his wife, and then continued sternly. "You may not be aware of this. It is common gossip, though. Prince Emthoro is thirty-two years old, and unmarried. His various mistresses have not complained of their treatment, but they have borne him no bastards. A prince who has not fathered children by the time he is thirty-two is probably not going to produce any children at all. Rumor blames an attack of mumps in early manhood. His brother died at Karthin. Now Shandie. Ma'am, that child of yours is unusually precious!"

"She is infinitely precious to me."

"To all of us, ma'am. Don't you see? The Affaladi branch is morganatically disqualified. I do believe that without the princess, Agraine's house may be effectively extinct. That means change of dynasty, and changes of dynasty almost invariably bring civil war."

The old man was forgetting that the effective impress at the moment was Ashia, and Ashia might see her duty to the Impire in ways that would shock the count out of his stoop. In the circumstances she almost certainly would. Eshiala was not going to mention that complication, though.

"Prince Emthoro is not a very likable person," Ionfeu said, "but he is not a monster. He will not harm an innocent child."

"Unless he produces children of his own, perhaps." *Or my sister produces them for him.*

"A son would take precedence. I admit the temptation will exist if he sires daughters and no son, but I repeat that he is not an evil man! I see it as my duty, your Majesty, to return your child to court so that she may come into her inheritance."

The countess made a small sound that conveyed both scorn and anger, but she did not speak. She would have spoken earlier and been overruled. Eshiala must fight this alone.

"You surrender to the Covin, Proconsul? You yield your rightful impress into the hands of a mad dwarf?"

A rosy tint bloomed in the pearly-gray skin over his cheekbones. "The chances that Shandie could overthrow the Covin were never very good, ma'am; although I swore to aid him, we all knew that. With Shandie himself dead, the odds are impossible. We have no leader. We must assume that the Protocol has ended. From now on, for all our days, there will be a single supreme sorcerer behind the throne. We must hope that the rule of the One will be no more onerous than that of the Four. He will certainly outlive all of us, and I expect he will establish a successor for future centuries—I don't know. My concerns are mundane, not occult. I know that your daughter's place is in Hub and my duty is to return her there."

She raised her voice. "Shandie would not agree!" The words came out too blustery, and the old man remained unmoved.

"With respect, ma'am . . . He left no instructions for this event. I must therefore use my discretion and best judgment. I have known him all his life. He always placed his duty to the Impire before anything else, and I believe he would expect the same dedication from his family."

Meaning, *A grocer's daughter cannot understand how aristocrats think.* She felt her face burn like the noonday sun.

"And I? Do I relieve my sister of her temporary promotion?" She held his gaze, and it was the proconsul who looked away. The roses were ugly blotches on his face now.

"That must be your own choice, ma'am." His voice was growing harsher. "We do not know what sort of magic has been used. The prince and your sister may be their usual selves, except for their appearance. They may be collaborating willingly with the Covin out of a sense of duty, to maintain the rule of law and order. Or they may have been coerced. At the extreme, they may actually be convinced in their own minds that they are who they seem to be."

Her anger flashed out then, but it could find no more useful weapon than an unfamiliar vulgarity. "Either way, I shall likely end up under Emthoro!"

"Your decision, ma'am. If you do not wish to accompany the child, I shall not force you. I can see what might await you."

Eigaze spoke up for the first time, her voice dry and bitter. "Of course, when the usurper is done with her, she may not realize it is Emthoro at all. He may look just like Shandie down to the mole on his toe, and she may have forgotten that the original died. What a wonderful chance to undo tragedy and regain a lost marriage!"

Eshiala had never heard the countess use sarcasm before.

"Be silent!" the count snapped furiously. "Ma'am, I have made my decision about your daughter. Whether you choose to accompany her is up to you. My wife and I can testify to her identity. You are free to depart if you wish. I am preparing a letter to send to the palace. Please advise me of your decision as soon as you can."

"How long have I got?" she asked. Her throat was so tight that every word hurt.

"A day or so at most. There may be panic in the streets if the goblins head south. Who knows how close on Ylo's heels they may be? We must act swiftly."

Countess Eigaze surged to her feet. "Ion, you know what I think! Write your stupid letter! Then read it over and try to find the honor in it. Eshiala, my dear, let's you and me go and have a cup of tea and talk this over."

Eshiala rose, also, feeling grateful. She wondered what Ashia would say in her place. The mind boggled.

As they reached the door, Eigaze seemed to have second thoughts. She turned. "What are you going to do about Ylo?"

Her husband frowned. "We need him to certify the emperor's death."

"I know you do. And I expect he does."

"He isn't going anywhere. He can barely walk."

"He can ride, can't he?"

Metal jangled from the direction of Centurion Hardgraa. He held a large bunch of iron keys. "The stables are secure, ma'am!"

"Ah!" Eigaze nodded. "You think that will stop Ylo, do you?"

Hardgraa scowled. "What do you suggest?"

"Me? I'm only a fat old woman, Centurion. As I recall, there are some rusty fetters down in the wine cellar, but it really is not my business. Come, then, my dear." She ushered the impress before her.

As they went out, she heard the count say, "He is a material witness, I suppose."

The two ladies walked together across the Great Hall. Eshiala could barely see it. Her head was spinning and she felt close to panic.

Eigaze stopped suddenly. "I have been married to that man for forty-two years, and we have never had a cross word! Now, all of a sudden, he is behaving like a drunken mule!" Her chins wobbled with outrage.

"Ylo?" Eshiala said suddenly. "If they are going to turn him in, as well, shouldn't we warn him?"

"Bah! Ylo can look after himself."

"But ..." It was a terribly slim hope. "If I appealed to Ylo—"

"*Never* appeal to Ylo!" the countess said firmly. "He would only despise you, although he might not realize that himself. Regardless of what they think, my dear, the Ylos of this world are far more interested in the race than the prize. The worst thing you can do is to throw yourself on their mercy, because that ruins the sport. They don't have any anyway—mercy sours the fruits of victory. With men like Ylo you must *always* play hard to get."

"I don't have time to—"

"As dear Aunt Kade always used to say, you will be gotten soon enough! Of course that's the idea, and the only way to play the game, and you mustn't think he's not enjoying it just as much as you are." Why was she standing here, in the middle of the Great Hall, babbling such nonsense? There was a curiously distracted look in her eyes. "They value what they get by what they pay to get it, even if they don't under— . . . Ah!"

A faint *Boom!* rolled through the mansion.

"What was that?" Eshiala demanded, sensing a sudden gleam of satisfaction in her companion.

"The cellar door, I expect. Mistress Ukka was standing behind it. Ionfeu will be busy with his letter . . . Come!"

Eigaze set off as fast as she could move, heading for the main door like a runaway haywain. Bewildered, Eshiala followed, into sudden dazzling sunshine.

At the foot of the steps stood the gig, with a sorrel mare between the shafts. Ylo was sitting on the bench bouncing Maya on his knee. He was tickling and she was shrieking with glee.

Eshiala said, "I thought the stables—"

"Mistress Ukka had duplicate keys, dear," Eigaze said soothingly. "Up you get! Ylo, have you got the bags?"

"Two under my eyes and two under the seat, Aunt. Impress, is this brat housebroken?"

The countess took Eshiala by the shoulders. "Gods be with you, my dear!" There were tears in her eyes. "I divided the gold in two. Don't let Ylo cheat!" She smiled bravely and dropped her voice to a whisper, "And remember to play hard to get!"

"She knows that!" Ylo said. "It won't work. Up you get, wench. I don't think the cellar door will hold Hardgraa for long."

Even here, out on the driveway, the cellar door could be heard protesting.

"Mistress Ukka will keep the servants away," the countess

said, forcing a brave smile, "but Ion isn't quite deaf enough. Hurry, then!"

A kiss and a hug . . . a scramble up to the bench . . . take Maya from Ylo . . . a crack of the reins and a final wave to the old lady as the gig went bouncing down the driveway . . . bewilderment . . .

"Where are we going?" Eshiala exclaimed.

"I'm going back to Qoble," Ylo said. "Wonderful climate and a long way from goblins. I've got some heiresses in mind there. You're welcome to come along, or I'll drop you off somewhere. Please yourself. And I don't cheat with gold. Virtue, certainly. Always! That's what it's for. Gold, never."

Escape? Hope glimmered before her like a mirage. Hope sang like a skylark, high out of reach. She saw the long wooded driveway ahead through rainbows of hope.

"But they'll chase us!" she said.

The count would release Hardgraa. The centurion would rally the footmen and the grooms. He would be after the gig with a posse in minutes. Even if Ylo could reach the road, that would only offer a choice of Faintown or Moggly. Moggly was a dead end, and long before . . .

"Where are you going?"

The gig had turned off the driveway onto a side track.

"Down to the lake!" Now Ylo's grin was pure delight. "Auntie didn't go to Faintown. She went to Moggly. She ordered a boat."

"Boat?"

Maya squealed in gleeful terror as the gig bounced on the ruts. Cenmere came in sight through a gap in the trees, and a small sailboat was gliding toward the jetty.

"She lied to them!" Ylo added joyfully. "The news isn't out yet! She made it all up! We've got a day's start on the panic, at least. Quite a lady, isn't she?"

The ice had broken, and the pond was only ankle deep.

"But . . ." Eshiala's head swam with the intensity of relief. "That's why you were such a boor to me? To deceive Hardgraa?"

Or could it have been to stop her throwing herself on his mercy? Was that what the countess had been hinting?

Ylo took a corner on one wheel. "Me? Boor? That was merely a tactical feint—you don't mean you believed me?"

She ducked as branches swept low overhead.

"You should have remembered I always lie," Ylo said happily. "I worked it out when the daffodils blew away. Nothing like a country walk to clear a man's thinking! The pool had warned me off Rivermead, but it also trapped me into coming back here. Then I saw how Ionfeu and Hardgraa would react to the news." He was too occupied with driving to look at her just then, but he smiled at the track ahead. "I realized that this was a perfect opportunity to use my damsel-in-distress gambit."

Eshiala's hair blew in the wind, she hugged her daughter, who was yelling with mingled joy and terror at the wild ride.

They had escaped from the trap!

"Oh, Ylo! I'm so grateful!"

He flashed his most sinister grin at her.

"Gratitude I can handle," he said.

Remedies refusing:
Love is a sickness full of woes,
All remedies refusing;
A plant that most with cutting grows,
Most barren with best using.
SAMUEL DANIEL, *LOVE IS A SICKNESS*

CHAPTER FIVE

SIGNIFYING NOTHING

1

"MY MISSION IS EXTREMELY URGENT!" ACOPULO BLEATED.

"If you will explain this urgency, then I am sure your departure can be expedited," Lop'quith said soothingly.

"I have told you! My business is secret!"

"How can that be? You are a priest, and while the Gods' business is naturally confidential to the uttermost in individual cases, in general terms it concerns us all."

Balked again!

Acopulo had been trapped in Ilrane for two weeks. *Star of Morning* had avoided shipwreck in Dragon Reach, although barely. Battered and leaking, she had limped into the elvish port of Vislawn. When the customs officials had come aboard, they had ransacked her from stem to stern. They had uncovered Shandie's letters to the caliph. *Star of Morning* had departed without her passenger.

An elvish prison was admittedly very pleasant. When forced to build cities, elves concealed them. Vislawn was a great sprawl of islands at the mouth of the river, all its buildings hidden within trees. Acopulo had a pleasant cabana all to himself. He had a whole island all to himself. It had flowers and shade and a silver beach. The meals that were delivered twice a day were the sort of cuisine that Lord Umpily dreamed of. But a prison was a prison.

Every few days, someone new would come to interrogate him. Politely, of course—an elf became ill at the very thought of whips or knuckle-dusters. The questioning took place under the trees in bowers of scented blossoms.

The present inquisitor, Lop'quith, was fairly typical. He wore nothing but skimpy pants of scarlet and turquoise silk, and had no more fat on him than a dead twig. The skin stretched over his bones was a shiny gold. He claimed to be exarch of the Olipon sept of the senior branch of the Quith clan, and surrogate speaker of law for the Sovereignty of Quole—which might mean a lot or absolutely nothing. He looked no older than fourteen, but one could never tell with elves. He might be exactly what he seemed, a kid playing a practical joke on the foreigner, or he might be what he said, an important government official. In that case, he shaved his armpits.

Acopulo dabbed at the sweat streaming down his forehead. The priestly robes he wore over his normal garb were very uncomfortable in this hot, sticky climate. He suspected that a genuine priest would wear only the robes, but to him that would seem like a confession of weakness. He shifted on the bench, trying to ignore the cloying sweetness of the flowering shrub at his back.

"You believe I am lying. Then bring forth a sorcerer, and I shall be happy to repeat my story for him." Oh, how he would like to talk with a sorcerer!

Lop'quith shook his head regretfully. "The law does not recognize sorcery. If a judge had to admit that witnesses' memories could be altered, or the physical universe itself changed on an ad hoc basis, then he could never reach any verdict at all!" His tuneful voice turned the nonsensical words to song.

"You used sorcery to discover the letter I bore, and my money belt! I expect you have already had the letters read for you, without breaking the seals."

The kid's eyes widened, flickering from rose and aquamarine to cobalt and malachite. "You wish to make this charge?"

"What if I do?" Acopulo asked uneasily.

"It will be a serious matter! The Office of Occult Manifestations will have to be advised, and the Mundane Affairs Inquisitor of the gens will certainly want to become involved."

God of Torment!

"Then I withdraw the accusation. Please, sir—"

"Do just call me by my name, or 'Deputy,' if you prefer."

"Please, Deputy, then. I did not intend to disembark at Vislawn. All I ask is to board a southbound ship as soon as possible. I do not see where Ilrane need be at all concerned with my affairs."

"But you are carrying letters from the sovereign of a realm with which we are bound by the Treaty of Clowd, 2998, to the ruler of one with which we may in this instance be in alliance under the Concord of Gaaze, 2875, as amended by the Covenant of Seven Liberties, Clause 18, Paragraph 14.b(i). As a cleric, you are also subject to the Law of Religious Harmonies of the Syndic of Elmas, 2432, or specifically to a codicil—"

"Enough!" Acopulo wanted to weep. "I don't suppose there is any chance of appealing to Warlock Lith'rian, is there?"

The kid gasped. He ran the fingers of both hands through his curls of shiny gold wire. His voice soared an octave. "The warlock? The Supreme War Leader of the Eol Gens? Have you any *idea* of the bureaucratic complexities that you would invoke if you filed such a request? Indeed, I am not at all sure that even by raising the possibility, you may not have already—"

"Forget it!" Acopulo screamed. If the complexities alarmed an elf, they terrified him. "Is there any way at all that I can just . . . What's wrong?"

"There!" Lop' exclaimed, sitting up suddenly. "Did you see?"

"See what?" Acopulo twisted around to stare where the golden finger pointed.

"A Serene Ocarina! I have never seen one so early in the year!" The opal eyes flamed in sienna, cerulean, and ivory. Lop'quith's childish face had flushed bright copper with excitement.

"A *what*?"

"A Serene Ocarina! A butterfly."

Oh, God of Scorpions!

2

THE IMPEROR SUMMONED THE SENATE AT LAST. FOR DAYS the capital had boiled with rumors of goblins and dwarves and disasters. Umpily had gathered up all the theories being circulated at court and reported them to Shandie as he was supposed to. Maddeningly, Shandie had just listened and grunted, but not confided in him.

Without question, Shandie had changed since ascending the throne. The old intimacy Umpily had treasured so long was missing now. Some nights he awoke in screaming terror, shattered by nightmares in which he had been right the first time and the ruler was the imposter and the missing fugitive the genuine imperor. In the clear light of day such ludicrous fancies were untenable, of course, and especially so when he was in Shandie's presence—although those occasions were much rarer now than they had been.

A turnout of the full Senate would almost fill the Rotunda, leaving very few seats for other dignitaries. With the court still in mourning, though, many aristocrats had retired to their country estates to catch up on personal affairs. There were more spare seats available than usual, and Umpily was able to order his toga brought out of storage and squeeze his generous bulk in among the lesser nobility.

By chance or craft, it was an East day, which was traditional for military matters. The Senate all sat on that side, therefore, a solid bank of scarlet togas behind the Gold Throne, so that the imperor would be facing them from the Opal Throne in the center. The minor peerage had to settle for the western seats, in back of the Red Throne. Umpily was put very high, near the back, where he would look down on the proceedings, but he had the Marquis of Mosrace on his right and the Duke of Whileboth on his left. Whileboth was frail now, but a shrewd soldier in his day. His comments would certainly be worthwhile if he managed to hear what was being said. His many acid remarks about old Emshandar had kept him out of the Senate, but he had slaughtered more than his share of dwarves in his time, had Whileboth. The legions had called him "Ironjaw."

As always, the proceedings failed to start on time. The audience fidgeted and muttered. Both Mosrace and Ironjaw were convinced that Umpily must know what news would be announced. He parried their queries as well as he could without actually admitting his ignorance. They gave up on him at last and pointedly fell into talk with their other neighbors, leaving him isolated.

He wished he could tell them that they need not worry. Whatever the truth behind the rumors, the evil, scheming wardens were gone forever. The Almighty had replaced them, guaranteeing that the Impire would prevail. Umpily could not say so, of course. He could not mention the Almighty to anyone, no matter how hard he tried.

The trumpets sounded and the consuls in their purple-hemmed togas led in the procession, trooping in from the west door, dividing behind the Red Throne, and circling around. Bronze and gold flamed in the bright spring sunshine flooding down through the great dome. Marshal Ugoatho shone in gold armor and scarlet-crested helmet; his replacement as legate of the Praetorian Guard was very nearly as splendid. The impress in a simple chiton was enough to draw breath from every man present under the age of eighty, and most of the others, too. Shandie in purple mounting the Opal Throne . . .

Consul Eerieo was a new appointment, and a nonentity. No one could imagine why the imperor had chosen such a nincompoop to run the Senate for him.

"One gets you ten he makes a botch of the invocation," Mosrace muttered. He had no takers, and Consul Eerieo made a memorable botch. After all that, it was with a strong sense of relief that everyone sat down again to hear what Emshandar V had to say on this, his first formal act as imperor.

"Honored Consuls, your Eminences . . ." His voice was strong, and quite audible. He wasted no breath on preliminaries. He threw the facts before them like gruesome relics.

The truth was much, much worse than the rumors, and the Great Hall seemed to grow colder and colder as the report unfolded.

Without the slightest provocation, the Impire's boundaries had been violated by both goblins and dwarves. Four legions—the IIIrd, IXth, XVIIth, and XXIXth—had ceased to exist, with hardly a survivor to tell the story. The immensity of the disaster was stunning. As an augury of the new reign, it could not have been worse. As a portent of the millennium, it was terrifying. With the old man barely cold in his grave, the young Emshandar, who had been Shandie, the darling of the army, was telling of twenty thousand dead. And what of the civilians? In harsh, unemotional tones, he read out lists of towns and cities sacked.

All around Umpily, hardened, cynical old politicians were sobbing. Some of their distress came from patriotism, but many of those men were learning of their ruin, of herds and lands and wealth destroyed. The towns of Whileboth and Mosrace both were mentioned—devastated. The implications were even worse than the facts. The news must be weeks old. What had happened since? How close were the vermin now? Destruction and looting must be continuing even as the imperor spoke.

Old Ironjaw was mumbling obscenities, his ancient face as pale as chalk.

The litany of disaster drew to a close, and silence fell. Shandie turned a page. This young imperor was a strategic genius, wasn't he? Enrapt, the Senate waited to hear his response. It was impressive.

"We have set in motion the following countermeasures . . ."

First, he said, the Home Force, the four legions always stationed around the capital, had been regrouped to build a *wall of bronze* across the northern approaches to Hub—the Vth,

XIth, XXth, and XXIInd. A sigh of relief rustled through the Rotunda. The capital itself was safe, then.

"Wall of bronze!" Ironjaw roared, in a voice like a rusty windmill. "The vermin have *eaten* four legions already!" The comment had been too audible—faces turned and grimaced when they saw who had spoken.

The imperor continued unperturbed. "Recruitment to replace the losses has already begun. Substantial reinforcements are on their way. From the Mosweeps we have summoned the VIIth, and the XXIIIrd from Lith. The Ist is already marching up from the Ilrane borderlands, and the XIVth will cross from Qoble as soon as the passes open. We have sent to the Guwush theater for the IVth, VIIIth, XVth, and XXIVth. The IInd, normally charged with garrisoning the shores of Westerwater, has been ordered to retake Pondague Pass and cut off the goblins' supply lines. You need have no fear that we can repel the invaders with this massive response!"

Flimsy applause flowered amid the senatorial benches and then withered into silence. Umpily had raised his hands to join in the clapping when realization came to him also.

Massive? It was altogether too massive. The cure sounded far more dangerous than the disease. *How many* legions? If Emshandar-who-had-been-Shandie thought he needed half the Imperial Army, then the danger must be close to mortal.

At Umpily's side, old Whileboth reeled to his feet.

"Idiot!" he screamed. "Twelve legions? No man has ever attempted to control twelve legions!" The cracked old voice echoed through the Rotunda, too plain to be ignored.

The imperor swung around on his throne and glared up at the heckler, his face flushing scarlet. The assembly muttered as it recognized Ironjaw. Umpily cowered away from the maniac and tried to hide his face in the folds of his toga.

"Idiot, I say!" the old soldier bellowed. "You are stripping the whole Impire of its defenses—the jotnar and djinns and gnomes and elves will be right on their heels! How can you provision twelve legions? What supply lines do goblins need? How long until your orders arrive in Guwush? How long for those legions to march across Shimlundok?"

Umpily worked it out as everyone must be working it out: a thousand leagues at seven or eight leagues a day ... *four months*! And they could not even begin until the orders reached them.

Consul Eerieo sprang up, but his words were lost in the sudden tumult.

Ironjaw tried to say more, stopped in apparent surprise, and toppled forward over the noble lords in front of him, slithering to the floor. They bent to his aid and then recoiled. Umpily heard the appalled whispers. Whileboth was dead.

In the shocked hush that followed, Shandie resumed his speech as if nothing had happened. "Turning to financial matters, we lay before you the following proposals ..." He began to outline expenditures enormous and taxes unbelievable. Julgistro had always been one of the richest contributors to the Imperial fisc, but it would not be contributing now.

Why did he not mention the Almighty? Why did he not explain that the Impire was safe because it was guarded by the greatest army of sorcerers Pandemia had ever known? Umpily wanted to jump to his feet also and shout the good news, but of course he could not speak of the Almighty.

The speech ended. There was no ovation, only horrified whispering. While the imperial couple and the officials trooped out, peers and senators remained slumped in their seats as if dazed. Four legions destroyed! Innumerable cities burned. Two invading armies still at large. Ruinous taxation.

And months until Shandie could assemble the gigantic force he seemed to think he required.

It was the coming of the millennium!

If the emperor had expected his response to soothe the nation, then he had gravely miscalculated. If he had deliberately set out to ignite a panic, then he had succeeded very well.

3

DWANISH WAS A DRAB, GRAY LAND, DRAINED BY THE DARK River, brooded over by the grim Isdruthud Range on one hand and the even greater North Wall on the other. The straggling convoy of wagons had entered the realm of the dwarves through massively fortified gorges. Phalanxes of border guards had questioned, inspected, and grudgingly allowed it to pass.

Thereafter it had continued its snaillike progress over rutted, stony roads. Dwanish was more populated than the northern reaches of the Impire, but still bleak and stark. Its farms were lonely patches on the bleak moors, its towns squalid huddles of cramped cottages without pattern or plan. Trees were rare, flowers nonexistent. Except for waterwheels and windmill sails, everything was made of stone. Slag heaps of ancient mine-workings blighted the landscape and the air stank of smoke. Spring was an affair of mud and slush and bitter wind.

By and large the inhabitants ignored the caravan, or stared with surly, unfriendly eyes. Even the tiny children seemed uninterested, except when they caught sight of the two goblins or the young jotunn. Then they would run screaming home to their hovels.

Shandie had taken up wagon driving to keep himself from brooding over the fate of the Impire. As far as he knew, the invading armies must still be looting and destroying, for he had no information except the negative certainty that the Covin had not intervened. Warlock Raspnex had detected no major sorcery, so the war remained mundane. The legions would be marching, and the imperor was not there to lead them. Weeks were slipping away in waste and worry.

Shifting from global view to personal was no improvement. Shandie could see no progress in his pitiful campaign against the usurper. Umpily had been captured; Acopulo had arrived in Ilrane and then fallen silent. King Rap had stopped communicating, also. The counterrevolution seemed to be over before it had begun, and the remaining conspirators were resolutely marching into a trap in Dwanish. There seemed to be no way to accomplish what they had come to do without blundering into disaster.

One afternoon he was urging his weary ponies across a very boggy meadow. All Dwanishian rivers flooded in springtime, filling the air with a stench of mud. He was startled out of his black reverie by an apparition scrambling up on the bench beside him.

Young Gath was still growing at an incredible rate, visibly taller than he had been back at Kribur. His odd assemblage of clothing was worn to rags; pipestem wrists protruded from the sleeves. He walked as if his boots pinched his feet. Yet, way up there, under a mop of golden hair, his face was still absurdly boyish, despite the jotunn jaw beginning to emerge from childhood softness. He perched on the seat, adjusted his long limbs into position, and smiled nervously down at the imperor.

"You want me, sir?" His voice never strayed from its adult register now.

"I do?"

"Well, you will. You're going to hail me as I go by. I mean, you were going to."

Shandie forced a welcoming smile and scratched his bushy black beard as he disentangled that information. "I still can't understand how you do that! It's a paradox!"

"Dad used to say that, too," Gath admitted glumly.

Shandie winced. The lad must be just as worried now about his father as he was about his sister.

"Well, never mind. What do you think of beautiful Dwanish?"

"I never knew the world was so big! Mom says most of it looks better than this, though."

"It certainly does. Er . . . I expect you miss your friends back in Krasnegar?"

"I miss Kadie! And my friends, I suppose. Yes."

"Boys or girls?"

Gath's pale face blushed bright red. "Both."

If he was trying to put the lad at ease, Shandie thought, he was doing a horrible job of it. "I wonder why I was going to call you, though?"

"You want me to tell you, sir?"

God of Madness! Conversations with Gath were like no others. "Might save time."

"You were beginning to think you needed some fresh ideas, you said . . . will . . . would have said, I mean."

"Yes. Well, that's true. Do you like puzzles?"

The boy shrugged uncomfortably. "Not much. I either can't do them at all or I see the answer right away. No fun."

The imperor chuckled. "I don't think you'll see this one right away. It's got the warlock baffled, and the other sorcerers. I'm only a mundane, but I'm supposed to have a knack for strategy, and I'm stumped, too. Maybe if I explain it to you, it'll help me see it better myself."

Day after day, in pairs or larger groups, Shandie had been debating with the sorcerers, arguing over the problem awaiting them in Gwurkiarg. Talking about sorcery was agony for them, but gradually he had gathered up all the hints and slivers they had been able to confide. He prided himself that he had now gained an overall knowledge of sorcery that few mundanes in history had ever matched. It wouldn't hurt to enlighten the young jotunn, also, and talk out the problem.

After all, the preflecting pool had recommended Gath to him. Perhaps there was more to the prophecy than that miraculous rescue from the goblins' tortures. And Raspnex still felt the kid might be useful somehow.

"You know a lot of it already. We must enlist the help of the Directorate without alerting the Covin. If Zinixo does not have agents actually within the Council itself, he will certainly have spies near it. He has a compulsive greed to enslave every possible sorcerer into his army. He craves vengeance on his uncle Raspnex and on your father, which puts you and your mother at risk, too, of course, because he is madly vindictive. This little caravan of ours would be a real prize for him."

He paused for comments, but the clear gray eyes waited solemnly for him to continue.

"Do you know all this already—what I'm going to say?"

"Pretty much, sir," Gath said politely. "But you want to talk it out."

"Er, yes." Feeling oddly foolish now, Shandie continued. "And we assume he wants to get hold of me, too, although he may be managing all right without me. So if he ever finds out where we are, then he'll probably strike with everything he's got. And that's plenty!"

Sorcerers could detect sorcery in use. That was the crux of

the danger. A sorcerer could escape detection only by doing nothing. The stronger his power, the less detectable he was in action, and the better he could detect others. Even if Zinixo had no votaries nearby, the Covin could probably sense power being used almost anywhere in Pandemia. If Zinixo's agents were present and could be detected before they alerted their master, the effort of silencing them and liberating them might itself be detected . . .

"This was your father's idea, you know! He was the one who invented the new protocol. He suggested we spread the word by telling mundane authorities, like the Dwanishian Directorate. Trouble is, we've picked the most difficult one to start with."

"Dwarves are hard-headed you mean, sir?"

"True, but also this is Zinixo's home territory. He's certain to have left a watch on it. Worse, there's no fast, easy road out for us afterward."

Gath thought about that for a while, scowling. "Where do we go next?"

They would be lucky to go anywhere except to Hub, as captives. The imperor cracked his whip over the team to encourage the little ponies, which were game enough, but tired by a long day. "Likely the Directorate will want us out of here as fast as possible, and that means down the Dark River, to Guwush, or Nordland."

Those cagey, hard-headed dwarves might just try to turn the fugitives in, of course, hoping to win the usurper's favor, but that was not something to worry a kid with.

"Or sell us to the Covin?" Gath was there already.

"Er, yes. It's not easy to betray a warlock, though."

"You didn't mention loyalty spells, sir?"

"What about them?"

"Our sorcerers don't have loyalty spells on them, and the Covin's do. So ours can see theirs even when they're not doing anything."

"You know, that had slipped my mind. Who told you that?"

"Oh, I've been talking to the goblins . . . and Master Wirax. And the warlock."

Shandie should have guessed that any son of Rap's would

be likely to have brains and an interest in sorcery. He wondered if the boy perhaps knew almost as much as he did.

"Good for you! Carry on."

"Beg pardon, sir. The pinto has a stone in its front right shoe."

Shandie directed his attention back to the team, doggedly plodding over their shadows in the mud. Lead left did have a faint limp, but it did not seem anything to worry about. "He's probably just tired. Couldn't have picked up a rock in this muck."

Gath said nothing, and his silence said much.

"Tell me," Shandie said.

"You stop and one of us goes and gets the rock out."

"Which one of us?"

The young jotunn clenched his big jaw for a moment, suddenly reminiscent of his father. He stared straight ahead at the ponies. "If I try to, you tell me to stay here and you go, to see if I've told you the truth. If I say you're going then you send me."

"You can see both futures?"

"Yes, sir." Then he blurted, "And one where you really lame that pony, too!"

Shandie reined in. "I'll do it," he said, and jumped down into the bog. The shaggy pony was a walking swamp and balked at letting him lift its leg. There was indeed a rock in the little shoe, as he discovered when he had cleaned the foot enough to locate it. By the time he slopped his way back to the wagon, he was coated in mud from collar to toes. He thought he detected a gleam in the gray faun eyes looking down at him, and wondered if he had just been manipulated into making a certain adolescent's day.

With much whip-cracking and horrible sucking noises from the wheels, the wagon began to move again. Shandie hoped the dwarves had some dry shelter in mind for the night. They had been known to pitch camp in worse terrain than this.

"Let's hear some more of your ideas."

"Sir!"

"I mean it! You talk for a while."

Gath squirmed, then said, "Well, Moon Baiter says that just

because the Covin is all-powerful doesn't mean that every loyalty spell has that much power in it. So if we—our sorcerers,
I mean—can corner one of theirs by himself, they may be able
to free him if they all act together. And if they're lucky the
Covin won't hear them. Warlock Raspnex said he'd sooner
drop plate armor in chapel service, sir, but he admits it may be
possible."

"It's not a comfortable prospect," Shandie agreed, amused
at the breathless telling.

"If we could get them into a shielded building, like that
cottage at Kribur where we met with Death Bird and the general—then it would be safe, wouldn't it?"

"But we can't count on them being so stupid."

"No, sir."

"Can you suggest any other plans?"

Gath chewed his lip for a minute. "I gotta question."

"Let's have it, then."

"Why walk into their lair at all, sir? Why not just write them
a letter?"

"It's a very good question!" Shandie said, thinking that it
was an unexpectedly cold-blooded one from a fourteen-year-
old. "I did write letters to Caliph Azak. I might have tried it
here, too, except events sort of swept me up and brought me.
And dwarves are just about as stubborn as fauns . . . What's
wrong?"

"I'm part faun!"

The young pup had actually clenched his fists! His faun part
would matter greatly to him, of course, especially now.

"Nothing wrong with that and nothing wrong with being
stubborn," Shandie said. That was not much of an apology!
Could it be that his all-over coat of mud was rankling him a
little? "Anyway, the Directorate knows the warlock by sight
and will certainly listen to him. They may be impressed by
having an imperor ask for help. Or they may throw me in a
dungeon, of course. We're even thinking of having your
mother accompany us. Krasnegar isn't quite a neighbor, but
it's a sovereign state. That's our plan, and we know it's about
as safe as lion shaving. If you've got a better idea, then I'd love
to hear it."

Gath thought for a while. "I know what my dad would do, sir."

"You do? What?"

"He'd ask my mom."

Shandie choked back a laugh lest he hurt the boy's feelings yet again. "Your dad's a smart man, Gath," he said.

So much for advice and consultation! Well, it had helped pass the time.

4

SHANDIE WAS NOT THE ONLY MEMBER OF THE CARAVAN TO brood. Inos had more than enough troubles of her own—Kadie abducted by goblins, Rap off in Gods-know-where, inexplicably failing to report on the magic scroll, her kingdom neglected and likely tearing itself apart. Compared to those worries, the possibility that she and her son were heading into disaster tended to sit near the back of her mind.

Nevertheless, she was aware of the problem. She and Gath had become very close on this strange pilgrimage, and she soon heard all about his chat with the imperor. It taught her nothing she had not already known. Being the only woman in the group, she had a unique status. Few men of any race would resist a chat with an attractive woman once in a while. Like Shandie, Inos had passed time by talking with the sorcerers— Wirax and Frazkr the dwarves, Moon Baiter the goblin, Warlock Raspnex. The other goblin, Pool Leaper, was only a mage, but he was the youngest of the group, and a rarity—a goblin with a real sense of humor. He had told her more than he perhaps realized. Among all living mundanes, probably only she had ever visited the occult plane of the ambience, because Rap had taken her there once when he was a demigod. She knew every bit as much about sorcery as the imperor did. And she was not going to allow Gath to be used as bait.

Her friendship with Shandie was a matter of convenience. Neither sought real familiarity, and their respective responsibilities as monarchs would have made that impossible anyway. She admired his self-control, but it made him too cold and humorless for her taste. She resented very strongly his reluctance to discuss business with her. It was an attitude she had seen carried to absurdity in djinns, and she knew that goblin women were no better than slaves, but it was not normally an impish trait. She would have expected better of the imperor himself. The idea that a famous warrior might be intimidated by women never entered her head.

As the convoy drew closer to Gwurkiarg, it also drew near to the Dark River itself. It was in flood, bloating over the landscape like a dirty lake, spotted with ice floes and tree trunks from the mountains, plus many squat barges and lug-sailed boats emerging from winter shelter. Near the capital the towns were more numerous—some of them knee-deep in water and stinking of mud. At night the sky was blotched with the fires of foundries, while the smoke-dulled days were clamorous with the sounds of mills and wagon wheels and metal shops. The dwarves' was an ugly land, as humorless and prosaic as its citizens, devoted like them to business and profit, devoid of soul.

In the Impire spring was proclaimed by the arrival of swallows and in Krasnegar by geese. The news was brought to Dwanish by mosquitoes. Inos was heartily sick of living under canvas. Common sense would have suggested that the travelers seek shelter within some of the many houses and other buildings now available, but Sergeant Girthar continued to order camp pitched every night. Presumably dwarvish householders demanded rent and dwarvish travelers refused to pay it. Mud and mosquitoes and tents were an unholy combination.

Men came and went within the convoy. Part of the armed escort was relieved and replaced. Old Wirax went off to visit his family, promising to catch up later. Saturnine government officials arrived to tally the loot, which they persisted in doing even when the wagons were on the move.

Halfway through a particularly unpleasant day, Inos learned that she was now in Gwurkiarg, capital of Dwanish. She was not impressed. The road was deep in mire, and cramped between unending rows of stone buildings whose doors opened right on the street; there were no pedestrian sidewalks or gardens. The convoy was now merely part of a continuous line of carts creeping into the city, matched by another line creeping out. At intersections they knotted up in chaos.

Gwurkiarg had a mysterious reputation. Few non-dwarves were ever admitted—perhaps because the inhabitants were ashamed of the noise and the smell. Having almost no timber, they burned black stuff they mined, which made their chimneys smoke horribly. Hour by hour, hundreds of melancholy ponies fouled the streets. The skyline of drab slate roofs was unbroken by domes or temple spires; the largest building in the city, she had discovered, was the Treasury, and most of that was underground.

The day was gray and rainy.

When evening brought it to a merciful end, Sergeant Girthar pitched camp in a muddy wasteland apparently reserved for the army's use. The gloomy buildings enclosing it might be a notorious example of urban decay or the heart of uptown Gwurkiarg—Inos neither knew nor cared. She was much more interested in the sight of Shandie in conversation with a couple of strangers. Jotnar were not inconspicuous in dwarfdom.

She slopped over through the mud and took up position at his elbow, waiting expectantly. He reacted with a formality she considered absurd, considering that they both resembled shipwrecked scarecrows.

"Your Majesty, may I have the honor of presenting his Excellency the Nordland Ambassador to Dwanish, Thane Kragthong of Spithfrith?"

The jotunn was huge and broad, almost as large as Krath, who won the Krasnegar weight contest every year now. He was swathed in leather breeches and a fur shirt that bulged open to expose an equally furry belly with a noteworthy overhang. He wore a sword, a shiny steel helmet, and high boots. His silvery beard was long and forked, and although he was well into middle age, he looked capable of entering a castle without using the door.

"An honor, your Majesty!" He bowed—slightly. Thanes came in one flavor, male, and queens regnant were an absurdity.

"The honor is mine, Excellency!" Willfully mischievous, Inos thrust out her hand.

He barely spared it an icy glance. To kiss her fingers would be unthinkable and a jotunn handshake was a test of strength and resistance to pain, not a greeting that could be offered a woman. The ambassador's sea-blue eyes were perhaps less bright than they had been in his youth, and well padded now in fat, but they could still register devilry. Too late she realized that a thane would not be outmaneuvered so easily.

"Nay, let us not stand on formality, kinswoman!" His great hands shot out and lifted her bodily, folding her into a crushing bear hug. He then kissed her, with considerable fervor. There was a beery odor to his mustache and his beard tickled. By the time her feet were allowed to return to the ground, she knew that she had been outflanked, outmatched, and outsmarted, and Shandie was probably fighting off an urge to roll on the ground and gibber.

She staggered back, gasping to regain her breath. "Kinswoman?"

The ambassador was rearranging his beard with an expression of great satisfaction. "We are distant kin. If you want details, then I confess I shall need to wait for my skald to return from Nordland." The old man smirked. "Thane Kalkor, of blessed memory, was a second cousin of mine."

Ah! "Then my great-great-grandmother Hathra comes into it somewhere." Inos bore a lingering grudge toward that ancestral lady and the relatives she had towed into the family tree. The royal house of Krasnegar had other, older connections with the aristocracy of Nordland, but most of those would have been forgotten by now had it not been for Hathra. "I confess I was not aware of you, kinsman. I am sure I have many other worthy and noble relatives whom I could not list either—but I do not mourn Thane Kalkor. My husband did the world a favor there. Nor do I mourn his loutish half brother, Greastax."

Her candor earned a frown from the snowy eyebrows. "It may be that we shall journey to Nordland together, kinswoman. If so, then you must learn discretion. To speak such words in the hearing of the present Thane of Gark or any of his brethren would compel bloodshed."

Inos had just been outflanked again. "Truly said, kinsman! I shall guard my shrewish female tongue more carefully in future."

"It's all right in private," the thane said mildly. "I admire a woman with wit." He grinned down at her triumphantly.

She decided the battered old colossus was considerably sharper than he looked; she might even learn to like him, provided he let her win a point or two sometimes.

"And the ambassador's daughter, Mistress Jarga," Shandie said. He must have noticed the byplay, but he was diplomatically not reacting.

Jarga bowed, also. She was shorter than her father, but still half a head taller than Inos, raw-boned and weatherbeaten; she wore leather breeches and jerkin.

In Shandie's account of the escape from Hub, Jarga had been the name of the sailor who . . .

"Kinswoman!" Inos said. "Jarga? Then you must be—"

"I had the honor of meeting your husband, ma'am," Jarga said quickly. Her ice-blue eyes were alert with warning.

"I am very grateful for the help you gave him on that occasion," Inos replied swiftly. There were mundane dwarves around, but none close. Was it possible that the ambassador did not know his daughter was a sorceress? She did not seem very much younger than her father, and probably wasn't.

"Master Raspnex will be here in a moment," Shandie said. "He is seeking a suitable site for our discussions."

"Then I shall depart," the ambassador rumbled.

Shandie looked startled. "You would not rather—"

"I think you will talk of things I prefer not to know." The big man was hiding a smile in his silver beard. "At least, not know officially. Jarga may care to remain and reminisce with her old friend the warlock."

And that was that. If the thane wished to leave, obviously only sorcery or a small army would dissuade him. Shandie went along, escorting him to the edge of the camp, while Kragthong moved through the dwarves like a gander in a chicken run.

"Sailors have superstitions about the occult," Jarga remarked wryly.

That was true, and Inos knew what sort of sailor he must have been. How many more bloodthirsty demons did she have in her family? Thanes were killers by definition.

Dismissing the doubtful past, she brought her mind back to the future. What was to be discussed at this meeting? Jarga had been one of Raspnex's votaries. If the old dwarf was honoring the new protocol, then she had now been released and was a willing helper. She was also free to be a traitor, of course. Meanwhile, the ambassador had made an interesting comment—

"Your father will escort us to Nordland?" Inos inquired cautiously.

"That depends on many things, ma'am. Will the local authorities allow you to leave? Will the usurper catch us? And timing is important. We shall be pressed to reach Nintor by Longday, and there is no reason to visit Nordland except to attend the moot."

Inos shivered. "I have never been to Nordland, but I have seen reckonings fought."

Jarga sighed. She gazed over Inos' head, and for a moment seemed to stare intently at something far off. "I never have," she said harshly. "I could go—I am a thane's daughter. To attend the Nintor Moot has long been an ambition of mine."

Her bony jotunn face had turned hard and melancholy, stirring prickles of the uncanny on Inos' scalp.

"Then why do you not do so?"

The sorceress blinked and lost her preoccupation. She glanced down at Inos with a wintery smile. "Even a thane's daughter may not set foot on Nintor unless accompanied by her husband, and he must be a full thane. There are limits to my ambition, lady!"

Inos grinned. "Your father might tell you to guard your tongue!"

Jarga dismissed the grin with a scowl. "He does not take his belt to this daughter anymore! But come, ma'am, there goes the warlock."

"Is this to be a council of war?"

"So I understand, ma'am."

"Then I think I want my son present."

"That might be very wise."

Grr! Obviously the jotunn sorceress had been told more than the mundane queen had. Angrily, Inos went off to find Gath.

That decision proved to be an error. Gath was not to be found and when she went in search of the meeting itself, everyone of any importance had disappeared, also. Eventually she tracked them down, in one of the nearby cottages. The room was tiny, and now crammed with people. Two men had to move before she could even squeeze in through the door, and others stood in front of the tiny windows, blocking the light. She made out Jarga's pale hair, and then—to her intense annoyance—Gath's, also. There was nowhere left to sit, so she stood where she was, head bent under the low ceiling.

An elderly dwarf was speaking, and the others' respectful silence showed that he was someone of importance. All she could see of him was a white beard.

". . . remain in session at least two more weeks. Everyone is very anxious to head home at this time of year, you understand. Crops to plant. Rivers open." He coughed. "But of course we shall certainly spare time to hear an address by the warlock of the north."

Raspnex's guttural voice came from roughly the same direction. "Who else? Suppose we produced, oh, let us just assume that the new imperor was passing by and wished to convey his respects? Would the Directorate agree to hear him?"

"If he was brief."

Inos felt a sort of silent chuckle shimmer through the group, but no one laughed aloud. There were complex politics at play here. The Nordland ambassador was going to be told what had transpired, but did not wish to attend in person. Superstition was only an excuse; he had other reasons. The imperor was present, but not officially, because officially he was a prisoner of war. That assertion would declare the imperor in Hub an imposter. There was a lot of deniability about. Dwanishian politics were notoriously labyrinthine at the best of times.

"And what of the queen of Krasnegar, were she here?" Raspnex inquired.

The old man sighed. "If the proctor insisted her topic was important, the directors might stay for her opening remarks. She would find herself addressing an empty hall very shortly, though. We have no business dealings with Krasnegar, you see."

"Could you arrange for such a session without announcing who the guest would be, Proctor?"

There was a long pause. Inos was thinking furiously. Dwanish was ruled by the Directorate, and the proctor was the current presiding officer, so that white beard belonged to the ruler of the realm, as much as there ever was one. The two goblins were standing together off to her right. Frazkr was probably present somewhere; Gath and Shandie and Raspnex certainly were. Who the four or five others were, she had no idea. If any of them was a spy for the Covin, surely Zinixo would not be able to resist such a catch?

"You frighten me," the proctor said, as if his thoughts had followed her own. "Even if I convene a secret session, suppose the usurper learns of your presence? He may smite the hall with thunder." Clearly he was well aware of the situation.

Raspnex spoke harshly. "He would prefer to take us alive, I think. But is Dwanish prepared to submit already? Will you tender your allegiance with no struggle at all? Before he even threatens?"

"The Directorate would have to discuss the matter."

"What course of action will you offer for its approval?" the warlock demanded angrily. "Debates require a motion."

"Tell me what you plan to ask of us." The old man was wily.

Raspnex sighed. "Only that you spread the word of our resistance so that all the sorcerers may hear of it and take hope. We ask their aid; the usurper extorts it. We cannot alert them occultly without revealing ourselves to the enemy. Mundanes will not be involved otherwise."

The old man coughed painfully. "You underestimate your nephew. I remember him as a child. As soon as the meeting breaks up, he will know of it, if not before. He will learn you are in Dwanish and will hold our land to ransom. How do you plan to depart?"

"Quickly!"

"Not quickly enough. If you go by sorcery, he will follow. If you take a boat, he may boil the river."

There it was. The proctor had expressed the problem exactly.

Raspnex sighed. "We shall ask each member of the Directorate to keep the secret for two weeks. During that time, we shall make our escape."

The old man snorted. "Three hundred men? Keep a secret from sorcerers? Most certainly the usurper has agents in Gwurkiarg, and they will be curious to know what the Directorate discussed in camera."

"The risk is ours."

"No. You may bring down vengeance on all of us. I know his spite. Your petition is refused." The old man stirred, as if to rise.

The warlock shrugged. "Your term expires when?"

"In ten days. You are of course free to approach my successor. He may reopen the matter or not, as he chooses."

"If we decide not to do so, would you allow my friends to depart in peace?"

The proctor was shuffling toward the door. "The ambassador has interceded on their behalf. We have no quarrel with her Majesty of Krasnegar or her son, and the imp obviously cannot be who he claims to be. Personally I wish you all good fortune. Go with my blessing."

Men scrambled to their feet from the floor and the scanty furniture. Inos moved away from the door. The fresh air that poured in was a big relief. As the room emptied, she slipped over to the solitary little bed and sat down beside Jarga.

In a few moments the dignitaries had departed. The door remained open, giving welcome light. She glanced around and saw only the pitiful handful she expected—Raspnex, Shandie, Frazkr, Gath, Pool Leaper, Moon Baiter, Jarga and herself. Old sorcerer Wirax was there, too, and she had not known he was back.

The grubby little room was still crowded. She wondered

briefly who lived in this cramped squalor, and what it would be like to spend a lifetime in it. A bed, a stone chest, a couple of stools, and a table—no pictures, no flower vases, no rugs or bright cushions . . .

"We came a long way for nothing," Shandie said sadly.

"Not at all!" Only Raspnex had remained standing, solid as a granite tombstone on his great boots. He rubbed his beard, making a scratchy noise, and his expression was the grimace he used as a smile. "The plan remains unchanged!"

"It does?"

"Certainly. Officially the old rascal wants no part of it, but you heard what he said at the end. He was telling us to go ahead—and definitely warning us against his successor!"

Deniability, Inos thought. Gath was sitting on the floor, peering between his bony knees at her. He was grinning, too, which was an ominous sign.

The imperor sighed. "Explain."

"Tomorrow we gatecrash," Raspnex said jovially. "Remember that I'm still warden of the north as far as that bunch of mineowners, wheelwrights, and ironfounders is concerned. If I march into one of their meetings and demand a hearing, I'll get one."

Shandie was uncomfortably perched on a coal scuttle. "So how do you know there isn't a Covin agent in the hall?"

"That's where he comes in!" the warlock proclaimed, jabbing a thick finger in the direction of Gath. "He and I stand by the door as they convene. If I see a votary spell going in, I depart, smartly."

Shandie frowned. "Why Gath?"

"Because he'll know if I'm going to, so he'll tell me beforehand. He's our advance warning! If he foresees disaster while we're speaking, again he'll tell us before it happens." The warlock shot an apprehensive glance at Inos, who was breathing fire and pawing the ground, figuratively.

"Can my son foretell the future better than you can, your Omnipotence?"

He waved his hands like shovels. "Not better, no. This is hard to explain. I can foresee things. Most sorcerers can, some better than others. But it's a noisy, conspicuous thing to do, and most of us don't do it much, because it can be extremely confusing, and even dangerous. Sorcerers have been known to fall into unbreakable trances trying to decide between conflicting futures, and others stumble upon their own deaths. Your son does it all the time because he can't help it, so he's learned to live with it. If he wasn't the sort of young man he is, it would have driven him insane. Fortunately his range is short, and his power is so weak that it barely shows up. It's sort of diffuse. Like a fly buzzing in the background. Unless you're looking for it, you don't see it. Hear it. Whatever."

Gath was positively leering now, watching Inos. Perhaps *bait* was not quite what Raspnex had in mind for him, but it was close enough. She clenched her fists and restrained her temper, waiting to hear what Shandie would say.

He was obviously unhappy. "And if you detect Covin agents, what's the alternative?"

"Then we try to spread the word privately among the other directors, as many as we can reach. Later, in small groups."

The imperor glanced around the little room, studying the faces of the dwarves and goblins. He seemed to find little comfort in them. "That kills any chance of reaching Nordland by midsummer."

"We'll have to split up anyway, sooner or later."

"I suppose so. If that's the best we can do, then we have to risk it. How about the escape afterward? The proctor was right, you know. The Covin will want to know what's been discussed, and it can certainly find out."

Raspnex shrugged his massive shoulders. "You and I and the boy remain. The others should leave right away. Jarga's got a boat waiting. As for us—as you may have guessed, this cottage is shielded. I know of several other shielded houses. We'll hole up in one of them and wait until the hue and cry dies down."

Shandie said, "Umph!" He did not look at Inos. Nor did he look overjoyed at the thought of half a year under house arrest in beautiful downtown Gwurkiarg. Gath was still grinning.

"Give up, your Majesty?" Raspnex jeered.

Shandie scowled. "I don't like it, but as they say you can't make chickens without breaking eggs."

The warlock turned to Gath. "You willing, young 'un?"

Gath sniggered. "No, sir."

Raspnex glared. "No?"

"Ask my mother, sir."

All eyes swung to Inos. Her skin prickled. What she was about to suggest might provoke an attack by the Covin within minutes. Faking a calm she did not feel, she smiled innocently at Shandie. "I believe you made my husband a promise?"

The imperial scowl deepened. "I did. I'm not sure it's still valid, though. I take it you don't approve of your son being involved in this?"

"I think it's the craziest nonsense I ever heard and I certainly won't let him be dragged in. I won't have anything to do with it myself, either. I think you're going about this the wrong way."

The men all stared at her, and she wondered if the sorcerers were prying into her mind. They might find a few surprises in there.

Raspnex had certainly become very thoughtful. "Tell us."

She pointed to a little shelf above the hearth. "Can you make that candlestick fall down?"

"Yes."

"Can you make it fall down tomorrow?"

He nodded, his eyes like agates.

"When do you rattle the ambience, as my husband calls it? Now, when you cast the spell, or later, when it takes effect?"

"I dunno." The warlock scratched his beard again. "Let's try it."

There was a moment's silence, and then the candlestick fell off the shelf.

"Well?" he demanded, looking around.

"When it works, mostly," Moon Baiter said, and the others were nodding.

"I felt almost nothing at the beginning," Jarga said.

"What I thought," the warlock agreed. "That's when the power acts. Holy rocks! She's got it!"

With a surge of relief, Inos turned to the jotunn beside her. "How long would it take us to run to your ship and set sail?"

Jarga smiled broadly. "About an hour. Less."

"Gath?"

He nodded vigorously, as if so full of mirth that he did not trust himself to speak.

"And he does it?" she asked.

More gleeful nods. "Yes he does, Mom."

"Wait a minute!" Shandie barked. "You've lost me."

"Oh?" Inos said. "You need me to spell it out for you?"

He glared. "Please!"

"Quite simple. The warlock appears before the Directorate in a couple of weeks. But he does it now. Then we depart."

Shandie blinked. "Is that possible?"

Raspnex had his gruesome leer back. "I don't see why not. I've never tried it, but if I can do it to a candlestick, I can do it to me."

"And the Covin won't notice you doing it? Now, I mean."

"How can it? I told you this room is shielded. I transport us two weeks into the future. Proctor said they'd still be in session in two weeks, so we might as well use that time. I send us there for ten minutes, or an hour, however long we think we need. We do what we want to do, and then we're not there any more." He uttered a dwarf's millstone chuckle, more amused than Inos could ever recall seeing him.

Shandie looked ready to tear his hair. "How do you get the power through the shielding? I thought—"

"Don't. We walk out that door two weeks from now and I transport us to the Treasury."

The imperor shook his head disbelievingly. "This is really going to work?"

"Ask Prince Gathmor."

"We do go on the ship," Gath said quietly. "*Gurx*? That's its name. Her name, I mean. I saw that earlier. All of us, and the ambassador, too." He pulled a face. "And dreg Vork."

The imperor wiped his forehead with his sleeve. "God of Madness! We go before the Directorate two weeks from now, but they can't follow us because we left today? Inos, who taught you this?"

Triumph felt very, very good. "I worked it out. It's just an extension of the kind of paradox Gath pulls off all the time. I don't suppose it would work backward, would it?"

"Ugh!" Raspnex shuddered. "Go and do it yesterday, you mean? I certainly won't try that! But I can't see why not tomorrow, or two weeks from now."

"And you can take me, too?" Shandie asked uneasily.

"You don't go!" Inos said. "I told you you've been going at this the wrong way. Forgive me, Omnipotence, but I don't think begging is the best way to influence a collection of, er, mineowners and whatever else it was you called them."

Raspnex was glaring now. So, she saw, were Frazkr and old Wirax. They must be reading her thoughts.

So, apparently, was Jarga. "Gang of ornery, miserly, bull-headed, rockbrained dwarves," she remarked with a smirk.

"Oh, I wouldn't go that far," Inos said gratefully. "But remember that Dwanish and the Impire are at war. If Sh—if his Majesty appears before them, claiming to be rightful imperor, it is going to distract . . . Well, let's say that the debate may stray from the subject you wish to discuss."

There was an ugly pause, then Shandie said tactfully, "I can see how the discussion could become quite prolonged."

It would take hours, or weeks, and achieve nothing.

"What are you suggesting?" Raspnex growled, but there was a sudden glint in his stony eyes.

"I think that a push might work better than a pull, your Omnipotence. I think the man who gatecrashes the Directorate should be Zinixo himself."

Shandie said, "Holy Balance!" and started to smile. The two goblins laughed aloud.

Then so did Raspnex. He guffawed. "Have you been talking to *elves*, ma'am? I see! Well, this could be more fun than I thought! A lot of them will remember . . . I wonder if I can match his taste in foul language? Insults? Threats? Absolutely forbid them to tell anyone about the new protocol, of course?"

"Make it up as you go along," Inos said. Now the tension was flooding out of her and she was beginning to shake. "Don't forget that rockbrained bit."

The warlock glanced around at the others, the sorcerers. "Any arguments? Good. Then let's try it. Help me with the change."

He flickered and became Zinixo. Inos caught her breath. It

had been almost twenty years, and he was no longer a youth, but she would never forget that sneer, that vicious face.

"Well, swine?" He laughed sepulchrally, and she remembered too how incredibly low-pitched his voice was, even for a dwarf.

"You're not dressed for the part," she said shakily. "Gold chains and jewels."

"He doesn't! I mean, I don't."

"But it will impress the Directorate."

"So it will, so it will. There!"

Gems and silks—now the fake usurper glittered in glory. He couldn't quite match dear Azak, perhaps, but he would certainly rile any dwarf who saw him. Frazkr looked nauseated already.

"Any last advice?" the imposter rumbled. "No? Jarga, why don't you take the mundanes down to the ship right away, just to be on the safe side? Then I'll go and tell those moneygrubbers what I think of them and what I'll do to them if they help me, er, you. Us, that is."

"Don't threaten their profits," Shandie said weakly. "Or you really will scare them off."

"Ha! By the time I'm done with them, they'll be so mad they'll take up a collection!"

As Inos rose, Gath jumped up and banged his head on a beam, which was a remarkable error for him to make. He used a word she hadn't known he knew. Rubbing his yellow mop, he turned around in a crouch and grinned at her. "Well done, Mom! I knew you'd do it!" He reached the door at the same time as the imperor. "Are we really going to the Nintor Moot, sir? I get to come?"

Shandie smiled at Inos, wearing a very appropriate shamefaced expression. "You'll have to ask your mother. She's the strategist."

It was a fair apology—she bobbed a curtsey.

He bowed her out ahead of him, and they blinked in the daylight and drizzle. The air was about as fresh as it ever was in Gwurkiarg, and welcome after the stuffy cottage.

Shandie glanced behind him and then said quietly, "That was brilliant!"

She grinned at him, still shivering a little with relief. "Oh, it was nothing, Sire! Live with Gath for a while and you begin to think backward and sideways."

"No, that was brilliant, too, but the Zinixo thing! Of course they'd never have listened to us. As you said, the best way to move a dwarf forward would be to try to push him back. How did you ever think of it?"

"Just muddled female thinking," Inos said demurely. She was tempted to explain that she'd been married to a faun for eighteen years, but it would sound disloyal.

Gath emerged behind them, still gabbling with excitement. "Mom? I don't have to fight Vork, do I? I mean, you don't mind that he calls you a fraud, and—and worse things?"

"What are you . . . who's Vork?"

He pulled a face, showing the broken tooth that always annoyed her so much. "Red-headed idiot. I mean, you told me not to listen when Brak insulted Dad, so you won't mind if I ignore what Vork says about you, will you? You should hear what he calls me . . . Never mind. *He spits on my feet!*"

Inos clenched her fists. "Who is Vork?"

Jarga had appeared also, ducking under the lintel. "Vork," she said, "is the terror of the four oceans, five years from now, my youngest half brother. He's about your son's age, and if Gath would just break his neck quickly, he would be doing us all a favor."

Signifying nothing:
> *Life's but a walking shadow, a poor player*
> *That struts and frets his hour upon the stage*
> *And then is heard no more. It is a tale*
> *Told by an idiot, full of sound and fury,*
> *Signifying nothing.*
> SHAKESPEARE, *MACBETH*, V, v

INTERLUDE

Spring was mellowing into summer in that fateful year of 2999, and people were on the move all over Pandemia.

As a rock falling in a pond raises a wave, the goblins' attack had sent a catastrophe of refugees pouring southward, and all roads led to Hub.

Behind the fugitives, the goblin horde zigzagged across the deserted landscape, burning empty farms and deserted towns. Death Bird and Karax had agreed upon a brilliantly simple strategy. Goblins moved much faster than dwarves, so Death Bird would let the Imperial Army catch his scent and thus lure it northward. Then the goblins would be the hammer and the dwarves the anvil.

Like most brilliant ideas, it did not work. They had not considered the refugees.

Four legions stood across the ways to Hub, the wall of bronze Emthoro had described to the Senate. When the human tide surged down upon them, they moved aside to let it pass, but it choked every road and lane with people. Cohorts stood as islands in the flood, unable to advance upon the enemy even had they wished to. The army's own supplies could not get through. Soon the wall of bronze itself was in danger of starving. Hub trembled as the torrent of frantic humanity swirled into its streets.

Deprived of rape and torture, the invaders became bored. The imps' apparent inactivity made them apprehensive. Goblins had no tradition of discipline or loyalty to supreme authority; they began grumbling about returning home. Feeling his control weaken, Death Bird abandoned the agreed plan and struck out southwestward, apparently hoping to outflank the legions. His messengers never reached Karax.

He eventually crossed the Ambly River into Ambel, and continued south. Had he turned east, the capital would have been easy pickings, and his reasons for not doing so were never established. Perhaps he suspected a trap. Perhaps he preferred a rapid advance into virgin country because it fed his men a satisfying supply of victims. The horde raced southward, meeting no resistance. Death Bird was undoubtedly one of the greatest military geniuses ever to torment Pandemia, but he was also a savage, and limited in many respects. Had he known more history, he would never have led his host within range of the worms of Dragon Reach.

General Karax, hearing nothing of his unreliable allies and being unable to transport any more loot, turned his army around and headed back toward Dwanish. The Directorate later judged this eminently sensible act to be treason and put him to death.

•   •   •

Couriers had already poured out from Hub like hornets to summon the legions. Men in thousands shouldered their burdens, formed up in columns, and began marching. Day after day they wore out their sandals on the endless straight roads of the Impire.

In Gwurkiarg, capital of Dwanish, the former warlock Zinixo burst in upon a meeting of the Directorate, ranting about an obscure conspiracy of sorcerers no one had ever heard of and denouncing the warlocks for attempting to amend the Protocol. Two of the directors were observed to fall on their knees when he entered the hall. They knew that this was merely an occult projection of some sort, of course, but they did not question the actions of their beloved leader. A couple of other Covin agents in the city detected the release of power, but they, too, refrained from interrupting the Almighty. By the time Hub inquired what was happening, the apparition had vanished, leaving no trail to follow. Word of the outrage spread rapidly throughout the land.

By that time the riverboat *Gurx* had been riding the spring flood down the Dark River for two weeks. That inconspicuous little craft was later to be the subject of a famous ballad, for during those fateful days it bore an imperor, a queen, a thane, two princes, and the second largest collection of sorcerers in the world.

In Thume the rainy season had ended and the dry season begun. Life went on there undisturbed by the clamors of war, as it had for a thousand years. Novice Thaïle pursued her studies in the College.

Sir Acopulo, released at last by the elvish officials, took passage on the first available southbound ship, which happened to be a smelly little fishing boat from Sysanasso.

·   ·   ·

In Zark, the caliph learned of the Impire's troop movements and hastened his preparations for invasion.

In far-off Krasnegar the unusually bitter winter drew to a close. The royal council ruled in the queen's absence under the efficient chairmanship of the deputy she had appointed before her mysterious departure. His authority was often challenged, but he remained undeposed because the council could never agree on a replacement. In one of the few actions it did agree on, it ordered the rack-boned herds driven across the causeway to the hills of the mainland, the traditional first rite of spring.

The people of that barren little land would have been very surprised to know that their king was fighting his way through the jungles of the Mosweeps in the company of a jotunn and two trolls.

The torrent of refugees that poured into Hub had released a second flood, heading east and south. Racing in advance of them on the road to Qoble went a one-horse phaeton, bearing a man, a woman, and a child. After they had been traveling for over a month, they arrived one night at an inconsequential hamlet called Maple, where the man pulled up in the middle of the only street and gestured to the inn signs displayed on either hand.

"We seem to have a choice of two," he observed with a roguish smile. "The Imperial Crown, or the Daffodils."

And Eshiala, who may have become bolder during the past few weeks or perhaps merely tired of resisting the inevitable, blushed and announced, "I think I'd like to try the Daffodils."

So it was in Maple that Ylo gained his reward and Eshiala learned how an expert made love. It was a very prolonged affair, at times gentle, at times extremely energetic. It began with her toes, and involved a lot of laughter and eventually tears that were not tears of sorrow, and it lasted until dawn.

By coincidence or divine irony, it was during that same night of rapture that a solitary rider thundered through Maple without stopping, passing below the chamber window. He thus drew ahead of his quarry. He had always known that this absurdity might befall his solitary pursuit, but he had heard Ylo speak of a warmer climate and guessed that he planned to return to Qoble. There were very few passes into Qoble, and they were all guarded by detachments of the XIIth legion. Its officers would listen to Centurion Hardgraa; every man in the ranks knew Signifer Ylo.

In Qoble the child would be recaptured and the traitor who had abducted her would pay the penalty.

CHAPTER SIX

WESTWARD LOOK

1

THE FOREST GIANT HAD TOPPLED YEARS AGO, AND ITS TRUNK
was thickly encrusted by moss of an especially nasty green.
Higher than Rap's head, it lay across his path like a wall. "Path"
was a misnomer, of course. There was no path. There was
almost no light to see by, or solid ground to stand on, or space
to squeeze between the branches and suckers and vines. The
rain did stop sometimes, briefly, but such momentary droughts
made no difference at the bottom of that sea of vegetation,
where water dribbled and dripped continuously. He had been
clawing his way through this nightmare for more weeks than
he could bear to think about. Had there been any way to give

up, he would have given up long ago. Even fauns were not that stubborn.

Thrugg had found handholds somewhere and swung his great form onto that fallen trunk—peering up, Rap could see his enormous feet and calves like flour sacks. The rest of him was hidden in leaves. Then he crouched down, coming into view with the usual spray of water. He bared teeth in a grin. "Coming?"

He went naked and there was not a single mark on his doughy hide. Rap was swathed in garments of stout linen, yet he had almost no undamaged skin left between scars, scrapes, rashes, bruises, and insect bites. He had renewed his entire outfit from hat to boots just three nights ago, and put a preservation spell on it, but already it was rotting and falling apart.

The surprise was not that the Impire had never conquered the Mosweeps; the surprise was that it had ever wanted to.

Stop! He was veering perilously close to an attack of self-pity, and he seemed to be doing that far too often recently. Go on, or sit down and die—those were the choices. Or use sorcery and be snapped up by Zinixo, of course, which would certainly be a worse ordeal than this. Fauns did not sit down and die! Nor did jotnar.

Thrugg's big paw was waiting. Rap grabbed it with both hands and felt a familiar humiliation as the young giant yanked him effortlessly skyward. A rush of wet leaves in his face, and he was standing at the troll's side, feeling childlike and helpless.

Thrugg pushed aside vegetation and peered at him with an expression of bestial ferocity that would have given a professional torturer nightmares for months. Rap could identify it now as mild concern, just as he had learned to make out the slurred mumble of trolls' speech—the words were all in there, if you listened carefully enough.

"Not long now. You manage?"

Was his frailty so obvious? "Sure I can manage! Race you to the next castle . . . if you'll just tell me where it is."

Thrugg chuckled, a deep rumbling noise inside the barrel of his chest. He thumped a friendly hand on Rap's shoulder in approval. The moss crumbled under Rap's feet, and he shot down into a soggy, crumbling paste, coming to rest with his arms on the green carpet and the troll's horny toes in front of his face. *Oh, Gods!* Again he felt black blankets of despair envelop him. What was the use?

"Not down there!" Thrugg said.

Rap summoned his resources. *Fight on!* There would be humor in this situation somewhere, if he could find it. "I think you're cheating!" he moaned. "Do troll rules let you nail your opponent into the ground?"

"Sure. Now I stamp on your head."

"It's not fair, you know! You must outweigh me three to one, and I'm the one who falls through?"

"Standing with feet wrong way."

"Well, it is restful, like a warm bath."

"That's good! Dead trees usually full of many-legs. No bites? Stings?"

At once Rap's skin began to crawl with a million tiny feet, real or imaginary. *"Get me out of here!"* he yelled, close to panic.

Thrugg lifted him out and jumped, still holding him like a child. They came down on the far side of the tree with a splash, knee-deep in mud. The brief stay in the rotted wood had been long enough for Rap's clothes to be invaded by the many-legs, and several no-legs also. With howls, he began stripping them off.

"Use sorcery?" the troll asked urgently. He hated to see anyone else suffer, although he had endured months of slavery at Casfrel rather than wield his power against another human being.

"No!" Rap said. The Covin seemed to have abandoned its search, but the fugitives had agreed to continue their avoidance of magic in the open, and he would not be the first to give in. He clawed at something squishy feeding on his thigh. "Ugh!"

"Next castle's shielded."

"Wonderful! How'd you know that?"

"Been there before. Almost there now." How Thrugg found his way though this impenetrable maze was a complete mystery. Rap thought he did it by smell. He could navigate just as well in the dark during a thunderstorm. He never lost his sense of direction, and he invariably found some sort of shelter for the night—not that he needed shelter, but the visitors did. He did not use sorcery, for Rap would have detected that.

"Then I'll clean up there. Lead the way." Leaving his infested clothes where they were, Rap set off in only his boots and a bare minimum tied around his middle. When he wore clothes, he sweated to death in the steamy heat. When he didn't, he was stung and scratched unbearably. He could never decide which was worse. But if there was shielding ahead, then he could put everything right in a few minutes. New clothes, new skin. *Cold beer!*

Today they had crossed a single ridge, covering less than a league, and Witch Grunth's home was a long way off yet. Insidious voices whispered that this expedition was a terrible mistake. The moon was past the full again, so Rap had been floundering around in the mountains for more than two months. He had no idea what was happening outside in the real world. He had no way now to communicate with Shandie or the warlock. For all he knew they might both have been captured, leaving him to fight a hopeless single-handed battle against the Covin. At the present rate he was going to die of old age before he achieved anything at all.

Krasnegar itself might no longer exist. He could not bear to think of Inos and the children. In the letter he had sent with Shandie, he had urged Inos to leave and take refuge at Kinvale. She might have sent the kids away, but he doubted she would have abandoned her kingdom. She took her royal responsibilities more seriously than anything else in her life, and at times she could be as stubborn as a faun.

Would he ever see her again? More likely he would die of old age in this Evil-begotten morass. What had ever possessed him to come here? Lith'rian would have been a far better bet than Grunth.

And always, that haunting half memory that whispered he had forgotten something important and was overlooking a winning move . . .

Thrugg had been right again, though. In a few minutes they heard running water and the ground dipped steeply. Rare was the stream that had no castle on it. Trolls spent their lives home-making, building huge edifices of rock, almost always straddling running water. A cataract in every room seemed to be the most desired feature in domestic architecture, except possibly incompleteness. As soon as he saw his work nearly finished, a troll would wander away and start again somewhere else. A man's gotta do something, Thrugg said, and what else was there to do in the Mosweeps? Most of the jungle was edible for trolls, so there was no need to farm. Once in a while they would run down a deer—usually just for sport, but rarely for a taste of meat. Wood and paper and cloth turned to mush in days. Fires would not burn. Heaving rocks around creatively was better than doing nothing.

Every stream bore abandoned castles, many so ancient that they were buried in jungle. A surprising number of them showed evidence of occult shielding. That abundance of shielding was the only encouraging thing Rap had discovered on this mad pilgrimage. It confirmed his theories about the best places to look for sorcery. For untold centuries, the gentle folk of Faerie had been exploited for words of power. The Nogids and the Mosweeps were barriers on the road home to the mainland. Many geniuses and adepts must have been shipwrecked, and words of power outlived their transitory owners. He had assumed that the trolls and anthropophagi would include more than their share of mages and sorcerers, and so far his guess seemed to be working out.

Gathering them together, even with Grunth's help, would be another matter altogether. One lifetime would never be enough.

Somewhere just ahead, though, was another troll castle. Soon he would discover who lived in it, if anyone. Many trolls were completely solitary. Others lived in strange groupings—two or three men and one woman, or the other way around. Once or twice he had met bands of children living together with no evidence of adults to care for them. Little Norp had attached herself to one such band without even a word of farewell. Trolls were peaceable and could eat anything. They had no need for social organization.

Yet they had a culture, of a sort. He had not known of their singing and dancing before, but they existed. Although they were strange to him, he could appreciate them as art. Trolls made strangers welcome—indeed their hospitality toward other trolls was unlimited. They would share even their mates without jealousy. Rap had refused several offers in the last two months, always with as much tact as he could muster.

Darad had no such inhibitions. Even after exhausting days of scrambling through impenetrable vegetation, he could never resist challenging the men to wrestling matches. He never won, and he never learned. His activities with the women had perhaps been more successful, but he had suffered numerous broken bones in both sorts of encounter, despite his partners' efforts not to hurt him. Had Thrugg not cured his injuries, Darad would have long since been left behind, a helpless cripple.

Darad and Urg were following, probably quite close, but the dense undergrowth blocked noise.

A glimpse of weepy gray sky showed through the trees ahead, and the noise of water grew louder. The day was far from over, but the promise of rest was too tempting to refuse. At this rate, Rap was going to be as old as Sagorn before he even met up with Witch Grunth.

His gloomy meditations were interrupted by a thunderous roar from Thrugg. Trees shuddered and cracked as the giant hurled himself forward and disappeared down a bank. Rap scrambled after, hearing more ferocious bellows, and then others in answer. He emerged from cover at the edge of a small pond. Thrugg and another man were rolling around in the center, roiling the water to spray, punching, roaring, and struggling as if bent on mutual murder. Such was the normal friendly greeting between male trolls. Fortunately, they were rarely so affectionate toward men of other races.

Beyond them stood a wall of gigantic rocks, with the stream cascading down from the front door. Venturing a peek with farsight, Rap established that the castle was indeed shielded against sorcery. That was welcome news, and so was the relative absence of moss on it. It must be very recent—and that suggested a sorcerer in the neighborhood.

Shortly thereafter, Rap was reclining at ease in a comfortable chair identical to his favorite chair in Krasnegar. Cold drinks stood on a table nearby. He was clean and garbed in loose cotton slacks. He had healed his scrapes and bruises, including the dislocated shoulder he had suffered in being introduced to Shaggi, his new host. Sorcery had a much greater appeal in the Mosweeps than it did anywhere else.

The room was troll size, a modest cathedral, although in shape it was more like a cave, with few level or vertical surfaces. It was dim and relatively cool. A waterfall cascaded down the rear wall to feed a series of pools crossing the floor to the entrance. Jungle was already clambering in through the windows. Apart from Rap's innovations, there was no furniture.

Thrugg and Shaggi sprawled side by side on a rock ledge, growling and gabbling at each other incomprehensibly. They appeared to be old friends, for they laughed often, and jovially swung killer punches at each other. Shaggi was something of a mystery. If anything, he was even larger than Thrugg, and of about the same age. He was not, apparently, a sorcerer. Or else he was concealing the fact superbly.

Just when the mayhem seemed to be slowing down and Rap thought he might manage to enter the conversation, a shadow darkened the doorway. Urg came striding in, carrying Darad. He was delirious, thrashing and struggling vainly against her greater strength. Thrugg leaped up in alarm, and his image brightened in the ambience as he inspected the damage. Snakebite, Urg explained casually. A sorcerer of Thrugg's power could heal anything short of death, and in moments the jotunn was sitting up and looking around with his usual ferocious grin. Rap organized another, very solid chair. But of course Darad would have to meet his host, and there would be more violence.

Rap could contain his impatience no longer. "Shaggi?" he demanded hastily. "Who put the shielding on this house?"

"Uh?" Shaggi scratched his head. "Shielding?"

Thrugg chuckled. "I did." He was sitting on a rock by the stream, crunching on a thick tuber he had magicked up for himself.

Rap's mood turned black again. "Oh."

"He's my brother."

"Oh!" Well, that explained the joviality. "I was hoping maybe we'd met up with another sorcerer."

"You did!" a new voice said. A monstrous old female came lumbering out of the shadows under the waterfall. Her hair was gray and tied behind her head in a ponytail, which was an odd affectation for a troll. She wore a loose cotton gown, which was even odder.

Thrugg leaped up and tried to embrace her. She swung a sideways punch that would have smashed any normal skull like an egg. It bowled the young giant right off his feet, and he flipped into the pool with a splash that soaked half the chamber.

"Idiot!" she snarled. "Why did you bring these vermin here?"

Wiping water from his face, Rap sprang to his feet. He had done it! All those weeks of torment in the horrible jungle had not been wasted—he had found the woman he came to seek. He bowed low.

"Greetings, your Omnipotence!"

Grunth glared at him and then spat. "Go away!" she said. The ambience flared dangerously, with images of molten rocks. "Go away before I burn you to ashes."

2

SHAGGI BOUNDED OVER THE STREAM TO RAP AND EN-folded him in a bone-creaking hug. "He is my guest!" he bellowed, apparently believing that his mother would be unable to damage Rap without hurting him at the same time—which was far from the case, of course.

Even before he had spoken, though, or Darad had stopped blinking his surprise, Thrugg spoke out in the much faster world of the ambience. In a stream of images almost instantaneous, he described Rap's attempt to rescue the slaves at Casfrel. He explained how that had been an act of pure altruism, and a very dangerous one. His appreciation and gratitude were obvious—embarrassingly so. Rap himself had almost forgotten the incident, and thought nothing much of it anyway.

But it cooled the witch's anger. She sat down on a convenient rock and scowled at him. "My thanks, then," she said reluctantly. "But you are not welcome here."

"I see that," Rap muttered, still breathless from Shaggi's embrace. "Can we talk about it?"

The molten rocks glowed again briefly. *"Talk. I'll listen."* Grunth turned her attention to Urg, holding out her arms in welcome. While the two hugged in the mundane world, Rap started to speak in the ambience. Thrugg introduced Darad, who was as far out of his depth as usual, and Shaggi went splashing out down the stream. He returned very shortly with a double armful of branches for supper. And while all this was going on, Rap was bringing Witch Grunth up to date on everything that had happened since she had made her brief appearance in the Rotunda. It was a real shock to realize six months had gone by since that fateful day the old imperor died. During those six months, the usurper had undoubtedly been consolidating his grip on the world. Time was slipping away.

Only once did Grunth comment. When Rap described the new protocol he hoped would bring peace to the world, she projected a fragrant image of an ill-kept barnyard. Somehow that did not seem like a very hopeful sign.

As soon as he had done, her son flashed some queries at her. To his astonishment, Rap now learned that the two of them had been corresponding mundanely, by messenger, ever since Thrugg reached the forest. He had never bothered to mention the fact, but many of the trolls he and Rap had met on their journey had then gone off to summon known sorcerers to this meeting, here at Shaggi's castle. Outside the Mosweeps no one would believe that trolls were capable of such organization, and the idea of them acting as messengers would be a joke, a contradiction in terms.

Grunth's scowl grew more hostile, and for a moment she sat in silence, giving away nothing.

"Well?" her son demanded. "Did they come?"

"Some," she admitted. She turned her gruesome glare on Rap. "You bring trouble! If that dwarf monster suspects what you do here, then he will enslave us all. No one can resist the power he wields."

"Will you do nothing? He will come for you anyway, when he gets around to it. He'll settle with Lith'rian first, I expect, then he'll come for you."

He thought he had scored a point; angry flames flickered again.

"How many sorcerers are there in the Mosweeps?" he demanded.

Thrugg was sitting with his knees up like a child, chewing a wad of leaves. *"Thousands!"*

"Silence!" His mother hurled a bed-size boulder at him in the ambience.

He deflected it easily, grinning a disgusting cud at her. *"How many, then?"*

"Fifty, maybe. No more."

Fifty sorcerers together would wield power to move mountains!

Grunth jumped on Rap's thought. *"So they would, faun, but how do you find them all? How do you bribe a troll, faun? And do you think all fifty together could hurt the Covin?"*

Worry it a little, maybe. And how did one bribe a troll? Apparently Thrugg had invited some of those sorcerers to come here for the meeting. Either they had declined, or the witch had sent them home again, or she was keeping them out of sight. Rap had always known that she might refuse to aid his quest, but he had never considered that she might seek to block it. She was vastly more powerful than he was, and so was her son. Although Thrugg seemed more inclined to support Rap at the moment, surely in a crunch he would side with his mother?

Perhaps Rap had endured this nightmare journey to no purpose—the thought was crippling.

"And how many in the Nogids, would you suppose?"

The witch's muzzle wrinkled in a sneer. "None."

Rap's heart sank even farther. He sat down again to give himself a moment to consider and took a swig of cold beer. "Zinixo got them already?"

She nodded contemptuously. "You thought you were so smart that no one else would think of that?"

The dwarf had once been warlock of the west. He would

have investigated the anthropophagi's islands very thoroughly in those days.

"When?" Rap demanded.

"About three months ago." There was a hesitancy there, though. It showed in the ambience, where lies were impossible and even evasion improbable.

"And he conscripted all the sorcerers?"

"Most." She would volunteer nothing.

Rap took another drink, feeling more despondent than ever. His quest was starting to seem utterly hopeless.

Thrugg gulped down his fodder and said aloud, "Come on, you mangy old hag! What're you hiding behind that new shielding?"

Her response was a blinding bolt of lightning that shattered rocks in front of his toes. The cave rocked with the blast, the three mundanes yelled out in terror—and Thrugg just sat and leered while gravel ricocheted off his hide. As the echoes died away and ears stopped ringing, a newcomer came strolling out of those sinister shadows at the back. Darad growled. Rap scrambled to his feet. He had never seen such an apparition before.

The man's skin was a dark molasses shade, but his face and chest and limbs were scrolled with bright white and blue and green tattoos. In size he would rank as taller than an average imp and skinnier, but it was only fat that was missing—the muscles were there and he moved with grace, even barefoot on rock. He wore an apron of white beads that jangled as he moved. He had a red flower in the bush of his hair and a bone through his nose, and when he flashed a smile at Grunth, he revealed very white teeth that had been filed to points.

"Begging your parson, your Omnivorous," the newcomer said apologetically, "I feel it is time for me to include on your deliverations." He turned his chilling smile on Rap and advanced with both hands out and the white beads of his garment clattering. They were human finger bones.

He was a sight to curdle the blood, and yet an enormously exciting one. He was a sorcerer, and probably a strong one. He was also an anthropophagus. Rap knew almost nothing of such people, and had never heard of them leaving their native

Nogids, because any other race would kill them on sight. Was this some of Grunth's doing? Or a Zinixo trick? He bore no loyalty spell that Rap could detect; could even the powers of the Covin achieve that?

"Your repudiation has proceeded you, your Majesty King Rap. I am horrid to make your acquaintance."

"I am likewise honored," Rap said warily, submitting to an embrace. He thought of a stormy night many years ago, and a terrified sailor boy running along a beach with several hundred cannibals in close pursuit. None had come this close, fortunately. Those gruesome teeth were smiling much too close as the man continued his speech.

"My full name you would find quite unrenounceable, but you may abominate it to Tok." The dark eyes shone with amusement over the ends of the bone. It was probably a clavicle. "My title is Tik, convoying a heretical right to certain delicacies when my village feasts. My friends call me Tik Tok."

"And you call me Rap. I visited your native lands once, Tik Tok, but only briefly."

"Ah!" The anthropophagus sighed. "It was a shame you could not stay for dinner."

"The invitation was extended, but I felt I had to rush off."

Sharpened teeth showed again. "But your green friend remained behind? That was at Fort Emshandar. I was there, as a child. My first feast! But I should like to hear the perpendiculars from you some time."

"You mean that was how the goblin escaped? You let him go?"

"Of course. My grandfather and some others defected his destiny. Even we do not argue with the Gods, Majesty Rap!"

"You speak impish very well."

Mischief gleamed in the shiny black eyes. "I picked it up as a youngster, in the kitchens." Tik Tok swung around in a clink of bones to face the trolls. "And I am delighted to meet Sorcerer Thrugg, the great libertine. Your brother has been telling me how you emasculated so many slaves!"

Thrugg did not rise. "Looks as if I have some more to free," he said, still grinning like a hungry grizzly.

A line of trolls came lumbering out of that shadowed corner—male and female, ranging in age from a couple of youths up to white-haired oldsters. Big as it was, the chamber began to seem crowded. There was not enough level floor for them all, and some climbed up the slopes and peered down like living gargoyles from shadowed ledges. Darad was backing to the door, looking worried by such impossible odds. Shaggi wore a shamed expression at this treatment of guests.

Three of the newcomers barely showed at all in the ambience and thus were probably not full sorcerers. The other eight were. Every one of the eleven wore a sheen of ensorcelment. Grunth's occult image seemed to swell and solidify, and her glower had become even more threatening. These were her votaries. No question who ruled here.

Rap cursed himself for a reckless fool. He had blithely let himself be trapped in a shielded building at the mercy of a deposed witch. What sort of woman lurked within that hideous bulk? She was very old. She had been overthrown after ruling a quarter of the world for twenty years, falling back from absolute power to heaving rocks around in a jungle. Had she managed to convince herself that she was enjoying an honorable retirement, or did she see it as humiliating exile? Either way, she would not want him intruding and reopening the wound. And why the gown? All the other trolls were nude. It showed she was not the innocent savage she must have been in her youth. She must know from her years in Hub how trolls were regarded by the rest of the world—and she could read his thoughts much better than he could read hers.

"Will you go now, faun?" she barked. "Or must I use force?"

Again the ambience gave her away, and Rap felt a surge of hope. She was not quite as implacable as she was trying to convey. Moreover, the limber anthropophagus at his side seemed completely unworried. He was studying the trolls, wriggling his nose thoughtfully to make the bone in it wiggle up and down.

"What do you think of the odds, Tik Tok?" Rap asked cautiously.

"Mouth watering!"

If one's taste ran to such beef, there was certainly a year's supply in view.

"The lady can overpower us," Rap said, fishing for information.

"But it would be unwise under the circumcisions."

"What circum . . . To what do you refer, exactly?"

Tik Tok smiled his nightmare smile. "When the Covin invaded my homeland, I was not the only one to allude capture. Several of us made our escapade in a large canoe and came in search of her Omniscience. My companions are not far off, and are aware of my thereabouts."

"And how many companions do you have?"

"Nineteen sorcerers and five mages."

God of Battle! Rap felt a rush of relief and excitement. The witch was outnumbered! . . . but was she any worse than a cannibal chief would be?

Only Thrugg was still sitting, munching noisily on the stub end of a branch. *"You will have to repeat your proposal, faun. They were behind the shielding."*

Rap glanced at Grunth but she made no move to stop him. Quickly, in case she changed her mind, he repeated the story he had related earlier, outlining the new protocol. The trolls listened with stolid faces, unmoved.

But Tik Tok beamed and slapped him powerfully on the shoulder. "This is a preposition of hysterical significance, your Majesty! I should like to hear our meaty friends' reactants."

"Well, Mother?" Thrugg asked, picking splinters out of his teeth with a claw.

"They don't approve!" she snapped. "Trolls do not make war."

Rumbles of agreement echoed through the great chamber, momentarily drowning out the rush of the waterfall.

"But their views cannot differ from yours," her son said. He rose to his feet, moving lightly despite his enormous bulk. Then he could look down on her. "Why is what you have done to them better than what the imps do to us?"

Amen! Mother and son bared teeth at each other as if this was a long-standing dispute between them.

"Both would appear to be invaluable solitude," Tik Tok murmured.

Failing to move Thrugg, the old woman turned her anger on Rap. "I repeat that war is not our way. And suppose I did agree? I could loan them to you, to aid your cause. If I free them, they will just vanish into the jungles."

"No!" Rap said. "They join of their own free will, or not, as they please. They will not need to use violence. If they wish to limit their help to defense, I will still welcome them. We do not seek to destroy the usurper's agents, but to liberate them."

"There is much to be said for violets," Tik Tok muttered.

"Mother?" Thrugg demanded. He towered in the mundane chamber as a column of muscle, and in the ambience he was still the most solid of them all.

Grunth sighed and waved a great paw. "Do it then."

The ambience blazed as the young sorcerer stripped away the loyalty spells. For a moment the released votaries just stood and stared, mumbling with surprise as they adjusted to their new thinking. Then, with deafening roars, they converged on their liberator, men and women both, some even leaping down bodily on him from their higher perches. Thrugg disappeared below a bellowing, squirming riot of monsters. Dust rose in clouds.

Tik Tok sighed and licked his lips.

Speech was impossible in that din. *"Well, your Omnipotence?"* Rap sent. *"You seem to be mistaken so far. Will you also join our cause?"*

The witch nodded sourly. *"I suppose someone must keep you from blundering into disaster."*

Incredible! Rap yelled in glee and, when he could not hear that himself, flashed a blaze of rose-pink joy in the ambience. He had founded an army—a small army, but a start on something greater. His sufferings had not been wasted after all. *"Thirteen trolls and twenty-five anthropophagi?"*

"And a faun for dessert." The bone in Tik Tok's nose wiggled. *That makes thirty-nine of us, if my calcifications are correct. An impassive display of millinery power!"*

3

THE HORDE HAD ENJOYED AN UNUSUALLY GOOD DAY. AS
was his custom, Death Bird had deployed his men in two columns. When they converged at sunset, they entrapped a large
band of refugees. Camp was pitched earlier than usual to enjoy
the spoils: women for rape, horses for food, men for sport—
everything a goblin's heart could desire.

For Kadie it had been an exceedingly bad day. The weather
was unbearably hot now, bringing dust and insects, but in the
last few weeks she had learned to endure those. Her cramps
and nausea did not come from weather alone. Even goblins
came down with fever, and why should she expect to be
tougher than them? Trouble was, sickness was weakness in this
army. The ones who couldn't keep up were killed by their
friends. Sympathy was about as common hereabouts as killer
whales. By afternoon, she was barely managing to stay on Allena's back. Running alongside as always, Blood Beak naturally noticed her distress, but he jeered much less than she
expected. Indeed, he seemed almost concerned.

The goblin army camped by totems. The prince himself was
a Raven, but his bodyguards came from a wide variety of tribes.
The little band would attach itself to a different group each
night. Blood Beak was gaining authority. The men had begun
to regard him more as their leader than their ward, and would
generally do what he said, as long as he did not try to overrule
their standing orders. This night he insisted on joining the
Beavers, who were setting up alongside an unburned barn. He
got his way, probably because it was a good campsite, near a
well.

With the magnanimous air of an imperor bestowing a duke-
dom, he told Kadie she could have the barn. Shelter and privacy were rare treats, and she was grateful. Then he ordered
one of the guards to unsaddle the mare for her, and again was
obeyed, although not very willingly. Blood Beak could be quite
pleasant at times, for a goblin.

Ignoring her own light-headedness and aches, Kadie first
established Allena in a corner by the door with hay and water,

and only then made a nook for herself at the far end, behind some bales of straw. She had no desire to eat, but she felt even more sticky and filthy than usual. She must wash before sleeping, she decided.

That was when she discovered what the trouble was. Her mother had warned her, of course, that such things would happen. Most of her friends had started long ago, and back in Krasnegar she had been quite worried that she was taking so long. Lately she hadn't thought about it. Well, now it had started. It should be an exciting milestone in her life, the start of womanhood. Thousands of leagues from home in the middle of a barbarian host, it was a very unwelcome development indeed. Fortunately she had some spare garments to use as rags—there was no shortage of such plunder and it wasn't really stealing because anything she did not rescue would just be burned by the goblins.

As the sky grew dark, she settled down to try to sleep, sore and unhappy. She laid her magic rapier within reach as she always did and pulled a tattered old cloak over herself for warmth. More than anything, she thought she would like a hot brick wrapped in a blanket, just to cuddle. She had barely closed her eyes before a nerve-curdling shriek rang out close by. It was followed at once by another, even louder. The goblins had begun the evening's entertainment, and the Beavers' fire was right outside her barn. She was used to it by now, of course. Even Allena hardly flicked her ears any more at the sounds or smells of torture, but it was rarely so close. There was rarely so much of it.

Every time Kadie began to settle, another scream would jar her awake. The night outside was bright with moonlight and campfires, and loud with torment, far and near—agony and raucous merriment in Evil-spawned choruses.

Tonight of all nights she needed to sleep. She needed her mother, whom she had not seen in over two months. In fact, she had not spoken with any woman in that time. She spoke to hardly anyone except Blood Beak.

Blood Beak, her future husband, the goblin prince. By his standards, she supposed, she would now class as nubile. The wedding could come any time now. She wished she had a breviary, to know the right prayers to say and the right Gods to invoke. But she would not be able to read it in the dark, and probably there was no proper prayer for this situation. Mom had told her that exact words didn't really matter. She hoped they didn't, because she'd done a lot of very unorthodox praying lately. She'd even prayed to the God of Rescues, and she wasn't at all sure that there was a God of Rescues. Perhaps she had prayed wrongly—to the God of Battles to send the legions and kill all the goblins, for example. The God of Battles had not heeded her appeal. And the God of Rescues, if there was one, was not rescuing those poor men and women outside. At least nothing that bad had happened to her, at least not yet.

If only they would be quiet outside there and let her sleep! There were so many victims tonight that the torments might go on till dawn.

"Kadie?"

Perhaps she had floated off into a half sleep. It was not a scream that wakened her, it was a whisper. She sat up with a stifled cry that was half a groan. Her hand fumbled for her sword. "Who's there?"

"It's me."

"Go away!" And yet she was relieved that it was Blood Beak. She could see him now. The barn was not completely dark.

"I need to talk with you."

"We talked all day. You can talk all tomorrow. Go away. I'm sleeping."

"You were weeping. I heard you." He came closer. "Why were you weeping?" He spoke impish very well now, when no one else was listening.

"I wasn't. Why shouldn't I weep? What does it matter to you? Go away!"

She had her sword ready, although her palm was so slippery wet and shaking that she doubted she could use it. Her heart was pounding madly. She had driven Quiet Stalker to his death and she would kill Blood Beak if he tried to touch her. Yes, she would! He did not come close enough. He knelt down by her wall of straw, just out of reach.

"Don't want you to weep."

She couldn't think of an answer. The more she thought about it, the more that remark seemed totally wrong.

"Kadie, I'm worried."

And that one, too. "What's the matter?" She saw a gleam of firelight on his face and chest, and dark stains. "You're hurt!"

"No."

"That's blood!"

"Yes. I cut an artery by mistake."

Her insides lurched. She never let him talk about what he did in the evenings. She tried to pretend to herself that he didn't join in, but she knew he did.

"You killed him?"

He made a noise that sounded perilously like a sniff. "I made a fool of myself, Kadie! They give me first scream, and I was so excited my hand slipped . . ." He banged his fist on the ground. "What an idiot trick! He was the best we had, too! Would have lasted for . . . you really want to hear?"

"No." She could sense his hurt and pain, though. The other goblins would have jeered at him. He must feel like a failure, like Brak must have felt at losing a fight to skinny Gath, or an imp getting cheated. Probably the guards would be a lot less inclined to do what he said now.

"I'm glad the man died easily," she said. "I'm sorry you're upset. Now please go away."

He didn't answer, just wiped moodily at the drying blood that had sprayed all over him.

"What's wrong?" she whispered.

"Father's gone mad." He spoke so softly she barely heard.

Death Bird had always been mad, but she mustn't say that. "Why? What's he doing?"

"Nothing. That's the trouble. It's not just me! Other men are saying it, too. He won't turn back. We keep going south. You know those mountains we saw?"

"They were clouds."

"The sort of clouds you get above mountains. They're the mountains on the other side of the Impire! The Mosweeps, they're called. He's brought us all the way across the Impire!"

"I know. You knew. We talked about it."

"But . . . But the legions are behind us! We should be going back, and he won't."

"He'll have to when he gets to the sea." She wished she'd paid more attention to geography lessons.

"I suppose. Then we'll have legions on one side and the sea on the other."

She had never heard a hint of this from Blood Beak before.

"You think I can change his mind?" she said disbelievingly.

"You? Gods, no! I think he's forgotten all about you. He hardly even sends for me anymore." Blood Beak's voice trailed off uncertainly.

A sudden powerful shriek outside told her that the goblins had started on a fresh victim. She ignored it, waiting.

"Kadie . . . No one's come to rescue you yet."

"They will!" She wished she still believed that.

"Kadie . . . If I could help you escape . . . Would you like that, Kadie?"

She began to shake all over. "How?"

"I don't know!" he said miserably. "I don't think I can. But I would if I could! If I see a chance . . ."

She couldn't think of any way he could help her escape, either, but her heart seemed to explode with excitement. She thought of herself marching up to one of those great houses she had seen, a mansion like Kinvale, except it wouldn't be burning and there would still be people living in it, rich people, imps. They would be clean and well dressed. *I am so sorry to drop in unexpectedly like this, but I am Princess Kadolan of Krasnegar, and I have just escaped from the goblins . . .*

"But why?"

He was quiet so long that she thought he was not going to answer at all. Then he said, "Because we're all going to die!"

"You've beaten the legions before."

"Only two at a time." His voice went shrill. "They *must* be after us by now! We've outrun them, that's all. But when we turn back, we'll bang into dozens of legions. Hundreds of legions!"

It must be true, of course. And not a goblin would be allowed to escape. Not one would straggle back to Pondague across the whole width of the Impire. Especially not the king's son.

"I expect your father's thought of this, you know. He must have some sort of plan that he hasn't told anyone."

"I hope so! That's what everyone's hoping."

"But—If I could escape, yes, I'd like that very much, Blood Beak. I'd be very grateful. I'd tell everyone how you helped me, and ask for you to be pardoned."

"I don't want that!" he said angrily. "You think I'm a coward?" His voice rose in outrage. *"You think I'm trying to save myself!"*

"No, of course not! I know you're brave. I think it's wonderful and romantic that you're offering to help me." But she had upset him, had said the wrong thing.

"Just like one of your stories!" His voice wavered. "Trying to make me into an impish prince, aren't you? Well, I'm not an impish prince. Maybe I'm clumsy with a knife, but I'm going off to the women now, and I take a lot of satisfying! No one laughs at me there! So just don't you forget who I am!" He jumped up.

"Blood Beak!"

"What?"

"I'm sorry. I didn't want to upset you. You had bad luck tonight, but I'm sure you can make up for it with the women. I'll let you tell me all about it tomorrow if you want. And I would be very, very grateful if you could help me escape."

He grunted. "If you see a way, then let me know and I'll think about it."

He stalked out.

Kadie lay down again and stared wide-eyed at the dark. Did he mean it? Could he help her? Now she had a whole new terror to deal with. Despair was much easier to bear than hope.

4

RAIN WAS FALLING IN THE MOSWEEPS, OF COURSE, BUT IT was a warm, soothing rain, and the night was pleasant in spite of it. Rap sat by himself on a rock at the front door of Shaggi's castle, alongside the waterfall. He was brooding about his family and worrying about the future. His grand design was starting to fall apart already.

Today had been a holiday. For the first time in half a year, he had sat around and relaxed and not gone anywhere. One of the youthful trolls had been sent off downstream to fetch Tik Tok's anthropophagous band; two more troll sorcerers had wandered in and been released from their servitude. A wild party had hatched and was rapidly growing to a full-fledged riot. The noise inside the castle was incredible.

Nevertheless, there was a war on, and riotous parties were vulnerable to surprise attacks. Rap himself had insisted on posting guards, taking one of the first watches himself. All he need do was keep a vigilant eye on the ambience, and it was remaining silent. Growling and crunching noises in some bushes at the far side of the pool told him where the two mundanes, Urg and Shaggi, were consoling each other in traditional fashion. Thrugg would not mind, so Rap should not; although he was reminded that he had enjoyed no time alone with Inos since the great storm washed out the causeway.

He recalled himself to duty, taking a glance at the ambience. He detected nothing within a hundred leagues. He went back to meditating on what happened next.

Obviously there was little point now in visiting the Nogid Archipelago, for Zinixo and Tik Tok between them had emptied the closet. The Covin was thought to have captured forty or so recruits, which meant that the bad guys' power was still growing faster than the good guys'.

So what next? Rap had gone fishing for an ally and landed an army, and he had no idea what to do with it. Probably nothing. Zinixo had nurtured his Covin in secret until he was ready to strike, and Rap had told Shandie that they would do much the same. No rendezvous, he had said, no preordained day of uprising. To set a time or place would be to invite discovery. Sneak attacks might betray the entire movement. Bizarre as it seemed in mundane terms, that strategy had been accepted by both imperor and warlock.

The troll sorcerers would fit in well with it. They would very happily vanish off back to their castles and wait until trumpets of the Last Battle rang in the ambience. Whether they would then respond, of course, was a problem for the future.

But the anthropophagi must find some safer refuge. They were already homeless refugees and would enjoy life in the Mosweeps no more than a faun did. Inevitably they would start preying on the imps, if not for meat then just for sport. As soon as their presence became known the army would start hunting them, and the Covin would come to assist.

Had any would-be leader ever commanded a force so grotesque: trolls and anthropophagi? Rap was yoking the ox with the tiger. His own occult powers were trivial, good for little more than fairground juggling, and yet as the only outsider in the group he must somehow keep the peace between the two sides. It would be a marriage of fire and water, but if he let his army sit still and do nothing, it would rot. So follow me! Where to?

Faerie? Dragon Reach?

Always he came back to that nagging feeling that he had forgotten something.

Then he had company . . .

A slender woman stood in the doorway, silhouetted against the light of the bonfires within. She stepped closer with a familiar jingling sound, and he found himself looking at a skirt of white bones, human ribs. He stood up quickly.

She was young. Mostly she wore tattoos of red and blue, but take those away and she would be very pretty. She had flowers tucked in her air, and bones through her nose and earlobes, but take those away . . .

She was very close. "I am Sin Sin," she said huskily.

Rap gulped, sweating in the damp night. *Inos, come here, I need you!* "I'm, er, I'm Rap."

"I know," she breathed.

Her bra seemed to be fashioned out of two juvenile skulls, one slightly larger than the other. He realized that he had been staring at it rather too long.

"Isn't that very uncomfortable?" he asked.

"Yes. Do please take it off."

"Er, no. I'd rather not."

"As you wish." She sighed and tried to embrace him.

He backed away, almost falling into the pool below. "Sin Sin, I'm on guard." A long time since Inos . . . too long with only trolls . . .

"I came to relieve you. But you needn't go."

"I wouldn't want to distract you while you keep watch."

"You won't."

"Yes, I will. I mean, I might."

"Fauns are so-o-o handsome!"

"No, they're not. Please, Sin Sin!"

"Yes, yes!"

"I'm married."

"So? You still look good enough to eat." She smiled seductively, but the effect was spoiled by her sharpened teeth. Rap's self-control came back with a rush.

"That's what I'm afraid of!" he said firmly, and slipped by her. He splashed through the stream into the castle.

The largest bonfire was the size of a small cottage, and its glare blinded him. The noise of drums and singing was mind-crippling, and the tumult in the ambience even worse. Forty or so sorcerers and mages were making merry, and that must be a rare event in the history of the world. Until now, power had always brought danger, and the sorcerous had been reclusive people. This infant brotherhood he had created was changing the rules already.

He must not claim all the credit—Thrugg had not enslaved him, despite his greater power, and Tik Tok's band had kept their individual freedom—but it was Rap's vision of a society of free sorcerers that had inspired this party.

What a party! Had Pandemia ever seen its like? Incandescent dragons circled near the roof. Naked troll maidens were dancing erotically—and it took him a moment to realize that they were illusory, as was the band of anthropophagous muscle men parodying them on the other side. A fountain of wine was spouting into the stream. The air was filled with smoke and colored balls and half a dozen albatrosses and giant bats, apparently playing some sort of team game. A bewildered camel brayed in terror on a high ledge. The great chamber was a madhouse of mirth and foolery.

Trolls and anthropophagi? Probably there had never been

such a meeting before. Were they mundanes, half the gathering would be cooking the other half, but these were sorcerers, united in a common cause. So far. They were all drunk on magic. Was he just being a nervous maiden aunt, or could he already detect dangerous undertones in the horseplay? If it went too far, there were no limits on what might happen. And even if it didn't, there would be the emotional hangover when it ended and reality returned.

Poor old worrywart Aunt Rap!

He checked the upstream rooms and discovered several strange orgies in progress, some of the participants real and some occult. In an obscure chamber he located the people he wanted. Of course there was no such thing as privacy around sorcerers, but the little room was secluded—off the main stream, watered only by seepage. He transported himself there, into calm and sanity. Or maybe not.

Grunth was reclining in an elaborate chair large enough to be called a throne, decked out like an impress in jewels and scarlet satin. Her tiara flashed with a fortune in rubies and sapphires; her great clawed feet were encased in golden sandals. She beamed a toothy baboon snarl at him and he saw that she was drunk.

Tik Tok sprawled in a wicker chair, wearing a blissful idiot look of extreme intoxication. He had rearranged his tattoos in yellow and magenta, and festooned his hair with pink rose-buds. He was gnawing on a juicy bone that Rap carefully did not inspect carefully.

Thrugg had chosen to squat on the floor as usual, nude as usual, munching noisily on nuts and roots. He looked up with a sour glance that was very unusual—for him—and must mean trouble.

The fourth member of the party was Doctor Sagorn. Darad had needed little persuading to make him depart from such alarming company, and he had summoned the old jotunn in his place. The scholar sat erect on a high-backed chair. He wore a thin gown of pale-blue cotton. It was sweat-stained and rumpled, but his customary arrogant disdain for once seemed to be hiding an agreeable mood. His pale-blue eyes gleamed when he saw Rap, and the withered lips trembled on the verge of a smile.

The stuffed penguin in the doorway defied explanation.

Rap materialized a seat for himself and a mug of Krasnegarian beer. He sat back and, after a moment's reflection, added a local cool breeze. The mundane environment was satisfactory, then. The ambience continued to rock, flash, riot, boom, stink, and swim as the party continued, downstream in the sprawling castle. He tried to ignore it. When nobody said anything, he began with Thrugg.

"What's wrong?"

The troll's mouth was too full for speech. *"Wurnk and Vog."*

Sagorn spasmed with surprise, so he must have been included in the sending.

"The old fellows?" Rap asked.

"Yes. They don't like crowds. Wanna go."

"Not surprising! I expect the rest will follow them in a day or two."

Abandoning words, Thrugg flashed an excruciating image of a slave being beaten by a gang of imps. Everyone winced, and yelped. The implication was one of strong disapproval, which seemed out of character for the unwarlike troll. Why should he want to keep the army together?

"Isn't that the plan?" Sagorn muttered. "To hide out individually until battle is joined?"

Again Thrugg replied without words, and this time the image was a relative measure of the strength of forty sorcerers and a couple of dozen lesser magic-users. Not only was a larger group inherently more powerful, it was also much less detectable. Sagorn's mouth fell open.

"Good point," Rap admitted. "If we must have an army, then the larger the better." Sorcery would become possible again, if it was used with caution.

Thrugg nodded more cheerfully, pulping timber in his monstrous jaws.

Rap readjusted his thinking yet again. "So we keep the trolls enlisted. We need to hunt down the rest of the fifty you mentioned, though. That means organizing messengers. It means setting up a central headquarters. Two might be better. Would Vog and Wurnk do that much?"

Thrugg shrugged, but even before the gesture was complete, he had located the two old trolls, explained, persuaded, and won agreement. It was all over in a blink, and he nodded.

Grunth belched and said, "They'd better!" in an ominous voice. The witch had not yet adjusted to the idea of voluntary servitude.

"And what do the rest of us do?" Rap asked. "If we stay here, we'll achieve nothing. Where do we go, and how?" He thought of the vast expanse of rain forest surrounding him and mentally shuddered.

Tik Tok paused in his gnawing. "Downstream. Watercourses felicitate travel in jungles."

"Good point. But that takes us to the coast, and there will be imps at the coast."

"Mm!" The anthropophagus nodded and licked his lips. Then he flashed pictures of forty or so sorcerers standing on the shore, calling in a ship, compelling the crew to row to shore in their longboat, marooning the sailors, and rowing back out in their boat. The imagery was not as vivid as Thrugg's, and rather spoiled by an alcoholic unsteadiness, but it obviously represented a feasible plan when there was so much power available. The final scene showed the ship sailing away with its rigging full of sorcerers, all lustily singing sea chanteys. A large, unidentified carcass was being roasted over an improbable bonfire on the deck.

"I fail to see how carnal self-indulgence will promote the cause," Sagorn remarked dryly.

Tik Tok turned to stare at him thoughtfully. "Where I come from, jotnar are regarded as speciously tasty morals."

"I am sure my old meat would be unpleasantly stringy." The haggard old face had turned a little paler, though. Rap repressed a grin. It took a lot to discomfit the sage.

"We steal a ship of course," Grunth said sleepily. "Easy."

"And go where?" That was the ultimate question.

After a moment's silence, Tik Tok said, "Did you and your fellow compositors not set up a revenue?"

"No," Rap said. "It seemed too dangerous."

"Not much help!" Sagorn snapped, resuming his disdainful pout. "With so much power available, why not just go on the attack? If you can create a diversion, the Covin will send a party of sorcerers to investigate. You overpower them, break their loyalty spells, and win them to your cause; then skedaddle and pull the same trick somewhere else."

Groaning like a constipated bull, Grunth subsided into the depths of her throne and closed her eyes. Sagorn's pale cheeks flushed pink.

"It won't work, Doctor," Rap said gently. "Sorcerous armies move instantaneously. You can't run away from them. Remember the trouble Raspnex went to when he rescued us in Hub? It was a miracle, what he achieved that night. It had taken weeks to prepare, probably, and it cost him half a dozen votaries. Guerilla warfare won't work in the ambience. As soon as we show our hand, Zinixo will cut it off."

The old man scowled. He was out of his depth with sorcery, and that discovery would be unwelcome.

Downstream, the party was waxing even wilder. Half the dancers were airborne, and so were some of the lovers. The games were developing into occult tests of strength. A bear was wrestling a giant squid near a tug of war between a team of trolls and six white stallions—

"Go and drop in on Lith'rian," Grunth muttered without opening her eyes.

"I am inclined to agree with that, I think." Rap sighed and quaffed some beer; the flavor made him homesick. If there was organized resistance anywhere, it would be among the elves, in Ilrane. He realized he was hungry, and began to contemplate the prospects of a plate of chicken dumplings.

"Sysanasso?" Tik Tok mumbled, his mouth full of meat.

"Another good idea. There's a nasty rumor about fauns being stubborn, though. I don't know where to start there, or how we can persuade them even to spread the news."

Rap knew who was the logical agent to assign to Sysanasso, and he didn't want the job. He had never thought of himself as indispensable before, but he suspected he was the only glue that might hold this improbable legion together.

He heard a strange noise he could not recall ever hearing before. Doctor Sagorn was laughing.

"Doctor?"

"I was just imagining the elvish customs officials at Vislawn or Mistrin when you dock and they meet your crew."

"I am not familial with elves," Tik Tok remarked. "Singers, not fighters?"

"Elves are people of exquisite taste!" Sagorn said primly.

Rap expected Tik Tok to say he was ogrely looking forward to meating them, but he didn't. Perhaps mere puns were beneath his dignity. He just licked his lips again.

"Zark has sorcerers," Grunth said, and yawned like a hungry crocodile.

"I'm sure it does," Rap agreed. "It also has a central authority, the caliph. We wrote to him and hopefully he will spread the word. Dragon Reach might make a very good refuge, if we take no metal and use no sorcery. Or the Keriths— sorcerers should be able to resist the merfolk, shouldn't they?"

Thrugg leered. "Resist the men."

Sagorn snorted. "Your Majesty, I am inclined to think you initiated this counterrevolution without adequate preparation."

"I'm certain of it. We had very little choice at the time."

Silence fell in the rocky chamber, broken only by the quiet trickling of water down one slimy green wall. The ambience, on the other hand, was approaching the boil. A couple of the older anthropophagi were trying to calm things down, with little success. Perhaps the shielding would fail, and the whole castle just explode.

Rap clawed his hair, making a mental note to shorten it in the morning. "Listen, Doctor. Maybe you can help me. Ever since we began this adventure, I've had a nagging hunch that I've forgotten something, that I'm overlooking something."

"I understood that sorcerers had perfect memories."

"I'm not much of a sorcerer. But that's a good point. If I have forgotten something, maybe I've been made to forget it!" He glanced around and saw that the others were listening. He hoped he was not about to make too much of a fool of himself. "You're not a sorcerer. Can you think of anything we saw, or anything that came up in conversation . . . any plan we discussed and then set aside, perhaps?"

"A forgetfulness spell specifically directed at the sorcerous?" the old man muttered. "Is that possible?"

"Probably. Almost anything is possible if there is enough power available. Could Zinixo have blanked my mind?" He felt he was really conjuring bubbles now, but having gone so far he might as well wade in until he sank.

"If he had managed that much," Thrugg growled, "then he would have been able to call you to him."

"I suppose so."

"What sort of something?" Sagorn said thoughtfully. "What would be useful? A strategy? A place of refuge? A weapon? A possible ally?" His eyes glinted coldly, like sunlight on a northern sea. "What about that preflecting pool the imperor saw? Nobody ever quite explained that episode!"

"A pixie!" Rap yelled. "That's it! You've got it! Shandie met a pixie near Hub!"

Grunth yawned again. "If you're starting in on bedtime stories, then I think I'll organize a bale of hay and catch up on my beauty sleep."

"Unfortunately pixies are instinct," Tik Tok said sadly, and yawned, also. "Would have been nice to invite someone diffident for dinner."

"Pixies still exist," Rap said firmly. "My wife met some, many years ago. *The imperor met a pixie!*"

Three sorcerers stared at him as if he had taken leave of his senses.

He was so excited now he could hardly sit still. "Don't you see? The War of the Five Warlocks? What happened at the end of it? Who won? Grunth?"

"Don't recall," she said uneasily.

"No one does!" Sagorn was beaming.

"It was the second millennium!" Rap shouted. "There was more sorcery around then than there ever has been since—until now, the third millennium. Anything would have been possible with that kind of power loose! Now do you understand? There is an aversion spell on Thume! An inattention spell, and it's directed more at sorcerers than at mundanes, although it obviously affects them, too. Shielding blunts it, because the last time I thought of this I was in a shielded house, like this one. When I went outside I forgot again."

"You were otherwise engaged," Sagorn murmured, but he was obviously relishing the mad suggestion and the audience's reluctance to accept it.

"I want you to stay close to me in future," Rap said, "and whisper 'Thume' in my ear every half hour."

All three sorcerers were cold sober now.

"That kind of spell wouldn't last that long," Thrugg protested, glaring at Rap like a hungry grizzly taking aim.

"No, it wouldn't. Of course it wouldn't! So who is maintaining it?"

No one answered. What sort of power could maintain a spell over an entire country, let alone establish it there in the first place?

"Whole armies can vanish in Thume," Sagorn said gleefully. "Or not, as the case may be. Travelers disappear or return with tales of an empty, deserted land, yet not even the Impire has been able to commandeer that emptiness! *And no one wonders why?* Ma'am, gentlemen . . . This does not make sense! Why has it never worried you before?"

Rap glanced around the group and saw the dawning of belief, the dawning of excitement, even. Could the War of the Five Warlocks have left some secret behind in Thume, a secret still active after a thousand years?

"I wonder if we could even approach it?" He looked down at his bare arm and wrote *Thume* on it. No, that would not be enough. "Thrugg, you're strongest, I think. Fix this tattoo for me so I can't wipe it off in a fit of absentmindedness. Give it all you've got."

The result was an explosion in the ambience that almost stunned him. It rocked the castle. The wild melee downstream came to an instant halt, shocked into sobriety. All Rap actually felt, though, was a momentary tingling.

"Thank you!" he said weakly, still dazed.

"Couldn't do it harder or the shielding would have burst," Thrugg explained apologetically.

All the other sorcerers and mages in the castle were staring at their leaders in consternation, wondering what had provoked that immense outburst of power. For some reason most seemed to have picked out Rap as the culprit. They should be informed of the new theory, but whom would they believe? Well, there was one person there who would never refuse an audience.

"Tik Tok, why don't you explain?"

Tik Tok beamed his dagger teeth and sprang to his feet in a shower of rosebuds. *"Fiends and alloys!"* he proclaimed. *"I am pleased to denounce that we have made a significant breakdown in understudying!"* He paused and glanced at Rap. "Good start?"

"An inedible performance," Rap said dryly. "Carry on."

Westward look:
> And not by eastern windows only,
> When daylight comes, comes in the light,
> In front the sun climbs slow, how slowly,
> But westward, look, the land is bright.

CLOUGH, SAY NOT THE STRUGGLE NAUGHT AVAILETH

CHAPTER SEVEN

WE HAPPY FEW

1

"FOR THE HUNDREDTH TIME, NO! I WILL NOT MARRY YOUR daughter! Not tomorrow. Not next year. Never! Not ever! At no time between now and the end of the world!"

Sir Acopulo spun around in a swirl of black robe to slouch against the railing. His move was too violent—the railing creaked ominously and even the balcony itself seemed to sag, as if in sympathy. He backed hastily into the room, seeking safety. The water was a long way down, and none too clean. One of the harbor's responsibilities was to remove the village sewage, but the tide was in at the moment.

"But it is your duty to marry my daughter," Shiuy-Sh wailed.

He was scraggy little man, small even by Acopulo's standards. Years of seawater had shriveled his skin like old brown mud, and his scanty hair was turning silver to match the fish scales that embellished his arms to the elbow. His only garment was a twist of dirty cloth, although like all fauns he always seemed to be wearing furry black stockings. Now he stood in the middle of Acopulo's living room and wriggled his hairy toes in emotional agony, twisting and torturing the straw hat he held in his hands.

"It would be blasphemy for me to marry your daughter. Or your nephew. Or your grandmother!" Acopulo wanted to weep. He had been over this argument thousands and thousands of times, and he knew it was useless. He never got anywhere. Arguing with fauns was like trying to eat marble.

Raw.

"But my grandmother is already married," Shiuy-Sh said, seeming puzzled. With the widespread nose and large mouth of his race, he looked none too intelligent at the best of times.

"I wish she had never been born!" Acopulo wiped sweat from his brow. Ysnoss had a wonderful natural harbor, or so its inhabitants claimed. The price of that harbor was that the village nestled at the bottom of a gorge, a notch cut in high cliffs. Steep rocky walls beetled up on all sides, capturing the noon sun and deflecting the wind. Ysnoss was a gigantic oven. Perhaps "stew pot" was a better description, if one considered the foul steamy stench arising from the harbor itself.

There was no road out of Ysnoss. Most of the shanties were built on stilts, because the land was so steep. Acopulo had been given one of the finest houses in the whole village, two rooms directly over the water.

He had been there a month, and expected to remain there until he went utterly insane, in about another ten minutes . . .

"Tcch!" Shiuy-Sh exclaimed in annoyance. "Bad dog, Imp! This is the priest's house! Where is your shovel, Father?"

Imp was the size of a small pony, filled with the jubilation of youth and totally lacking in manners. Twice already he had stolen the gift of fresh bass Shiuy-Sh had brought, and he had eaten half of it before the faun rescued it the second time.

Wearily Acopulo pointed to the shingle he retained for such

needs. That was another curse of living with fauns—there was livestock everywhere: dogs, cats, pigs, chickens, parrots. No faun ever seemed to go anywhere with less than his own pack of hounds and a couple of tame macaws. Monkeys and geese were the worst pests. Fortunately there was not enough flat ground in Ysnoss to stand a cow or a horse on.

"My brother has promised a whole pig for the feast," Shiuy-Sh remarked cheerfully as he scraped the offensive mess through a gap in the floorboards. "And his wife is preparing wreaths of purple and white—"

"I don't care!" Acopulo screamed. "It is nothing to do with me!"

He stared miserably out over the water to where the sea shone in the gap between the cliffs. About five weeks ago the Ilranian authorities had finally given him permission to leave. He had taken the first available boat out of Vislawn—*Curly Nautilus*, a smelly little faun fishing dory blown off course and forced into port for repairs.

For a fee so reasonable that it should have made him suspicious right away, *Nautilus*'s crew had promised to deliver him to a port in Sysanasso. There he had expected to catch a more reasonable craft to carry him east to Qoble, or perhaps even all the way to Zark. He would have sailed in a basket to get away from those elves. Fauns, he had soon discovered, were much worse.

Ysnoss was a port, of course. He had not stipulated the port he was to be taken to—like most imps, he had no clear picture of Sysanassoan geography at all. The fact that nothing but the locals' own small craft ever stopped in at Ysnoss was not a violation of the contract. Nor had the negotiations considered the fact that Ysnoss had no priest and both its neighboring villages did, although that had turned out to be a very material detail.

Shiuy-Sh completed his small chore, tossed the shingle back out on the balcony, and wiped his hands on his furry thighs. "If you do not wish to come to my house, Father," he suggested with the air of a man making a significant compromise, "then my daughter and nephew will be most honored to be married here, in your residence. Unfortunately . . ."

"Unfortunately what?" Acopulo demanded, scowling at the little man's woebegone expression.

"Unfortunately, this house is one of the oldest in Ysnoss. Even my grandmother cannot recall who built it. The whole village will be coming to the wedding. Do you not feel we shall be tempting the Gods by filling this place with people? Your faith is very ennobling, Father, but you must forgive the rest of us our doubts."

"I forgive the rest of you nothing! I have told you a million times that I am not a priest!"

"But you dress like a priest!"

Acopulo put his face in his hands. He knew exactly what was coming if he persisted with the conversation: "But the elves said you were a priest." "But it is very impious to dress like a priest if you are not." "But if we believed that you had been guilty of such sacrilege we should have to hold a court . . ."

There was no way to argue with fauns. One might as well wrestle trolls, trust djinns, throw oneself on jotunn mercy, or beg charity from dwarves. A race that had gained a worldwide reputation for stubbornness was not going to start listening to reason now. There were dozens of small boats in Ysnoss. Acopulo had offered more gold than the entire population would see in centuries just for passage around the headland to Ushyoas, and not one owner was willing to take him. Ysnoss *needed* a priest. Other villages had priests.

"I will not marry your daughter! That is final."

"But that is most unkind of you, Father! Would you have her live in sin with my nephew? We have given you a fine residence and we bring you ample provision—"

"Report me to the authorities!" *Please!*

Shiuy-Sh sighed and shrugged his shoulders, causing fish scales to twinkle like sequins. "But," he said—most faun sentences began with that word—"but I have explained many times. Several princes claim to have authority here."

"Any of them will do!"

"But to favor one over another might cause trouble."

"Then choose the nearest!"

"But I don't know which is the nearest, Father. We pay no attention to any of them."

Acopulo uttered a heartfelt groan. The humiliation was unbearable. That he, a distinguished scholar, a widely traveled man of letters, a trusted confidant of the imperor, should prove incapable of delivering a letter! Almost six months had gone by since he left Hub on a simple journey to Zark, and yet in those months he had gone barely a third of the way and looked likely to die of old age before he went any farther.

He spun around to the skinny little fisherman and gripped him by the shoulders. They felt like iron. At close quarters his stink of fish made Acopulo's eyes water. Shiuy-Sh was a nasty little runt, yet when Acopulo tried to shake him, his skimpy form proved quite immovable.

"I am not a priest!" the scholar yelled in his face.

Shiuy-Sh blinked in astonishment, as if he had not been told that hundreds of times before. "But the elves said . . ."

2

THE FIRST THING GATH DID WHEN HE AWOKE MOST MORNings was to think over what was going to happen in the next few hours. Probably everybody did that, but in his case he *knew*. Sometimes he was reassured and just went back to sleep. Other days he came awake with a rush, foreseeing events that had sneaked up on him in the night.

This morning the first thing he thought about was a very smelly foot in his face. He rolled over, and there was another one on that side. Vork was up to his silly tricks again, obviously. Gath selected the best future, chose a toe at random, and bit it. It tasted really bad, but the yell was just as satisfying as he had seen it would be, and so were the thump and yelp as Vork jostled one of the sailors and provoked a jotunn reaction. He was going to have a thane-size bruise. Serve him right!

The crew slept in the hold, on top of the cargo. Vork could have had the floor in his father's cabin, and the imperor had offered Gath the spare bed in his, but bunking down with the sailors had a lot more appeal. There was something manly about it, even if a load of shovels and picks was not the most comfortable mattress in the world. The talk at night was manly stuff, too, all about sailoring, and being a raider, and women. Gath had learned a lot of new things and confirmed some things he had suspected but not been sure of. Very educational.

Then he saw what the morning had in store for him and woke up with a rush. *Holy Balance!* God of Madness! Wow!

For three weeks, *Gurx* had been riding the spring flood on the Dark River. She was a wallowy old tub. Most of the officers were dwarves, because that was the law in Dwanish, but Thumug the bosun was the real captain, and the hands were all jotnar. The ambassador regarded them with downright contempt, calling them discards and freshwater fish, and of course Vork did, too, although he was careful not to let the men hear him. The crew's ability or lack of it had mattered little on this trip. The current had carried her like a leaf in a gutter, whirling past the dirty, dismal Dwanishian towns. Today she arrived at Urgaxox. All sorts of things were going to happen at Urgaxox.

Gath emerged on deck and looked around, shivering. He dressed like a sailor now, in leather breeches and nothing else. He did sailor things when he was allowed to—pulled on ropes and scrubbed decks, and it was a lot of fun. He'd developed some good calluses and he thought he had a little more muscle in his arms, or at least his biceps felt harder. Of course it took rowing to make real sailors' arms, and *Gurx* was no longshsip. Unlike Vork, he wouldn't want it to be, but any ship was better than a dwarf wagon. A jotunn was a jotunn. Even half a jotunn.

There was frost on the deck. The sun was just over the horizon. The Zogon Mountains had disappeared two days ago, and now the Kalip Range was in sight to starboard. At Urgaxox the river turned east in its final rush to the sea, and this was the end of Dwanish. Urgaxox was a frontier post of the Impire and the start of Guwush, gnome country. It was where *Gurx* would unload her cargo, and her passengers.

Vork was forward, just tipping a bucket of water over himself. For a moment Gath stood and studied him, sizing him up in view of the very surprising things that were going to happen in the next couple of hours. After three months away from Krasnegar, Gath pined for some friends of his own age. A girl or two would be especially welcome because it was time he got some practice in talking with girls, but Vork could have been an acceptable fellow traveler. So far he had been anything but.

He was Ambassador Kragthong's son, the youngest of Jarga's six half brothers and the only one still living with his father. He was a year older than Gath, but not as tall. He still had his puppy fat and he still spoke soprano. He was one of those freakish jotnar with red hair and green eyes. His nose was well flattened already—and he seemed to think all these misfortunes were Gath's fault.

Vork had three aims in life and would talk of nothing else. On a scale of years, he planned to be a great raider like his unlamented cousin Kalkor. More immediately, he longed to go home to Nordland and especially to visit the great midsummer moot at Nintor. Gath could agree with him on that one, although he had some reservations about watching men chop each other to bits with axes. Once, maybe, just so he could say he'd seen a reckoning.

Vork's short-term ambition was to smash Gath to jelly. He missed no chance to pick a fight, and Gath's refusal to cooperate riled him frantic. Traditionally, fighting must be done ashore. *Gurx* had tied up only twice in the last three weeks, and both times Gath had stayed on board. Vork called him a coward and Gath didn't care—much. He knew he could beat Vork if he wanted to.

Clenching himself up to hide his shivering, he stalked over to Vork, then stepped back quickly as Vork tried to drop the bucket on his toes.

"Know what happens today?" Gath said, snatching the bucket.

Vork paid no attention, squeezing water out of his red hair.

"Clean your ears out, you've got fish in them."

"I don't talk to cowards."

"I'll tell you what happens today, then. We tie up at Ur-gaxox."

Vork swung around with a gleam in his blue-green eyes. "And?" The bruise on his cheek was a great pinky-yellow lump already.

"Time you came ashore with me," Gath said, blandly giving the sailors' challenge in shrill falsetto.

Vork flushed scarlet. "Time? . . . I've been trying to get you ashore for weeks, you jelly-boned half-breed!"

Gath smiled. "And the other thing that happens today is that I rub your face in the dirt." He put a foot on the line and tossed the bucket overboard.

It wasn't quite certain. He had a very faint foresight of Vork kneeling on his chest and pounding with both fists, but he wasn't going to mention that.

"You're a seer!" Vork said, suddenly wary.

"You don't have to come if you don't want to. I mean, if you're scared."

Vork was jotunn. That settled that.

There wasn't much time. Gath sluiced himself off sailor fashion and rushed down to the galley to grab some breakfast and turn from blue back to pink. Then he hurried up on deck again, still dripping, still gnawing on a hunk of gritty black bread.

Already *Gurx* was approaching the docks. Urgaxox was even larger than he'd expected, but the river was so high that much of it was hidden behind the shipping. He saw sunlight flashing off metal on the quays and guessed it came from legionaries's helmets. There would be gnomes, of course, and dwarves, and jotnar, because this was one of the greatest ports in the world. But he wasn't interested in the people at the moment. There were more ships in sight than he'd ever seen in his life—river craft like this one, and oceangoing galleys. They clustered along the piers like suckling piglets. Here and there he saw longships, low and sinister. Not *the* longship, though—not quite yet.

Ambassador Kragthong was leaning on the rail with the emperor at his starboard side, a bull and a pony. Gath hurried over. This was the bit he was looking forward to least of all, but it had to be done. He just managed to beat Jarga to her father's port side. He was taller than she was now, and he didn't think that had been the case three weeks ago. He hoped she wasn't reading minds this morning, but he knew she was not going to stop him.

"Anything happening?" the thane rumbled, speaking over Gath's head to his daughter.

"Much the same. Just have to be careful."

She meant the level of magic, of course. Ever since the warlock's appearance before the Directorate, a week ago, the sorcerers had been reporting Covin activity all over Dwanish. There was a hunt in progress.

The imperor had shaved off his beard in the night and looked surprisingly younger. "Smell that mud?" he said. "The river must be falling."

The thane grunted. "Place always stinks. It's the gnomes."

"It would probably be a lot worse without the gnomes."

The big man grunted. "Depends. Uh? . . ."

He had seen *the* longship. Then *Gurx* swept by the end of that pier and it was out of sight.

"Something wrong?" the imperor asked sharply.

"No. No, nothing." Kragthong shot a side glance at his daughter.

"Saw no details," she said softly. "I'd better not look now."

"No, for Gods' sake don't do anything to give us away."

They were alarmed, though.

"Do we have to find billets ashore?" the imperor inquired. "Or can you line up a ship right away?"

"You'd best all stay aboard," Kragthong said. "I've got men here I can talk with." He mostly meant he wanted to check on that longship, but the imperor probably didn't know that. Gath did.

The imperor thumped a fist on the rail. "I wish I knew what had happened to Rap! It's not like him not to report. If they got him, then Nintor's a deathtrap for us. On the other hand, if he's been turned, he would probably have tried to string us along. I'm very much afraid he . . ." He had just noticed Gath, concealed by the thane's great bulk.

"I would rather he had died than been enslaved, sir. He would, I'm sure."

"Perhaps," Shandie said icily. "He may just have been robbed and lost the scrolls, of course. I'm assuming that he's all right."

Gath ignored that obvious lie. Dad would never be so careless as to lose his magic scrolls. Would never *have been* so careless. Oh, Dad, Dad! "But even if Nintor is dangerous for us, sir, it's very important to get your message to all the thanes, isn't it, sir?"

"Yes!" The imperor's tone was even icier. "Have you seen your mother around?"

"I think she's having something to eat, sir."

"Thanks." The imperor walked away.

"Good idea, that," Jarga said, and followed him.

The ambassador remained, still frowning at the shipping. Odious Vork slid into the place his sister had left. He scowled hideously at Gath, obviously suspecting that he was up to no good.

Which Gath was, of course. "Er, Excellency?"

The big man did not look around. "Mm?"

"At the Nintor Moot, it's only thanes get challenged, isn't it?" Gath knew the answer perfectly well. Only thanes or thanes' sons could go to the moot. Only thanes could vote. Only thanes could be challenged to reckonings. He just wanted to be sure that Kragthong knew he knew.

"Right."

"Sir, would you please lend me some money?"

That got the ambassador's attention. He blinked down at Gath with wintery disapproval. "Money? You're not supposed to leave the ship. What d'you need money for?"

"Er, Vork and I were just going to go ashore for a few minutes to settle something. Winner buys the beer, sir."

The silvery beard quivered into a smile. Kragthong seemed to swell even larger, and he looked thoughtfully past Gath to his son. Then his approval faded. "Looks like you started on him already."

"No, sir. Not me. He slipped on the companionway."

"Did *not*!" Vork squeaked, although Gath could not imagine what explanation he would prefer to offer.

"I'd ask my mother, sir, but I don't think she would understand."

"Of course not." Kragthong chortled. "But I ought to give
the money to him, surely?"

"Certainly not!" Gath said, faking the anger that would be
expected. "He hasn't a hope. I know he's only a kid, but he
gives me no peace and I just can't take his crap any longer."

The thane beamed with pride. "Suppose I hand you both a
crown and the loser gives his back?"

"That's very generous of you, sir. I'll see he does."

"He talks big for a half-man!" Vork trilled. "He doesn't
know what real Nordlanders are made of."

"That's the spirit!" Kragthong said jovially, fishing in his
pouch. "Make a good match out of it, lads. Men shed blood
and women tears, remember. Wish I could come and watch,
but I've got some business to attend to."

Gurx was just tying up.

3
_____

"COME ON!" GATH SAID, AND RAN DOWN THE PLANK WITH
Vork at his heels. He almost fell on his nose, because the plank
was much steeper than he had expected. With the crest of the
spring flood in town, *Gurx* was riding high. The pier was almost awash. There was a longship tied up ahead, and a squad
of legionaries keeping watch on it. They paid no attention to
two barefoot jotunn youths running by.

Beyond the levee, the streets were knee deep in dirty water
and the stench would have stunned a troll. There were some
very unhappy dogs. There were dwarves, but Gath was sick
of dwarves. There were horses, some of them huge, bigger
than anything Krasnegar had ever seen, plodding along with
their great feet splashing and wakes behind their carts. Seeing
horses made him think of Dad.

There were jotnar galore, mostly dressed like him, just in
breeches. The sailors had big silvery mustaches. The ones with
beards as well were probably raiders when they were farther

from Imperial authority—to paint an orca on a sail was the work of a few minutes. Many of both types were so smothered in tattoos that they looked like the chintz chairs Mom had imported last summer. There were imps, both civilian and military. Urgaxox was unofficially a free port, the imperor said. It was so valuable to Dwanish and Nordland and the Impire— and to Guwush when Guwush wasn't part of the Impire—that whoever happened to be holding it never closed it. Even with a war on, dwarves were going about their business under the legionaries' noses. Under their armpits, too.

There were gnomes, and they were finding the water especially troublesome. It came up to their waists, and higher than that when a wagon went by. Gath had only ever met six gnomes in his life, the royal ratcatchers in Krasnegar: Pish, Tush, Heug, Phewf, and their two tiny babies, who could lie on his hands. He had never seen gnomes out in daylight. He had never seen them taking a bath, either, he thought with a chuckle. Then he noticed that they were eating things they picked out of the floating muck. He lost interest in gnomes.

"Where're we going?" Vork demanded at his back.

"T'find a dry place. I don't want to drown you."

"Drown me? I'm going to give you the thrashing of your life. I'm going to teach a mongrel to watch his tongue around his betters . . ." Vork had started talking himself up. Lots of jotnar had to do that. Some could flash into fighting madness right away, but most needed to work on it. Gath had to get Vork on his back while he could still listen to reason.

Then he saw the archway and turned into it.

Vork said, "Hey!" and came after.

The courtyard beyond was deserted, as Gath had known it would be. There was ample mud on the ground, juicy black mud, but not much free water.

He swung around. "This'll do, Carrots. Prepare to meet thy doom!" That faint image of Vork systematically reorganizing Gath's face was more solid than it had been earlier. The one with Gath on top was still stronger.

Vork was paler than usual, his green eyes wider. The odds were not on his side. His opponent was taller, and a seer. Such things wouldn't matter to him in a few minutes, but he wasn't quite there yet. He was insulting Mom now.

"Oh, shut up!" Gath said, and swung a feint. Yes, attack was the secret. He poked a few more, and Vork kept blocking and backing away, still gabbling nonsense.

Gath swung a slow right; Vork blocked; Gath caught his wrist and heaved, thrusting out a leg to tip him over. That was all it took. He threw himself on top, twisted Vork's arm up out of the way, and grabbed red hair with his other hand. Vork's nose was right on the mud and Gath's teeth were at his ear.

"Give up?"

"I'll kill you. I swear it. I will kill you!"

"If you won't give up, I am going to rub your face in the mud."

"I will k—"

Gath rubbed his face in the mud, then pulled it out again. "I can keep this up for hours. I can rub all the skin off, so you'll have a red beard to match your hair, and everyone will know how you got it—"

Vork squirmed helplessly, scrabbling with his free hand to find something to hurt. "I don't care what you do to me, I'll kill you afterward. I will kill you kill you kill you!"

Any wriggle he made, Gath could counter before he even tried, and yet the image of him winning grew stronger. The kid was about to lose his temper and then Gath lost the battle. More ruthless! He pushed Vork's face hard in the mud and held it there. He bit his ear to get his attention.

"Listen to me! I'm bigger'n you, and I'm a seer. You never had a hope. I could probably beat your father, even, given enough time. He could never lay a boot on me, and I'd wear him out. D'you hear me?" He let the kid take a breath.

"Kill you!"

Back in the mud. "I'm a seer. You can't ever beat me. You are not going to Nintor. Your dad is not going to Nintor." Gath gave him a moment to think about it, and the possibility that Vork would win suddenly faded away to nothing.

Gath let him breathe again.

He choked out a jugful of mud and said, "Truth?"

"Swear it by God of. I'm the better fighter?"

Reluctantly Vork muttered, "Yes."

Gath stood up. He offered a hand. He was a mess, but when Vork scrambled to his feet also, he was an awesome apparition, and it was too soon to laugh.

Then came the strangest moment in the whole strange day, at least as far as Gath's prescience reached. Vork grabbed his hand, squeezed it, pumped it. He grinned, showing white teeth in mud, and his green eyes were shining in mud. "You won! Thought you would. Glad that's over. Buddies?"

And that was when Gath said, "Buddies. This is what you wanted?"

And Vork would explain that of course he'd wanted to be buddies all along, but jotnar couldn't be buddies until they'd found out which one was the better fighter.

Crazy! "Then let's clean up and go have that beer."

Vork hesitated, impressed. "Serious?"

"Dead serious," Gath said. "I want your help, kinsman-buddy."

They found a pump and cleaned up. The water was even browner than the stuff in the streets, but it took most of the mud off. Then Gath set off as fast as he could stride, with Vork almost trotting to keep up and babbling questions by the score, as if he'd been bottling them up for weeks. He wanted to know all about Krasnegar and howcum the jotnar there would accept a queen ruling over them, or failing her a faun. He wanted to hear about the goblins. He was a different boy altogether. It was weird.

"There's a place," he said. "What's wrong with that one? Where're we going?"

"We're going to the True Men and we haven't got much time."

"Where? Why? What're you planning?"

"Just wait and see. Do what I tell you to do and you're going to learn why you're not going to go to Nintor." Except he almost certainly was.

"What's it like to have prescience, Gath?"

Now that was an impossible one! "It's like memory, except it works forward, not backward." It was harder to describe how sometimes he could see more than one future, and he couldn't possibly explain that Vork's witless chatter was welcome in the sense that he didn't quite know what to expect because it was trivial. Important things he knew in advance but not trivial things, just as he remembered important things in the past and forgot unimportant things. How could he possibly put into words the fact that sometimes he had to go places and do things to learn things, even when he knew in advance what he was going to learn, because if he didn't, he would set up a paradox that even he couldn't handle? And he wasn't going to explain how sometimes the really important things—

Then it happened, right there in the street. Prescience became present and suddenly he was lying under the table, looking at the boots. He staggered and said, "Where am I?"

"Gath! What's wrong?"

"Where am I?" Gath whispered, in case the owner of those boots heard him.

"You're in Urgaxox. In the street! What's wrong?"

Gath shuddered, and found his way back to the present, shaking and sweating. Yes, he was in the street, leaning against a door. A group of gnomes stood at the far side, staring at him with their beady black eyes. He hadn't pulled that trick since the night he saved the imperor! And he remembered what the warlock had said in Gwurkiarg about foresight driving people mad. He wished Raspnex hadn't said that, because he'd often wondered if he was going mad and it didn't help much to know that it could happen.

All right! Concentrate. You're still going to the True Men. You're not there yet. Don't think about the important things that are going to happen. Think about what's happening now.

"Come on!" he said grimly, and began walking again.

Vork was quieter after that. But soon he wanted to know why the True Men, and how Gath knew about the True Men, and what was so special . . .

"There it is," Gath said.

There were no words on the sign, of course, just three crudely painted male faces, all heavily forested with golden

beard and mustache. Any nonjotunn who walked in under a
sign like that could expect to come out in pieces. Gath pushed
open the door and marched in, wondering whether he would
have had the courage to do that if he were by himself. He was
showing off to his new friend. New follower, really—that was
what Vork was. He said he wanted a buddy, but he really
wanted a leader, even if he was a year older. He wanted a
better fighter to follow.

Gath had been in saloons in Krasnegar a couple of times, so
the scene was vaguely familiar. Once he'd been sent to fetch
Krath, the smith. Twice he'd been tagging along with Dad
when Dad was on business. *Oh, Dad, Dad!*

Even so early in the morning, the big room was crowded
and noisy. The air was thick enough to drink. There was not
one dark head to be seen, and Gath felt small, suddenly. Along
one side were three rows of plank tables, where men were
eating fish soup. Along another was a bar. He headed for the
bar. Getting close was tricky. One didn't jostle jotnar, especially drunk jotnar. Eventually he squirmed his way through,
though.

The bartender was massive and shirtless, all fat and hair and
tattoos. His face had been taken apart and put back together
so many times that it wasn't quite a face anymore. He turned
it sideways and inspected his two new customers out of the
corner of one eye.

"Don't serve *milk*," he said.

Gath produced the ambassador's coin and clinked it on the
bar. "Two beers. The small beer." His insides were dancing a
gavotte with excitement.

The bartender turned away, dipped two mugs in a bucket,
and slopped them down in front of the customers.

"The small beer, I said." Gath knew what happened if he
drank *that* stuff. Nintor didn't happen, for one thing.

The bartender's face twisted as if in pain, but it might have
been a smile. He removed the mugs, tipped their contents back
in the bucket, and filled them from another bucket. Then he
reached for the coin, and Gath let him have it. He grabbed his
drink and began edging back out through the knots of shouting men.

"He cheated you!" Vork squealed behind him. "You ought to get change. Or a meal. Or something."

So go wrestle him for it? "Be quiet and follow me!"

The center of the room was fairly empty. Gath hurried across to the tables and went round behind the first one, carefully not jostling any of the men on the stools. Some were slurping up the soup—it smelled good—and others had passed out. Some were red-faced and arguing. It was hard to think straight in so much noise. He found the stool he wanted, facing the door.

Vork flopped down beside him, green eyes big as eggs.

"Kinsman!" Gath said, raising his tankard.

"Kinsman!" Vork beamed. He drank. He choked.

It was awful stuff compared to Krasnegar beer, and Gath didn't even like that. He forced himself. "Drink up." he commanded, but his eyes were on the door. He could tell when it opened and closed, because of the light, but it was hard to see who was coming in because of all the men standing in the way.

"Gath?" Vork whispered, worried now. "What happens?"

"You won't believe me."

"Yes, I will!"

"No, you won't! Just do what I say, and—"

It happened again. He was marching up the plank, holding his hand out and trying to smile and saying "Kinsman!" Seagulls cried overhead and the deck moved under his feet and a hundred blue eyes . . .

"Gath!"

Gath had his eyes shut and his fists clenched. "I'm in the True Men, right?"

"Yes. What's wrong?"

Thane Drakkor had a very babyish face, and yet there was something chilling in his brilliantly blue gaze. Gath stepped off the gangplank and felt the thane's horny hand take his and he braced himself for the crushing grip . . .

It passed again. Back to the present, and the True Men. Madness! He wiped his forehead, which was streaming wet. "Nothing. Just a big day, you see. I live things too often when . . . Ah!"

There was no mistaking who had come in now. He gripped Vork's pudgy arm. "Now! Down on the floor!"

In a moment they were both under the table. If Vork's eyes had been eggs before, now they were poached eggs. But no one had noticed. No one laughed or came to peek.

"Lie down," Gath whispered. "If anyone sees us, pretend you've passed out. Keep quiet, and listen!"

Staring at him as if at a madman, Vork sank back on one elbow. Gath stretched out, rolled over on his belly, and laid his head on his arm to keep his face off the floor, which was almost as filthy as the streets.

Feet went by. A real drunk was snoring under the table not far away.

A very small voice—"Gath?"

Gath said nothing.

"Gath. I need to go pee!"

"Pee then!" Who'd notice in here? And why did he have to mention that? Gath said nothing, cursing the beer. He hadn't drunk that much of it! Vork whimpered.

Then a pair of very large boots came into view, one of them hooking a stool back so their owner could sit down. They had been very fine boots once, with silver buckles and fancy stitching around the tops. They were wet and muddy now. Gath had never seen them before, but he risked a look at Vork. His face was paler than a fresh snowdrift—Vork recognized those boots, obviously. A tankard clumped down on the table.

A pair of dirty feet and bare shins joined the boots and another stool scraped. A second tankard thumped down beside the first.

"What's going on?" Ambassador Kragthong demanded in a low voice. "Why so many in town?"

"On their way to the moot," the other man said.

"I know that, fool. But why come to Urgaxox?"

The other man chuckled. "To see if it's true."

"If what's true?"

"The Impire's pulled the legions out of Guwush. Four of them."

"Gods' ballocks!" the thane said. There was a sound of gulping, and then a tankard thumped again on the table. Beer slopped through the planks onto Gath's shoulder.

"The XIIIth's still here in town, and the XXVIIth's inland,

but that's all. They're jumpy as fleas, too. Hardly got enough men to watch all those longships."

"God of Slaughter!" Kragthong muttered. "It's an open door! It's money on trees!"

"That's it. And Drakkor's here."

A grunt. "Thought I recognized his outfit. Heard he'd gone south this year?"

"He came back. You can guess what he's going to say at the moot!"

"They'll follow him now! War!"

"You bet they will! Chances like this don't come in a hundred years."

There was a powerful silence, then, as the thane digested the news. More beer dripped coldly on Gath. In the end it was the other man who spoke, but much less surely than before.

"The imps suspect. They've got half a cohort on Pier Twelve. If they knew for certain that was Drakkor's longship, things might—"

A crash of thunder made both eavesdroppers jerk in alarm. Apparently someone had banged a large fist on the table.

"If you're hinting that I would—" The ambassador's hairy hand had closed on the hilt of his dagger.

"No! No!" the other man said hastily.

"Thinking of selling him yourself?"

"No, no, no! Of course not!" The other man was keeping his hands under the table, and they were shaking.

"Then don't even dream it," Kragthong growled. "Men have seen their own lungs for less."

He released his dagger. Hands disappeared and there was another pause for drinking . . .

"You heading to the moot, Thane?" the other man asked.

"Course."

"He's been bragging about adding Spithfrith to his collection."

"Ha! I'm not scared of that pipsqueak," the big man growled. "Drakkor gives me one crooked look I may just waive ambassadorial immunity and do the world a favor." The words seemed oddly unconvincing to Gath, although he could not tell why.

DAVE DUNCAN >> 227

"They may strip it off you anyway. He'll have the votes this year, with everyone breathing fire like that."

There was a pause.

A long pause.

"You might be right," Kragthong muttered. "God of Blood! I got some important news for them. Was going to take some guests along."

"Your decision," the other man said cheerfully. "Been nice working for you. Get the chance, be sure and mention my name to your successor."

The thane rumbled a few obscenities and made more swallowing noises. "Anything else to report?" The tankard thumped down again, sounding empty.

"Rumor has it the legions have gone from Ollion, too. The caliph's bidding high on shipping."

"Fire and blood!" The old man belched thunderously and moved his boots back, preparing to rise. His hands came into view, taking a small bag from a pocket. It clinked as the spy's hand accepted it.

"I'll also give you some free advice," the ambassador said. "Get out of town and stay out."

"Thanks. Kinda thought o'that myself, though."

Thane Kragthong half snorted a laugh. "You know, I'm afraid it might prejudice my standing in Dwanish if I was present at a war moot. Just remembered an important engagement!"

"Wise," the other man said softly.

"You'd best keep reporting to the same address. Gwurkiarg's not so bad a fleapit after all!"

The other man laughed dutifully, both rose. Boots and bare feet moved away together.

Gath sat up, feeling very shaky. He'd known every word in advance, and yet the real thing was terrifying. He knew what he did next—was he truly as crazy as that?

Vork looked as if he'd died, painfully. He licked his lips and said nothing.

"You're not going to Nintor, kinsman," Gath said hoarsely.

Vork shook his head. "You knew?" he muttered.

"I knew."

"Gath . . . You don't think Dad's *scared*, do you?" Vork's world had just been shaken to its roots. "Scared of Drakkor?"

"Course he's not scared, he's a thane. You heard—important business. Come on."

No one noticed as they emerged from under the table. Neither suggested finishing the beer. They headed for the door.

The streets outside were muddy and smelly, but the cool air was a blessing. Gath drew in great gulps of it. His heart was thudding painfully around in his chest and his throat hurt. There was no sign of the ambassador. Pigeons strutted on the street, and a pair of gnome children were stalking them like cats.

"Back to the ship?" Vork said.

Gath shook his head. "I said I needed your help, right? Want you to do something for me, a favor."

Vork nodded agreement, but he wasn't going to do it when he heard what it was, of course.

"Wait an hour?" Gath said confidently. "Then go back. When they ask you where I am, tell them—but not before!"

"What?" Vork shouted. "Where are you going?"

"It's important that the message gets to the thanes," Gath said. "Your dad isn't going. If he doesn't, then the imperor daren't, and probably not any of them. Mom can't, obviously."

Vork somehow managed to produce two red patches on his cheeks while the rest of his face stayed chalky white, except for the bruise, which was purple now. "You can't!"

"I've got to!" Gath said, wishing he didn't more than he had ever wished anything. "It's my duty." It was hard on Mom—first Kadie, now him—but he thought Dad would have approved, and that was all that mattered now. Dad had given his life for the cause, so he could risk his.

"You can't!" Vork said again.

They both moved aside as a wagon went by, and neither of them even noticed it.

"Yes, I can. I'm a thane's son! I can go to the moot!"

"How? You've got no money!"

"Drakkor's in town," Gath said, and already he knew what Drakkor looked like. "You heard. He's a thane of Gark, and he's another kinsman, and he's going to the moot. I'm going to go to his ship and ask him to take me with him."

"He won't!" Vork squealed.

"He does," Gath said sadly, wishing it wasn't so. "He laughs a lot, but he does. He's leaving very shortly."

The redness spread all over Vork's baby face. "I'm coming with you!"

Yes, he was. "It may be dangerous," Gath warned. "Didn't sound like your dad's friends with Drakkor."

"He's my kinsman, too! Besides, only thanes get challenged."

"I know that. You're sure?"

"Sure I'm sure!"

Gath grinned. There was no use arguing, because this was how it happened. "All right. Come on then. Pier Twelve! Let's go, kinsman!"

4
———

THE WORST PART OF WAR WAS THE WAITING. NO ONE should know that better than Emshandar the Fifth, by the grace of the Gods rightful imperor of Pandemia, lord of the four oceans et cetera et cetera, former proconsul, former legate, former tribune. Yet, while waiting to *do* something was bad enough, as he knew from a score of battles, waiting to do nothing was even worse.

Shandie had taken a brief stroll along the levee and was now heading back to the ship. Half the town was underwater, and he was familiar enough with the dreary place that he had no desires to investigate it further. It breathed unhappy memories. Just to be back in the Impire, his Impire, was a strangely unwelcome sensation. Even the sight of legionaries brought a lump to his throat. They should be springing to attention and saluting, and instead they ignored him totally. They all bore the hourglass symbol of the XIIIth Legion, which was both curious and infuriating. The XIIIth had been stationed at Fort Agraine. Someone had moved the XIIIth into Urgaxox, the IVth and VIIIth out. Somebody was tampering with *his* army, and if it wasn't the odious dwarf it must be Cousin Emthoro, who was almost as odious and an idiot besides.

Shandie had worked with the XIIIth during his days in Guwush. He passed a tribune he thought he knew, but no one would recognize him. Anyone who saw the imperor walking around the docks of Urgaxox dressed as an artisan would assume he was a hallucination.

Besides, every man was busy keeping watch on the Nordland longships. As well they might! Even civilized jotnar on trading ships were unpredictable and dangerous. The undomesticated variety was about as trustworthy as hungry white bears, and uncommonly evident in town at the moment. Fifty men to a longship . . . the army's records showed that one longship was at least equal to a maniple, two hundred men, odds of four to one. More than once a single longship crew had bested a whole cohort, ten to one. Those records were locked in a vault in Hub, as secret as fear of death could make them.

The sight of so many blond heads naturally brought Shandie's thoughts back to the Nintor Moot. According to the ambassador, as many as fifty thanes might attend, although only a score or so were of much importance, meaning they could outfit more than one longship. The longships drawn up on the beaches might number over a hundred—five thousand men, the equivalent to a legion. No, thank you. Were Shandie ever to take on the men of Nordland, he would want much better odds than even. When the war horns sounded, there were plenty more where those came from, too.

The Nintor Moot was an experience he would give a hand for. Very rarely in history had foreign visitors been invited to the moot and even more rarely admitted. A couple of his remote predecessors had attended, although not as reigning imperors. For an outsider to be invited was incredible good fortune, and especially when the invitation came from an ambassador, who could provide the diplomatic immunity other thanes could not. Heading along the pier, back to *Gurx*, Shandie slavered at the thought of going to Nintor.

Alas, Nintor would be suicide, not just for him, but for any of his companions, also. He had come to that conclusion days ago, and it became more obvious every time he thought about it. Whoever went to the thanes' moot would be snatched by the Covin. He had not said so yet; no one had, but he was sure they were all just waiting for someone else to break the ice. They all dreaded the reaction such prudence would provoke from Thane Kragthong. Despite his peaceable retirement occupation as Nordland's ambassador to Dwanish, the big man was still a fearless, bloodthirsty raider at heart. He had enough battle stories to freeze a salamander. The old rogue must be relishing the thought of the thunderbolt he would release when he asked the moot's indulgence to hear the imperor, or even the female thane of Krasnegar: Outrage! Uproar! He would spurn the danger, and spurn those who considered danger.

Shandie climbed the plank—and dodged. A huge airborne mass hurtled toward him, with two brawny blond giants clinging underneath, slithering across the deck, sweating and cursing. How much they were guiding it and how much it was towing them was not clear. They crashed into the side and their dangerous burden swung free, out over the pier and the wagon waiting. They rushed off, bare feet drumming on the planks. The cargo was being unloaded. Jotnar worked as fiercely as they fought, hurling the ironware into nets, running instead of walking, hauling ropes, all in a frenzy as if every second counted. The dwarvish officers watched in saturnine silence, doing nothing to help.

The hatch covers had been piled near the bow. Inos and the warlock were using them as a bench, sitting side by side in the morning sun. They were an ill-matched pair. The dwarf was garbed in black mineworker clothes, shabby and well-worn. Only his broad nose and gray-agate eyes showed between his bristly beard and the brim of his hat. He had his boots planted on the deck and his troll-size hands on his knees, and he gave the impression he was going to stay there until the mountains washed to the sea.

The seat was too low to be comfortable for Inos. Her knees stuck up and she was leaning back on her arms, but she was laughing at something and sunlight lit gold highlights on her honey-blond hair. No longer young yet still a striking woman, neither imp nor jotunn. Such mixtures were usually awkward misfits, but in Inos a man could see possibilities the Gods had overlooked when They made the standard races. A very remarkable woman, Queen Inosolan! She was accustomed to getting her own way and did not see why she must change her habits just because she no longer ruled all she surveyed. She could flash from guile to fury in seconds; stab to the heart of a problem like a rapier; juggle humor and flattery with logic and a line of invective that would embarrass a centurion. Her arms and legs protruded from sailor's breeches and jerkin. Such garb for a lady was utterly bizarre, and yet she was obviously a woman to be reckoned with. Shandie had learned at last not to underestimate her.

Her smile of welcome flashed emerald and ivory. He knelt down in front of her and sat back on his heels. That made his eyes about level with the dwarf's.

"Any news?" he demanded.

Raspnex scratched at his beard. He had been staying out of sight for the past few days, holed up in his cabin as if sulking. "Nope. Too slaggy much power around, is all. This place is giving me the shivers."

"It's natural they would watch for us here. It's the front door to Dwanish."

"You didn't see Gath anywhere, did you?" Inos asked, sitting up.

Shandie shook his head.

She frowned. "Apparently he went off with Vork. I hope they're not getting into mischief."

"He's fourteen!" Raspnex snorted. "At fourteen mischief is an obligation."

"Vork's fifteen."

"Worse."

"How about sixteen?" Shandie asked.

"Sixteen is better. By then at least you know what sort of mischief they're after."

Inos and Shandie exchanged winks. The dwarf's dry humor was rare as raw diamonds, but equally worth collecting.

With oaths, cracking of whip, and much squeaking from axles, the loaded wagon moved away. The shirtless giants drooped for a moment in sweaty silence and the dwarves tallied their records. Then another, empty, wagon rolled up and the whole noisy business started again.

Shandie got down to specifics. "How do you two feel about the Nintor Moot? Inos?"

Green eyes studied him carefully for a moment. "Crazy. If Rap's been taken, he'll have told them he suggested it to you. Even if he hasn't, it's just too obvious."

"I agree," the warlock growled.

"So do I," Shandie admitted, surprised that there was to be no argument.

Inos said, "The trick we pulled on the Directorate won't work twice."

Pause. "No, it wouldn't," Raspnex said.

"What would happen," Shandie asked, "if you did try the same trick again and they caught you? I mean, if you projected yourself into the future and they were waiting for you there?— Then, I mean? However you put it."

"Sizzle!" the little man said. "I'd come back fried. Anyone stands up at the moot and starts to talk about sorcery, he's going to be blasted by thunderbolts. None of us three'd set foot on the island before being nabbed. Even if we hadn't sapped the Directorate, the Nintor Moot's just too high grade for my nephew not to keep an eye on it. Now he knows where we are, roughly, and what we're up to—now he'll have pits dug. I say we forget the thanes and head south."

Inos sighed, and smiled. "I wanted to say so sooner, but I thought you'd call me a nervous old maid."

"Me, too!" Shandie chuckled. "I'm not suicidal yet! Besides . . . how many sorcerers are there in Nordland anyway?"

"Damn few, I think," Raspnex growled. "Jarga doesn't know of any."

"Thane Kalkor was a sorcerer," Inos said. "The one Rap killed."

The dwarf shrugged his thick shoulders. "Well, he was an exception, then. Jotnar have no truck with sorcery as a rule."

"So the game isn't worth the candle," Shandie said. "We'll forget about Nintor. I just hate the thought of breaking the news to old Kragthong. He's relishing the thought of setting the moot by its ears. He's going to be very disappointed, to say the least."

"Bloodthirsty old killer." Raspnex snorted. "We can tell him to go ahead by himself, but I'm sure he won't get five words out before his beard goes on fire."

After a moment Inos said, "If not Nordland, then Guwush?"

Mm! Shandie shivered. Zinixo might be keeping less of a watch on the gnomes, but the mundane dangers would be even greater. Rebellion still festered in the hills and forests. Shandie himself had earned great hatred when he helped put down the gnomes' last-but-one revolt. He had slaughtered thousands of the little horrors at Highscarp. Moreover, it was hard to imagine asking gnomes for help in anything, they were such inconspicuous, secretive people. Yet they could be implacable fighters when they wanted, like rats.

"I think we should split up here," Inos said. "Some of us go overland across Guwush, and the rest sail around it by ship. We can join up somewhere on the Morning Sea. Maybe even Ollion itself."

"Goblins." Apparently the warlock meant the word to convey agreement. The two goblins would have to be smuggled off *Gurx* by night, or in sacks maybe. They were probably the first goblins ever to venture near Guwush since the coming of the Gods.

"We can ask the thane to find us a ship," Inos suggested. "We may as well charter our own vessel. Here he comes now."

"The old villain will despise us for a clutch of cowards," Shandie warned. "Who wants to break the news that we're not going to Nintor with him?"

Kragthong's great bulk had been rising into view like a surfacing whale. He stepped off the plank and headed ponderously across the deck toward the conspirators, totally ignoring the crew, which had just raised yet another iron-filled net from the hold. Free of the hatch, it began to swing on its cable. Sailors screamed warnings, which he did not heed. A dozen men scrambled to catch the deadly mass, jotnar and dwarves both. Inos and Shandie and Raspnex sprang to their feet with cries of alarm. For a moment disaster seemed inevitable. Then the squirming heap came to a screaming, cursing halt just inches away from the ambassador, who strode on by it as if it did not exist.

Inos and Shandie remained where they were, the warlock stepped up on the bench. The thane stopped and looked down at them all, his battered face flushed and his forked white beard sparkling like ice in the sunlight.

"I have bad news!"

"Namely?" Shandie asked.

"This is in confidence. You're not to tattle to the imps!"

Shandie almost said, *But I am an imp! I am the chief imp!* That wasn't true, though. Much as he hated it, he was an outlaw now, a rebel against his own impire, an enemy of his people. He felt his fresh-shaven face flush. "In confidence, then."

"*Blood Wave II*'s in port."

God of Murder! Shandie wondered which of the longships he had passed was the notorious raider. They had all looked equally lethal. Drakkor! Shandie himself had put a price on that man's head, a huge price, although he had known it was an empty gesture. Even the semicivilized, Impire-born jotnar would sooner die under torment than ever betray a thane.

Inos said, "Pardon my ignorance?"

"The thane of Gark!" Kragthong barked. "Drakkor, son of Kalkor. Another of your kinsmen."

"Ah!" She nodded, her green eyes glinting cold like pack ice. "Indeed he must be, for his father was. I thought . . . After my husband ended that monster's career, I understood that one of his brothers succeeded to the thanedom?"

"Three of them held it, in turn. Then Kalkor's sons began to come on the scene. The latest is Drakkor, who won it two years ago. Four reckonings in one day! No one is likely to dispute his claim now. He is cast in the same mold as his father, although he must be too young to remember him."

"A bad mold. Why is this bad news, that he is in town?"

The weathered old face glowered down at her. "Because he is on his way to the moot. I understood he had gone south. His father almost circumnavigated Pandemia, and Drakkor was thought to have the same ambition. But he is back, breathing fire as usual." The old man hesitated, then added, "A ruthless and very dangerous killer."

If a Nordland thane described another in those terms, then he was talking of someone worth watching. Were the notion not so absurd, Shandie might have supposed that Kragthong was nervous.

"His father laid claim to my kingdom," Inos said furiously. "The issue was settled at a reckoning in Hub. You are saying that Drakkor might reopen the matter?"

The big man took his beard in both hands and tugged, as he did in moments of stress. Perhaps that was why it was so forked. "If you go to the moot, he will feel compelled to do so. The reckoning in Hub was suspect—so he would claim. There was some doubt, was there not, whether your husband killed him in fair combat or by sorcery?"

"Kalkor himself was a sorcerer!"

"That statement alone would be enough to provoke a challenge!" The thane continued before Inos could answer, his voice growing louder. "Even an orthodox reckoning—held at Nintor in proper fashion, witnessed by the assembled thanes . . . even an orthodox reckoning may be set aside by another. His father's failure would not stop him challenging you. He would plead a blood feud, and no one would argue."

A very odd gleam showed in the queen's green eyes. "Well, we cannot let a boor like this Drakkor fellow keep us away from the Nintor Moot, can we? I am thane of Krasnegar, after all!"

Imperor and ambassador opened their mouths simultaneously, but this time it was Inos who brooked no interruption.

"A noble thanedom! If I wanted to, I could probably outfit more longships than almost any of them. I thought an ambassador's guests were protected by his diplomatic status?"

The big man harrumphed, looking quite abashed now. "The challenge would be improper and could be refused. That would not look, ah, seem . . ."

"Quite!" Inos said crossly. "In practice one cannot hide behind points of law without casting doubts on one's courage. So we must accept the challenge, right? I certainly cannot lift one of those axes the boys fight with, so I shall have to find a champion. Some husky young . . . But it's usually a relative, isn't it? Of course! I should have realized. Honor will compel you, as host and kinsman, to waive your immunity and take up my cause!" She smiled gratefully.

The ambassador stiffened. "My pleasure, ma'am. But I shall see that Drakkor is warned of the danger in advance. That should give him second thoughts." He turned quickly to Shandie. "You are aware that Hub has pulled four legions out of Guwush to fight the goblins?"

"Four?" Shandie recoiled. "Pulled four . . . You are joking!"

Obviously he wasn't joking, though. What in the Name of Evil was Zinixo thinking of? The gnomes would explode instantly. It was amazing they had not poured down out of the hills already. A generation of warfare had not completely pacified Guwush, and now it would be all thrown away. Surely the crazy dwarf was not letting idiot Emthoro actually run the Impire?

He wanted to scream.

There was worse to come . . .

"Ever since he won his thanedom," the ambassador said grimly, "Drakkor has been preaching fire and sword against the Impire! He claims his father was betrayed in Hub. Again, a blood feud."

"A blood feud against the whole Impire?"

"It is a good excuse. He almost carried it last year. Now, with Guwush and Urgaxox lying naked, not a voice will rise against it."

Shandie sat down on the hatchcovers, feeling ill. *My people!* Goblins, dwarves—and now gnomes and jotnar, also? The millennium come in blood? He tried to speak, cleared his throat and tried again. "I don't suppose that slime-brained cousin of mine weakened the garrison at Ollion by any unlucky chance?"

"I'm told he did," the thane said.

So the caliph had his chance, also? Goblins, dwarves, gnomes, jotnar, and then djinns? And could the elves and fauns ever turn down the chance to join in?

"What is Zinixo doing?" Shandie howled. "He has stolen the Impire—will he now destroy it?"

No one answered.

Finally it was Inos who spoke. "Ambassador, you are saying that none of us should go to the moot?"

He flushed scarlet above the edges of his beard. "That is my view, ma'am. Not because of the danger, you understand! Please believe that! I should be your champion most willingly, and honored to serve a noble kinswoman so. But you see, Drakkor will have the votes for war. I saw a war moot once, when I was young. It was as if the very air reeked of blood. Not a man but was shouting at the top of his lungs. Your message will not be heard!"

Jotunn bloodlust was notorious. Shandie could imagine what it would do to an assembly of thanes, the killers' killers—or at least he thought he could imagine it. He could imagine it as much as he wanted to.

"You make sense, Excellency," he muttered. "They will have no time for improbable tales of sorcery."

"I'm not arguing," Raspnex growled.

The ambassador sighed and visibly relaxed. "Maybe next year."

If there was a next year.

"I am so sorry," Inos said fretfully, "that you will not be able to settle the insolent Drakkor for me. It seems, then, that we must press on to Guwush and preach to the gnomes."

"I bid you good fortune," Kragthong murmured. "I wish I could have been of service."

Meanwhile was he going to scuttle home to his lair in Dwanish? Perchance even jotnar found wisdom in their old age! Shandie refrained from comment.

Certainly there could be no thought of going to Nintor now. Quite apart from both the Covin and Drakkor lurking in the background, the thanes themselves would be ravening mani-acs. Shandie was ashamed to feel a life-giving sense of relief. The moot would have been a great opportunity, but a very dangerous one. Now it was clearly out of reach and really not worth bothering about anyway, since Nordland had no sor-cerers.

"Guwush indeed," he said, wondering if that were any less dangerous for him. "We three head inland by coach, and send the others around the coast by ship? Has anyone got any ideas how one gets in touch with rebel—"

Kragthong let out a cry. Shandie looked up and saw that the others were all staring at the river. He sprang to his feet. A longship was going by, heading downstream. Riding the current, the low shape streaked through the water, its banked oars moving in perfect symmetry. With every stroke it surged forward, its dragon prow lifting, deadly and beautiful as a hunting shark. Beside the helmsman at the steering oar, two boys were jumping up and down waving. Their shouts drifted faintly to the watchers. One of them had red hair.

Inos rushed over to the rail and waved in reply, and then the raider had vanished beyond the end of the next pier.

Shandie looked at the warlock's glare, and then at the thane, who stood aghast, his face as white as his beard. For a long moment no one spoke at all.

"Nothing will catch them," Shandie muttered.

Raspnex shook his head.

The thane must know whose longship that was, for his dismayed expression mourned a lost son.

Inos was still at the rail, staring downriver, perhaps waiting for a distant glimpse as the vessel rounded the first bend.

Shandie walked over and put an arm around her.

"Inos, I am truly sorry! It is partly my fault. I suppose they think it's a great joke to beat us to Nintor. This morning Gath asked me how important it was to get the word to the thanes and—"

"This morning Gath avoided me," she said quietly, not turning. "Don't blame yourself. When he spoke to you he must have known even the name of the ship he would go on. He knows we are not going and has taken our place."

"How can he possibly—"

She sighed. "I don't know, but I am certain. Gath does not play jokes. He never has. It is my fault. I should have told him of the God's prophecy." Her voice was calm and steady. She did not even sound bitter. "But how could I tell him?"

How could she be taking this so serenely? Shandie felt completely out of his depth. He removed his arm. "What has that to do with it?"

Now Inos did turn to look at him. Her eyes seemed a brighter green than usual, but there was no trace of tears in them. "Strange that a warning that sounded so awful at first should now be a comfort, isn't it? Don't you see? Gath fears that his father is dead. But the God gave the message to Rap, that he must lose a child, and that makes no sense if Rap is never to know what happened to his children. I should have told Gath of that."

Shandie groped for words. Her courage bewildered him. It seemed so cold, and yet he knew she was not cold.

She smiled quirkily. "You expected hysterics, Sire? A woman need not be pureblood jotunn to feel pride in a brave son. He seeks to honor his father's memory, and this is exactly the sort of thing his father might do." Suddenly her eyes sparkled like crystal and she turned away.

Shandie had underestimated her again. "You do not want to go after him?"

Inos shook her head. "I could not help. I would probably make things much worse. He may just possibly escape the Covin's attention, unless he actually gets to stand up and address the moot and announce who he is. That may be what he's planning, but it isn't very likely, is it?" She sighed. "His grandfather was a raider, you know—Rap's father, Grossnuk."

"Oh, come! Gath is not going to turn into one of those!"

"No, of course not. So what do they do with him? Set him working in the fields? I'm more worried that he'll run into that Drakkor man without realizing the danger."

Whose longship was that?

"Drakkor?" Shandie repeated. "Even he won't harm a child, surely?"

Inos smiled pityingly. "A Nordland thane? Scruples? Perhaps you don't remember Kalkor, his father?"

"But what quarrel—"

"Kalkor did not recognize my right to succeed my father as thane of Krasnegar. So Drakkor won't. So who is the present thane of Krasnegar?"

"*Gath?*"

"Gath," she said sadly. "Holindarn's grandson. And Drakkor will challenge him to a reckoning for it. Or just kill him to settle the blood feud—Gath's father killed his father. I'm not sure if Gath knows that."

We happy few:
   . . . *from this day to the ending of the world,*
   But we in it shall be remembered;
   We few, we happy few, we band of brothers . . .
             SHAKESPEARE, *HENRY V*, IV, iii

CHAPTER EIGHT

AFTERWARDS REMEMBER

1

THAÏLE WAS WALKING THE WAY WITH TEAL, THE MASTER OF Novices. He was a long-winded man of middle years whose only notable eccentricity was a devotion to the color blue. He invariably dressed in blue—usually a pale sky blue when he was relaxing, a conservative ultramarine for business, and navy blue or indigo on solemn occasions, but always one blue or another. This curious idiosyncrasy did nobody any harm. He was patient and even-tempered, and he commanded respect. He was a great improvement upon his predecessor, the muddy-eyed Mistress Mearn. Thaïle had never discovered what had happened to Mearn; she had vanished completely, and was never spoken of. No one seemed to mourn her absence, least of all the novices.

"These are known as the Central Hills," Teal remarked, unable to resist a chance to lecture. "We are in almost the exact center of Thume here. You might mistake them for the foothills of the boundary ranges, but you will observe that there are no true mountains in sight."

"It is a pleasant spot," Thaïle commented respectfully, carefully not asking how she could observe what was not there. She was very weary of classes and studying, and glad of a chance to walk in such pleasant woods. A younger and less talkative companion would be an improvement; no one at all would be even better. There must be some reason for this excursion, but Teal had not yet explained and she had not asked.

He discoursed upon the stately elm and silvery birch, the monumental oak and chestnut. "Note that copper beech! Magnificent. A pity the rhododendrons are over." The day was stiflingly hot, even in the Central Hills, with not a hint of a breeze.

Thaïle was still a novice and would remain one for several years yet, but she was no longer the naive peasant girl who had walked the Defile. A second word of power had brought her an adept's ability to master any mundane skill. She could read and write and calculate. Day in and day out she sat with her fellow novices and trainees as the tutors filled their heads with history and geography, the sociology and politics and languages of the Outside, genealogy and the lore of magic. She read until her eyes ached and listened until her head swam. She talked with sorcerers. She heard rumors of terrible events stalking the world Outside, and knew that prophecies were being fulfilled. She understood that these were not normal times; the College was nervous as it had not been for centuries.

The second word had confirmed her Faculty by bringing her the beginnings of occult skills, very rare for a mere adept. They frightened her, for they implied that she was destined to be a mighty sorceress one day. Dread years lay ahead, and she might find herself playing a part in them, and for that she had no ambition. She suspected she had no ambitions at all, except to do her duty as it had been shown to her that terrible night in the Defile.

"Ah!" Teal exclaimed. "There—see the lake?"

Thaïle peered through the foliage and admitted that she could just make out a tiny scrap of polished blue in the far distance, between two hills.

Teal nodded fussily. "Now you have seen it, I can leave you. There is only the Baze Place, so you can't be mistaken. He is expecting you. When you've finished, come and see me at the Library." His eyes twinkled, waiting for her question.

"Finished what?"

He beamed. "You are to learn another word."

The baking heat of the day seemed to chill. For a moment Thaïle wondered if she was being teased or tested in some strange way. She, a mage? What insanity was this?

"But, Analyst! I have been here less than four months."

"We are well aware of that."

"But surely it takes years—"

"It is a great honor for you, Novice." He paused, surprised. "Of course as a mage you can hardly still remain a novice, can you? I shall arrange to have you registered as a trainee, or perhaps even as recorder, although I don't suppose you will ever be asked to perform a recorder's duties. How difficult!"

She was frightened now. The future threatened like a shadow across a path. She wanted no more occult abilities, nor the self-knowledge they might bring. "But I have years of study ahead of me yet before I will be capable of handling the powers of a mage."

"Now, now! That is not so, my dear, and you should know that. Why, Outside people become mages or sorcerers without any studying at all. We teach you about Thume and the College; we can't teach you anything about using power. That wisdom comes from the words themselves." He saw that she was about to argue further. "It was an edict, Thaïle."

A stronger breath of fear dispersed her faint rebellion like smoke in the wind. "The K-k-keeper? Why?"

"I have no idea," Teal said peevishly. "As I said, it is a very great honor that her Blessedness even knows you exist, let alone takes an interest in your progress or orders it accelerated.

I am sure she has her reasons. Now, off to the Baze Place with you. Remember to be patient. He is very old. Address him as 'Archon.' "

Thaïle started. "Is he?"

"He was once. He may bore you with many stories. Just remember that he has dedicated his whole long life to the College and deserves respect for that. His goodwife's name is Prin. She must be almost a hundred herself."

"That is old for . . ."

Teal's nod held a hint of reproof. "For a mundane? Of course she is a mundane, and yes it is. He preserves her as he preserves himself. Do you grudge him that?"

She felt her cheeks flush hotly. "Of course not."

"When he dies, she will die, also. Remember therefore that what you will take from him today is doubly precious to him."

"But—"

"No, I do not think you will kill him. Just be understanding if he seems reluctant, or takes a long time to get to the point. I am sure he will eventually. Baze has always been loyal to the College, and will not shirk this final duty. The *Oopan* word. He knows that, but remind him, just to be sure."

Teal swung on his heel and walked off along the Way. In a few moments he rounded a bend, and disappeared behind shrubbery in a final flicker of blue. Reluctantly Thaïle continued her journey, heading down to the little lake.

In a few moments she emerged from the trees at a small clearing by the shore. The cottage under the willows was old and furry with moss, like some great forest animal dozing in the sun. In size and shape it resembled the Gaib Place where she had been born, except that the logs of its walls were thicker and sturdier. A man sat on a bench by the door, just as her father might even now be sitting by his door, wondering how his lost daughter fared. There was no sign of Goodwife Prin, either inside or outside the house.

Baze was spare and weatherbeaten, but he did not seem especially old. His back was straight. He held bony hands on the boss of a thick staff propped upright between his legs, and he

246 «THE STRICKEN FIELD

was staring fixedly at the water. His hair was thin, silvery streaks on his brown scalp, his ears very long and pointed. His shirt and pants were of drab brown stuff and he was barefoot.

She approached, expecting formal welcome, but he surprised her before she was even within earshot. *"Come and sit by me. You are younger than I expected."*

She moved faster, panting in the sticky heat. "Archon Baze?"

"Who else?" He did not turn his head at all, but he smiled toward the lake. *"And you are Novice Thaïle, sent here to become a mage. So young. Troubled times."*

Nervously she crossed the somber deep green of the grass before the cottage and seated herself on the end of the bench. Still he did not turn his head. Of course he had no need to look at her to see her, and perhaps the very old learned to dispense with unnecessary movements, but she found his immobility disconcerting.

"You are frightened." His voice was raspy, and sounded forced.

"Er, a little, sir."

"No need. I am quite harmless."

"Yes, sir. I mean, I don't doubt that, Archon."

He did not answer for a while. A jay shrieked in a maple.

"You should, perhaps. I have slain many men in my time. Women and children, also."

She could not think what he wanted her to say to that. She wished she was not there. A squirrel bounded out of the shrubbery and stopped abruptly to stare warily at the couple on the bench.

"Most Keepers execute their own judgments," the old man told the lake. "After all, what more pain can guilt bring a Keeper? Puile, though, had a hatred of violence. When he was Keeper he gave the worst work to the archons. Once he had me destroy a village." Still he sat in perfect stillness. He sighed, but even that hardly moved his chest. "Merfolk, settling on the coast. They meant no harm."

Horrified, Thaïle said, "A whole village?"

"Even the babes. I came in the night, and they knew nothing. By morning there was only grass. Do you know the worst thing about being an archon, Novice?"

No one had ever spoken quite like this to her, and she was not sure how much she should believe. She could guess the answer to that question, though. "Fearing you may be the next Keeper?"

Baze did not reply, but his head moved in a very slight nod. The squirrel decided it was safe to make three more bounds.

Thaïle jumped at a sudden outburst of song. She twisted around and saw a wicker cage hanging under the eaves, a yellow bird pouring out incredible streams of golden melody, finer than anything she had ever heard. She glanced at the old man. He was smiling toward the lake, but obviously listening to the song and enjoying her surprise.

It ended as suddenly as it had begun.

"That is Sunbeam," Baze said softly. "She is an old friend. My goodwife enjoyed her company in the days when I had to travel."

Thaïle nodded.

"You think it unkind to keep a bird in a cage, Novice?"

She started to shake her head and then remembered that no one could lie to a sorcerer. "It seems a little unfair."

"But Sunbeam has lived ten times as long as any of her nestmates could have done. Should she not be grateful for that?"

Thaïle would not think so. Perhaps birds were different.

The sorcerer sighed. "I think she is happy. If you wish, you may go over there and open the cage and release her. But do you know what will happen then?"

"No, sir, er, Archon I mean."

"She will be terrified! All her life her world has been that safe little cage. Without it, she will do what birds do when they are frightened—fly. Fly and fly. She will fly up and up, and on and on, never daring to come down. And eventually she will exhaust herself and fall helpless from the sky. Unless a hawk catches her first, of course."

"I see. Then I won't."

He nodded, satisfied. "*Oopan*, wasn't it?"

"Yes, sir." The College catalogued the words by their first two syllables.

"A very strong word," he mused. "It has made many archons. It may even have been one of Keef's own." A thin smile twisted his bloodless lips. "But the records are unreliable so far back and that claim is made for many. Everyone would like to think he had been given one of those most sacred and blessed words. I had *Oopan* of old Geem . . . eighty-three? No, eighty-five years ago. What happened to Quair?"

"Who? Quair, Archon? I have not heard—"

"Two days ago, I felt my power grow stronger. Now you are sent to me to learn *Oopan*. So it was Quair who died." Very slowly, the old man rotated his head to look along the bench at her with golden eyes as bright and clear as a child's. "How?"

She quaked. "I have no idea, sir. No one mentioned Quair to me."

"He sat where you are sitting now—oh, forty years ago, perhaps. A sturdy young man, brash for one still fuzzy-cheeked. I shared *Oopan* with him, and it hurt more to speak than any word I have ever shared. Very strong, you see."

"Yes, sir."

"But the years dealt with his fuzz. He turned out well. We considered him for archon more than once. His talents included some unusual . . . Forgive my discourtesy! I have forgotten how to treat guests. So few friends left now! A cool drink? Lemon, perhaps?"

Before she could speak her thanks, a beaker appeared on the bench beside her. She was hot and dry from her walk and the day was muggy. She realized that there were no bothersome insects, though.

"Quair was not old as sorcerers measure old," Baze continued, still staring steadily at her, like an owl. "So how did he die? What kills a sorcerer?"

She choked on her drink. "Sir, I do not know. No one mentioned him to me. They did not tell me how he had died."

"He was an appraiser."

Novices, trainees, recorders, archivists, analysts, archons, the Keeper. . . .

"So you have not yet learned of the appraisers?"

"No, sir. Archon, I mean."

"There are eight archons," the dry old voice said. "Although only seven at the moment, as Sheef has not been replaced. I wonder why? There may be many appraisers or none at all, at the Keeper's whim. I do not know how many there are just now." He sounded petulant about that.

Thaïle muttered something meaningless. She did not want to know about appraisers. She was learning many things that she did not really want to know, and if appraisers were a secret reserved to higher ranks than hers, then she would prefer that they remain so.

Very slowly Baze turned his head again to face the lake. "Appraisers travel the world. They go in disguise, and study in detail that which the Keeper sets them to study. They are extensions of the Keeper, additional eyes for the Keeper."

Two days ago Master Teal had specifically said that no pixie ever left Thume, except for the Keeper. The Keeper watched Outside and might choose to travel Outside in person. The Keeper could do whatever she, or he, wished and need account to no one, not even the archons, who must remain within Thume. So Teal had said, and it was not the first time he had said it, either. Had he lied, or did Thaïle now know an arcane archon secret that a mere analyst did not?

Baze sighed. "Troubled times."

"Yes, Archon."

"They are spelled to die, of course. If they are discovered, if their disguise is penetrated, if others' power comes upon them—they are consumed."

Thaïle shivered and laid her beaker down on the bench with a clatter. Baze raised a hand and rubbed his eyes.

"Now Quair is dead and I must share the word lest it die with me."

She nodded.

"I make you unhappy, child," Baze whispered to the lake. "What do the young care of an old man's maundering? Sixty years I was an archon, and you—you will be one for so little a time! Come close and I will share *Oopan* with you and let you go."

2

THAÏLE RACED ALONG THE WAY, FLEEING FROM THE MEM-ory of glory and the old man's pain. The word of power reverberated in her mind like thunder or the drumming of waterfalls. It had illuminated the world for her as lightning might brighten a night sky, but on the Way all power was curtailed and shut in, restricted to fear and memory. When she left the Way that splendor would blaze again; she wanted help and protection.

The Way twisted beneath her urgent feet and in moments brought her unwitting to the Library. She stood in the rank sea grass upon the cliff top, seeing the breakers far below churn whiteness around the rocks and hearing the cry of the gulls. Even the spray seemed distinct, a myriad cloud of diamonds flying in the sun. The ancient buildings towered around her like sea stacks, grim and secret. They were closed to her, but the world had opened up again. She sensed the insects creeping among the roots and how the stubborn mussels clung against the tugging of the surf. The blue curve of the sky was alive above her and she understood the needs in the birds' calling.

A stone bench stood in the long grass near the ending of the Way. Two people rose from it as she arrived. She saw four. Her eyes made out Master Teal, fatherly and fussy in his middle-blue shirt and breeches, clutching his doublet over his arm because the day was hot. Beside him stood Analyst Shole, tall and dignified in a golden blouse and patterned skirt. They smiled a welcome.

But with her new occult vision she also saw them as they truly were. Teal was grossly fat and hairy, no more fatherly than a cave bat. Shole was far older than she normally appeared, a scraggy relic, patched like an ancient cabin whose logs had rotted and been replaced. His smile was a drool of naked lusts and hers a grimace of tiny teeth in the mouth of some predatory fish.

Hideous in body, deformed in mind, the two old sorcerers reached out together to grope inside Thaïle's mind. She saw images of slimy, sucking tentacles and struck them away with horror. Teal and Shole recoiled, exchanging shocked glances.

"Archon Baze has shared the word with you?" Teal asked, smiling falsely. The silver fur on his flabby breasts was matted with sweat. His lust had shriveled and been replaced by fear. She sensed the fear sprouting on him like mold on bread and knew that this was madness. The word had driven her insane.

"Your Faculty is remarkable, child," said Shole, her small teeth glinting and stirring heinous memories. "We must establish now what power you wield, for we shall be asked." She stood behind a wall of transparent bricks, her image blurring and shifting like a reflection in water. Was she doing that deliberately? Hiding, concealing? Somewhere, sometime, Thaïle had met that smile in a buried, forgotten past. . . .

A clawed hand reached for Thaïle's face. She smote it aside. Shole fell back a step and cried out.

"Take care!" Teal cried. "You may do her an injury!"

"Injury?" Thaïle shouted. "What would you do with me?" She spun around, meaning to flee, and was restrained. Soothing melody and soft pillows—the two sorcerers were at her side, creamily calming and reassuring, quieting the clamor of life from the grass and the birds and the distant forests.

"It is a normal reaction," Teal murmured. "In an hour or so you will feel better."

"You are a mage now," the woman said. "It takes time to adjust. Come inside, out of the sunshine."

The tentacles writhed about her, becoming scaly limbs like those of a giant insect or perhaps young dragons, and then thickets of thorns. Surely power had brought madness? Thaïle struggled against the occult delusions, striving to see her companions in their familiar forms. A flash of sorcery dazzled her, transporting all three of them to the steps of the Chancery. Its bulk loomed dark against the sky, thick ancient stone promising sanctuary and coolness and a blessed shielding to shut out the clamor of the overbright world. As she was guided to the doors, she saw the tiny cracks in the grain of the wood, the rust on the hinges, little silver spiderwebs. She sensed the millions of feet that had trodden the granite of the steps, and the weight of years.

Then she was within; there was peace and cool twilight. She let her companions guide her to a bench and sank down thankfully, shivering in the sudden chill held captive by the walls. There was no one else in the Chancery except a couple of trainees poring over documents on the topmost floor. A beaker was thrust into her hands, and she drank, her teeth chattering on the rim.

She sat then for a moment, huddled over and staring miserably at the flagstones, and yet well aware of the two sorcerers lurking alongside. Slowly she became aware of a low sea-sound rising out of the silence, a soft rumble like distant surf, or wind playing with a forest. Or a murmur of thousands of voices. Growing.

"The old fool has told her two words," Teal said furiously, but he had not spoken aloud, and he had intended the message only for the sorceress.

"I fear not. I think just one."

"A mage so strong? It is impossible!"

The background voices were growing more insistent, an uncounted multitude muttering, trying to speak to her, Thaïle.

She looked up in alarm, realizing that she was hearing the books themselves, the myriad volumes that filled gallery upon gallery in the Chancery. The most sacred and ancient records the College possessed were stored here, and she was hearing them. Teal and Shole stood over her, pulsating phantoms of terror and jealousy obscuring their mundane selves. Why were they so frightened?

Out of the sibilant muttering of the books, one voice was starting to emerge . . . It alone was speaking her name.

"Are you feeling any better now, dear?" Shole asked. Hatred and fear burned in green fire about her.

"A little, thank you," Thaïle said weakly. Where and when had she seen this woman before? Before she came to the College. Deep anger stirred, fighting for memory.

Her Feeling had returned. She had almost forgotten her talent in the last few weeks, because it worked only on her fellow novices and trainees, and not even on all of them. As an adept she had learned how to suppress it, and had taken to doing so out of respect for others' privacy. Now she could read her companions' emotions as easily as mundanes'. She could not ignore their feelings, for they bore a rank smell of danger. They were as repellent as their owners: apprehension, jealousy, resentment, and a seething desire to dominate and *use*.

"Do you see that chair?" the sorceress asked. "Can you lift it? From here, I mean?"

Startled, Thaïle looked where the woman pointed. Some distance away along the hallway a massive throne of carved oak stood against the wall, old and dusty, abandoned there ages ago, serving no especial purpose.

"Work magic, you mean?"

"Of course. Try it."

Thaïle thought, and wished, and the chair wobbled, then began to rise.

"Well done," Shole said, but her cheerful tone hid an angry, frightened hiss. "Keep lifting."

The chair grew heavier. The sorceress was pushing downward. Thaïle resisted, lifting harder. The hall began to pulsate with power. Shole's withered form glowed with effort, and yet the chair continued to rise.

"Help me!"

Teal joined in. A deep throb seemed to permeate the whole building. Anger and fear grew stronger, and provoked anger in Thaïle also. The battle of power was hurting her. Resenting the unequal odds, she summoned all her will—

With an echoing crash, the chair exploded into dust. Power dissipated in a flash like a lightning stroke. Thaïle fell back against the wall, and the two sorcerers staggered. *God of Mercy!* On the topmost floor, the two students raised their heads, startled by the noise.

"Incredible!" Teal thought to Shole, but Shole was too stunned to reply. The contest had pained her.

In the occult silence that followed, the multitude of voices became audible again, most just clamoring impersonally for Thaïle's attention, but that single voice still rising out of them, one book calling out to her by name. She could not distinguish the words. It spoke in an unfamiliar accent, an antique dialect.

"Well, you are a mage of uncommon power, Novice," Teal said with a heartiness belied by the envy that writhed over him in snakes of fire. "I must stop calling you by that name! You need no tutors now."

"I don't?" Thaïle said, looking up at him in alarm. These new abilities overwhelmed her. She wanted guidance and support and reassurance—and yet she would trust nothing these two twisted antiquities told her.

"Look!" He snapped his fingers and a thick leather-bound volume appeared in his hand.

It could not have come from outside, because the building was shielded. Somehow Thaïle traced it back and found the shelf he had taken it from, and the gap. How had she done that?

With a smirk, Teal blew dust from the book. Then he held it out to her, unopened. "Read it!"

She did not need to take it from him. It was a catalogue of all the men and women who had known the word *Istik* in the last seven hundred years—analysts, archons, and even a couple of Keepers. Their lives and deeds were listed, and some notes on their powers. Many of them had been especially gifted at foreseeing trouble, as if that were a characteristic of that particular word. They included Archon Foor, one of her own ancestors, a distinguished member of her Gifted family.

"Try," Teal said.

"I don't need to. I can see what it says. But there is another . . ." She listened, seeking to isolate that one insistent voice from all the thousands of others. She dampened those others, and then the One gleamed more brightly. It was on the topmost gallery, on a high shelf, coated in webs. She reached for it and it jumped easily into her hands, solid and heavy and slightly warm.

She sneezed at the dust that came with it. Her eyes watered, but she did not need eyes in this dark hall.

"This one," she said. "The writing is strange. Why, it is full of prophecies! I can't—"

"Give me that!" Shole screamed, and the book vanished.

Thaïle jumped to her feet in fury. "How dare you! Where did you put it?" It must still be in the building. "Ah! Down there!" In the cellar. Again she reached.

Shole blocked her, Thaïle shoved her aside, yet neither had moved.

"Stop!" the sorceress cried, her panic brightening the corridor. "That one is not for you, not yet!" She hurled a shielding over the littered, cobwebby table where the book lay. The occult noise was another clap of thunder, louder even than the chair had made.

Of course creating a shield was always a very conspicuous use of sorcery—how did Thaïle know that? The book's voice had stopped. She wondered if she could break a shielding now. It was just a matter of strength, she saw . . .

"Thaïle!" Shole said in violet and gold urgency. "Please! Do not meddle with that book! That one needs authorization from the Keeper."

"I think we should go now," Teal said shrilly. "You must go home, Thaïle, and rest awhile. Use your new powers sparingly at first, won't you?" He was very worried, planning to report to the archons and unload his responsibility as soon as possible.

Thaïle looked at his sweaty, bulbous, white-furred image and shuddered. "Yes, I shall go home," she muttered.

Home? What Place? Again old memories stirred under the tumult of the day, but she could not reach them.

3

A PIXIE IN TROUBLE WENT TO HER PLACE AND SHUT THE door on the world. If the trouble was serious enough, she curled up on the bed. Perhaps a married pixie needed her goodman there, also—that aspect Thaïle did not know, not having a man. Silence and solitude were enough. After a while she felt calmer and could begin to explore the new powers she had gained from *Oopan*.

By evening she was feeling better. She was feeling hungry, too. She would have to face people again eventually. She decided she must seek out some company—after all, occult promotion was cause for celebration, usually. Lying on the bed, sucking the end of a curl, she ran through her mental list of acquaintances. Rather to her surprise, she discovered that the women on it had much less appeal at the moment than the men. Reassurance from a deep-pitched voice would be more convincing, a male smile more gratifying—something to do with the chin? She laughed at herself and decided it must be the bed making her feel that way. She rolled off, straightened up, and ran to the bathroom.

As she made herself presentable, she reviewed her list again, the masculine part of it. Three novices and two trainees survived her first pruning. Most of the novices were too juvenile, most of the trainees not juvenile enough. Mist, of course, was long gone from the College. Of the five novices in that class, only she and Woom had survived the test of the Defile. Woom had his faults, but by the time she was slipping on her shoes, she had decided to brighten Woom's evening for him. In fact, she had known from the start that her choice would be Woom.

She trotted down her steps and started across the glade, sensuously aware of the warm summer night. The western sky was streaked with gold clouds and long shadows lay on the grass. She opened her mind and detected someone a long, long way off to the south. How strange that such beautiful country had no more people in it! The Gaib Place had been isolated, but the Thaïle Place seemed to have the world to itself.

Just as she was about to set foot on the Way, she heard something, and stopped. There it went again! Woodchucks? Jays? Squirrels? Reluctantly she admitted it was children laughing. She tried again to Feel someone, and found no one. She scanned the forest with farsight, and although her range was many times greater than it had been before, she again detected no sign of human life.

The ghostly laughter had gone. Perhaps new magical powers were just hard to get used to and she would return to sanity in a day or two. Calling the Woom Place to mind, she set off along the Way.

Two or three bends were enough for that journey, because the landscape hardly had to change. Conifers became more common, hardwood rarer, the temperature dropped slightly.

The cottage came into farsight and then into view. It was a very good Place, in a rocky clearing with a crystal stream. Woom was not home. She could hear him, though. Even without magic she would have located him, a few minutes' walk uphill. He was chopping wood.

What an absurd thing to do! How typically male! The greatest joy of belonging to the College was freedom from drab toil. Let the rest of the world spend the whole of its days digging and plowing and pruning and harvesting and scrubbing—and chopping! With sorcery the monotony vanished and life was freed for living, Jain had explained that to her long ago and she had not believed him. She had not seen Jain around lately.

She came through the trees behind Woom. There he was, stripped to the waist, whacking viciously with an ax at the corpse of a tree. The steady thump of his blows, the play of light on his back and shoulders . . . Memories stirred. Not her father, for he never worked without a shirt on. Who? Who had chopped wood like that while she watched? Perhaps Wide, her sister's goodman? No, he was so lazy he sent his wife to gather sticks. Yet Thaïle had certainly watched someone doing that. She suspected that the next stage was for him to throw down the ax and her to jump into his arms. What a strange notion!

Woom was an adept, he could hear sparrows blink. He turned around and watched her approach.

She waved. He had been a dweller-under-rocks when she first met him, human slime. The Defile had changed all that. He had emerged as a solemn, stolid young man. He was half a year younger than she, not quite old enough to rouse serious intentions in either of them, but old enough that they both knew the idea was possible.

He wiped his forehead with his arm, ran fingers through wet hair. "I am Woom and welcome you to the Woom Place."

She knew no one else in the College who clung to such mundane formalities. She knew no one who smiled so seldom without ever seeming surly.

"I am Thaïle of the Thaïle Place and how are you planning to move the logs home?"

"I'm not." He unhooked his shirt from a twig and flipped

it over one shoulder; he swung the ax up on the other. "You can have them all."

They began to walk.

"Seems like a very foolish waste of effort."

He looked at her with eyes of somber amber. "I do it because I enjoy doing it. Why did you come?"

"Thought we might eat supper together."

"You'll cook?"

"Yes."

"Why?"

She laughed. "Because I enjoy doing it. You win."

He did not react. Winning had no importance to Woom, nor losing either. He took the College very seriously; he worked very hard. He was completely dedicated to his duty to the Keeper and the preservation of Thume. Nothing else had mattered to him since he walked the Defile.

He was very ordinary-looking, was Woom. He could not have much growing to do now, if any. He was not tall, or burly, but he was neither short nor skinny, either. He was not handsome nor plain. He was just . . . well, ordinary. His powers were ordinary, too. He would never be an archon. She shivered.

As they emerged from the trees, something flickered at the edge of the clearing—a goat? No, there was nothing there. Thaïle stopped and stared, and probed with magic.

"What's wrong?" Woom asked.

"Thought I detected . . . Ah!" She had it. There was another Place in this clearing, another cottage close to Woom's. The two were somehow offset, as if on opposite sides of a sheet of glass. That explained lots of things, like why such wonderful living sites had not been inhabited sooner and why no mundane ever blundered in unexpectedly. There must be another Place right beside hers, also. The whole College must be like that—in Thume and all over Thume, and yet not quite the same Thume. The Gates were just a pretense, obviously, nothing but admitting points for new recruits. The recorders would not need the Gates, they would just—

"Excuse me," she murmured, and *stepped sideways*. She transposed herself into the other clearing. There was the goat, and the cottage. Woom's house had gone, of course. A small boy was washing a pot in the stream. He looked up in alarm. Even as his mouth opened, Thaïle *stepped sideways* back again.

Woom's eyes were a little wider than usual, but he said nothing.

"I'm having a very strange day," Thaïle said airily, and led the way to his door. There were two chairs there that he had made himself. They were heavy and solid compared to College furniture, but surprisingly comfortable. She had sewn a couple of cushions for them. She sat down with a sigh of pleasure.

"I'll clean up," he said.

"Sit and talk first. Care for a drink? Pineapple juice?" She made a pitcher and two beakers on the table.

Woom stared at her thoughtfully, and then pulled on his shirt and sat down. She could not tell what he was thinking—
Despair!

She gasped. She had peeked at his emotions without meaning to. His impassive expression hid a horrible bottomless melancholy that she had never even suspected. She watched as he filled the beakers and passed one to her.

"Woom! What's wrong?"

"Nothing's wrong. Very good juice."

He held her gaze, but now she could see how thin the shell was, how black the heart. Hopelessness.

She had made cushions for his chairs. He had accepted them, knowing that her gift did not mean . . . How could she have been so cruel, so blind?

"Oh, Woom! I never realized. I am sorry, very, very sorry!"

"You're a sorceress now?"

"Just a mage. They gave me another word today."

He nodded. "You're special, very special. We all know that. You know what they call you behind your back?"

"I don't think I want to. How long have you felt like this?"

"Like what?"

"About me."

He shrugged. "Since I first set eyes on you. Mist knew, of course. But it can't be, can it? The rules won't allow it." He took a long drink of juice, as if rules settled everything.

"You hid it very well. At first I thought you hated me."

"I expect I did. I hated everyone. You most of all, likely. The Defile showed me there were better things to hate."

She stared at her hands, but her powers could still see his impassive face and the desperate longing behind that mask, the longing to be wanted. Had that always been his trouble? Was that why he was so single-minded about serving the Keeper? Wanting to be wanted?

"What do they call me behind my back?"

"The Little Keeper."

That, too. Wanting to be wanted.

"I wish I had known sooner," she said. "Perhaps I could have helped a little. It's too late now."

"Helped how?" he demanded. "That rule is never broken."

A mage did not blush. "Nothing."

"Bed, you mean? That isn't what I want."

He believed that, she saw. Oh, poor Woom! Mist had confused love with sex, as if one was the same as the other. Woom thought they were totally separate, unrelated. Both men were wrong. She was certain of that, although she did not know how she knew.

"And what's different now?" he said harshly. "Oh—five words? We know five words between us, is that it? You're afraid we'd start whispering words of power in each other's ears?"

His face was shinier now than when he'd been chopping wood. Oh, poor Woom!

"I thought it hurt to share words of power?" he said.

She had never thought about it. She thought about sorcery in other ways now, somehow, knowing things she had never learned. "It does. Four's the limit."

"So Teal told us. Why? What's so special about four words? Why not five?"

"Too much power?" she said uncertainly. Suddenly red-hot hammers were beating in her head. "It would tear you apart. That's some of it, but . . . But not all of it. It's love, Woom. Not just sex, but love." Love and sorcery, an unholy mixture, or a holy mixture perhaps, and together . . . The world swayed nauseously and her eyes felt ready to boil. "I can't talk any more!" she gasped.

She let the elusive thoughts slide away, and her pounding headache eased. What to do about poor Woom? Shreds of forgotten talk floated into her mind, hints and innuendos . . .

"Speak to Teal," she said suddenly. "He can arrange for you to, er, go visiting outside the College. Meet girls." People from the College always married mundanes; that was the rule.

Woom stared hard at her. "I don't want to go visiting outside the College. I don't want to meet girls. I have a job to do here and I'm glad of the chance, and I wish we hadn't gotten on the subject. You going to feed a hungry man or just talk?" From him, that was a rib-splitting joke.

"I'll magic something," she said irritably, staring at the darkening clearing. Memories kept nudging at her mind, man memories. That might be why she had pried into Woom's thoughts, or even why she had come here at all. Not Mist. Not Woom. Who? The new word of power in her head was trying to tell her something. Man. Man. Man? Leéb?

Oh, what a strange day.

"Thaïle?"

"Mm?"

"Why did Keef kill her lover?"

"Huh?" She looked hard at Woom's steady amber eyes and the inquiry in them.

"Teal won't tell. It's the heart of the legend, but he won't say. Or can't. Maybe he doesn't even know. Keef slew the man she loved. *Why?*"

Love and sorcery . . .

"I don't know."

He was right, though. Why had the first Keeper slain her lover? That was the heart of mystery, and no one ever said why it had happened, why it had to happen. How strange that Woom should have seen that and she had not. And he had more—

"What's the Keeper, Thaïle? What is she? Why is she different?"

Chill and horror . . .

"I don't know that, either." The pain came rushing back.

"I think you do," he said solemnly.

'No! No, I don't!" She didn't want to know that. She would know that soon enough. Woom never would.

Poor Woom in his sweat-soaked shirt! Just an ordinary adept, barely more than a mundane, destined at best to be a very ordinary sorcerer all his days.

Behind him, the image of the Keeper was beckoning, transparent and faceless.

"Come to me, Thaïle. You don't need directions now."

"Yes. No."

Thaïle stood up. "Sorry, Woom. I mustn't talk about such things. I have to go." She walked away without waiting for an answer. He did not call out to her, as most men would have. She came to the Way and told it to take her to the Keeper, and in a moment she was gone from the Woom Place.

4

SHE DID NOT KNOW WHERE THE KEEPER LIVED, BUT SHE DID not have to know. No longer need she be familiar with a place to make the Way take her there. Now she could control the Way.

The moon was rising. She could have managed as well in the dark, but she admired the beauty of the silver light angling down through gaps in the forest canopy. The trees became even larger, damp and monstrous. Soon the black jungle cut off the moonlight completely, but the Way went on. It was very narrow, very twisted, winding between the great trunks, a tunnel through foliage. There was no sound except the soft pad of dripping water.

The Way ended at a mossy cliff, thick moss completely burying the stones beneath. There was a great building here, wrapped in jungle, but it was shielded. She left the white gravel and had to take several squelching steps over soggy humus to reach an alcove and an inconspicuous little door. The flap creaked open for her on corroded bronze hinges.

Inside was brighter, and empty. The moon shone through vacant windows that still held a few remnants of stone tracery and stained glass to hint at their former glory. The ceiling was intact, though, preserved by sorcery, along with most of its ribs and carvings. The floor was a barren plain of uneven flags, but something had kept it clear of dust and leaves through all the silent centuries. The air was still, as if frozen.

She knew what place this must be. In a far corner was power. It radiated up from the floor, but it was cold power, dark power. If this was the Chapel—and it must be the Chapel— then that was Keef's grave. Thaïle resisted the urge to approach it, refusing the call.

She had tried to go to the Keeper. Instead she had gone to the very heart of Thume, the resting place of the first Keeper. Did Keef rest? Remembering the wraith that had guided her in the Defile, Thaïle wondered. Her guess about that wraith might be wrong, of course—but she did not think it was.

She looked around at the emptiness. At one end two doorways led out to a vestry and the main entrance. There was nothing else, no altar or holy balance, no lamps. The Gods had forsaken this place. The Good and Evil were not worshipped here.

She had made no mistake. This was a test. Again she surveyed the curiously misshapen and asymmetric hall, although her mundane eyes could see only shreds of moonlight on stone. Two corners held doors; one held Keef's grave. The fourth corner was empty.

She recalled the duplicate cottage she had visited so briefly at the Woom Place. There had been two Places, set apart in the same Place. That was the answer, then. The Chapel was in the occult Thume. What occupied this space in the mundane Thume?

She *stepped sideways.*

The Chapel remained unchanged, and Keef's grave, also, but now a cluster of furniture stood in that fourth corner: a desk, a chair, a high shelf of books, a closet. A bed—why a bed? The Keeper never slept. Perhaps she sometimes rested. She was sitting at the desk now, waiting.

Thaïle walked to her, half the length of the Chapel, thinking "What a horrible Place." Not even a rug. As she drew near, she saw a thick book lying on the desk and recognized it. Beside it stood a slim silver vase holding a single white lily. That was sad.

As always, the Keeper was shrouded in a dark robe; her cowled head was bent over her hands. Thaïle arrived and sank to her knees on the icy, greasy stone. The head lifted, but the face within was dark and shielded. Not even eyes showed.

She felt strangely calm. "The Little Keeper" the novices called her, so Woom had said, and Woom never joked. She knew the book, although its voice was muffled now and its text concealed from her. Her name was in that book. She was important, she mattered! Perhaps now she would find out how, and why.

"Your power is beyond belief," the familiar rustling voice said. "Baze swears he told you only the one word."

"He did, ma'am."

"You have not learned a fourth elsewhere? No pillow whispers?"

"*No!*"

"Do not raise your voice to me, child! I can still apply discipline. You can suffer more and yet be useful. Mayhap another visit to the Defile is needful."

Thaïle shuddered. "Threats demean you," she said with all the courage she could muster.

"Insolence!" the Keeper said, but more gently. "You have yet much to learn, and time is short. Time is desperately short. Had you come to the College when you should . . ."

Memories stirred.

"What?"

"Never mind." The hidden eyes were studying her. Doubtless the power she could sense was reading her thoughts. "So with three words you have been working sorceries. You clamored all over Thume like temple bells and some of what you did was true sorcery. And with only three words! There is no record of that since . . . for a long time."

"Since Keef?"

"Since Thraine. Oh, Thaïle, Thaïle, do not be stubborn and willful! The Evil is almost upon us. The atrocities have begun, and now the Usurper stirs. *The dragons are rising!*"

The last words prickled goosebumps on Thaïle's arms. "Dragons?" she whispered.

Yesterday Analyst Teal had sent her off by herself to read a dismal, gruesome book about the Dragon Wars. It had brought back memories of the Defile and being slain in torment by the heat of a dragon. She knew about dragons. Her flesh crawled. She jumped as a something began to hiss overhead, then realized it was a burst of rain falling on the roof, wind lashing the trees.

"He is raising the dragons!" the Keeper cried, her voice breaking with horror. "From Gralb nest and Kilberran nest, even the few still at Haggan, and of course the Wurth blaze, the greatest of them all now. The worms brighten the sky. May the Gods be merciful!"

"Coming here?"

"No, not yet, but he plans a fiendish mischief with them, and great slaughter, a needless evil such as your mind will not conceive. Shall I show you? Close your eyes."

"No, please! Please don't! I believe!"

The Keeper sighed. "I hope you do. I hope I am reading the prophecies correctly, else I am about to make a grievous error."

"Error, ma'am?" Thaïle trembled at the thought of the Keeper—the *Keeper!*—making an error.

"Error. My instincts tell me I am, and the auguries are black, yet the prophecies say I must do what needs be done. We shall see before the night is out, I think. You must go now and keep a Death Watch."

"No! I just became a mage. I cannot yet control the power you have given me."

The Keeper sighed. "One learning is as easy as two. In the Outside, when a sorcerer dies, he usually bequeaths all his words at once. Men go from mundanes to sorcerers in an instant. Do you wonder that so many go mad?"

Thaïle did not want to go mad. She was not supposed to answer the question, though.

"Your Faculty will sustain you," the old voice murmured. "Go back to the Way. Raim will call you on it."

"Raim?"

"An archon. He is keeping the old man alive until you get there."

Thaïle rose unwillingly, very shaky.

"And child!"

"Ma'am?"

"Be very careful he tells you only one word!"

Five words destroyed.

Thaïle tried to speak, and failed. She *went*. The Chapel was empty, the Keeper and her furniture gone. She scurried off to the door, ignoring the lament from Keef's grave.

5

INOS EMERGED FROM THE FRONT DOOR OF THE INN AND paused to look up and down the main street of Highscarp. It was a quaint little place, reminiscent of Krasnegar in some ways. The moon shone peacefully over rooftops; candlelight and firelight gleamed in the windows. The night air was wonderfully refreshing after the heat and stink of the tavern.

A party of legionaries had come out ahead of her and was now making its way unsteadily along the road, but there was no one else in sight. She knew that gnomes tended to be nocturnal, and she had expected to see some of them around. This was gnome country, after all, even if it was also part of the Impire.

Behind her, the raucous drunken singing rose to a crescendo in the chorus of "I Loved a Hot Little Gnome." The chorus was obscene, but most of the verses were even worse. As a hostelry for gentlefolk, the Imperor's Head left much to be desired. Just about everything, in fact.

She had spent the whole day in a bumpy, smelly, grossly overcrowded stagecoach, listening to meaningless chatter from witless wives of Imperial officers and fending off their prying questions. Shandie and Raspnex had ridden on the roof, and suffered even more, no doubt. All the male passengers had been required to walk up the hills. Even the Impire could not build straight, flat roads across Guwush.

Even the Impire could not guarantee the safety of its high-ways there, either. The stage traveled with a mounted escort.

And after all that, the Imperor's Head—four women to a room, and a thousand fleas apiece. The food could only have been cooked by gnomes—carrion soufflé, fricassee of offal. In retrospect, Dwanish had been a pleasant vacation.

She would go uphill, she decided.

The door flew open and a man almost cannoned into her.

"Inos!" It was Shandie.

Wearing a sword.

"Just where do you think you're going?" he demanded angrily.

"Needed some fresh air. Remember it? I thought I'd take a stroll."

He snorted. "Take a stroll? Here, in *Highscarp?*"

"Where else? Why, is that unwise?"

"You'd be lucky to live long enough to be raped."

"Oh." Inos tugged her cloak around her and took another, hard look at the empty street. "Well, thanks for the warning. It seems peaceable enough."

"Believe me, it isn't! They'd come out of the alleys like swarming rats. Even the legionaries go round in groups—haven't you noticed?"

"No, I hadn't." She laughed. "Glad you mentioned it! I'll settle for the fresh air."

"You're welcome." He folded his arms. Obviously he was going to stand guard while she breathed.

Neither spoke for a while, and the silence darkened into melancholy.

"Wasn't Highscarp the scene of a battle a few years ago?" she asked, seeking a safe topic.

"Yes."

His tone alerted her—not a safe topic.

"One of yours?"

"One of mine. A glorious victory!"

"Why do you speak of it like that? Wasn't it?"

He took so long to answer that she was just about to apologize for asking. Then he said, "Yes, it was. We guessed that they lost ten thousand men, but it was probably more. It set Oshpoo back a long way." After another pause he went on. "We'll pass the field in the morning, just over the first bridge. I don't suppose there's anything to see there now except a monument."

"A monument to . . . ?"

"To the gallant legionaries who died serving the Impire, of course."

Inos recalled some of the stories that had filtered through to Krasnegar, months later. Highscarp had been a notable victory. The imps had partied for days, *her* imps.

"There will be more battles soon, you think?"

"Sure to be. I don't know what he's waiting for."

Oshpoo. The rebel. She supposed he was Oshpoo the Patriot to the gnomes. Shandie had been very reticent the last few days.

"You should not have come with us!" Inos said sharply. "You should have taken ship with the others."

"I'm in no more danger than you are. Probably we should all have taken ship."

"But if we do manage to contact the People's Liberation Army, and you're recognized—"

"I said don't worry! The best we'll manage will be a letter."

She felt unconvinced. How would the gnomish rebels feel about the general who had inflicted such a devastating defeat on them?

"How do you feel about Highscarp now?"

Shandie shrugged. "Why do you ask? How do you think I feel?"

She should not be wandering on such dangerous ground. "I'm not sure. It was a great triumph for you personally, wasn't it? I suppose you were proud of your success."

"Yes, I was. Very. In a way I still am." He looked up at the sky. "Bats?"

"I do not scream at bats!"

He chuckled. "I didn't expect you to. I'd forgotten the bats of Guwush . . . Yes, I was a soldier and I served my grandfather as I hoped others would serve me when I succeeded. Did my duty. I hoped it would end the war. Now I know that it solved nothing in the long run, nothing at all. Few battles do."

"Is it addictive?" she asked. "Victory, I mean. Soldiers who win and reap fame, who get medals pinned on them and speeches made to them . . . Do they yearn for other wars and other victories?"

"This one doesn't," he said harshly.

She nodded in the night. The singers had gone on to another song, one she did not know. She thought she could see movements in the shadows now, and was glad the inn door was right behind her. Were there eyes watching, ears listening?

"I believe you," she said.

"Thanks."

"Truly!" She held out a hand.

Surprised, he hesitated, and then took it.

Inos said, "When we first met, I thought you were a very cold person. Hard, unfeeling. Lately I've been catching glimpses of a much nicer man underneath." Surely moonlight was making her reckless!

He did not seem to mind her prying. "Gods! I shall have to be more careful in future."

"I thought you were a man of war. You're not, are you?"

"Not really," he said. "At least, I believe peace is better. That was my excuse. I thought that once I'd proved I could be a fighter, then I'd be able to choose peaceful solutions without being called a weakling." He turned his face away from her, as if to study the shadowed doorways nearby. "Perhaps it wouldn't have worked."

"I think it would. Think it will. It does you credit. And some wars are just."

"Are they?"

From Shandie, that ought to be a very surprising question, but she knew him now. He took nothing for granted.

"Yes," she said. "When the jotnar seized my kingdom, I had them all killed, every one, and most of them were not much older than Gath. Well, they were quite young. But none of the thanes has menaced us since."

"If a war is just for one side, then must it not be unjust for the other? Have I mangled the problem successfully?"

"No, you're right. I'm sorry if I offended."

"I enjoy talking with you. Know something? No one has ever spoken to me in my whole life like this. Not the way you do."

Poor, poor Shandie! His mother had been the worst sort of bitch, of course. He had had no brothers or sisters, and probably no real friends, even as a child. What of his wife? But to speak of the impress would be too cruel. The man was probably frantic with worry about her. However, there were limits to the amount of comfort Inos was willing to provide lost husbands, even emperors, and this conversation was drawing very close to those limits. She wondered if moonlight had this effect on people. Or was it loneliness calling out to loneliness?

"Highscarp is not a happy memory!" Shandie said firmly. "What's unsettling you?" He moved closer.

Fair enough. She had wrung confidences out of him, so now it was his turn, and this private little chat was becoming altogether too intense and intimate.

"Riding in that coach."

"I thought maybe it was dinner."

She smiled, then chuckled in case he couldn't see the smile. "That, too. No, I kept remembering the last time I rode in a grand carriage like that."

"When?"

"When I left Hub. Many years ago. We drove all the way to Kinvale before lunch!"

Shandie sighed. "Then I can guess who was driving."

"Yes," she said. "You want to hear something funny? The footman on that journey was Death Bird! Me and Aunt Kade, seven hundred leagues in a morning!" She laughed.

Rap driving.

Rap gone. And Kadie and now Gath.

Shandie took her in his arms.

The tears came at last. He held her tight in the moonlight while she soaked his shoulder.

6
___

THE JOURNEY WAS THE LONGEST THAÏLE HAD EVER TAKEN
on the Way, except perhaps her first trip to the Defile. She had
a strange conviction she was going around in circles, so perhaps the archon was having trouble making the Way work
backward for her.

Eventually she saw a light ahead and heard a distant boom
of surf. The moon was higher, riding through milk-tinted
clouds. Wind sighed over the bent grass on the dunes.

A strange group crouched around a bonfire, their shadows
writhing on the sand behind them. No, there were two groups,
she realized. On one side an old woman huddled, distraught,
weeping in the arms of a bewildered boy. On the other sat a
couple of young men she knew, novices from the College.
They looked at her with pale, strained faces, but she could tell
they were greatly relieved to see her come at last. The dying
man must be a full sorcerer, and these two would be granted
the other two worthwhile words.

Beyond them was a cottage. There was no light in it, but
archons did not need light. She trudged over the soft sand with
her heart laboring. One word only! Only one word!

The door stood open on darkness.

A voice said, "Enter!"

She recognized him, a blocky man with very gold eyes, and
much younger than she would have expected of an archon.

"Yes, we have met," he said impatiently, and gestured to
the bed. The face on the pillow was wrinkled and pallid, its
eyes closed. Under the mundane salt tang of the sea lurked the
occult scent of death, old and stale and cruel.

"You want the *Tylon* word," Raim said brusquely. "I will
rouse him. Give me a moment." He strode past her, out the
door and away, leaving her alone with the dying man.

Why? Oh, to move out of earshot, of course. Words could
only be heard mundanely, not by sorcery. Had she ever been
told that, or did she just know? Remembering her great-
grandmother Phain, she moved softly over to the bed and knelt
down beside it. This would be a much shorter Death Watch

than Phain's. The man's breath rattled like snakes. She wondered if she would ever know his name.

Minutes wormed by. If she wanted to pry, she would be able to Feel his agony. An insane urge to do so began to niggle at her like an itch. His features had the immobility of old ivory, reminiscent of the portrait busts in the Library. She lifted a corner of the sheet and wiped the trickle of spittle trailing from his lip.

His eyelids flickered and opened a little. The mouth pursed as if in pain. What a horrible way to die! She felt like a buzzard, picking at a corpse.

"Which?" The word was not spoken aloud.

"Can I get you anything? Water?"

"No. I am in something of a hurry, Novice. Which?"

"Tylon."

He tried to speak, and no sound came from his lips. He ran the tip of his tongue over them; she leaned closer, offering her ear. He croaked, gasped for breath; tried again.

He spoke.

The world exploded in glory and power.

She reeled out of the cabin, almost knocking over Kweeth, poor kid, only a boy, hurrying white-faced to the dying man to learn a word and become an adept . . . His fear was a luminous marsh fog around him.

The night was filled with splendor and majesty. It trumpeted. She could ride the clouds, embrace the moon. The ever-restless sea filled her with wonder. Her soul danced in the night wind.

Raim blocked her path. "Sit by the fire a moment, Archon, until you collect your wits."

"Archon?" she said. "Did you call me Archon?"

"You are to be the eighth archon," he snapped. He was a very brusque person, this Raim. "That is why Sheef was not replaced. Now go and sit. I am busy."

Without moving a finger, she slapped his face, hard. He reeled, astounded.

"I remember you," she said, feeling exultant. "You came

and snatched poor Mist away from my Place. My guest! Mind your manners better in future."

Anger burned red embers in the night. "You have soon become arrogant, Sorceress!"

"Did you need longer?"

Raim snarled and stepped away from her, rubbing his cheek. He was engrossed in keeping the old man alive and watching young Kweeth's nervous efforts, too busy to spare time for squabbling.

Thaïle walked away, over the top of the sand. Sorceress! The sheer delight of power was intoxicating. This was what Faculty was for. This was why she had come to the College.

Come to the College?

She had never come to the College! She had been kidnapped, abducted to the College. That first day at the Meeting Place . . .

Leéb!

As the great breakers offshore, no matter how high they rose, must topple at last in welters of foam, so memory crashed down upon her: Leéb, her goodman, and the Leéb Place, and their loving. Leéb weaving the walls of the cottage, Leéb building a boat, Leéb teaching her to swim, Leéb's hands on her body. His skin against hers. The missing months flooded back, months of love and laughter.

Now she knew where she had first met Analyst Shole. It had been Shole and Mearn who had come to the Leéb Place and abducted Thaïle and stolen—

Her baby!

She screamed to see the full extent of the College's treachery. Not only her goodman! Her baby, too! With a howl of pain and fury, she gathered her powers for vengeance.

She entered the Chapel in a blast of thunder, right before the Keeper's desk. The hall echoed. Dust billowed away across the flagstones.

"You stole my child! You stole my love! You stole my memories!"

The Keeper seemed not to have moved at all. She looked up slowly, a blankness in a cowl, conveying sorrow.

"You asked me to take your memories." Her voice was dark as buried rock.

"The second time I did! After I came through the Defile I did! I was barely sane that morning. I did not know what I was asking! You took advantage of me!" Never had Thaïle felt such rage, choking her, beating in her temples. "And I certainly did not ask you the first time!"

"It had to be."

"No, it did not! You could have explained! You could have asked me! You could have told me what was required, and why Thume needed me." Was that true, though? Would she have given up her man, her child?

"It had to be," the Keeper repeated, her voice a rustle of dry leaves.

"Why?" Thaïle yelled. "What evil do you battle that is worse than that? Who are you to commit such crimes against me?" She ripped away the shielding to see the shriveled face—and recoiled from the agony in it.

She froze as the sheer immensity of the College registered upon her for the first time: the vast complex pyramid of power and service, the centuries of noting, planning, watching, guarding. Spiders! She sensed the web that enfolded all of Thume, a web of ancient, implacable purpose. Horrible, lifeless, stultifying denial!

"Not just me! All of us, the whole race of pixies!"

And in those terrible stark eyes she read what Woom had wanted to know, what made a Keeper. She saw the suffering, and the warning.

She saw the future.

"No!" she screamed. "Not that! I never will!"

She fled the Chapel in another roar of thunder.

Leéb! Leéb and her child—now she would go to them! Now they would be reunited and she would spurn the College and all its works.

She rode the night sky like a wave among the clouds. She brushed the stars, soaring higher than the icy peaks of the Progistes until she saw the great river far below, a thin scar of silver. She plunged down into blackness as a sea beast seeks the ocean floor.

She came to the Leéb Place quietly, soft and silent, like a hunting owl. In the dark clearing the cottage stood deserted, the door flapping loose in the wind. No light shone through the windows or the chinks of the wicker walls. No chickens roosted in the coop that Leéb had made for her, exactly as she had asked. No goats waited in the paddock to give milk for her child. Weeds flourished over the vegetable patch.

The cottage was a hovel. Now she saw what Jain had tried to tell her once, and she had not believed. Such life was squalor, utter poverty. The Leéb Place had held only three metal tools and virtually nothing else not made by the goodman himself, or his goodwife. Compared to the elegance and comfort of the College, this was a sty for beasts. And oh, how happy she had been here! The only tears she had shed had been tears of happiness.

Oh, Leéb, Leéb! Leéb with his clumsiness, his pure-gold eyes, his silly sticking-out round ears. Leéb with his self-mockery, his quirky smile, his gentleness. Leéb, where have you gone? A pixie never leaves his Place! Have you gone to seek another goodwife to bring back here? Or did you take our child and go searching for me?

No, of course not. The Keeper had explained that. Leéb thought she was dead. He had buried a body.

She moved through the darkness surely. She saw all the heart-wringing familiar things—the chopping block, the clothesline, the stone Leéb sharpened his ax on. The boat he had made with so much labor, pulled clear of the water . . . would he not have found it easier to travel by boat than by land when he had a child to take?

Or had he left the child with old Boosh at the Neeth Place? Thaïle peered upriver with sorcery and saw the two old folk asleep in their decrepit little shanty, and no child or sign of a child.

The night was empty. The night was cold.

Then she knew what she must seek, and in among the trees

she found what she expected, three of them, one of them very small.

Behind the graves stood the Keeper like the God of Death, leaning on her staff, darker than the darkness. For a moment sorceress and demigod confronted each other in silence, while Thaïle struggled to control her sobs.

"It had to be," the Keeper said quietly.

Fury and hatred bubbled up in Thaïle's throat like acid. "Why, why?"

"You know why," said the Keeper. "We can never love."

"Evil!"

"Do you think I do not know, child?"

And again Thaïle screamed what she had screamed in the Chapel: "No! Not that! I never will!"

She tried to flee. Great as her power was, she was only human, and was pinned by the Keeper's greater power.

"It is prophesied!"

"Then unprophesy it!" Thaïle rent the night with a blast of sorcery that flattened the cottage, igniting it in a blizzard of sparks. She would wipe away the remains of this awful crime. A second blast struck woodshed and chicken coop to fiery fragments. A third smashed the burning ruin of the house and fired the shrubbery around.

"Stop!" the Keeper shouted. "I say be still! You are willful! You disobey! You are sworn to obey me!"

Again Thaïle smote the Place with fire. Thunder echoed back from the hills.

"Sworn? What choice did I ever have? When did I ever agree to serve you?" *Smite!* "Your evil infected my parents so that they would infect me, and I infect my own children in turn, slaves commanded to make slaves." *Smite!* "You have bred this iniquity from generation to generation—"

Bolt after bolt of sorcery struck boat and paddock, log pile and midden, everything. The ground was melting, but still the Keeper endured and held Thaïle there, also. The graves were gone. The last glowing remains of the cottage whirled away in the blast. Storm roared through the forest. Far off upstream at the Neeth Place, the two old folk were wakened in terror by the rumbling and shaking of the earth.

"Iniquity?" the Keeper screamed. "You would compare me with the Evil that waits Outside?"

Still Thaïle hurled destruction, fighting against the power that pinned her. On both sides of the river, trees crashed down in flames. Wind howled, and the icy peaks of the Progistes reflected the fountains of fire spouting in the valley.

"I say you are a greater evil! You slaughter babies in the name of love!' Maddened beyond reason by her pain and anger, Thaïle threw power at the Keeper herself.

The ground erupted, rocks flew, glowing like coals, and the Keeper recoiled before the outburst. *"Fool! You will bring the usurper upon us!"*

"Then let him come! How can he be worse?"

The river had begun to boil, the Progiste Ranges glowed red in the night. *"Fool!"* the Keeper cried again, and released her. Thaïle rushed into the sky and hurtled away, up over Thume and the darkness, and was gone to the Outside.

Afterwards remember:
> *Yet if you should forget me for a while*
> *And afterwards remember, do not grieve:*
> *For if the darkness and corruption leave*
> *   A vestige of the thoughts that once I had,*
> *Better by far you should forget and smile*
> *Than that you should remember and be sad.*
>   C. G. ROSSETTI, *REMEMBER*

CHAPTER NINE

PRICKING THUMBS

1

THE SUN WAS STILL HIGH, BUT IT GLOWED RED. THE GOBLIN army jogged steadily northward, while the smoke of their passing drifted away to the west. Finding the unwooded country of South Pithmot not to his liking, Death Bird had changed direction at last, and turned east. Now he had come upon a river and was heading up it, seeking a place to cross. His horde filled the plain.

Kadie rode in a mindless daze, as she always did now. Often she felt as if she had never lived any other life except this dawn-to-dusk horseback existence and it would go on until the Gods died. Poor Allena was worn away to bones, yet she was still willing, and Kadie could not bear to seek a replacement for her, because goblins ate horses. They were not eating many these days. The imps had stripped the countryside—gone themselves and taken their livestock with them. They had not torched the crops and buildings, leaving that pleasure for the invaders. She suspected the goblins thereby betrayed their whereabouts to the Imperial Army, but she had not mentioned that theory, even to Blood Beak. And where was the army? Why had the Impire let the barbarians ravage unmolested for three whole months? There must be a reason, but she could not imagine what it was.

"Kadie?" Blood Beak trotted alongside her stirrup as he always did, untiring. His bodyguard followed.

"Yes, Green One?"

"This river? Where does it go?"

"To the sea, of course."

"Which sea?"

"Home Water, or the Dragon Sea. I'm not sure. Ask someone before you burn his tongue out."

"Don't burn tongues out. Spoils the screaming. Do you still want to escape?"

She almost fell out of the saddle. He had offered to help her escape once, weeks ago, and then changed his mind. Was he serious now, or was this some sort of cruel joke? She glanced behind and noted that the bodyguard was farther back than usual. They were a new detachment, and none of them understood impish. Perhaps Blood Beak had thought of that.

"Yes, please!"

"I shall camp by the river tonight, then. In the dark, you could slip away and take a boat." He was not looking up at her, and she could see nothing of his face except a sweaty cheekbone. He was thick and meaty, but there was no fat on him at all.

"They use the boats for firewood."

"Then float on a log. It is too wide for wading. If you can come ashore on the far bank, you will be free."

She had never thought of escape by water. She did not know how to swim. No one in Krasnegar knew how to swim, but she would not freeze here. Goblins avoided water whenever they could—they would not even cross the causeway at Krasnegar—and they would not think of a prisoner escaping that way. Yes, it might work! Allena could swim and would be even better than a log. How supremely obvious and simple!

"I will be very grateful," she said, and felt tears prickle in her eyes. Just dust, surely? Dust would not cause the strange lump in her throat, though.

Not looking at her, Blood Beak said, "I shall come and visit you in Krasnegar one day."

"If you do, I shall make you welcome and send you away rich."

He did look up then, smiling. "You have taught me to dream impossible dreams, too, Little Princess. That is a bad habit for a goblin! I know really that none of us will return to the taiga, but I should like you to escape and remember me."

She nodded, not trusting herself to speak.

"Slow down a bit," he said. "If we camp near the rear you will have a better chance in the night."

Kadie eased back her game little pony and began whispering a prayer. She had prayed a lot in the last few months. She prayed especially to the God of Rescues, if there was one.

A wonderful hour of anticipation followed.

It ended in disaster. Perhaps she should have prayed a little harder. Perhaps she had prayed to a nonexistent God and summoned the God of Dashed Hopes instead, if there was one. After so many weeks, it seemed very cruel of the Gods to offer this wonderful chance and then snatch it away so soon.

Suddenly there were goblins standing across her path. She rose in the stirrups to see as far as she could across the plain. The horde had come to a halt. By the time she reined in, there were goblins everywhere, standing around panting, shouting questions to and fro. The sun was a red ball in the smoke, not close enough to setting yet to explain this unexpected stop.

She slid from the saddle and stood on her own weary legs. Blood Beak shot her a warning glance—meaning there were too many ears too close for the two of them to talk. She could guess what he was thinking, though. Her hopes of escape had just disappeared again.

· · ·

Blood Beak went in search of the chiefs. His bodyguard went with him, and so of course must Kadie. It took him an hour or so even to find the house, and a lot of arguing thereafter, but he eventually bullied his way into the conference. His guards remained behind, at the bottom of the stairs. He grabbed Kadie's wrist and towed her along as he went running up. That was the first time he had ever touched her. He had a crushing grip.

In the last few months, she had seen many great mansions and even palaces, but almost always they had been already burning, and she had never been allowed to look inside. She had made a very brief trip through Kinvale, but she had been too shocked that day to notice much of it.

This house wasn't as big as Kinvale, just a large country dwelling. It had been very beautiful, but already it stank of goblin and there was mud all over the rich carpets. She caught glimpses of chests left open and drawers tipped out and beds unmade, signs of a panicky departure. In the romances she had read as a child, princesses lived in sumptuous palaces, but she had always imagined something like the castle at Krasnegar, only warmer. This was no palace, and yet it surpassed her wildest fancies. She wanted to stay and admire the furniture and pictures, to touch the draperies, but she was given no chance.

The big upstairs drawing room was full of smelly goblins, naked savages, all standing around arguing at the tops of their voices. Blood Beak, having won entry to the council with lies and threats, had no authority to join in the discussion. He would very likely be thrown out at once if his father saw him. He released Kadie's wrist and left her standing by the door, while he went squirming off in the direction of the windows, which were the reason the chiefs had come indoors at all.

Kadie had a much better idea. She stepped up on a chair, muddy boots and all. Then she could see over the chiefs, and one glance was enough to show her the extent of their problem.

A tributary joined the river just a league or so ahead. There was a small walled town at the junction. More important, legions stood across the path. They were too far off to make out individual soldiers, but the sun shone on their shields and helmets. A glittering fence stretched from river to river—many, many legions. The Impire had reacted at last.

She stepped down to the floor again to be less conspicuous, and struggled to make sense of the guttural dialect as the chiefs argued. The sun was in the goblins' eyes, said some. It would set before battle could be joined, said others. Goblins fought better by moonlight than imps did. The men were tired. In the morning the sun would hamper the legions. The imps were trapped in the fork of the river. So were the goblins, because they could not use their greater speed to outflank their opponents . . . Talk flowed to and fro. No one seemed to be pointing out that Death Bird had strayed into a very bad position. He had a hostile army in front, rivers on both flanks, and a wasteland behind.

A loud crash of splintering chair was the signal for silence. "Am deciding!" the king shouted. "Fight at dawn. Kill imps then!"

There was a brief, halfhearted cheer. Chiefs moved rapidly out of the way as their leader headed for the door. He came face to face with Kadie before she had a chance to take cover. His angular eyes widened in shock at the sight of her and his hand flashed to his sword. The room went silent. Apparently he had forgotten about his hostage.

She had not seen him in many weeks. He looked older, and certainly thinner. The barrel chest was streaked with sweat and dust, there were lines in his face and gray in his rope of hair. He was probably doomed now, he and his horde, but he would live on in memory as the worst butcher ever to humiliate the Impire.

"Princess!" He grinned his big teeth at her, looking her over shrewdly. "Are not hot in so many clothes?"

Of course she was hot, because she always wore a coat to hide her sword. He had remembered that, too.

She bowed and tried not to look frightened. "No, Sire."

"Where son?" Death Bird looked around. Wearing a surly expression, Blood Beak emerged from the onlookers.

His father regarded him mockingly. "Are growing! Ready for wedding soon?"

Blood Beak hesitated, glanced at Kadie, and then puffed out his chest—which was quite large enough already. "Soon. Thinks carries baby."

Kadie felt herself blush scarlet at this outright falsehood. The spectators guffawed, the king pursed his big lips. He did not look very convinced. "Told you not to lie with her!"

The boy shrugged. "Begged me to. Get no sleep else."

There was more cruel laughter, but Kadie minded less now. She stared at the carpet, knowing that in some strange way Blood Beak was trying to protect her.

Death Bird thumped his son on the shoulder. "Guard woman well tonight. Camp at my fire." He glanced at Kadie again, eyeing that suspicious coat. "Don't get fancy ideas, Princess," he said in impish. "The legions won't save you." He leered disbelievingly. "And look after my grandson."

Then he strode forward and out the door.

Kadie relaxed with a gasp and a weak shiver. Blood Beak summoned her with a nod, and she followed him as he went after his father, leaving the chiefs to their jabbering talk.

There would be no escape tonight.

2

"THIS IS DULL!" JALON COMPLAINED. "DULL, DULL, DULL! YOU never used to travel like this. Where is the flying spume, the bare poles burning cold fire in the tempest? I want a lee shore, waves higher than the crosstrees, and all hands to the pumps!"

"Take my share, too," Rap said, easing the wheel around. "Rock this tub and she'd fall apart." The leaky, bedraggled old coaster had probably not ridden out a storm in fifty years. At the slightest hint of one, she would slip away into safe haven.

The sea was a lazy silver mirror, whose only claim to excitement was the crimson wound burned across it by the setting sun. A sickly wind barely gave *Dreadnaught* steerage way, let alone blew spume, but Rap was enjoying the challenge of keeping the sails filled. He was standing first watch while the minstrel kept him company, sprawled on the dry boards of the deck nearby, leaning on his elbows.

"Besides, it beats scrambling around in jungle."

"You have a point there." Jalon rolled his head around to grin up at Rap with dreamy eyes of cornflower blue. "But then I wouldn't! Darad is stupid enough to *like* doing that sort of thing. He finds hardship a challenge to his manhood. The rest of us are more than happy to humor him."

Jalon was the only one of the sequential five whose company Rap honestly enjoyed. He was short for a jotunn, but otherwise his appearance was unremarkable. With his silver-gold hair and fair skin—already peeling for the second time—he seemed barely more than a youth. His behavior, though, was anything but typical. Artist, minstrel, dreamer, hopelessly impractical, and unfailingly good-humored, he was a most unlikely jotunn.

But then Rap was a most unlikely faun, and for the same reason. Jalon was a hybrid, also, and the elvish blood in his veins might explain why he seemed no older than he had on the day Rap first met him, twenty years ago. He must have added about four years to his tally in those twenty, but not a single day showed.

It was enough to make a man nostalgic.

So was the low shadow to the north, for that was the island of Kith, which also brought back memories of youth and adventure, and another quest, which at times had seemed just as hopeless as this one.

Assorted anthropophagi sat around the deck, taking life easy. The multicolored tattoos on their walnut skins shone like flowers in beds of rich loam. The trolls were happier out of the sun, off by themselves. If a man opened any door on *Dreadnaught*, he would find a skulking troll. Larder or galley, cabin or pump room or chain locker—it made no difference, a toothy monster would be huddled in there, grinning sheepishly at being discovered. They were quite willing to be sociable if asked; they just could not keep it up for very long at a stretch.

"You're brooding," Jalon said softly.

Rap concentrated his attention on the sails. "No."

"You're brooding," Jalon said again, in exactly the same tone. "Tell me what's wrong, sonny."

"*Sonny!* What way is that to address a reigning monarch?"

"I am a hundred and ten years older than you are." The minstrel flashed a grin that made him seem barely more than adolescent. "Now, tell Grandpapa what's the matter. Not the Imperial Navy, obviously."

"No." There were no other sails in sight. *Dreadnaught*'s crew might not even have reported the theft of their ship yet. They had been set ashore with a plentiful supply of gold. Being jotnar, they probably would not sober up until all the gold was gone.

"Information," Rap said. "I wish I knew how Shandie and Raspnex are doing."

"They're doing fine," Jalon said, rolling over on his back and putting his hands behind his head.

"You don't know that!"

"Grunth says so. She says Zinixo must know roughly where her lair was. He's had the Covin hunting her, off and on, but not much lately. If either of your playmates had been captured, the dwarf would have been after Grunth, too, like flies round carrion."

Rap had heard that theory before and found it unconvincing. Losing his magic scrolls was about the stupidest thing he'd ever done in his life.

He was worried sick about Inos and the kids, back in Krasnegar. Had Shandie reached them and warned them? Had Inos had the sense to go into hiding at Kinvale? But he wouldn't discuss his family with Jalon.

"Sysanasso, then. Tomorrow or the next day, we'll make landfall. There must be sorcery among the fauns. In fact I know there is. My mother came from Sysanasso."

If anyone was going to be set ashore as a recruiting agent in Sysanasso, it would have to be Rap himself, and he did not want that. Although he was by far the weakest of the many sorcerers aboard, he was the only one who could keep the peace between the two ill-assorted groups. So far both had deferred to him. That situation might not last, but he was sure they would fall out very quickly if he departed. He also hated the thought of being left behind while the others pursued the war without him. It was *his* war, Evil take it! To ignore Sysanasso as a source of recruits was unthinkable; to send a troll or anthropophagus in his place was even more so.

"You need an agent in Sysanasso?" Jalon muttered sleepily. "Thinking about Sagorn, maybe?"

"Would he?"

"No. Beneath his dignity. Also boring."

Which is what Rap had already concluded. Indeed, he had discarded all of the sequential gang for the job. Jalon was unassertive and totally impractical. Andor would be effective if he chose to be, but could not be trusted. Thinal was even less reliable than his brother, and would not be interested. Darad was willing, but a moron. The gang of five had a man for almost any situation except that one.

A troll clambered out of the hatch and peered around, his huge form swathed in a length of sail to keep the sun off. Even jotunn garments would not fit trolls.

On the face of it, trolls and anthropophagi were the most improbable crew any ship could ever have. As almost everyone aboard was a sorcerer, *Dreadnaught* had no problem. A mere adept could learn any skill in minutes, and sorcerers did not even need lessons.

"Forget Sysanasso," Jalon said. "Ever been there?"

"Once, very briefly."

"You're looking for mundane authorities, you said. Fauns don't have any."

"They do so!" Rap retorted. "They have principalities galore. They even have some republics."

"But nobody pays any attention to any of them. Fauns do whatever they please. I know—I've been there. Well, Andor has. You'll just be shoveling water in Sysanasso."

Two more trolls emerged from belowdecks. The sun had not set yet. Then two more . . . what was disturbing them?

Rap wondered briefly about that, and then went back to considering Jalon's suggestion. Forget Sysanasso? It was certainly a tempting thought. But then where did he take his crazy army? Even if Lith'rian remained at large somewhere in Ilrane, the warlock of the south would not appreciate an invasion by a force of assorted trolls and cannibals. Rap had "Thume" tattooed on his arm, but that idea seemed very improbable in the cold light of day . . . the warm light of a summer evening, then. Thume was a dream. He could forget about Thume.

He might grow old in this war and achieve nothing.

Tik Tok came wandering aft, his bone kilt clinking. He was frowning. With his tattoos, the bone in his nose, and his pointed teeth, his frowns were enough to curdle arteries.

"Something amiss?" Rap asked.

The savage shrugged his brown shoulders and wiggled the bone in his nose. "Just a vague feeling of reprehension. You feel nothing wrong?"

Rap checked the ambience. "No."

"Others feel it, also, a sense of forebearing." He leaned on the rail and scowled northward.

Jalon sat up and yawned. "Ready to teach me more drumming?" He was fascinated by the anthropophagi's complex rhythms. They were unlike anything else in Pandemia, he claimed. He probably knew more about the music of Pandemia than anyone else did, so no one argued.

Tik Tok turned to look him over thoughtfully, and Rap laughed.

"He'd rather teach you cooking—the inside story."

The deck was becoming crowded now. Almost everyone aboard was in sight, and most of them were staring to the northeast. Rap's skin prickled. Again he sniffed the ambience. He was the least powerful sorcerer of them all. He ought to be the last to understand. But perhaps that brooding Jalon had detected in him had been a premonition?

There was something! He sniffed again—peered, listened, whatever . . . Something faint but tantalizingly familiar?

A sudden ripple in the mainsail brought his attention back to his duties. He spun the wheel. Then a bestial howl from Thrugg distracted him.

"Dragons!" Grunth roared from the bow. "The dragons are rising!"

Jalon, the only mundane aboard, scrambled to his feet and stared at the horizon, but of course there was nothing to be seen. Rap found himself clenching hands on the spokes and drawing deep breaths, fighting horror. Yes! Now he recognized that sinister, alien flavor, the occult spoor of dragons. He had almost been charred by a dragon once.

All over the ship, troll and anthropophagus stared at one another in dismay.

"South?" Jalon demanded, scowling. "Is Lith'rian starting your war, King Rap?"

"Can't say. But the witch is right. The dragons are rising."

Rap doubted Lith'rian was responsible—not unless he was cornered and desperate. For him to raise the dragons against the Covin would be suicide. He would reveal his own location and find the worms turned on him by the greater power. Far more likely, Zinixo had preempted South's prerogative and was stealing the dragons for some purpose of his own.

The usurper already controlled the world. Why did he need dragons?

3

THE WESTWARD ROLL OF NIGHT ACROSS PANDEMIA HAD already veiled Hub in darkness. The city was still under siege by its own people, with refugees filling every temple, huddling under every bridge and gateway. Starvation and pestilence were taking a grim toll, and the summer had barely started. The XXth Legion had been pulled back into the capital in a vain attempt to keep order, but the food riots continued to spread. Here and there burning buildings fountained sparks to the black sky.

Light still blazed in the great houses of the rich. The aristocracy knew where safety lay, and this year would not flee the summer heat of the capital for the comfort of country dwellings. They grumbled about the price of food and the expense of maintaining private armies to protect them, but they thrived.

Music drifted out from the high windows of the Ishipole mansion. A mere war would not deter the old senator from celebrating her birthday with one of her sumptuous balls. Official mourning for Emshandar had not yet ended, but Ishipole was a law unto herself. She had brazenly invited everyone of consequence and they had all come, starved for their accustomed gaiety. The imperor had promised to attend, thus putting a stamp of propriety on the occasion and guaranteeing that it would be an uproarious success.

Lord Umpily had never been much of a dancer. He spent most of the evening near the buffet, sampling every dish in the celebrated Ishipole cuisine and gossiping to his heart's content. The talk was mostly inconsequential scandal—pillage and rape were indecorous topics for social conversation—yet he could sense the brittle nerves under the paint and glitter. Almost every man he spoke to would put a small feeler eventually— had he heard any reliable news? Always he would sigh quietly and confess that he had not. The rumors told of such widespread destruction that no one could believe them any more.

Chandeliers glittered, orchestras serenaded, and death was denied. Outside, the wretched thousands huddled. Somewhere in Pithmot, the goblin horde continued its unspeakable rampage.

Umpily completed a mild verbal sparring match with elderly Marquise Affaladi, who was accompanied this evening by yet another in her ongoing collection of stalwart Hussars, this one even younger and larger than most of his many predecessors. He did not seem capable of speaking in complete sentences, but that would not be a necessary part of his duties.

Umpily headed back to the buffet in search of another taste of the peppered eels, or possibly the sumptuous lark tongue pâté, or—

"My lord?"

He stopped, aghast. She was incredibly beautiful, a vision in nacreous silk and a blizzard of diamonds. Her daringly low gown, her gems, her coiffure . . . She outdid every woman he had seen in the hall. Her face and figure would move mountains.

He had heard no announcement, no anthem—but the visit was unofficial, of course. He doubled over in the deepest bow he could manage. "Your Majesty!"

Eshiala laughed gaily as she bobbed her head in acknowledgement. "It has been a long time, my lord!"

"Er . . ." Suddenly he was speechless. When had he last seen the impress—the *genuine* impress?

"Taken any interesting boat trips recently, Umpy?"

Umpily said, *"Awrk!"* He felt his face blossom as red as any beetroot ever grown. Oh, what a fool he had been to be so deceived by the faun and the evil warlock!

The impress laughed again at his anguish. She seized his hand. "Come! Shandie is blathering to a lot of stuffy soldiers and senators. Let's you and me dance!"

He had not danced in years. He must not refuse an imperial command. Gibbering and sweating in panic, he let himself be led to the floor through a forest of astonished faces. He had no idea what music was being played or what the correct steps were. He was going to make an enormous fool of himself in front of the entire court. From the gleam in those lovely eyes, Eshiala knew that. She turned to him expectantly. He glanced wildly around to see what the correct hold was—

The orchestra wailed into dissonance and stopped. The dancers stilled in an angry murmur.

Then the imperor came into view over the crowd, holding up his hands for silence. He must be standing on a table. He was beaming that familiar but so-rare smile that brightened his nondescript features like summer sunshine on a rocky mountain.

"Eminences, Excellencies . . . and all the rest of you!" He laughed, and everyone laughed, bewildered.

Dukes and lesser nobility bristled at the insult. Umpily could hear the insidious thought throbbing through the hall: *His grandfather never used to behave like this!*

"I have some news! Good news!"

A cheer.

"Tonight I met with the wardens . . ."

A tumultuous cheer!

Umpily joined in, although his head was suddenly spinning. Had not the Four been deposed? The Almighty reigned in their place! What was Shandie playing at?

He was still grinning and nodding, waiting for a chance to be heard. Again he raised both arms, and the noise thinned.

"The goblins have been brought to bay at last! . . . Warlock Olybino has given me his word . . . Tomorrow they die! . . ."

Chaos.

The impress was frowning darkly, tapping her fan against her rosebud lips. Umpily felt quite certain what that frown meant—she had not been informed in advance of the announcement and perhaps not of the news itself. As if to confirm his suspicion, she plunged off through the crowd without a word, heading toward the imperor, although he had vanished down into the throng. Voices were rising in the Imperial anthem, but the cheering was drowning it out.

Limp with relief that he had been spared humiliation on the dance floor, Umpily peered around to locate the nearest source of alcohol. Everyone else had had the same idea. He directed his shaky steps back to the buffet instead, thinking that a mouthful of something sweet might settle him a little.

He almost ran down a very large elderly lady in blue satin. He muttered an apology—

Countess Eigaze!

The last time he had seen her she had been wrapped in a warm cloak on a tatty old ferryboat in a snowstorm on Cenmere. Six months ago.

For a moment that seemed to last a whole winter, they stared at each other. She had aged years. Her hair had turned to silver; her face sagged like hot wax.

She inclined her head, chins bulging. She murmured, "Lord Umpily," almost inaudibly.

"My lady!" At last, he bowed, but he never took his eyes off hers.

"Good news, is it not?" she said, a little louder. "About the goblins?"

"Very, my lady."

Still they stared.

The air reeked with unasked questions: How do you feel now about that delusion we shared? What did you tell Shandie when you came to your senses? Do you have bad dreams, much?

The countess shrugged her pillow shoulders. "Gods save the imperor." She almost made it sound like a question.

"Amen!"

She nodded again, grimly, and turned away.

For any guest to leave while the imperor was present would be an act of gross disrespect.

A little air would be permissible in case of faintness, though. Umpily reeled out through the great doors, past the petrified Praetorian Guardsmen standing guard. The big antechamber was just as bright and hot as the hall, although the roar of voices behind him faded a little. He was moving in a daze. His head pounded as if he was being suffocated. Why had Shandie invoked the name of the Four, when he himself had told Umpily that they had been deposed—that they were, and always had been, servants of the Evil?

The men's room!

He pushed through the door. As it closed, the din died away into a subterranean mutter. There was no one else present. He sank down on a chintz sofa and tried to relax, to think, to stop himself shaking. He did not understand!

He could never speak to anyone of the Almighty, but Shandie could. He had done so—he had told the truth to Umpily. Was it possible he also was limited, that he could not tell the world at large?

It still made no sense. If the legions scored a significant triumph in the promised battle, then why in the Gods' names give the credit to the evil Warlock Olybino, warden of the east?

The Almighty ruled now, did he not?

Noise billowed briefly as the door opened at his back.

Still, it was certainly good news that the goblins had been cornered at last. The atrocity stories drifting in from Pithmot . . .

There was a sword in front of his eyes.

With a startled yelp, Umpily cowered back in the sofa. Two Praetorians stood before him. They were large, intimidating young men. They were staring at him with very cold eyes; and one of them had his sword out.

Had his sword at Umpily's throat.

"You will come with us, my lord," the other said. "If you give us any trouble, you will die."

4

PRAETORIAN GUARDSMEN DID NOT DRAW THEIR SWORDS when arresting unarmed fat old men—Umpily knew that from experience. As he tottered to the door, he realized that this was no orthodox arrest. If the imperor wanted him, he had only to ask. If the impress was still intent on that dance, she might just possibly send a guardsman instead of a footman, but no sword would be drawn unless he resisted. There was something very far wrong here. He paused, holding the handle. The men were right behind him.

"Who are you?" he demanded in a disgustingly quavery voice, addressing his remarks to the lacquered carvings of the door itself. "Where are you taking me?"

"Someone wants to see you."

"Who—*Oooo!*" Something sharp had just penetrated one of the tighter portions of his apparel. He yanked the door open.

The cheering was still in progress. The guards he had seen earlier were still standing by the entrance to the hall. For a moment he considered shouting to them, but he was hustled across to another door before he found the courage, and through into a pantry. Then it was too late. Another door at the far side brought him to a servants' stair.

"Down," said a voice at his back. He went down, into shadow and then near darkness, hearing the slithery slap of military sandals behind him. His captors were laden with armor, but he knew he could never outrun them, even on the flat. He would break his neck if he tried to do so on a stair. When he could no longer see anything, a heavy hand settled on his shoulder and urged him along.

His captor's night vision seemed to be infinitely better than his. They took him belowground, through deserted cellars, back up a barrel-loading ramp, and out into an alley behind the Ishipole mansion. He expected a coach or even a horse, then, but instead he was hustled across to another, low door and into what seemed to be an unused stable. It had a musty, deserted smell. Uneven cobbles snared his feet. He stumbled through the dark, guided by the iron grip on his shoulder. He thought he sensed solid objects near his path; he felt cobwebs on his face.

The fingers bit tighter. "Stop!"

He stopped. The hand was removed.

He jumped as another voice spoke in front of him, a woman's voice. "Very good," it said. "That's him. Let's give him some light before he shakes himself to pieces."

A lantern flickered into dim life overhead.

He was, as he had guessed, standing in an ancient, abandoned mews. The stalls were piled with litter and many of the partitions had collapsed. The center was still more or less empty, containing only a group of four ladder-backed chairs that looked new and might have come from any kitchen, but the shadows all around were full of mysterious shapes and corners. Anything could be lurking out there. Cobwebs hung like draperies.

The woman was unknown to him, of indeterminate age, wearing a dark cloak and a hat that shadowed her face.

"Be seated, Lord Umpily," she said, and took one of the chairs herself without looking at him.

He sat down quickly. The two guardsmen were already heading back to the door.

"Who are you?" he demanded.

"No one. Be silent."

The door clicked shut. He assumed that its hinges had been well oiled recently. Still the woman did not look at him, sitting as still as a statue. He shivered in the clammy cold, fervently wishing he had made better use of his time in the men's room. He could think of no reason why he should be abducted like this, right under the imperor's nose. He knew no state secrets now. He was comfortably wealthy, but there had been hundreds of much richer people at the ball.

Sudden horror—they had been able to see in the dark! How had the lantern been lit? "Sorcery!" he whispered.

"Be silent!"

So he was silent, thinking shivery thoughts of sorcery. The evil wardens had not been apprehended yet, so far as he knew. The fake Shandie was still at large, and so was the sinister faunish king of Krasnegar. He had assumed that they had fled to distant lands. Could it be that they still lurked around the capital?

Hooves and wheels clattered outside to a halt—just a brougham, from the sound of it. Then the door rattled, and opened. This time it creaked a little. Then it closed.

Two figures advanced very slowly into the muddle of light under the lantern. One of them was the taller of the two fake guardsmen. He was supporting a small man in civilian clothes, who leaned on a cane and shuffled his feet. His head was bent with age, only thin silvery hair showing. His breath rasped with effort. The hand clutching the cane was a bunch of twigs. The woman rose and helped the guardsman lower the old man onto a chair. They remained standing.

Umpily was not sure his legs would support him, so he stayed where he was. This ancient newcomer must be the person who had summoned him. He did not look as if he would live to the end of a long conversation. Yet, old and frail as he was, he commanded the assistance of sorcerers! For a few moments he remained hunched over, panting hard and loud. At last he raised a face eroded by unthinkable age and peered blearily at Umpily.

"Good evening, my lord!" His voice was a breathless croak.

"Good evening, er, sir." Umpily thought his own sounded virile and confident by comparison.

"Forgive my unorthodox invitation." *Wheeze.* "Ah—you do not remember me!"

"No."

The old man chuckled, and the chuckle became a hacking fit of coughing. The woman bent to steady him, seeming alarmed. Eventually he recovered, and wiped his mouth with the back of his hand. He gestured. The guardsman stepped back a pace, and the woman returned to her chair.

"Well, we have met several times. Perhaps this will jog your memory?" The shriveled carcass began to swell. Years fell away like snowflakes. He grew large, and larger yet. His nondescript clothes shimmered into bronze armor, arms and legs bulged with enormous muscle. Silver hair darkened and then vanished under a golden-crested helmet. The ladder-backed chair creaked under the weight of the giant warrior who now inhabited it.

Looking about a hundred years younger, Warlock Olybino leaned back and crossed his legs—and smiled menacingly at Umpily.

"Better?" he boomed.

Umpily's teeth were chattering so hard he could not speak.

The warden glanced across mockingly at the woman and then around at the guardsman, who now seemed a mere weed by comparison. "Considering the trouble he went to in trying to find me, he seems curiously overcome!"

"I cannot break his bonding, Omnipotence," the woman said. "I tried."

"Well then, we shall all have to try together, won't we? Can't leave him laboring under delusions! Ah, there it goes."

Sudden comprehension—stroke of lightning! Umpily doubled over and buried his face in his hands. Oh, what a fool he had been! How obvious it was now!

Nothing broke the silence except the hiss of the lantern hanging from the rafters.

"Well, my lord?" said that sonorous bull voice. "Which one seems like the real imperor now?"

Umpily groaned. "The one on the boat!"

"And who was that popinjay cavorting upstairs awhile ago?"

"Emthoro!"

"Right you are!" The warlock chuckled.

Slowly Umpily forced himself to look up at the mocking smirk on the face of that virile young warrior.

"And which one is the real Olybino?" he asked—and was at once petrified by his own audacity.

The giant scowled menancingly. Then he shrugged his great shoulders. "The one who came in, of course. This place is shielded. There were many shielded places in Hub a few months ago. The Covin is now dismantling those shieldings so it can watch everything that transpires in the city. There are very few sanctuaries left now."

"So you never left the capital?"

Olybino smiled sadly. "I had nowhere to go. I was a Hubban born and bred."

"You got my letters?"

"I heard of them." Again that dangerous scowl. "To have allowed any of them to reach me would have been dangerous."

He gestured again. The guardsman spun around and stalked away; the door clicked shut behind him.

Umpily sneaked a glance at the enigmatic woman, but her face was still curiously masked by shadow. He wondered if she was using sorcery to keep him from seeing her clearly. She might even be someone he knew. This little meeting would be a very deadly conspiracy if the usurper ever learned of it.

Olybino uncrossed his great legs and crossed them the other way. "I am dying."

"Dying, your Omnipotence?"

"You heard." His voice echoed like funeral bells. "I am more than a hundred years old. I had expected another hundred at least, but that is not to be. If I use sorcery or even magic to keep myself alive, I will be detected. Soon there will be no shieldings left." His expression was stony now, revealing nothing.

"I am sorry," Umpily whispered. He had never much cared for the warden of the east with his juvenile soldierly posturings, but he would not wish death on anyone, and this was a particularly cruel death. "Can you not flee from the capital as the others did?"

"I am too frail to travel." The words seemed ludicrous on the lips of that brawny colossus.

"Not even by boat?"

The warlock stared hard at Umpily for a moment, and then shook his head. "Your concern is touching, fat man— unexpected! Nevertheless, I assure you I have considered all options, and I can see no way out. My one resolve is never to fall into the hands of that cave-dwelling runt. I will not give him the satisfaction."

"He is around, then? I have not seen him."

"Oh, he is around! He was in the hall tonight, pulling Emthoro's strings."

Umpily shivered and at the same time felt sweat break out all over him.

Olybino snorted. "Do you not think the prince by himself could have done a better job of playing imperor than that preposterous performance?"

The night was growing stranger all the time. To cross-examine a warlock was an experience utterly beyond belief, but Umpily's curiosity was burning him like a rash and Olybino seemed willing to answer his questions. There was the matter of what was going to happen to Umpily himself after this meeting ended—but that was a concept too terrifying even to think about. He rummaged hastily through all the queries flitting around in his head and found a safer one.

"Why did he mention . . . I mean, why did he have the prince mention—the wardens tonight? If there is to be a great victory—"

"To discredit me!" the warlock growled. His face did not change, for sorcerers could control their appearance as mundanes could not, and yet a timbre of fury rang in his voice. "You skipped a couple of questions, my lord. First you should ask why he has allowed the goblin obscenity to persist so long. Then you ask why he is doing what he is doing to stop it."

"Oh! Well, er . . . why?"

The warrior folded his brawny arms and sighed. "The little monster is insane, you understand. He trusts no one, he fears everything. Even now, he cannot rest. Always he seeks more security, yet if he controlled every sorcerer in Pandemia and every kingdom, he still would not feel safe. So far he has kept his existence secret, yet he longs to be loved and acclaimed." He raised an eyebrow. "You appreciate your own danger, of course?"

"D-d-danger, your Omnipotence?"

"You hadn't realized? One day he may take a notion to destroy everyone who knows about him—including you." The warlock smiled grimly. "Or he may swing to the other extreme and have himself proclaimed a God so that everyone may worship him."

Umpily wiped his forehead. How had he ever become involved in this?

"I expect he is still thinking it over," Olybino said callously. "But he seems to be leaning more to the God solution at the moment. When the goblins and dwarves invaded and destroyed the four legions, he had Emthoro call in reinforcements on an enormous scale. You probably heard the speech yourself?"

"Yes, your Omnipotence."

"I was forced to deprive myself of the pleasure." The warlock's face was calm, but his great fists were clenched, the knuckles showing white. "He deliberately stripped the frontiers of defenses."

"But why? Everyone wondered that!"

"So that the inferior races will be tempted to attack, of course! They have probably begun already. *He* may know. I don't. But if they haven't started, they will soon."

Umpily quaked on his hard wooden chair. "All of them?"

"Enough. The jotnar certainly won't be able to resist the chance. The caliph was planning to attack anyway. The impire will be engulfed in fire and destruction. Understand?"

Oh, Gods! "And Zinixo will come forward to save it?"

The giant warrior beamed. "There! That wasn't so hard to work out, was it?"

No, it wasn't. It was beyond belief, and yet somehow it seemed logical when put in those terms.

"But why did he drag you into that speech tonight, predicting victory over the goblins?"

Olybino pouted. "I'm not sure of the details. I'm not crazy enough to be able to think the way he does, but I am sure he plans to discredit me somehow. Most likely there is not going to be a great victory."

"Not more legions destroyed!" Umpily cried.

"Possibly." A glint of amusement showed in the warlock's coal-dark eyes. "But if we are to debate strategy, then tell me what he plans to do with the dragons."

"Dragons?" Merciful Gods!

"The dragons have risen. All four surviving blazes are in the sky now, heading north."

Dragons? Not for a thousand years had the dragons been used in war. The millennium was going to live up to its reputation. Umpily licked dry lips and said nothing.

"No suggestions, my lord?" the warlock asked mockingly. "Well, let us move to more cheerful tidings. I know you escaped with the real imperor. I have heard rumors that the faun is in the game again. You tried to get in touch with me, and I have a rough idea of what you wanted to tell me. Now I want to hear the details. That was why I arranged this meeting. Speak! No, wait. Would you care for a more comfortable chair?"

Umpily nodded vaguely, striving to rid his mind of thoughts of dragons so he could recall what he needed to say about the new protocol and the imperor's counterrevolution.

"We have all night, my lord," the warlock said cheerfully. He stood up and stretched, his great arms almost reaching to the cobwebbed rafters.

"All night?"

"In the morning we shall learn what the usurper plans to do with his dragons." Something sinister burned in those potent eyes—madness, perhaps. What could be more dangerous than a dying sorcerer? "This is a very historical night, much too exciting for sleep."

In the morning what happened to Umpily? Would Olybino let him go, knowing of his whereabouts? Even if he did, Umpily's loyalty spell to the usurper had been removed. How long until some agent of the Covin noticed, and realized that he had changed sides again?

He was a dead man, too.

Pricking thumbs:
> *By the pricking of my thumbs,*
> *Something evil this way comes.*
>
> SHAKESPEARE, *MACBETH*, IV, i

CHAPTER TEN

POSSESS THE FIELD

1

DARK DID NOT LINGER LONG IN THE NORTHLANDS IN SUMmer. The sun had hardly withdrawn below the horizon before it rose again to deal out another day.

The sea rolled on forever, endlessly green and cold and shiny. A solitary ship rode the billows under a single sail, heading north. Although many others held the same bearing on the same ocean, not a one was in sight. The crew slept, huddled on their benches or on the gratings below, snoring in ragged chorus. A skinny youngster clutched the steering oar firmly, half choked with pride at the honor he had been granted. If he knew that three or four of the sailors were only faking, and keeping a wary eye on him, then he gave no sign. He watched the waves and the horizon and the wheeling white birds, and mused over the lesson in knot-tying that the bosun was going to give him in an hour or so . . .

Dawn came to Guwush, brightening the roofs of Highscarp. Working gnomes grumbled about summer nights and began to yawn. Day people slept on awhile yet in the overpriced, crowded rooms of the Imperor's Head.

The poor and the frugal had chosen less expensive accommodation in the hayloft. They slept on, also, all except one, an aging dwarf. He lay still, but his eyes were wide with horror as he followed the distant trace of dragons.

The sky brightened in Thume, wakening the larks in the meadows and the roosters of the humble farms. Over the densest forest, the light of day was blocked by clouds and falling rain, then branches and leaves, until only a vague brightness seeped through the ruined windows of the Chapel to where the Keeper knelt in prayer at Keef's grave. Alone.

Hastening west and southward, morning came to the bloated refugee camp that was Hub. Unseen by day as by night, the God of Death continued Their work, gathering the souls that fever and hunger had released.

Sleepy nobles bounced in their carriages, heading home from the ball, each one escorted now by mounted guards because of the rabble infesting the capital.

In an unused stable, Lord Umpily snored in a heavy armchair almost as well padded as himself. A sorceress sat nearby, stoically waiting on her master's orders.

Her master paced, pondering what he had learned in the night—pondering also what blow he might best strike against his enemy before he himself was felled. He had never been especially powerful by warden standards, but he was nonetheless a mighty sorcerer. He did not intend to be found unworthy at the end. In his time he had seen enough youngsters die bravely to know how it was done, and there were still a few blank pages left in the history books.

Warriors did not die unnoticed.

Sunlight danced joyously on the icy peaks of the Qoble Range.

Ylo opened his eyes.

He registered ceiling, drapes, blue sky through a chink in the drapes, silence from the crib in the corner . . . a bare leg next to his. He moved very slightly to increase the area of contact with that delicious smooth warmth.

He lingered happily over memories of the previous evening.

What a transformation, he thought proudly. What a wildcat. What a credit to his teaching. A most rewarding pupil.

Big day ahead. Long climb up to the pass. Must pick a good horse. Ought to make an early start, before the stock got too well picked over. He could not hear anyone else stirring yet, though.

He rolled over and cuddled closer.

"Mmmm?" she said.

He licked an ear, and felt a wiggle of pleasure.

"Should be on our way early," he whispered.

"Mmmph!"

He slid a hand around to cup a firm, warm breast. There was no resistance. Quite the reverse, in fact. Just two weeks ago he would have needed an hour to prepare that move.

"Ought to get up," he hissed.

"Maya's not awake yet," a sleepy voice said.

"So?"

"So what are you waiting for?"

Some time later, Ylo drove the phaeton around to the front door. Eshiala was standing there with the bags ready at her feet. He jumped down and went to fetch them.

Her face still seemed flushed, but perhaps that was only happiness. The smile she gave him now was the sort of thing men dreamed of all their lives. No longer would anyone call her the Ice Impress—Spring Queen, perhaps, with all that that implied.

People were coming and going all around, and every man squared his shoulders as he saw Eshiala, but she had eyes only for Ylo. Which was very, very nice.

"The air!" she said. "And those peaks! You know, I've seen pictures, but never real mountains before."

"I arranged them specially for you." He lifted the bags.

"I thought you must have. Careful with that one, it has milk in it."

"Trust me. And if you think these hillocks are cute, wait until we get to the pass." Ylo peered around to locate Maya, who was chasing cats, dogs, and pigeons indiscriminately. Satisfied, he turned with a bag in each hand and almost blundered into a man heading for the door. It was nothing serious. The other stepped aside easily enough, but then . . .

There are two ways of looking at another face.

One of them says: *I know you.*

And when that other face registers shock for just a moment and then goes blank—that means trouble.

Ylo stood and watched as the stranger clattered up the steps and vanished into the inn.

"Those scarlet blossoms . . ." Eshiala said. "Something wrong?"

"No. Nothing."

But there was. Ylo could not recall the stranger, but the stranger had obviously known Ylo. Although he had been wearing civilian clothes, he was the right age to be a soldier.

More than five thousand men in Qoble knew Ylo by sight. Twenty thousand might be a more realistic estimate, although he would expect few to recognize him without his uniform and wolfskin cape. And yet . . . And yet he was tall for an imp; to admit that his face was memorable was not entirely vanity. Men might not like to admit it, but they noticed his looks almost as much as women did. Shandie, now, had been able to disappear in his own office, but people remembered Ylo.

As he loaded the baggage and tied it securely, his fingers moved by themselves. His mind raced along other paths. The stranger had been surprised by the encounter, but that was understandable. The new imperor's personal signifer should be in Hub, at court, not here in the provinces. Perhaps there was nothing sinister about that reaction.

On the other hand, if the Covin had apprehended Ionfeu . . . If the Covin still wanted the baby impress . . .

He should not have come to West Pass. Qoble held many more cities than just Gaaze, where the XIIth was stationed. He should have continued east and crossed by one of the other passes and gone to Angot, or even Boswood.

Well, it was too late now. To change his plans would alarm Eshiala, and he did not want any clouds shadowing that new-found happiness of hers. He gave her a hand up and lifted Maya to her, smiling guilelessly without hearing a word she was saying.

One pass was as good as another, anyway. The army watched them all.

2

THAÏLE HAD RIDDEN THE NIGHT SKY LIKE A SHOOTING STAR among the aurora. At first she went north, and the balefire she had lit at the feet of the Progistes dwindled away into the dark, behind and below, until its tiny worm glow was lost to her.

Leéb, she thought. *Oh, Leéb!* And, *My child!*

I never knew my child.

Briefly, too, she sensed the hateful figure of the Keeper as a shadowy pillar of sorrow standing huge upon the mountains, staring after her.

Soon she crossed the coast of the Morning Sea, slipping easily through the sorcerous walls of Thume. She caught a momentary vision of the ambience of a startled old man, and knew him for the archon who kept watch over those shores. Then that was gone, also. All gone, and she was Outside, soaring just below the stars, heading north.

A coldness closed in upon her. She had left Thume, her birthplace, the land of her people. Down there in the darkness was the sea, the clean, cold sea. She sensed ships as pinpricks and ignored them and the sleeping souls within them, but soon the coast of Guwush was ahead of her and then below. People moved there in the dark, little folk going about their business like ants deep in the soil. They were alien. She felt their strangeness and was chilled by it. Outside! She was out among the demons, and although she knew now that the demons were only people like herself, the child she once had been whimpered its terror within her. She remembered being Quole, dying with her baby under the nails of hungry gnomes a thousand years ago.

So little magic! Here and there she sensed small glimmers, furtive movings, little flames of candle shrouded to hide their light from monsters prowling the dark, but Thume had been full of magic, warm with magic, and Outside seemed stark and cold and mundane. Then there was sea ahead of her again, blue-green northern sea that stretched on to icy, rocky, pitiless lands lit already by the first hard gleams of dawn.

She veered, shying off from day as a doe might shy from a hunters' fire. She headed west, into the heart of night. Far below her went cities, great huddles of people in numbers she could not comprehend. Never had she seen more than thirty or forty people gathered together, and these immense assemblages terrified her. She rose higher, higher, until she felt the stars above her head.

She was not a bird, or a flying woman, merely a thought traversing the night. Only great power could move like that, but she knew her strength was great, for great power brought wisdom, also. She might well rank with the legendary sorcerers of ancient times: Thraine, or Is-an-Ok, or Keef.

People and more people! Her mind reached out and everywhere found people. From Summer Sea to Winter Ocean, people. Where were the forests, the calm pools, the grassy slopes like those she loved in Thume? Overrun, all. Gone these many thousand years! Where could she find sanctuary in a world so busy? Where was peace when the land was all carved up by roads and blighted by cities and brutally disciplined into angular, working fields?

Onward she went, onward, seeking. Seeking she knew not what.

All her life her world has been that safe little cage. Without it, she will do what birds do when they are frightened—fly. Fly and fly. She will fly up and up, and on and on, never daring to come down. And eventually she will exhaust herself and fall helpless from the sky.

Baze had known, then! Or suspected, at least. So had the Keeper. Perhaps it was all written in that book of prophecies. Perhaps there was no sanctuary. Perhaps she was destined to circle back at last, to perch on the twig she had left, obedience returning to the Keeper's hand.

Never! They had slain her love, slain her child, thrust powers upon her that she did not want. Whatever the Gods had in store for the land of Thume, it could not be more cruel than what Thume had done to Thaïle. She would not save them, would not play their evil game.

Would not become what the Keeper was.

Still the land unrolled before her, cloaked in night that could not mask her sorcerous vision. People and more people. She would go on, go on forever and when she came to the western seas, still she would go on, never returning.

And then she sensed an evil. It had been there all along, perhaps, but too strange for her mind to grasp, a discordant shadow upon the ambience. Now it was closer and she could no longer refuse to recognize it. It was inhuman, alien, somehow almost *metallic*. Intelligence without wisdom, desire without pity, a different sort of sorcery.

The dragons are rising. Yea, dragons! That was what that black cloud signified—dragons. She knew dragons. In the Defile she had been slain by a dragon, a thousand years ago. But these were hundreds of dragons, a great blaze questing. She sensed their excitement, their joy in this glimpse of freedom, their remorseless hunger for gold or any lesser metal. She also sensed their anger and resentment as they were herded to another's purpose when they wanted to disperse and plunder the riches below them. Appalled and yet fascinated, she found herself being drawn to the dragons. Who or what had strength to constrain this mighty host?

Suddenly—danger! There was another entity in the night, another power in the ambience. Not inhuman, but more evil, enormous, and consciously evil. Dragons had no pity; they could not comprehend suffering, but this other could. It loomed over the ambience, a flickering beacon of darkness in the very center of the world. This was what drove the dragons, and now it had detected Thaïle. Black tentacles of power reached out for her, querying, groping as a hand might grope in a sack. She sensed two great stony eyes peering around, looking for her—wondering, worried, dangerous eyes.

Unless a hawk catches her first, of course, Baze had said.

There was the hawk! There was the evil that had overthrown the wardens. Now it had caught a glimpse of Thaïle. Not a proper glimpse, perhaps, just a hint. She had creaked a floorboard and the guard had raised his lantern. If the Covin was sure of what she was and where she was, it could snatch her from the sky and make her its own. Even she could not withstand so much massed power.

The Keeper herself could not, or so she had said.

As the tiny songbird might seek to dodge the plunging falcon, Thaïle swooped downward in panicky flight. She made herself small and elusive in ways that words would not describe. She flitted low over the world, seeking to hide her essence behind the great bulk of the Nefer Range—but mere rock would not block those stony eyes. She rushed south over Ilrane, barely taking thought to marvel at the towering crystal skytrees, and there she began to feel success.

It was the dragons that saved her. If the usurper took his full attention away from the dragons, they would scatter and start to ravage and that was evidently not his plan—not yet. Even the massed power of the Covin could barely control so many. Now was not the time to go hunting wisps. Angrily the eyes turned away, the tentacles withdrew.

Saved!

Thaïle stood in a garden. The house beside it was an odd affair of woods and colored stones, alien and impractical, but curiously beautiful. All around it were sleeping flowers and drowsy trees and small ponds of fish. Within slept a man and a woman and two children, golden-haired and golden-skinned. Elves, the gold-haired demons . . . they did not *look* very demonic. Apart from their coloring and their silly little ears, they looked quite like pixies.

There were other houses scattered around in the hills with

people in them. By Thume standards the landscape was crowded, but it was rural compared to any other place she had seen Outside. A skytree towered heavenward very far off, its top glittering in the moonlight. Its base was below the horizon. She called up visions of the books she had browsed through. This was Ilrane, the land of the elves. Could Ilrane be the sanctuary she sought?

"No," the Keeper said at her back. "There is no safety here."

Thaïle whirled and screamed aloud. *"Go away!"*

The familiar tall shadow leaned on its staff and made a cackling noise like a rattle of bones. "You are a pixie. You are a freak! No one will offer shelter to a pixie. Pixies no longer exist, remember?"

"Go away, or I smite you!"

"You will draw the usurper."

"Then I will draw the usurper!" She gathered power . . .

"You have seen him," the Keeper's mocking whisper said. Eyes glinted within her cowl. "You know his evil now. He will bind you, bind you forever. With you to serve him, the last hope dies. All will be his, to destroy."

"But you cannot bind me! Not that way! You have tried everything else, but that last obscenity is barred to you or you would use it. You cannot bind me to do what you will require of me—that which I will never do! Now be gone or I strike!" Thaïle brandished power like a fiery sword and the Keeper faded away.

Now even Ilrane was sullied by memory. Thaïle went also.

This time she was more careful. She was learning, mastering her skills, and she made sure that she remained unobserved. She headed west again, fascinated by the sinister song of dragons.

As the night drew to an end, so did the land. Only Westerwater lay ahead of her, cold and lifeless. Rosy dawn lit the peaks of the Mosweeps, icy ramparts soaring above the downy clouds, and she sank down again, to watch the sun rise and to rest. *Eventually she will exhaust herself and fall helpless from the sky* . . .

She sat on a snowy ledge above a pale abyss, hugging her knees and viewing the world of ice and white crags. It was cold, but it was clean. A sorceress could be quite comfortable where a mundane would freeze solid in seconds. She could see forever—see the dragons still questing northward, see the pillar of evil in the center. Probably she could even see Thume itself over the curve of the world if she tried, although she knew that Keef's mighty sorcery would conceal the inhabitants from her.

Hunger? She made a juicy-sweet mango, and a silver knife to cut it. When she had eaten the pulp, she turned the pit into a diamond as big as a pixie's ear, and tossed it away in the snow. There were only two problems a puissant sorceress could not solve, and the greater of those was death.

She remembered her few months with Leéb and the tears froze upon her cheeks. Keef and Is-an-Ok, Thraine and six or seven others since the world first turned, and now Thaïle—she knew now she could evade the usurper as long as she was careful. Her power was great enough, greater than he would ever look for. She could go anywhere and do anything. But she could not call back Leéb, or her baby. She had nowhere to go and no one to love.

The second problem was loneliness.

The sun shone on all Pandemia.

The world was hers and it was nothing.

3

LORD UMPILY HAD JUST COMPLETED BREAKFAST. THE SUR-roundings were somewhat bizarre—a filthy, cobweb-strewn stable littered with rubbish. Only a sickly gray light trickled through the little grimy windows, but better illumination might have spoiled his appetite. In the middle of this midden he sat at a damask-covered table laden with silver plate. The dishes contained scant remains of turbot, smoked sturgeon, roast venison, and an oyster-and-mussel omelette, but all of the excellent veal kidney pie had gone, and most of the warm, fresh loaf. He sipped at his goblet of porter, dabbed his lips with the crisp serviette, and reluctantly decided that he could eat no more. The surroundings might lack refinement, but he could not recall a more superb repast.

The sorceress was still sitting where she had been when he drifted off to sleep some hours before dawn. For all he knew, she might not have moved all night. Her face was just as indistinct by daylight as it had been under the lantern. Two young men had joined the group and sat now in silence on the ladder-backed chairs. They wore doublet and hose, but Umpily strongly suspected that they were the two fake guardsmen who had abducted him from the ball. They, too, were impossible to make out clearly now. Nobody was speaking, but the three glanced at one another from time to time, and he was sure that they were conversing by sorcery.

"His Omnipotence furnishes an excellent table," he said cheerfully.

No reply. No one even looked at him.

He sighed, wondering where the warlock had gone. The niggling problem with the excellent table was that it was so reminiscent of the hearty last meal traditionally furnished to condemned prisoners of rank just before they were led out to execution.

The door clicked, squeaked, squeaked again, and clicked shut. With a swirl of gray cloak, Warlock Olybino came striding in to join the meeting. He had discarded his gaudy armor and shed much of his size, although his face was still recognizable. He was apparently playing the role of a nondescript, middle-age artisan, but his bearing was much too arrogant. Who would tell him so?

He glanced at the ruins on the breakfast table and shot Umpily a contemptuous glance. "Moderation is not your strong suit, my lord."

"Moderation insults perfection, your Omnipotence." It was an old saying of Ishipole's, but Umpily thought he had used it rather well.

The warlock grunted and turned to his associates. Silence fell, but again a silence marked by glances and small gestures. Something was being discussed—and apparently something important, for Olybino suddenly turned on his heel and strode to the far end of the stable and then back again. In passing he reached out and lifted a rusty old horseshoe from a collection nailed to a pillar.

Then he came to a halt, idly bending and flexing the metal in his hands as if it were rope, shedding a blizzard of rust flakes. "That is how it will be!" he snapped. "No further argument!" He spun around to face the solitary mundane. "The legions are advancing on the goblin horde at Bandor. At least five legions, possibly six. I dared not look too closely. The dragons are almost upon them."

"Upon the legions?"

The warlock nodded grimly. "I suspect that is the plan."

Umpily shuddered. "But why?"

Seeming to apply no great effort, the warlock stretched the iron bar to twice its former length. "Who can plumb the horrors of the dwarf's mind? I may be wrong, of course. A couple of dragons per legion would be ample, yet he has summoned almost every worm there is. Four blazes could waste Hub itself in half an hour. Why so many?"

"I-I-I can't imagine, sir."

"Nor I." Olybino tied the iron bar into a knot. "But I still think the legions are his target. Remember that only sorcerers know anything about him and his Covin. Only they know of his usurpation. So far as the mundane world is concerned, young Emshandar sits the Opal Throne and the Four rule in their palaces. Now comes the millennium. After a thousand years it will be dragons versus legions again! It almost happened at Nefer Moor, remember. That probably gave the poxy runt the idea. How will the Impire see such a battle?"

It was obvious—South against East, warlock versus warlock.

"He seeks to discredit the Four," Olybino confirmed, scowling. "One or two more disasters like that and he can throw off his cloak of secrecy. He will step forward as savior, declaring that he has deposed the evil wardens. Then he will proclaim a new order."

He tossed the knotted metal away and wiped his hands. The former horseshoe clanged on the cobbles.

Umpily hugged himself. "Is there nothing we can do?"

"You, fat man?" The warlock glanced again at the empty dishes. "You might offer to create a famine for him."

"The genuine imperor found me useful in the past!" Why did that sound so sulky?

"True," Olybino admitted. He walked a few more paces, then returned and leaned his knuckles on the table. His eyes glittered. "What you told me last night was impressive. That faun has a flair for strategy! He found the only way to recruit a counterforce—that's assuming that there are enough sorcerers still at large, which I doubt. Nor do I believe that his absurd idealistic new protocol would work in practice, not for a minute. But it makes a good rallying cry. In fact his plan is the only hope, so we may as well try it. The problem is to spread the word to the frees before the Covin hunts them down—which it continues to do."

"I will help in any way I can, sir." Umpily could not bear to remember how he had been deceived by the fake Shandie. Sorcery or not, the humiliation was agony. He felt a burning need to redeem himself. He was ruefully aware that this remorse was out of character, and might fade in a day or two, but at the moment he was capable of anything . . . capable of *considering* anything.

The warlock snorted. "The best thing you can do, I suspect, is to keep scribbling gossip in that diary of yours. Oh—you didn't think I knew about that? Why do you suppose you so often happened to be present when I turned up to talk with Shandie?"

He straightened and turned to his three minions. "Did you know you are in the presence of one of the great historians of Pandemia? Future ages will turn to his records whenever they need to know what the prince imperial had for breakfast on a particular day."

They smiled faintly at the mockery. The warden turned his threatening gaze back to Umpily. Even without his grandiose armor and bogus muscle, Olybino could still intimidate. Indeed, he had more dignity without such ostentatious fakery. Who would tell him that, either?

"It is time to leave. We removed your spell of obedience. Do you want it replaced?"

Umpily shivered and shook his head. His mouth was too dry for speech. Everything he had written in his memoirs for the last four months was rubbish!

"Sure? You will be happier being deceived!"

"I am sure," Umpily croaked.

Olybino chuckled. "Good for you. Very well. We shall put a shielding on you instead. That way you will not be taken in by the Covin's illusions, and you will still have a visible sorcery on you. The Covin will assume it is the loyalty spell. Of course it will not withstand close scrutiny, so you must avoid attracting attention. When the dwarf learns what I have planned . . . Well, just say that very soon the little cave rat is going to be considerably out of sorts. He may go looking for scapegoats on whom he can vent his ill temper."

Horrors! Umpily shivered. "What must I do?"

The warlock showed his teeth in a sinister smile. "Just watch! This is going to be a very interesting morning." He turned to his votaries, his face suddenly grim. "What I must do now must be done quickly. I cannot give you very much time. Be on your way."

Apparently Umpily was already shielded from sorcery, for the three were no longer disguised. The two former guardsmen were recognizable again, although Umpily would not have known them had he not expected to. The tall one he recalled as a younger brother of Count Ipherio. The woman was the charming daughter of Senator Heolclue. She smiled at him; the two men nodded solemnly. They rose. Umpily heaved himself upright, also, with more effort than he had expected. Then the woman sank down on her knees on the cobbles, and the two men copied her.

"The Good be with you, your Omnipotence!" she said, her voice breaking.

"A soldier knows his duty," the warlock snapped.

The count's brother raised clasped hands in appeal. "Master, let us stay and help, I beg you!" His eyes glistened with tears.

"I told you there would be no more argument! Be off with you! Hub is no place for sorcerers now." Olybino turned his back on them all, folding his arms. The three rose to their feet and headed for the door, with Umpily at their heels.

4

"NOW WILL YOU TELL ME WHAT'S GOING ON?" JALON IN-
quired, his tone unusually petulant.

"I'll tell you one thing that been going on." Rap took the
wheel from the minstrel's unresisting fingers. "We have been
straying a mite off course, Helmsman."

Dreadnaught, in fact, was broadside to the weather and drifting aimlessly. Fortunately the wind was light and the waves
were puny. No one would trust Jalon with the helm otherwise.

"I was trying to find a rhyme for 'whelk,' " he explained
without a blush. "Forgot to watch the compass. Now, what is
going on?"

Rap grinned at him in disbelief. "Have you ever wandered
out of the house in the morning without remembering to
dress?"

"Oh, yes!" Jalon looked surprised that his friend would even
ask. "Dozens of times." He was apparently unaware that his
present shirt was inside out. "Now, *please*, what is going on?"

Rap studied the sails for a moment, taking the ship's pulse.
She was coming round slowly, turning her bowsprit to the
dawn. He was coming around slowly himself, recovering from
the extremely weird experience of being in concert with the
other sorcerers. He had spent the last hour as part of a meld
of sorcerers, and being just Rap again required some adjust-
ment.

"We were scouting."

"I thought that was too dangerous?"

"We decided we had to risk it. It's pretty safe if we all work
together. So much power is just about impossible to detect."

Jalon pulled a face. "Sounds backward. So what'yu find?"

"Dragons."

"Still?"

"Still. Just about every dragon in the Reach, we think. He's
got them flying north. It's an incredible display of power, because they keep trying to scatter. He's holding them together,
though. The Covin is. And we've found his target, we think."

"Well?"

"Goblins."

"Goblins?" The minstrel scratched his flaxen mop. "I know I'm no scholar, but I am sure it's a long way to goblin country! . . . isn't it?"

"The goblins are in Pithmot, at a place called Bandor. The Impire's got five legions lined up against them." Rap yawned. He was intensely weary, and sick of the alien taint of dragon in his mind. Goblins almost on Home Water! Yet why should he be surprised by that? Years ago, the Gods had decreed that Death Bird would live to be the scourge of the Impire. They had not mentioned dragons, though.

Jalon's blue eyes were wide. "You're quite sure Zinixo's on the legions' side?"

"That we are about to find out," Rap said grimly. "A few minutes more. We think he's going to destroy the goblins in front of the legions to demonstrate his power and compel respect. That's the best idea anyone's been able to come up with."

The minstrel shuddered convulsively, as if seized by a sudden ague. "That's awful! Can't you do anything?"

"Now, don't you start!" Rap had the ship under way again. He had spent half the night in argument with trolls who wanted to warn everyone in the dragons' path and anthropophagi who wanted to turn the blaze aside. Just a gentle nudge would be enough, they said, because if the worms once scattered not even the Covin would ever regain control. Knowing that, they said, Zinixo would not dare resist a little sideways nudge.

It had taken every trick and skill and argument Rap could muster to win his associates around to his own view—the sensible view, of course.

"We're going to do nothing!" he said. "We could make very little difference, and possibly make things a great deal worse. We might let the blaze scatter over half the Impire. We'd give ourselves away to the usurper, and that would be the end of the game. So we sit on the sidelines and puke, that's all we can do."

Jalon looked aghast at this cold-blooded decision. "You'll let dragons attack people and not even try to rescue them?"

"That's what we decided."

But would it work? Would all those kindly trolls be able to restrain themselves when the burning started? Would the anthropophagi be able to resist the lure of battle—not to mention the occult view of people cooking? And could the Covin continue to control such an enormous blaze once it had tasted metal? There was potential here for one of the greatest disasters of all time.

Rap would find out very shortly.

He smiled at the minstrel's woebegone expression. "Don't sing too many laments for the goblins, buddy mine. They didn't get to South Pithmot by hitching rides in haywains. Our old friend Death Bird has probably left a trail of bloody footprints all the way from Pondague. I'm sure there isn't a soul in that mob of his that doesn't deserve what's coming!"

Easy to say! Dragons were a bad way to die. The Gods had crafted Death Bird's destiny for him and he could not have evaded it. His ultimate end must be ordained, too.

Rap decided a few minutes alone with the wheel were just what he needed to soothe his tattered nerves. "Why don't you go and find me some breakfast, ol' buddy?" he asked. "I'll finish your watch for you."

Jalon nodded, blue eyes deadly serious. "I'll check out the galley. Which would you prefer—spruce bough salad or housemaid's knees?"

Before Rap could answer, a voice roared in his head.

SORCERERS, ATTEND! BEHOLD THE POWER OF THE ALMIGHTY!

"Rap?" Jalon said. "Rap? Rap, what's the matter?"

5

DAWN FOUND KADIE ALREADY AWAKE, GRITTY-EYED AND sour-mouthed, huddled in the corner of a stone wall that enclosed an orchard. She had slept very little, if at all. Goblin preparations for battle included more than the usual amounts of torture. Perhaps the screaming was partly intended to frighten the enemy, although the legions had been far out of earshot when darkness fell. More important, apparently, was the effect on the spectators, because the victims had not been impish prisoners but goblin volunteers, who had directed the horrors being inflicted on themselves. Thus few of the goblins had slept, either, and now they were roused to manic blood-lust, twitching and jabbering with excitement. Many of them bore bloody relics hung on strings around their necks—fingers and even more gruesome tokens, freely donated by their original owners.

There had been no opportunity for escape, and she could not hope for any now.

The orchard was to be the command post and was already full of goblins. Several of the trees had been lopped off and a platform built upon them to provide a lookout. Death Bird had yielded to his son's hysterical pleading and agreed that he might join in the assault instead of being held in the rear. The king himself was going to lead the first charge. To Kadie it all seemed very much like a suicidal last stand.

Death Bird had detailed a half-dozen men to guard her. They stood around her, sulking mightily, and glaring at her from their hideously angular eyes. They felt slighted, obviously, and she was convinced that they would cut her throat as soon as the battle began, so that they could go and join in. The one thing no goblin wanted was the shame of being taken prisoner.

She had eaten nothing the previous evening. Allena the Mare had disappeared, and had almost certainly provided the skimpy provisions she had seen handed around. Somehow Kadie resented that more than almost anything. How could they be so cruel?

Then Blood Beak came striding through the trees. He had his bow already strung in his hand, sword and quiver slung on his shoulders. A shapeless piece of raw flesh dangled in the center of his bare chest; it had dribbled blood all over him.

"Is almost time!" He bared his big teeth at her.

She cowered smaller, feeling the stones of the wall cold through her cloak. "Good-bye, then." She still had her magic rapier.

"Come! Will watch from lookout."

He was trembling with excitement. He would drag her there

if she refused. Reluctantly she rose. The surly guards closed in around her, and they all headed off through the trees.

There was no proper ladder, only a log with a few stumps of branches still attached. She clambered up, awkward in her long cloak and anxious not to trip over her sword, following Blood Beak. The uneven nest on top was already packed with chiefs, creaking under their weight. She found a place to sit, aware that her guards could see her and were waiting underneath.

The sky was blue already, with a burning wound in the northeast showing where the sun was about to rise in molten gold. A lark sang its heart out far overhead, and lesser song-sters whistled and chirruped in the trees. She had never heard birdsong like that in Krasnegar. It was a beautiful day to die.

"Are coming!" a man hidden from her proclaimed. She recognized the king's voice. The legions did seem closer, a wall of men and bronze, advancing slowly.

If I am to be rescued, then now is the moment, she thought, but her childish ideas of rescues seemed very foolish now. She was not going to be rescued. She was going to be killed by the goblins long before the imps arrived. As soon as Death Bird left, probably. Her parents would never know what had happened to her. She would never know what had happened to them, or Gath, either. If Gath was here, he could tell her what was going to happen. Of course she was glad Gath was not here—but it would be nice to have someone.

An edge of burning bronze broke over the horizon like a trumpet call. There was not a cloud in the sky, not even smoke. She shivered with cold and fear and lack of sleep. Still the birds sang. Death was a long sleep, but she wished she could have lived longer. She had not had time to collect very much good for the Gods to find when they weighed her soul. *"Nothing here at all,"* They would say . . .

A pair of bare legs came into view, then Blood Beak knelt down on the adjacent log, balancing precariously. He leered at her, his eyes full of madness.

"Kill many, many imps!" He had to raise his voice over the raucous babbling of the chiefs behind him. Their bragging and boasting were just bluster to hide nervousness.

"You're outnumbered," she said. She was not sure, but it seemed likely, and his scowl confirmed it.

"No matter numbers! Better men. Better killers."

She sighed. "Good luck. At times I almost came to like you, Blood Beak."

His eyes flashed within their tattoos. "Tonight will bed you!"

"Tonight will bury you."

She turned away and blinked at the glare. The sun was above the skyline now. To the north the Imperial Army glittered. If she watched carefully, she could make out its creeping advance, a fiery tide slowly engulfing cottages, copses, walls, coming on remorselessly like a breaker entering Wide Bay at Krasnegar.

Off to one side lay the river. It was not far away—a few minutes' ride on a good horse—and she would be safe if she could only somehow move herself to that far bank. She noticed then that the far bank was already crowded. A multitude of imps had come to watch the battle. They blackened every tree, every wall, every vantage point. Ghouls!

A sudden silence alerted her. The chatter around her had died away, although the murmur of the waiting army beneath was still rumbling like the sea. Men were turning around, moving cautiously on the unsteady footing. Everyone was staring south, and up. Kadie scrambled up to her knees, and took a firm grip on a stub of branch. A cloud? Birds?

Why should everyone be staring at birds? Had they never seen a flock of gulls before? Then she heard another sound, a very low note, surf far off. The birds were approaching steadily, not wheeling around as gulls did. They were moving awfully slowly, so they must be awfully high. Then how could she see them? And why did they glitter like that?

"Dragons!" someone said in a whisper. It might have been Death Bird himself.

Nonsense! She turned for a glance at the legions. They were almost close enough to make out individual men now, and they had stopped coming. The cavalry had drawn out in front, and the horses seemed to be giving a lot of trouble. She checked the spectators across the river, who were closer. No, they weren't! They were in full flight. The trees were bare.

"Dragons!" The mutters grew louder. The horde below the platform had noticed, also, and its mutter had stilled. The lark had fallen silent. There was only that sinister low rumble from the sky.

Yes, dragons! Oh, Gods be merciful! So the river would not offer safe refuge at all, and the spectators would die, also. Dragons rarely took out less than a county, even when there were only one or two of them.

"Metal," a voice nearby said, uncertainly. "Must throw away metal." Nobody answered. Nobody moved. How could a man throw away his weapons when an enemy army was almost within range?

The flock was closer now, the shivery deep note recognizable as the beat of innumerable huge wings, all blended into one like the sound of raindrops becoming the single roar of a storm. Kadie's heart drummed painfully in her chest. Dragons! The stories she had heard and all the books she had read had rarely ever mentioned more than one dragon, two at the most, and there must be hundreds up there. They were almost directly overhead now, a spray of glittering sparks. Like diamonds in sunlight—red and blue and white. *Blaze,* she remembered. Not a *flock* of dragons, a *blaze* of dragons. She had thought that dragons were almost extinct. She had never guessed there could still be so many left in the world.

Her neck was growing sore with staring straight up. She glanced at the river, and the far bank was completely deserted now. But the chiefs beside her were beginning to mutter again, making unbelieving sounds of hope. The dragons were passing overhead, high as clouds, but not changing their flight. They were going to fly on, not stop to attack, fly right over the goblin horde—to where?

Then there was change. The blaze seemed to slow its advance, seemed to grow brighter. *They were coming!*

A torrent of rainbow light poured down. Like a shower of jewels, the blaze fell from the sky. It was so beautiful to watch that she had no time for fear. Nobody had seen this in hundreds of years, a blaze of dragons stooping! She could make out individuals now, big ones, small ones. The big ones were in the lead, glittering monsters with outspread wings, and the lesser dragons followed like a shower of glittering dust. Some of them must be huge, bigger than any ship she had ever seen, big as houses. Still they fell, still they grew larger, spiraling down from the sky. Almost she thought she could feel heat from them, even at this distance. They were spreading out in a vee, the foremost heading for the Imperial center, the laggards aiming for the flanks.

And they were not stooping on the goblins—they were heading for the Imperial legions. The dragons had come to rescue the goblins!

She scrambled to her feet, wobbling on the log, heedless of the risk of falling. All around her the goblins' voices were growing louder in a steady growl of astonishment that seemed to contain no words and grew rapidly into a roar of excitement. The dragons were attacking the legions!

"Are saved!" Blood Beak screamed. "See imps run!"

The wall of bronze had broken. Maddened horses wheeled everywhere in wild disorder and foot soldiers scattered like chaff. Some were even running toward the goblins.

The lead worms impacted the center of the line. Dust and smoke billowed out from the ground as the great wings slowed their fall. Flame erupted from grass and trees. More and more dragons followed, two showers now, until a great sheet of flame engulfed the whole Imperial Army; wind roared and smoke billowed. Still more dragons descended into the holocaust. Faint screaming told of death agonies as men were burned or eaten.

Refugees came fleeing out of the smoke, racing for the goblin horde, and dragons flashed in pursuit, worms of fire streaking over the ground faster than racehorses. The baby latecomers came straight down on some of the fugitives. Kadie knew she was screaming, and could not hear herself over the deafening cheers of the goblins. She watched men being run down, flattened, engulfed. She saw stony dragon jaws seize them as dogs would seize rats, lifting them high to gulp them down. Usually they exploded in clouds of bloody steam before they were even swallowed. Terrified men fled across the smoking meadows, being chased by dragons of all sizes—some longer than long-ships, others no bigger than ponies. The little ones glowed a dull red, but the giants had a blue-white glare that hurt the eyes.

Yet there seemed to be an invisible fence halfway between the opposing armies. Dragons that had caught their prey wheeled around to return to the flaming center, ignoring the feast of goblin swords beyond. A very few legionaries man-aged to reach that occult border and cross into safety. Their pursuers turned back as if forbidden to come farther. The fu-gitives continued to run until goblin arrows cut them down.

The legions had disappeared, houses and trees had vanished, and there was nothing left to burn. Air shimmered above a fiery welter of dragons where the Imperial Army had stood. In the farther distance, the little town was a roaring inferno, already almost consumed. Whoever had sent these monsters was on the goblins' side, and the goblins were screaming themselves hoarse with excitement as they watched.

There was nothing left. Now what?

Now withdrawal. A white-hot dragon as big as a temple thundered over the ground with wings beating up clouds of flying ash. It launched itself into the air, heading straight for the goblins. The cheering stopped. Others followed it. Shivers of terror ran through the watchers, but they had no time to run before it became obvious that there would be no attack. The lead monster continued its painful climb, fighting its way up the sky. It passed over the goblins too high for a bow shot, had anyone been crazy enough to try, but even at that height, blasts of scorching air beat down from its wings. One after another, the rest of the blaze followed it. The charred and empty land they left glowed faintly red.

This was wrong! Something Kadie could recall reading long ago had said that once dragons had tasted metal they would ravage the countryside for days afterward. Perhaps the book had been mistaken, because all dragon lore must be very old, or perhaps someone held these particular worms under very tight control.

Still gaining height, the monsters streamed southward. The

heat of their passing was like a potter's kiln or the face of the sun. Far below them, sweating goblins were cheering again. Already the lead monsters were almost lost to sight in the far, high distance.

Then the cheering faltered. The smaller dragons were obviously more nimble in the air, and one last youngster broke out of formation. As if sensing the banquet of swords and arrowheads waiting below, it came spiraling down—warily, like a puppy approaching a strange cat. Goblins in its path screamed and fled. It was little bigger than a sheep, its scales glowing dull maroon and dirty orange, the colors of a smith's forge, but even one baby dragon could scatter an army. It sank below treetop height, wings thundering as it tried to hover, snaky neck twisting around, jeweled eyes gleaming this way and that. It seemed puzzled, or perhaps it had arrived too late for the feast and been cheated of its share and was still hungry. The meadow below caught fire, smoke streamed out in the blast. Then the monster changed its mind, or heard a call. It flapped harder, gained height again, and streaked off in pursuit of its fiery relations.

Cheering broke out once more.

The ruins of the town still burned, but of the Imperial Army nothing remained at all on the smoking black wasteland where the blaze had ravaged.

Death Bird began making a speech, screaming gutturally to his horde and waving his arms. The cheering kept drowning him out. The chiefs were embracing one another, almost dancing, making the platform rock and creak alarmingly. Kadie sat down and straddled the log she had been standing on. She felt sick. She was still alive. Thousands of men had been charred to nothing before her eyes and she was still alive.

Blood Beak knelt to speak to her, teeth showing in a ferocious mad grin. "Can hear?" he said. "Are going home! Sorcery on our side! Wardens help! Going back to taiga!"

"It's a long way to the taiga yet."

He leered. "Marry you tonight! Waited too long."

She turned away. He grabbed her chin and twisted her head around, thrusting his head so close to hers that she could see every black dot in his tattoos and the wispy hairs around his mouth and even the shiny drops of sweat on his forehead. "Will have you tonight!" he said furiously. "No magic sword tonight! Will tame Krasnegar girl tonight!"

"No, you won't."

His glee made his lips curl back, revealing his tusks. "Good, good! Enjoy struggle!'

"You're leaving," Kadie said. She felt quite calm, almost sad. It was all over. "You're leaving. You have to leave. There's no food here. You must find a way across that river, to somewhere you can loot, right? And I can't come. I have no horse now."

His face darkened, confirming what she had suspected about poor Allena. The horde would start to move as soon as the king had finished his speech. She could not follow.

"Run!" Blood Beak said menacingly.

"Don't be ridiculous."

"Will have men carry you."

Breaking free of his grip, she tossed her head angrily. "That's pretty stupid, too, isn't it? What will you offer them? Do you plan to let them join in the wedding celebration?"

He flushed olive, furious. Obviously he could see no solution, either. "Then do it now and leave you!"

Which is what she had been expecting him to say. The goblins were saved, but Kadie was not. Fear was a sick throbbing in her stomach.

Death Bird had finished his oration. The platform rocked and bounced as the chiefs scrambled down to the ground. Blood Beak jumped up to intercept his father, doubtless planning to explain the Kadie problem.

He never even began. Something hid the sun. Men screamed. She looked up in time to see an enormous blackness in the air above her. She recoiled in amazement and lost her grip and . . .

6

"IT'S THE LEGIONS!" RAP SOBBED. "HE'S SET THEM ON THE legions! Oh, Gods, Gods!"

Pain and terror flooded the ambience in lurid color, burning nerves, crushing senses. A ship full of sorcerers, *Dreadnaught* rang like a bell. Anthropophagi had become screaming mad-men. Trolls howled like dogs.

"The legions?" Jalon grabbed the wheel Rap had released. "Why would he do that?"

But Rap could spare no thought for the mundane minstrel. He stumbled to his knees with the effort of wrestling, reason-ing, shouting in the ambience, struggling to control his pitiful little army before it rushed into futile rescue. If just one sor-cerer broke away and was captured in consequence, then all would be betrayed. Waves of maddening pain poured out from Bandor Field. Five legions! Five times five thousand deaths.

Why? Just to demonstrate the Covin's power for the benefit of the sorcerers of Pandemia?

"You all right, Rap?" Jalon asked, kneeling down beside him and laying a cool hand on his sweaty brow. Rap unrolled. He was conscious of a bitten tongue, and the hard planks of the deck under his back, still cold from the night. He stared up at the concerned jotunn face above him, the blue eyes an exact match for the early-morning sky behind, so that a fanciful man might assume the minstrel had two holes through his head and the sky was smiling through . . .

"Yes," he mumbled. "Yes, I'm all right."

The battle was over, the suffering had ended. No one on *Dreadnaught* had broken ranks.

"It's done?" the minstrel asked, helping him sit up.

"It's done. The legions are dead. The worms are heading home." Every muscle shivered independently.

Five times five thousand men . . . for what? But at least the Covin had held the blaze together and prevented widespread disaster. The power required for that was appalling—which was why it had been done, of course.

SORCERERS, YOU HAVE SEEN! NOW WATCH AGAIN THAT HIS STRENGTH BE MADE KNOWN TO YOU!

"Rap? Rap, now what's happening? Tell me!"

Rap had reached his knees. He sank back now on his heels. No more! Please no more!

Thrugg answered for him, in a roar that filled the ship from stern to bowsprit. "The goblins! He's going to kill the goblins!"

Rap thought then of Death Bird, who had been Little Chicken—a very old friend and yet never quite a friend. They had adventured together, almost died together, almost killed each other . . . Long ago.

However Death Bird had led his horde to Bandor, he had made history and probably very bloody history. He was only a savage, born of savages, reared by savages, and yet he had hammered and quenched and forged until he wrought the independent savage bands of the taiga into a nation and a fighting force capable of humiliating the Impire. Had any invader ever done as much?

The Gods had thrust greatness upon him.

And Rap had helped, obedient to the Gods' will for once. Was the destiny ended now, the adventure over? Remembering their last meeting, at the Timber Meet, he saw how like old men they had become, trading stories of their respective children. Death Bird had bragged about a son who had slain a bear. Was the boy there at Bandor dying with his father, or had he remained behind in the taiga to continue the dynasty? Rap would never know.

Good-bye, Death Bird. Tell the Gods that what They find in your soul is what They decreed Themselves.

7

KADIE WAS LYING IN THE GRASS, HURTING. SHE VAGUELY remembered working out that she had fallen, but not the actual fall nor when exactly she'd worked it out, either. Why did everything have to be so fuzzy? Had she been there a long time, or only a few seconds?

There was a terrible amount of noise everywhere: crashing sounds, men screaming, and alien shrieks that certainly came from nothing human. There was something wrong with her eyes, so she didn't have to believe that the branches overhead were really, truly rocking against the sky like that. She wanted it all to stop so she could rest.

Then someone died quite close. At least it sounded like someone dying—a terrible scream, then a gurgling screech, and a thump. More thumps. Yes, that definitely sounded like someone dying.

She lifted her head and saw two black birds as big as horses. They had their beaks in two men, and were battering them against two trees. She rubbed her eyes and looked again. Now there was only one bird and one dead man. That was better . . .

She was on her feet, reeling in a dark haze of giddiness. Another man was slashing with a sword at another bird. It stood higher than he did, and it was jabbing with its beak, snapping at him, driving him backward. She leaned against a trunk and tried to keep her legs from folding up under her like razors. She was in the middle of a battle. There were goblins everywhere and giant black birds everywhere, and half the time she was seeing two of everything.

She watched a burly goblin swing his sword double-handed against a bird's neck. It bounced off. The bird closed its beak on his head, lifted him bodily, and shook him. Then it stopped shaking, but his body continued to swing as if his neck was now made of rope. The bird dropped him and planted a foot on him. Then it pulled his head off.

Kadie staggered under the platform and found another trunk to lean on. There were a dozen men sheltering under there already, and birds were trying to come in at them on the far side.

They were ravens, enormous ravens.

She laughed a little. Raven Totem. Death Bird. Blood Beak. Giant ravens! Obviously the wardens were playing jokes, and she was sure she would see how funny it was if her head would just stay still a minute. The goblins had eaten her horse. Allena the Fare?

Dragons belonged to the warlock of the south, Mamma had said, and the legions belonged to the warlock of the east. No one must use sorcery against the legions, but today South had sent his dragons against them, so now East had sent these birds against the goblins, tit for tat. Quite obvious. Warlock Rasp-nex had said that the wardens had been deposed, but he must have made a mistake.

All around her ravens were feeding, or chasing men through the trees, smashing branches and even trunks as if trees were weeds. She peered up, between the logs of the platform. The sky was dark with the monsters, still coming from somewhere. Over the low wall that enclosed the orchard, she could see them settling like starlings on the main host of goblins. Thou-sands and thousands of them—jet-black feathers, black beaks, black legs, bright golden eyes glittering. Their shrieks were the cries of ravens magnified a hundredfold. Arrows bounced off them, swords bounced off them.

There were bodies on the platform, one still dribbling blood.

"Kadie?!" A hand grabbed her.

She looked around, and saw two Blood Beaks, both grass-green with terror. She smiled at them vaguely. Oo, what a lot of noise there was! How was she ever going to get to sleep with all this noise?

Behind the Blood Beaks the ravens were winning the local skirmish, grabbing men and smashing them against trees. When they were dead, the birds fed on the corpses. There were only six or seven defenders left under the canopy, and all that was keeping them from being overrun was the congestion of feed-ing birds. The others could not pass to get at their prey.

The goblin king was fighting like a human whirlwind, hold-ing off two monsters. But the unequal struggle could not last forever. Even as she watched, a beak as big as two swords jabbed into Death Bird's chest. The points came out through his back in a wash of blood. The raven backed away, carrying him. He pounded fists on its head for a moment, then went limp. Bye-bye, Death Bird . . .

"Kadie, I'm sorry!" Blood Beak was yelling in her ear over the noise. "I didn't mean what I said!"

"Yes, you did," she said politely. There was only one of him, which is what she expected, really. She wished her head would stop aching. This was all very interesting and if she could see properly it would be even more interesting. She wondered if the birds would attack only goblins. How did they feel about jotunn-imp-faun mixtures? Perhaps she should take her clothes off so they could see she was pinky-brown, not green. Could birds tell colors?

She was going to find out very shortly. Only three men were left under the platform, and Blood Beak, and her. The noise was growing less, she decided, more bird shrieks but a lot less man-screams. The goblin horde was being reduced to carrion. Soon there wouldn't be any goblins. Two whole armies wiped out without even having a fight—even if she had survived to tell this tale, no one would ever have believed her.

Then Blood Beak yelled, and she turned. Two ravens were coming through the trees. From the way the closer one was looking at her with its beady gold eyes, it was obviously interested in more than goblins. She drew her rapier.

"I'll save you, Kadie!" Blood Beak waved his sword.

"I doubt that very much." Again she spoke so quietly that he would not hear. Her head was going round too fast for shouting.

The two monsters rushed in side by side. Blood Beak swung his sword at the one on his side, and the sheer power of his blow seemed to knock the great head back. Eyeing her own opponent blearily, Kadie decided she would dance forward lightly and lunge at the beak itself, hoping to hit the tongue. Tongues should be vulnerable, shouldn't they?

Her feet seemed to move in all directions at once. She stumbled forward, almost falling. She missed the tongue. The point of her rapier struck the beak, and the whole bird vanished with a sort of *plop!* noise.

Oh.

How unusual.

Blood Beak slashed again unsuccessfully, retreated before the next stab, caught his foot, sprawled over on his back. Fast as a whip, the raven's head flashed down and gripped his leg. He shrieked. It began pulling and lifting him.

Kadie lunged again, felt a hit, and the bird had gone.

She knelt down. "You all right?"

He stared up at her with wide square eyes in a face the color of green cheese. "What happened?"

"My sword. It's magical, you see. Good against magic birds. Of course I didn't know that until recently. How is your leg?"

"Broken."

She looked and saw white bones in the red stuff. It wasn't broken, it was crushed. She looked away quickly. Blood Beak would never run again.

"I'll make a bandage," she said, removing her cloak. A shadow warned her—she spun around just in time. As the monster lunged at her, she lunged right back. It vanished like a soap bubble. Another bird was right behind, so she took a step to meet it and dealt with that one, also. The men had all gone. There was only Blood Beak and herself under the platform. She glanced around and saw no goblins upright anywhere.

She did see an awful lot of giant ravens feeding, though, tearing at the corpses, and about as many again still hunting, most of them heading for her.

She reeled back to Blood Beak, who was whimpering and trying to sit up.

"You had better bandage your leg yourself," she said. "I'll keep the chickens off."

Suddenly she felt a thousand years old. Her arms were so heavy she could barely lift them, and the cloak lay forgotten at her feet. If the monsters came at her from all sides, she wasn't going to be able to get them all.

There were thousands of them.

8

COWERING IN HER VANTAGE ON THE HIGH MOSWEEPS, Thaïle wept in horror. The Keeper had known, or had guessed. *He plans a fiendish mischief,* she had said. Thaïle had never anticipated an evil so great. She could do nothing to stop it. No matter how powerful, one sorceress could not resist the Covin.

Very soon it was over. The dragons had destroyed the legions.

But then came the second message from the Almighty, and the second atrocity. Raw, naked power squirted out from the heart of evil in the center, enveloping the helpless mundanes of the opposing army and ripping them to bloody fragments. The illusion of black birds provided for the mundane spectators did not deceive Thaïle. She saw a single overall iniquity like a thundercloud, emitting random flashes of destruction. It was mindless and brutal and cold-blooded, a callous display of the usurper's might.

She could not identify the victims. None of the books she had seen had described such a race, but they were human, and they were dying, rent apart.

Again she could do nothing, and this time the butchery took longer. It ended when the horde had died and their corpses been reduced to gory pieces. Nauseated, she looked down upon the stricken terrain. All gone. She sensed others seeing and recoiling, also. Any sorcerer not alerted by the dragons would certainly have heard this slaughter. The Covin had made its point: *None can resist the Almighty.*

The last few stragglers were being hunted down and destroyed when Thaïle detected a tiny flicker of sorcery—sorcery of a different hue. The distinction was so subtle that she thought no other sorcerers would notice, unless they were very close, but someone was putting up an occult resistance; one man must be still alive among the dead. That pitiful spark of defiance caught her sympathy and her attention.

It was a woman? A girl! What had a girl been doing among so many thousand men? She was not even of their race.

A prisoner? Thaïle wondered. *Kidnapped? Kidnapped as she herself had been kidnapped from the Leéb Place?*

The spell of horror that had held her frozen shattered like ice on a pond.

She flashed to the rescue.

Yes, it was a girl, a woman just a little younger than herself. She had taken refuge under a sort of heavy wooden canopy. She was one of the dark-haired demons, but not quite an imp. Imps did not have green eyes, or those delicate features. Green eyes were found only on jotnar, the books said, and very rarely even then. How odd that the books should be so unreliable! Perhaps the races had changed in the last thousand years.

She was purely mundane, not a sorceress, because she did not show at all in the ambience. Her sword did. It was a minor piece of sorcery, but very cleverly crafted, and it was deflecting the stabbing flashes of power that the girl would be seeing as giant birds. It was wearing out, though. It would not last much longer.

Thaïle conceived a bubble of protection around them both. The illusory birds seemed to peck at it angrily. The girl looked around and saw she was not alone.

"Oh!" she said. Her face was haggard with shock and exhaustion. Then she managed a rictus of a smile. "You have come to rescue me!" She spoke in impish.

"Yes," Thaïle said, wondering why she was being so crazy. Who was she to oppose the monstrous evil of the usurper? If she lingered she would be noticed. She must move the child to safety on the far side of the river, and then leave at once.

"Thank you." The girl calmly sheathed her sword. "Can you rescue Blood Beak, too?" she asked hopefully. "He's hurt."

"He's dead."

"Oh." The girl looked down and then said, "Oh!" again.

"Was he your goodman?" Thaïle asked, thinking that the girl was very young to have the long hair of a goodwife.

"My what? Oh, no. Just a friend, sort of. He wanted to rape me."

The child was obviously delirious.

"Ready? I'll put you where the magic won't hurt you."

"You're a pixie?"

Thaïle started. Impossible! "How do you know that?"

"My mother visited Thume once." The girl leaned back limply against a tree, rubbing her eyes. "Years and years ago. She almost got raped there, I think, but she sort of glossed over the details when she told me. I didn't think they spoke impish in Thume. You have a funny accent, if you'll excuse my mentioning it, er, your Highness. I mean, it's a nice accent, just a little unfamiliar. Gods, I'm tired! Beg your pardon—I'm Princess Kadolan of Krasnegar. Please call me Kadie."

"I'm Thaïle of the . . . of the Leéb Place."

The big green eyes blinked. "Not a princess?"

"No."

"Oh. Well, a sorceress, of course. I knew someone would come and rescue me eventually. I wish you'd been a little sooner . . . Oh, I'm sorry! That does sound ungrateful, doesn't it? I am extremely pleased to see you, truly I am! You are going to take me to Thume, I suppose?"

Thaïle shook her head. She was not at all sure what she was going to do now. All she did know was that she was being very foolish and must hurry away, but the girl was not regarding her as a freak, a ghost from an extinct race, and now premonition was telling her that this meeting was important.

"I was kidnapped by the goblins," Kadie said, wiping her forehead wearily. "Months ago! I kept hoping Papa would come and rescue me, 'cause he's a sorcerer, but he's off trying to fight the usurper with the new protocol he invented, so he can't know what happened to me. And my mother's with the imperor, the real imperor, not the fake one, and I don't know what's happened to Gath, he's my brother, and I'm awfully afraid I'm going to start weeping like a silly kid."

Madness, surely? Thaïle probed in a way she had not known she could, wiping away the shock and exhaustion. She could find no trace of madness, or what she thought madness would look like. She did see the ravages of weeks and weeks of terror and hardship, like scar tissue on the soul, but some of that was part of growing up and would have come eventually anyway. Could all that strange babbling story have been *true*?

Kadie blinked again, straightened her shoulders, and smiled.

"Oh, that's a great improvement! Thank you!" She glanced down briefly, and shuddered. "Poor Blood Beak! It wasn't his fault, was it, the way he was brought up? I mean, none of us can help that. He didn't know any better."

"Your father is really a sorcerer? And you know the imperor?"

Kadie grinned, and nodded. "It's rather a long story."

Thaïle nodded, but did not grin. Did the Keeper know all this about fake imperors? New protocol?

Kadie glanced around nervously. She would be seeing massed

black birds, of course. Thaïle was aware that the power outside her shielding was changing. The Covin would detect this local disturbance very soon.

"If you're going to take me away from all this," Kadie said diffidently, "then shouldn't we maybe go now? We can talk on the way if you like." She grinned again. "This is a very strange conversation, isn't it? I'm awfully glad you've come."

Suddenly—astonishingly!—Thaïle found herself returning the second grin. How long since she had smiled? How wonderful it felt to be talking with a simple mundane instead of all the scheming sorcerers of the College! She detected no concealment in the girl, no guile. No demon, just an unfortunate victim like herself. "I expect you are glad! Where do you want to go?"

"Anywhere! Take me home with you."

"I haven't got a home."

Kadie's green eyes widened. "Oh, that's awful! How terrible! Well, let's go to my home. You'll be ever so welcome there. Stay as long as you like!"

"Where's that?"

"A little place called Krasnegar. Way up north. It's hundreds of leagues from anywhere, and dull as mud." She paused, frowning. "I will be glad to see it again, though."

"A little Place?" Thaïle said hopefully.

"Very little. Very rustic, I'm afraid. Oh! The birds have gone!"

"Quickly!" Thaïle shouted, holding out a hand. "Let's go! Think hard about where your Place is and I'll take us there!"

"Poor Blood Beak!" Kadie took the offered hand, but her eyes were on the dead boy. "I always told him I would be rescued."

9

DREADNAUGHT WAS DRIFTING AGAIN, ROLLING UNEASILY, and her sails banged and flapped in the morning breeze. Some of the trolls had curled up in balls. A couple of others were smashing things in mindless fury—barrels, pin racks, davits. Most of the anthropophagi were close to berserk. Grunth and

Thrugg and Tik Tok were trying to restore order, but the ship was a madhouse of emotion and monstrous flickering images.

Jalon, as the only mundane aboard, was frantic. "What's happening?" he asked yet again.

Rap grabbed him by the shoulders. "Get me Sagorn!" he yelled.

"What? I can't—"

"I need Sagorn! I can't tell you what's happening. I don't know what's happening. Zinixo's burned the legions and ripped up the goblins. I want to know what he's trying to do!"

The minstrel cringed before his anger. "But I can't call Sagorn. He called me—"

"Then get me one who can!"

Jalons' garments ripped to shreds as Darad's enormous form appeared in his place. The warrior stood there half naked, his hideous face turning pale. "Rap?" he mumbled, staring around the crowded deck.

"Not you!" Rap screamed. Idiot Jalon! "Call Sagorn!"

Darad frowned and licked his lips. "But I called him the last time, Rap . . ."

"Call another!"

SORCERERS! NOW YOU HAVE SEEN THE POWER OF THE ALMIGHTY! NONE CAN RESIST HIM. ALL MUST BOW DOWN AND SERVE!

Anthropophagi shrieked in fury. Trolls moaned.

Darad vanished. Rags fluttered around the puny form of Thinal the thief. His spotty face blanched as he saw the company he was in.

"Not you!" Rap shouted. "Gods, not you! I want Sagorn!"

COME, SORCERERS! YOU ARE COMMANDED TO COME TO HUB AT ONCE AND ENLIST IN THE SERVICE OF THE ALMIGHTY, THE GOOD, THE BELOVED. COME NOW!

Rap wiped his streaming brow. "Thinal, I don't think we need you just at the moment. Please will you call Doctor Sagorn?"

"Who does he think we are?" Tik Tok screamed. His dark face was suffused with fury, his tattoos stood out in vivid color, and the bone in his nose was jumping. "Monster! He expects us to serve him after *that*?"

Thinal's teeth were chattering. "Rap, I can't!"

"What do you mean, 'can't'?"

Thrugg rolled across the deck like a bullock. *"Rap, this is serious! Some of my friends are going to answer that summons!"*

"Stop them!" Rap screamed. If even one troll obeyed the Covin's command, then *Dreadnaught* and all her crew would be betrayed.

Thinal was shaking like a flag. "Rap, I haven't done enough time! I only just got away last time! I can't call anyone yet!"

Grunth's grotesque shape loomed in the ambience. "Rap, this is bad! What're we going to do?"

COME, SORCERERS! THE ALMIGHTY IS MERCIFUL AND HIS YOKE IS LIGHT. NONE CAN RESIST HIM! COME JOIN OUR HAPPY BAND. COME NOW, OR ELSE BE HENCEFORTH COUNTED AMONG THE ENEMIES OF THE ALMIGHTY.

"I will come with my spear!" Tik Tok screamed, and other anthropophagi cheered him. "If any of you oxen want to enlist, then speak up and I will kill you!"

"We fear the Covin more than you, Maneater!" bellowed one of the trolls.

Rap took Thinal by the throat. "I don't care how much it hurts, you are going to call Sagorn and call him *now*! If you don't call Sagorn, then I will choke the life out of you!"

Thinal gibbered. Strips of cloth were falling loose from him, leaving him almost naked. Sweat broke out on his face and his teeth chattered louder than ever. Uncaring, Rap began to squeeze. "Call Sagorn!"

ANY SORCERER WHO DOES NOT ANSWER THIS CALL IS HEREBY SENTENCED TO DEATH. COME NOW!

"Sorcerers! He lies!"

The pandemonium seemed to pause. Rap relaxed his death grip on the thief. Who said that?

"Sorcerers, hear the truth now!" The voice and face were faint, but in the ambience they could never be disguised.

Rap looked to Grunth. "Is that who I think it is?"

Registering surprise and delight, she opened her muzzle in a blood-curdling grin, flashing her huge horse teeth.

HEED NOT THE LIARS AND THE EVIL! HEED ONLY

THE WORDS OF THE ALMIGHTY. The Covin was trying to drown out the opposition, but that was not feasible in the ambience.

"Sorcerers, there is yet hope!" the thin and distant voice said. *"Rap the faun has returned!"*

"Oh, Gods!" Rap said. "Me? Who? Now what? Where is that coming from?"

"He outwitted Zinixo once and—"

IGNORE THE RENEGADE . . . The Covin's roar was a forest fire, a waterfall, an earthquake, and none of them could hide that solitary whisper of rebellion.

"—he can do so again!"

"Meld!" Tik Tok shouted. "To me, everyone!"

With a rush, the sorcerers began combining their powers in the ambience. It grew easier with practice. Rap found himself sucked in almost without willing it. They grabbed up the comatose trolls and the raging anthropophagi, joining, blending as if an occult snowball went rolling through the ship. Thrugg arrived like a falling temple . . . Grunth . . .

"Here is the promise!" the whisper said. *"The faun proposes and the wardens agree."*

The last anthropophagous mage was blended in, and the meld was complete, thirty-seven minds. "—Hub," they thought, "—it is coming from Hub—of course it is—I knew that—where else would it come from?—look out for the Covin—take it gently, I said—don't be so pushy."

They looked and beheld the City of the Gods itself, the City of Five Hills, with the Opal Palace in the center and the palaces of the Four around it. To Rap, and even more to Grunth, it was all familiar. To the others it was an overwhelming shock, a sprawling miracle of spires and marble, copper roofs and golden domes. Temples and mansions and parks filled the center, dwindling out for leagues into brick tenements and squalor in the suburbs. The entire population of the Nogids or the Mosweeps could have vanished within its teeming multitudes. For a moment the meld roiled in astonishment. A couple of the trolls almost went into withdrawal and had to be vitalized.

Then they sensed the hideous power of the Covin, raging like a storm over the city, unseen and unsuspected by the mill-

ing hordes of mundanes—the artisans, the merchants, the por-
ters and refugees, the soldiers and servants, beggars and thieves,
going about their business in the morning sun. Markets and
wagons and marching legionaries . . . And still that solitary
voice rang out in defiance, louder and clearer, a crippled old
man, near to death but burning bright with hate and fury.

*"The imperor in Hub is a charlatan, but the true imperor still lives
and he also pledges . . ."*

"—clearer," thought the thirty-seven, "somewhere around—
cannot locate him exactly—of course not—there he is—no, he's
not—see the Covin hunting, also—clever work—how is he
doing that?—it's Warlock Olybino—we must help him—no,
we mustn't."

"There shall be no more slavery among sorcerers . . ."

The trolls had no love for the sorcerer whose armies had enslaved them. The anthropophagi saw only a lone warrior battling
enormous odds, and their fierce fighting souls reached out to him.
A ferocious argument developed within the meld itself.

"—the Covin will catch him—of course it will—he knows
that—take it easy—you'll get us all caught if you jostle that
way—what do you suppose his range is?—well, it's a lot better
than it should be—you mean because the Covin's already gotten
everyone's attention—it's going to find him very soon—leave
him alone—it serves him right—his range isn't all that great, is
it?—how can we help him?—bet they can hear him down in
Zark—we can't help him—the Covin sure is mad, isn't it?"

The whirling darkness whirled faster. The stony eyes of a
dwarf glared angrily over the city, larger than thunderheads.
But for all its power, the Covin could not drown out that mocking voice. Nor could it catch the warlock. Giant hands of smoke
grabbed and found nothing, grabbed again, and again . . .

*IGNORE THE LIES OF THE RENEGADE. COME NOW
TO HUB AND ENLIST IN THE ARMY OF THE ALMIGHTY
THAT HIS NEW ORDER MAY EXTEND TO ALL HIS SER-
VANTS THE BLESSINGS ONLY THEY CAN KNOW . . .*

"—he moves like a flea—it's a random pattern—we must
help him escape—oh, no, we mustn't—he knew the risk . . ."

"A court of sorcery will judge all offenses . . ."

The contemptuous whisper continued remorselessly, rendering futile all the occult bellowing of the Covin and its frantic efforts to entrap its tormentor. On the Avenue Abnila, in the ground of the White Palace, on the lakeshore—Olybino was never in one place for more than a second and there was no pattern to his moves.

He must have prespelled this in advance, Rap thought admiringly, but how can he ever escape in the end?

"In future wardens will be elected by the sorcerers ..." Olybino was adding a few things Rap had never thought of.

Trolls and anthropophagi listened and watched and argued: "—we can't desert him—we can't save him—the dwarf will get him—he can't keep this up forever—if we do anything we shall be detected."

The mundanes of the city went on with their lives unaware, but all over the world, sorcerers must surely be listening to the conflicting proclamations, watching the conflict. Then the Covin changed its tactics. The illusory hands vanished. A bolt of power crashed into the street where the warlock had been. Pedestrians and carriages were blasted to ashes, houses collapsed in fiery ruins.

The meld stilled in shock.

A moment later the mocking voice came from a park near the Opal Palace: *"All this is promised by the rightful imperor, by the wardens ..."*

Soil and trees erupted in flame, but the voice came now from a bridge over Old Canal: *"... and by Rap, the faun, the sorcerer who long ago refused to become a warden, but who now leads the battle for liberty and justice ..."*

The bridge flew apart in dust, filling the air with scorched bodies of pedestrians and horses. Debris and corpses rained down into the water.

"... the battle against the evil of the Covin!"

Now the mundanes were involved, as pillars of smoke and flame sprouted at random across the city. The meld of the *Dreadnaught* watchers howled—trolls in horror, anthropophagi in fury. Somewhere in that joint consciousness, Rap struggled to be heard and was drowned out.

"Brothers and sisters—" the warlock cried, and destruction smashed down in the crowded street where he had stood.

The callous butchery roused even the trolls. The anthropophagi were already gibbering.

"*—wait for the summons, and when the trumpet sounds . . .*" A temple collapsed in flames. "*. . . liberty and justice . . .*"

"—this is slaughter—we must stop this—the maniac may blast the whole city next—quickly strike now—call for help from all the other watchers—the time is not ripe—it will never be riper—people are dying . . ."

Bloodlust roared. Tik Tok's band was incensed almost beyond reason, gathering hatred to strike. Even the meekest of the trolls wanted to rush to the aid of the wounded, at the very least, and most of them seemed ready to join the cannibals and do battle against the murderous evil. Rap himself could feel his self-control slipping, and his fragile authority had long since faded. Every sorcerer in Pandemia must be watching this. There would never be a better time to issue the rallying cry, to sound that trumpet the warlock had just proclaimed. Were the numbers enough? Would the Covin have risked this open confrontation were it not certain the odds were on its side? Was any victory possible now? Its power was mountainous.

"*Zinixo, you are a mad, odious, murderous, despicable little—*"

And that time the warlock held his ground. The Covin blasted it with a torrent of thunderbolts.

Silence and curling smoke.

Dead.

The meld screamed. Fury and power built like a pillar of fire, preparing to do battle . . .

In sudden panic Rap screamed a warning: "*The dragons! Remember the dragons!*"

Dragons?

The fire faded away.

Rap opened his eyes. *Dreadnaught* moved serenely over the waters of the Summer Seas in the morning sunshine. At the wheel stood the gaunt figure of Doctor Sagorn, unperturbed and dignified despite the wind-stirred rags he wore. The sails bent in curves and the wake was straight. Steering a ship, his stance implied, was a childishly simple operation.

Trolls sobbed and moaned. Anthropophagi glared and muttered curses. Wiping his face, Rap made a quick count. Nobody
missing! He sat up.

"It is all over, I presume?" Sagorn remarked calmly.

"Yes. It was East. Olybino."

"So I gathered. You were all shouting at once, but I made
out that much." The old scholar pulled a contemptuous smile.
"He made a proclamation? You explained that procedure on
White Impress, you may recall."

Rap nodded. He ached all over, as if he had been thrashing
around on the hard planks. He felt soiled. He despised himself.

He glanced around, seeing the fury on the faces of the anthropophagi and the trolls' shame. Grunth bared her baboon
teeth at him as if enjoying his failure. He was the voice of
sanity and therefore not popular at the moment.

"He died," Rap said. "They got him."

"Of course." Sagorn shrugged. "That was why neither you
nor Warlock Raspnex was willing to take that particular shortcut, wasn't it?"

"Partly."

"Only partly, your Majesty?" The scholar sneered. He was
a highly improbable jotunn, but he had all his ancestors' contempt for cowardice.

Rap opened his mouth and then closed it again. Both he and
Raspnex had assumed that to do what Olybino had just done
must lead to instant capture. The imp had found a way to
evade capture and force the Covin to kill him. Even if Rap had
thought of that technique, would he have had the courage to
throw his life away for the cause? He did not have enough
power anyway, but he was not sure enough of himself to say
so to Sagorn.

"So now your work is done?" the jotunn remarked, glanc-
ing at the sails and adjusting course as if he had been a sailor
all his days. "The sorcerers of the world have been informed.
I thought you were about to summon them all and start the
battle. What stopped you?"

"Dragons." Rap sighed, clambering painfully to his feet.

"Dragons?" The scholar lifted snowy eyebrows.

"The dragons are still returning to Dragon Reach. If we had

started a battle, the Covin would have released its hold over them and they would have scattered over all Pithmot."

"Ah. Then I apologize for doubting you."

"Don't bother."

Rap felt foul and hypocritical. He had always regarded the warlock of the east with contempt, despising his absurd posturing and his idealization of war. But in the end Olybino had given his life for a cause. He had probably not fully believed in that cause, but he had been true to his own ideals of duty and courage.

And Rap? How was he at duty and courage? He might well have missed the best chance he would ever get of overthrowing Zinixo. Yet only a fool let himself be goaded into battle on unfavorable terrain, and *Dreadnaught* was certainly that. Had the meld revealed itself, Zinixo could have just blasted the old tub out of the ocean. When did caution become cowardice?

When did setback become disaster?

There could be no doubt that the Covin had carried the day. The legions and goblins had been exterminated, the warlock destroyed, and perhaps even now sorcerers were streaming into Hub to enlist.

The emotions were all wrong, yet the logic felt right. Rap glanced down at that inexplicable word tattooed on his arm. Some sorcerous instinct was still telling him that his decision had been correct, even without the dragon problem. There was a piece of the puzzle still missing.

The time was not yet ripe.

It would come soon.

Possess the field:
> *If hopes were dupes, fears may be liars;*
> *It may be, in yon smoke concealed,*
> *Your comrades chase e'en now the fliers,*
> *And, but for you, possess the field.*

CLOUGH, *SAY NOT THE STRUGGLE NAUGHT AVAILETH*

ABOUT THE AUTHOR

DAVE DUNCAN was born in Scotland in 1933 and educated at Dundee High School and the University of St. Andrews. He moved to Canada in 1955 and has lived in Calgary ever since. He is married and has three grown children.

After a thirty-year career as a petroleum geologist, he discovered that it was much easier (and more fun) to invent his own worlds than try to make sense of the real one.